ANNA'S MEDALLION

A NOVEL ABOUT NAZI SLAVERY BASED ON A
TRUE LOVE STORY

KRIS DRAVEN

ISBN (paperback): 979-8-218-63976-1

For my grandparents, in loving memory

"*If only it were all so simple! If only there were evil people somewhere insidiously committing evil deeds, and it were necessary only to separate them from the rest of us and destroy them. But the line dividing good and evil cuts through the heart of every human being. And who is willing to destroy a piece of his own heart?*"

Aleksandr Solzhenitsyn
Author of The Gulag Archipelago *and 1970 winner of the*
Nobel Prize in Literature

CONTENTS

FOREWORD

The history of forced labor in Nazi Germany is well-recorded but often forgotten.

Following the German invasions of Austria, Czechoslovakia, Poland, Denmark, Norway, Belgium, Netherlands, Luxemburg, France, Yugoslavia, Greece, and the Soviet Union, the Nazis quickly began forcibly transporting POWs and civilians of those countries to Germany. Once there, the forced laborers were distributed to farms, construction sites, and factories to work without pay and under threat of imprisonment.

Many of the laborers were housed in concentration camps with attached armament factories operated by such firms as IG Farben, Krupp, Siemens, Daimler-Benz, BMW, Volkswagen, Hugo Boss, Mittelwerk GmbH, Gustloff-Werke, and many others. Altogether, approximately 12 million slaves worked in Germany during World War II, from 1939 to 1945. More than half of them perished from exhaustion, malnutrition, disease, hard labor, and Nazi extermination. These men and women came from all over Europe: 3 million from the Soviet Union, 2 million from Poland, 1 million from France, and the rest from seventeen other countries of Europe.

There were twenty concentration camps in Nazi Germany and approximately 1,200 sub-camps. In all the camps, the Nazis' goal was to extract as much wealth and labor out of the prisoners before killing them in gas chambers or through harsh working conditions.

Some of the camps served primarily as extermination camps, while others were labor camps designed to support the Nazi war machine. While it's extremely difficult to estimate the total population of the concentration camps due to many records being destroyed just prior to the liberation by the Allied forces, somewhere between 15 and 20 million people were imprisoned in the camps, and 11 to 17 million perished there (including 6 to 7 million Jews).

One of the biggest and most brutal labor camps in Germany was at Buchenwald. During its operation, from 1937 to 1945, Buchenwald concentration camp held approximately 239,000 prisoners from various nationalities, including Jews, but also political prisoners, homosexuals, Jehovah's Witnesses, Roma, and others deemed undesirable by the Nazi regime. It is estimated that at least 35,000 prisoners died in Buchenwald due to harsh conditions, forced labor, medical experiments, executions, and other forms of mistreatment, including starvation and lack of disease control.

While the camp held only 2,900 prisoners initially—mostly communists opposed to the Nazi regime—the population exploded to over 98,000 in the last full year of operation. While Allied forces advanced and the war situation deteriorated for Nazi Germany, Buchenwald's population surged as prisoners were evacuated from other camps and moved to Buchenwald.

Conditions worsened drastically, leading to a high death toll among the inmates.

The biggest labor camp for women—which was just as brutal—was at Ravensbrück. Approximately 132,000 women and children were registered as prisoners throughout its existence, from 1939 to 1945. Around 30,000 to 50,000 prisoners died in Ravensbrück due to various causes. The camp was initially built to incarcerate political prisoners, but it later expanded to include women from multiple backgrounds deemed undesirable by the Nazi regime. This included Jews, Roma, Jehovah's Witnesses, resistance fighters, socialists, communists, and women labeled as asocial or criminal (mostly prostitutes and lesbians).

The living conditions for the slave laborers in the camps and elsewhere throughout Germany were extremely harsh. Overcrowding, inadequate food, and constant abuse by the SS guards and ordinary Germans who found themselves as slave masters were daily realities. The laborers were treated like scum and discarded like used parts if they underperformed. However, despite all their suffering, some of them found a way to survive.

A few even found love.

1

APRIL 20, 1941

With the anti-Nazi leaflets tucked inside her white spring jacket, Anna Kogut hurried through the city, wondering if she had seen her parents for the last time.

She had willingly decided that today would be the day she fought back and enthusiastically accepted her assignment from Captain Mazurek of the Home Army—the Polish resistance against the German occupation. Yet, as she drew closer to her destination, the looming consequences gnawed relentlessly at the corners of her mind. Her innocent disguise—a petite seventeen-year-old with braided blond hair, light-blue eyes, and a yellow sundress—hid her dangerous mission. It could mean death for her entire family—just as it had for countless others who'd dared to resist. Nonetheless, her mind was made up.

It was a warm spring day in Tschenstochau, the German name for the once-Polish city of Czestochowa. Despite her anxiety, Anna inhaled deeply, savoring the sweet fragrance of blooming purple crocuses. The cherry trees were adorned with fresh young leaves, and their delicate white blossoms had already begun drifting down to the streets.

As she walked past the public park off Pulawski Street—now renamed Scharnhorststraße—she noticed German parents lounging on benches, watching their children play on swings, slides, and seesaws. The sign on the park gate read "Für Polen und Hunde Eintritt verboten" ("Poles and dogs not allowed entry"), so Anna had no choice but to walk past the police building instead. She felt cold sweat trickle down her ribs as she anticipated someone challenging her.

When no one stopped her, Anna turned left onto Hindenburgstraße and walked another block uphill to Freystädterstraße. She paused at the corner by the post office, pressing herself against the rough bricks, careful not to attract attention, and scanned the area for any sign of policemen or German soldiers among the passing crowd.

Captain Mazurek emerged from the alley behind her. He was a short man in his forties, dressed in civilian clothes that made him blend in with the crowd. However, she knew he carried a pistol beneath his wool jacket and would use it without hesitation.

"Hello, Niece," he said, kissing each of her cheeks.

"Hello, Uncle," she said.

He was not her uncle, but he said this would make their meeting less suspicious.

"Are you ready?" he asked.

She was surprised by how ready she felt despite her nerves. Most people who knew her would be shocked that Anna was doing something so dangerous. Her teenage peers would consider her the least likely among them to fight the Nazis. Why was she risking her life for a hopeless cause? It was not like she had ever been known to be a rebel or troublemaker. She was very proud, that much was certain, but she was never outspoken about anything. One of her three sisters would be far more likely to join a resistance. Most people, however, didn't realize that patriotism burned intensely within her.

Anna had found it inconceivable that Germans and Soviets had occupied her country in 1939. The Poles had fought back bravely but were severely outmatched, battling on two fronts: the Germans in the West and the Soviets in the East. It took only about four weeks for Poland to fall. Anna was deeply troubled by the hopelessness that had ensued in the two years that followed. Unlike her parents and grandparents, who grew up during the 123 years of occupation by Prussia, Austria, and Russia, she was born free—a citizen of an independent country. That was all she had ever known, and she was not planning to give it up.

"I'm ready," she said.

"Act natural. I can tell you're hiding something under your jacket."

She adjusted the leaflets under her jacket and stood up straight. "I'm sorry. I'm a bit nervous. There are too many things to think about at once."

"Just think about one step at a time. Don't get ahead of yourself."

"Yes, sir."

"Now, I must ask you one more time. Are you ready to give your life for your country? This is your last chance to back out if you want. There will be no hard feelings if you do."

Someone once told her that wild animals usually fought the cage after being captured but eventually gave in to their fate, so she should do the same. What she didn't tell that person was that she had always hated going to the zoo because she felt like killing the animals just to end their suffering. It was the same for her now; she would rather die than live in a cage.

"I'm ready to give my life," she said.

"Good. God be with you."

"Poland fighting."

"Poland fighting," he said, then walked away.

Reciting the partisan motto filled her with courage, but seeing him vanish into the alley reminded her that she was alone now. Mazurek would not be there to save her if anything went wrong. She would have to rely on her wits and training to survive.

The church bells rang, which was Anna's clue to move along. The liturgy was ending, and it was time for her to act. She took a deep breath, then ran across the street toward the Jasna Gora Monastery. However, this was not an ordinary monastery. Rather, it was a large fortress that housed Poland's most renowned chapel, which had served as a symbol of Polish resistance against foreign invaders since the battle fought there in 1655 against Sweden and its German mercenaries. The story went that the Black Madonna icon inside the chapel was responsible for a miraculous victory over an overwhelming enemy army. Anna was hoping for a similar miracle today.

Out of respect for the pilgrims always praying in silence, she bypassed the chapel where the revered icon was located and entered a church next to it instead. Even though she used to go into that church every Sunday as a child, she had to stop to take it all in today because the church took her breath away.

Giant red marble columns rose to a white marble ceiling intricately carved and painted with religious scenes. The altar was like a scene out of heaven. White sculptures of saints were seemingly meeting for a casual discussion in front of green and gold Corinthian columns while a giant gold cross hung above them, suspended from white clouds chiseled out of alabaster. All of that was accentuated by gold and silver carvings sprinkled throughout.

She shook off the feeling of mortality and ran up the stairs to the balcony. It was always busy on Sundays; people needed hope and swarmed the churches to get some. The crowds started to exit, accompanied by the chants of the famous Pauline monks, whose order had built this monastery. Anna took a couple of deep breaths and, out of habit, touched the gold medallion with a picture of the Black Madonna that hung around her neck. She'd planned to take it off long ago but kept forgetting to do so, perhaps still taking some comfort from its presence.

Then she threw the leaflets on top of the congregation and shouted, "Free Poland! Free Poland! Free Poland!" over and over until her throat hurt. This filled her with hope. At that moment, she felt as if she wasn't alone in the fight. The crowd's murmur of shock and admiration made her feel like she alone could lead the people to liberation.

Anna continued throwing leaflets for a couple of minutes until the church emptied. With her task completed, she rushed down the stairs and out of the church. She wanted to sneak through the city back to her parents' house, but her plan quickly evaporated because two policemen were waiting for her outside. She fell straight into their arms, which snared her like an animal in a trap.

"Going somewhere, stupid girl?" said one of them. He looked like one of those criminals who got the job after the Germans wiped out the pre-war police—all brute force and no brains, only out to prey on innocent people like vultures.

The crowds moved around them in silence as if she didn't exist. Anna knew they were afraid, but she still resented their cowardice. She expected them to be inspired by her and rush to her rescue. Instead, they cast their eyes down and shuffled away like dumb sheep. At that moment, she felt utterly alone and the furthest she'd ever felt from the liberation.

"Let me go, you brute!" Anna screamed as she twisted away just like Captain Mazurek had shown her. The policemen were surprised by her strength and couldn't hold on.

She didn't wait for their shock to wear off. Anna took off as fast as she could, pushing people to the ground to block the two policemen, per Mazurek's training. This was precisely why she had worn flat shoes instead of high heels.

A commotion and shouts from the policemen broke out behind her, but she didn't look back. Instead, she pumped her legs forward, ignoring the medallion, which was smacking her face with each stride, and focused on the ground before her.

Anna stopped a few minutes later in an alley off Hindenburgstraße. She watched and listened while trying to catch her breath, but no one seemed to be following her. She could see the wall around the Jewish ghetto, which reminded her why she was doing this in the first place. They were slowly killing off the Jews, and the Poles were probably next. But not if she had anything to say about it.

Anna was going to fight. She *was* fighting, she realized, and that made her smile. Her mission was a success. She didn't get arrested.

Anna stepped out of the alley and walked calmly toward her home. There were only a few people out and about. Nobody paid her any attention. She crossed the train tracks and reached her apartment building on Gartenstraße. She went through the B entrance, one of three to her building, and climbed the stairs to her second-floor apartment. The door was locked, so she pulled out a key hanging on a string around her neck and turned the lock. Anna breathed a sigh of relief as she closed the door behind her and leaned against it. She was safe.

She walked over to the kitchen, where her three sisters sat at the kitchen table, eating an apple strudel their mother had made the day before. They looked at Anna as if she were a ghost, their forks suspended midair. She realized her appearance must be disheveled.

"What's wrong with you?" asked Bozena, her older sister. She looked just like Anna, with the same blue eyes and blond hair, except she was a bit bigger and meaner. People wondered if they were twins, but boys sometimes picked on Bozena for being too heavy.

Strangely, her two younger sisters, Basia and Ewa, were brunettes with darker skin. They looked almost Mediterranean. People teased them and called them Gypsies, but boys chased after them relentlessly.

"Nothing," said Anna. "Just went to church."

"I thought you didn't believe in God anymore," said Bozena.

"Where are Mom and Dad?" Anna asked, trying to deflect.

"They went to visit Aunt Marysia."

"When are they coming back?"

"I don't know. It's Sunday. They might be there for a while. Why?"

"No reason," Anna said, then left the kitchen.

Something wasn't right. Now that Anna had a minute to think, she realized feeling safe was naïve. Why did she believe the police would abandon the chase? She had committed a serious offense. The leaflets she distributed called for an armed rebellion against the Germans. There were witnesses. Somebody would recognize her. They would tell the policemen where she lived. She was vulnerable, and now she also had to think about her sisters. She wished her parents were there to tell her what to do. Or Captain Mazurek. He would know what to do.

That was when the roar of the truck engines filled the air. Anna ran to the living room window. Below, in the street, stood two German army trucks. Soldiers were pouring out of them, rushing toward all three entrances to her apartment building. People on the street were running away. Screams and sounds of boots pounding the stairs echoed inside the building. Everything was happening so fast.

"BOZENA!" Anna screamed.

Bozena rushed into the living room, her eyes panicked. "What's happening?"

"It's a roundup," Anna said. "We have to hide."

They all knew the drill. This wasn't their first roundup. Germans were constantly rounding people up, either looking for Jews or kidnapping people for labor in Germany. Or arresting saboteurs.

Anna and her sisters scrambled to gather whatever clothes and food they could carry and hurried toward their parents' bedroom and its fake closet, which hid a tiny panic room. They were in the foyer when the front door burst open, and the policeman she had writhed away from earlier rushed into the apartment. Two German soldiers were right behind him.

"There you are," the policeman said, smirking with satisfaction.

Anna and her sisters screamed in terror. Bozena tripped over her feet and tumbled to the floor; Anna tripped over her. Basia and Ewa ran into a bedroom and slammed the door behind them.

The policeman stood over Anna. "Did you think you could just run away from Sergeant Podolski?"

"What do you want from me?" Anna screamed, unsure about what else she could say or do to save herself and her family.

"What do I want from you?" he said and laughed. "I want you to be a nice piggy. Round up the other piggies and come with me so I can get myself a nice bonus from our German friends."

"What did you do, Anna?" yelled Bozena.

Anna didn't respond. She stood up, cast her eyes down, and waited for the soldiers to round them all up. There was no point in fighting against trained soldiers with rifles. All she could do was stand there in her Sunday dress and let the guilt eat at her for bringing this upon her family.

The Germans pushed all four of them down the stairs and piled them into the trucks, together with two dozen other young people. Anna wasn't sure why they'd arrested all these people and not just her. Maybe it was only because they could. What would they do to all these poor souls?

Anna expected the worst: a shot to the back of the head as the Germans did to many people in her city.

2

APRIL 26, 1941

Filip Wolny had been packing his suitcase since the fight with his stepfather that morning. He didn't want to leave his village, but he had no choice. The thought of departing the only place he'd ever known was terrifying. The world was huge, and he was nothing but a little ant in it. Yet he smiled at the idea that his life finally had a chance to improve.

He'd turned eighteen two months earlier but never had any money. His wool pants, jacket, and cap were patched-up hand-me-downs from his older brothers. Even his undergarments were old, including the stained underpants. He still lived in his stepfather's two-bedroom farmhouse and had to share a bedroom with five siblings. Going to Germany for work would change all that. He'd finally have some money. Of course, he had to give most of it to his stepfather, who would spend it on vodka instead of fixing up the half-sunken roof and rickety wooden floors, but Filip's portion would be enough to buy some land and build his own house.

"Hurry up!" his stepfather shouted from behind the door.

Filip finished packing, opened the door, and entered the kitchen, which also served as a bedroom. His entire seventeen-person family—including his stepfather, mother, ten siblings, and some of their spouses—waited for him in complete silence. Although he didn't get along with all his siblings, they respected him for his hard work in putting food on the table. They were all there now to say goodbye—some of them because they liked him, the others just to make sure some of what he sent home fell on their plate.

"What are you so quiet for? This isn't a funeral," Filip said, breaking the silence.

His stepfather rose from his chair, his massive body swaying slightly, and said, "You will be late, goddamn it!"

Filip's blood rushed to his brain, and he charged toward his stepfather. "Don't worry. I'm leaving. You don't have to worry about your money."

"Stop it, Filip," said his mother, stepping between them.

She was not the same woman Filip had known when his father was alive. Her hair was grayer, and her eyes sunken. He knew she felt the burden of caring for the family and keeping the peace. She'd had to remarry and didn't have many choices. His stepfather was a drunkard but the only man willing to marry an old woman with eleven children. Filip felt guilty because it was all his fault, but he still hated the man.

"Well, you know he just wants me to slave away for him," Filip argued because the big fight with his stepfather had been about how they would split the money he'd earn from his work in Germany. His stepfather wouldn't budge from his three-quarters share. As long as Filip lived under this roof, there was nothing he could do to change that.

His stepfather sat back down and poured himself a shot of vodka from a half-empty bottle.

"It's for the family, Filip," pointed out his mother.

Filip knew arguing was pointless. He put on his cap, picked up the suitcase, threw his laced shoes over his shoulder, and said, "I guess I don't have a choice. It's not like we can feed twenty mouths on a farm that's supposed to feed four."

One by one, his family members said goodbye, kissing him on both cheeks—a custom he never enjoyed. His brothers remained calm, almost indifferent, but his sisters and mother cried profusely, as he knew they would.

He was relieved to exit the house and breathe in the familiar farm air—a mixture of sweet morning dew and musky dung from several cows passing by on their way to the pasture. He strode down the village dirt road with his mother following.

"Filip, slow down," she complained.

"I must catch the ride," he replied, pointing to an approaching horse wagon. "I'll have to wait until next week if I don't."

She ran, trying to catch up. "Why do you want to leave me so quickly?"

He stopped, grabbed her by the arms, and looked into her eyes. "Mother, it's only for four months. I will be back before you know it." He wanted to tell her he loved her, but expressing love just wasn't something they did. "I will write to you as soon as I arrive," he said instead.

"Maybe we can convince your stepfather to let you stay," she said, her voice quavering.

"You know we need the money. And the Germans said we must volunteer now, or they'll take us later without pay anyway."

His mother nodded in reluctant agreement but started to cry. She reached inside her blouse and pulled out a handker-chief. She opened it, revealing several gold coins. "It's the only money I have. If you ever get in trouble, use this to get back to me and our village."

He felt guilty for taking money from her, but he was desperate. He was going to Germany with enough food to last only a few days, and he needed emergency money. So he took the coins and hid them inside his jacket.

"Thank you," he said, kissing her on the forehead. "I'm grateful to have such a wonderful mother."

"And Filip," she said, "please don't blame yourself—"

"Stop it, Mom."

"I mean it, son. It wasn't your fault. The Germans killed your father. Not you."

Filip appreciated her words, but they were not true. If he hadn't threatened the German soldiers when they first arrived in his village two years before, forcing his father to shield him, he might still be alive today.

"Thank you, Mom, for everything," he said. "I will never forget it."

The horse wagon pulled up next to them. He threw his shoes and suitcase in the back, then jumped in. There were seven young men on the wagon, all around his age. He knew most of them, but he recognized some only from the local village dances. He imagined he must have the same look on his face that he saw on theirs: bewilderment, fear, and excitement.

The wagon moved slowly, the driver letting the horses walk at their own pace. Filip watched his mother for a while as she stood crying on the side of the road. He tried to look away but felt guilty, so he kept staring at her.

"Poor woman. I should have married her instead," said a freckled-faced, blond young man sitting beside him when the wagon was a safe distance away from Filip's mother.

"Shut up, Leszek," Filip said.

He knew Leszek from their village school. He was popular with women, which made him arrogant, and he liked to run his mouth.

"Didn't you say she had to remarry after your father was shot?" Leszek asked.

"Don't disrespect her. She's a good woman . . . and my mother."

Leszek smiled and leaned back. "Whatever you say, Filip. I don't think she could have done better."

Filip knew not to jump him. They'd gone through that routine many times, and he never came out unscathed. He could not afford to get injured at the very start of his trip. He stared back at his mother and watched her disappear behind the surrounding wheat fields and cherry orchards.

It now occurred to him that he wouldn't see his village and his family for the next four months. He was also going to another country, and he'd never been outside his village. Not to mention that the world was at war. Anxiety gnawed at him underneath all the excitement.

They reached the small town of Grodziec about half an hour later, and the driver informed them this was as far as he could take them. They piled out of the wagon and stood on the asphalt road. Filip stepped to the side, onto the dirt, because his bare feet didn't feel comfortable on this unusual surface.

"Where to now?" he asked.

Leszek scratched his head. "We have to keep going north toward Konin. It should be about twelve more kilometers from here."

"Are we going to make the train?" asked one of the others—a scrawny little kid who looked no more than fifteen years old.

"My stepfather said the train is at noon," Filip responded,

looking up at the sun. He didn't own a watch and knew none of the others did either. "We have about four hours to get there."

"Then we better get going," said Leszek.

They picked up their suitcases and marched north. The day was warming up, and the sun reflected off the asphalt like it was a mirror. Filip's body was conditioned for labor, but he was sweating profusely in his wool pants and jacket while carrying a suitcase and shoes strung around his neck.

They walked for an hour until they reached the town of Rychwal and a road that ran toward Konin. It was twice as wide and busy with car traffic. A car passed by every few minutes, so Filip saw more cars in twenty minutes of walking than he'd ever seen in his whole life.

Then a truck appeared around the bend, traveling in the same direction as the group of men. Filip had never before seen this sort of monstrosity. It was four times bigger than a car, and its engine roared like an airplane he had seen drop bombs on his village during the war two years earlier.

"Let's catch a ride," Leszek suggested.

"What if it's the Nazis?" said Filip.

"So what? We're going to Germany anyway," Leszek said, waving his arms at the approaching truck, now only about a hundred meters away.

The truck drove on without stopping, even though its folded canopy exposed an empty bed beneath. The driver grinned as if mocking them, but he continued past at a horse's trot.

"What an asshole," said Leszek, then he ran after the truck. "Let's go!"

They all ran after Leszek, who threw his suitcase inside the truck and grabbed the tailgate to climb in. Filip threw his shoes in first, then his suitcase. But he tripped and fell, his hands and elbows scraping on the asphalt and getting bloody. He rose and chased the truck, watching five other men get on. The truck picked up speed, and his knee hurt from the fall, so he stopped.

"Don't lose my suitcase!" Filip screamed after them, but he could barely hear himself over the shriek of the truck engine.

Leszek laughed, waving at him.

The scrawny kid hadn't even tried to get on the truck. He now walked up to Filip. "That's your friend?" he asked.

"Leszek? No. More like my enemy."

"Then you'll never get your stuff back," he said. "You should probably go back home."

"What's your name, kid?"

"Kazik."

"Listen, Kazik," said Filip, walking in the direction the truck went. "I'm going to Germany no matter what—even if it's just in my underpants."

"You're like me. You're afraid to go back to your father, aren't you?" Kazik said, following Filip.

"Shut up, kid," he snapped, his voice betraying his fear. Kazik was right, but he didn't want to admit it to him. His chances of surviving this trip had diminished significantly without all the clothes and food he'd packed in his suitcase. He still had his mother's coins tucked inside his wool jacket, but he wouldn't spend them unless his life depended on it. The smart thing would be to turn around and go home—maybe try this another time. Yet he couldn't bear seeing his stepfather's face again. He would rather die.

He trudged forward with Kazik behind him. Slow and steady, they walked for three hours, passing the towns and villages of Glowien, Posada, Modla Krolewska, Stare Miasto, and Posoka until they finally reached Konin.

They were utterly spent and famished when they arrived at

the train station. Even though Filip didn't have to carry anything, his strength had waned without food. Kazik told him he had no food in his suitcase. But if he did, Filip figured he probably didn't want to share because of the long journey ahead. He suspected Kazik had occasionally eaten something out of his suitcase while going to pee in the woods. What was Filip supposed to do? He wouldn't steal from Kazik or force him to give him his food. His own foolishness had landed him in this predicament, and he had to face the consequences.

When they arrived at the train station, it was packed with more people than Filip had ever seen gathered in one place. Even the church in his village didn't pack so many. Thousands must have been there, everyone trying to climb onto a gargantuan train. He had seen trains in the distance before, passing by while he worked in the fields in the summers. But standing right next to the locomotive was awe-inspiring. It was ten times the size of the truck he had seen earlier. It huffed with smoke as if it were some giant dragon. Many cars were attached to the locomotive, going back as far as the eye could see.

"To the back!" screamed a German soldier, using his rifle to push Filip and Kazik away from the passenger cars and toward the cattle cars at the back of the train.

"Are we taking the cattle cars?" Kazik asked.

"You need tickets for passenger cars," said a man beside them. "If you're going for work in Germany, they'll take you for free. But it's going to be in those cattle cars."

"I need to find Leszek," said Filip, rushing off. "You take care of yourself, kid."

"Good luck," Kazik responded, jumping into one of the cattle cars.

Filip went from car to car, shouting Leszek's name. Many

men responded because it was a popular given name, but none of them were the Leszek he was looking for. *What if Leszek never got on the train?* he wondered. Even if he had, how would Filip ever find him among the thousands of people on this train? He could starve to death by the time he found him.

Then a whistle blew, and the conductor and the German soldiers started to yell. The crowd pushed Filip into the train's last cattle car. He almost tripped and fell again but held onto a door handle, and somebody pulled him up. Once he got on, it was standing room only. People were shoulder to shoulder, like the chickens in a cage that his father used to take to the flea market. This was extremely uncomfortable, even at his young age.

The train lurched forward, tossing everyone around like rag dolls. Filip stared at the landscape outside, which was passing faster and faster. He thought about jumping out, but somebody squeezed in front of him, pushing him against the back wall. Then the door slammed shut.

There was no going back. He was off to Germany.

3
APRIL 27, 1941

Anna hung from the cell's ceiling by her wrists. Her bare feet hardly touched the ground—just enough for her toes to feel the cold floor but not enough to lift herself. Her torn spring dress shook violently as her body convulsed from the excruciating pain in her shoulder joints. She wanted to cry, but her tears had dried up a long time ago.

All she could do was stare at the concrete floor of her empty prison cell, which was void of any furniture. There were no windows—just a metal door—and no air to ventilate the smell of feces trickling down her legs. She wondered if this was how wild animals felt when thrown into a cage for the first time. Did they have the same feelings of panic, anger, and hopelessness? Having so many emotions and no way to express them made her numb.

She heard footsteps, and the door opened. Three figures appeared, all wearing the same black Gestapo coats with the silver skull insignia on the lapel. She recognized two of them. They had been interrogating her for days. Anna couldn't tell how many days exactly. It could've been two days or thirty. She had lost track.

The third Nazi was new, and he now stood in front of her. He had in his arms a kitten the color of pure snow. He petted it gently as if it were a newborn baby. The kitten purred softly, unaware of the horror in Anna's soul. She wanted to tell the kitten its life was in danger and to run away, but she suspected the kitten had about as much free will as she did.

"How are you today, Miss Kogut?" the new Nazi said in German, which Anna spoke fluently after taking classes for the last ten years.

She didn't respond.

"Let her down," he ordered. The other two goons lowered her to the ground and untied her hands. "Is that better?"

Anna nodded. The blood slowly flowed into her arms again, returning some of the feeling.

"Good," the Nazi continued. "My name is Neitzel. Captain Neitzel. First, I want to apologize for all the . . . brutality. I'm not a big fan of it. But, as you can imagine, we must maintain order. We can't have people running around disturbing the peace. Don't you agree?"

Anna disagreed but said nothing.

"Well," Neitzel continued. "I know you're just a messenger. You're a young lady the terrorists took advantage of. That's how they work, you know. They find naïve boys and girls and use them for their evil deeds. Of course, they would never get their own hands dirty. No, they are too cowardly for that. And that's wrong. That's just immoral. Don't you agree?"

Anna stared at him for a moment, then said, "Where are my sisters?"

"Your sisters are waiting for you," he said. "All you have to do is tell us about your handler."

"I don't know what you're talking about," she lied.

"Of course you do," he said. "We need to know his name and address. That's all."

"I don't have a handler."

"Then where did you get the leaflets?" Neitzel challenged.

"I printed them at my high school," she said, which Captain Mazurek had instructed her to say in case of capture.

Neitzel smiled. He lifted the kitten by the fur at the back of its neck and held it in front of Anna's face. "This is for you."

Anna was relieved that the kitten's life might be spared. She took it into her weak arms and snuggled it as if it were her child.

"I believe you, Miss Kogut," Neitzel said. "However, the law is very clear. All acts of sabotage and terrorism are punishable by death. We cannot make any exceptions—not even for nice young ladies like yourself. Otherwise, the world would be in chaos. I'm sure you understand." Then he looked over at the other two men. "Take her!" he ordered, and the two goons sprung to action, grabbing Anna at each side and twisting her arms to stand her up.

Anna screamed in pain while trying to hang onto the kitten. She tried to walk as they rushed her out into the hallway, but her legs were too weak, and her feet dragged along the floor while they hefted her limp body.

"No! Please don't . . ." she pleaded, but it was hopeless. She didn't want to die, she realized. Anna was not going to tell them anything, but she was not ready to die either. She was too young. There was still so much ahead of her. She had never traveled anywhere exciting and had never driven in a car. She'd never even had a boyfriend. Anna had seen couples walk in the park, holding hands and sneaking kisses, and she wanted to know what that felt like before she died.

The goons dragged her down a flight of stairs and into an enclosed courtyard, where they tied her waist and legs to a pole next to a brick wall ridden with bullet holes. Facing her were three soldiers with rifles slung over their right shoulders.

"GEWEHR UBER!" shouted one of the Gestapo officers.

The soldiers swung their rifles forward.

"ANLEGEN!" he shouted.

The soldiers aimed their rifles. Their muscles visibly tensed.

Anna sobbed as she stared into the gun barrels facing her. The kitten looked up from her arms and meowed as if begging her to save its life. Tears began to flow out of her eyes, apparently not all dried up. She had never imagined it would come to this when she picked up those leaflets days earlier. She felt like a coward, crying and trembling before her enemy. How stupid she'd been to think herself so invincible.

Seconds passed—maybe a minute—but no order to fire came. The soldiers just stood there, aiming their rifles at her. The silence was excruciating. Anna's nerves stretched as tight as a violin string. She now wanted to tell them everything. She wanted this to end. That was when she realized it was what they wanted. They wanted her to scream for help. To tell them who her handler was.

"FUCK YOU!" she screamed at them. She was not going to die a coward. She was not going to give them more people to kill. "FUCK YOU!"

They didn't move for another few moments.

"WEGTRETEN!" the officer shouted finally.

The soldiers slung the rifles around their shoulders and stood at ease. The two goons approached Anna and untied her, then dragged her out of the courtyard and up the stairs again. They took away the kitten—apparently just a prop in their game to make her talk—and threw Anna unceremoniously back inside the empty concrete cell.

She lay on the floor and sobbed. The tears were soon gone again, but she kept crying. It made her feel better. She imagined herself as a baby, sobbing on her mother's shoulder for comfort. Anna didn't know what else to do or think. She was exhausted and cried herself to sleep.

She woke to screams and slamming doors. There was a commotion outside her cell. People were crying, and the Germans were yelling out orders while thumping their army boots. Then her lock slammed, and the door swung open. The two goons stepped inside.

"Time to go, bitch," one of them said as he pulled her out by her jacket collar.

"Where are you taking me?" she said, fearing a real execution this time.

"You're going to Germany. They'll put you to work and get some dirt behind those pretty fingernails."

"I have to see my sisters—" she said, but the goon threw a furious punch at her stomach and knocked the wind out of her lungs.

They dragged her out into the hallway, where she was joined by other prisoners also being pulled out of their cells. The Germans rushed them down the stairs and back into the same courtyard where she'd faced the firing squad.

Anna and about a hundred other prisoners stood shoulder to shoulder, surrounded by the SS and their dogs, which were barking as if ready to tear them to shreds. She wanted to talk to those around her—predominantly young men and women her age—but the situation felt so hopeless that trying to get information seemed like a lost cause. Their faces told her everything she needed to know. They were all just trying to survive this nightmare.

One of the Gestapo officers barked orders, and the SS guards pushed the prisoners toward a tunnel between two buildings. They squeezed through in a column five people wide and emerged on the main street, where more guards were waiting.

The guards walked them through the town until they arrived at a train station. People walked past the prisoners as if they did not exist. Anna could not find anyone's gaze; everyone just stared at the ground. *Cowards!* she thought. She was mad at all those people for not doing something to help.

The SS pushed them into the train cars like cattle. Some prisoners tried to resist, but they were quickly trampled or kicked by the guards. It took only about fifteen minutes for the train to load up. Then the SS locked the doors of each car, and the train surged forward.

Anna slid down to the floor of her car and covered her head in resignation. She could now feel what she thought those zoo animals felt. She remembered a male lion who just lay on the ground and stared blankly at the crowds across the ditch. He probably knew his freedom was gone forever.

She realized this was the end of her freedom too.

4

APRIL 30, 1941

As Filip crawled around the sleeping men, his stomach grumbled louder than the monotonous banging of the train rail wheels skipping rails every few seconds. He paused for a moment, looked around to make sure no one saw him, then crept forward again. He reached inside a bag tied around a sleeping man's neck, then pulled out a slice of bread and a piece of sausage. Salivating, he wanted to take a bite right then. But he hid the food inside his wool jacket instead and crawled back against the car's wall.

Stealing was the only way to survive. He was ridden with guilt but had no choice but to live like this. He couldn't find Leszek or his suitcase, and nobody dared share their food with him voluntarily. Everyone on the train survived purely on what they'd brought from home, and that supply was running low after four days of travel. The only water they drank came from frequent rains along the way. The Germans let them leave the car only once when they changed trains in Berlin. They didn't even provide bathroom breaks. The sixty or so of them had to share a bucket in the corner of the car. They threw the contents out through a narrow window near the ceiling.

When Filip confirmed that nobody had noticed him, he pulled out the sausage and took a large bite. It was the best sausage he'd ever tasted. The combination of fat and garlic made him feel intoxicated with ecstasy. Maybe it was because he hadn't eaten in two days—not since he stole some onions from an unsuspecting youth.

Filip took a few more bites of the sausage and the bread, then snuck his cold, bare feet under a guy sleeping beside him to warm up. He closed his eyes and quickly fell asleep. He dreamed about his home village, envisioning himself throwing bushels of wheat onto a horse cart while village girls watched him with admiration. They smiled at him mischievously and giggled like they did at the village dances. He wanted to kiss one of them, but she laughed and ran away.

"Get up, peasant!" said a man's voice.

Filip jerked up. He checked his pockets to make sure all his valuables were still there, including the money from his mother. Everything seemed in order.

"We're in Fulda. Adolf Hitler would like to welcome you personally," said the man beside him. His name was Wlodek. He was much older than Filip, already in his mid-twenties, and had been to Germany many times for work. "Make sure you have all your papers and be quiet. Whatever you do, don't argue with the Germans, or you'll get shot."

The train stopped, and the large car door swung open. Filip pushed toward it, wanting to see the town, but he didn't get a chance to examine it in detail because the German soldiers rushed everyone out of the cattle cars like sheep.

"Schnell!" yelled the soldiers, pushing everyone into a small brick building around the corner from the train station. About one thousand scared souls—mostly teenagers and young men in their twenties—stood waiting, arranged in multiple lines. The soldiers quickly separated men from women and pushed them into two different halls. The soldiers yelled some more, waving their arms.

"What do they want?" asked Filip.

"I think they want us to take our clothes off," replied Wlodek.

Some must have understood because they had started to remove their clothes. Filip did the same. He held the coins and the rest of the bread close to his chest, hoping nobody would rob him. They were ordered to throw the clothes into kettles full of boiling water. The clothes were then quickly removed and placed in ovens, where they cooked dry.

The men stood completely naked, holding their hands over their private parts while the clothes were going through the process. An uncomfortable silence hung in the room as they waited. They all pretended this was normal.

"Either they're trying to kill the fleas or they are going to feed us our own clothes," somebody shouted, trying to break the silence with humor, but nobody laughed.

"Why are they doing this?" Filip asked.

"They don't want fleas and ticks to spread to their superior race," said Wlodek.

Filip had never had either, but he wondered why his skin had itched so much in the last few days. He took a bath every week back home, which took care of most bugs. He thought that maybe he had gotten them and didn't even know it. Perhaps the Germans were at fault themselves for transporting the workers in old cattle cars meant for animals.

When Filip got his clothes back, they were so shrunk that he could barely wear them. While others had extra clothes in their suitcases, he had nothing else to wear, so he was forced to put them back on.

As soon as he exited the building, he spotted Leszek pushing through the crowd—the only person with two suitcases.

"LESZEK!" Filip shouted.

Leszek saw Filip and hesitated as if considering what to do. Filip rushed toward him, excited to finally find him. He'd never been so happy to see Leszek, and he almost cried when he grabbed his suitcase.

"I can't believe I found you," he said. "Thank God you have my suitcase."

Leszek scratched his head and said, "Yes, you owe me a huge favor. I've been dragging this thing around through all of Germany for you."

Filip hugged him. "God bless you! I thought I'd never see it again. How about my shoes?"

"They're inside."

Filip opened the suitcase. His shoes and clothes were still there, but the food was all gone. "What happened to my sausage and cheese?"

"Sorry, Filip. I ate it all. I ate my food in two days, so I had to eat yours. This trip was so long, and the fucking Germans wouldn't let us out. Plus, I never thought I'd see you again."

Filip thought Leszek probably still had his own food and ate just Filip's, but he was so happy to get his clothes back that he quickly forgave him. "I'm glad to see you, Leszek. Let's not get separated again."

"By the way, you look like a clown in those shrunk clothes," Leszek said, laughing at his own joke.

Filip wanted to punch him but thought better of it and laughed instead. "Where to now?" he asked.

"They want us on a train to Kassel in fifteen minutes. It's a regular train with seats and everything. They say there are good jobs up there. About a hundred of us are going on that one."

"Let's go then!" Filip declared, enthusiastic about not needing to travel inside a cattle car anymore.

They ran across several tracks to a passenger train parked closest to the station. The conductor was already signaling to leave when they boarded one of the carriages in the back.

"It's third-class seating, but it's free for the laborers," said Leszek.

They sat on a bench across from a few men Filip didn't recognize. The car had thirty benches, each designed to seat only two, but about a hundred people squeezed in together. Some Germans, easily identified by their fedoras, occupied the front of the car, but the passengers were primarily Polish men and women traveling for work. Despite the overcrowding, people were laughing and singing. Somebody pulled out a bottle of vodka that made its rounds. Even Filip and Leszek got to take a sip.

Filip was excited that his long trip was finally coming to an end. He spent most of the ride grinning while observing the German countryside through a big window. He wanted to take it all in. Strangely enough, Germany didn't look much different than Poland; it had the same wheat and rye fields, apple and cherry orchards, villages, and towns filled with red tile roofs and stucco walls. The only difference was that Germany seemed cleaner and more organized, with more asphalt roads.

"Do they have somewhere to pee on this train?" Filip asked. "I didn't have time to go at the train station."

"Yeah, in the front," said one of the men sitting across from them.

Filip got up and walked toward the front of the car. He

lowered his cap when he walked past the Germans, not wanting to disrespect them. There was a door that looked like it might be the place with a toilet, but a blond gal stood in front of it. She was beautiful, with blue eyes and white skin that looked almost angelic. But her yellow dress was torn up and splattered with blood. She stared blankly out the window as if in a trance.

"Excuse me," he said. "Is that the toilet?"

She turned her head and stared at him for a moment, furrowing her brows as if trying to comprehend the world around her. Then she moved away from the door and pushed her body against the wall without saying a word.

"I'm Filip," he said, feeling sorry for her.

"Anna," she responded, her voice barely audible.

Filip pulled a piece of bread from his jacket and handed it to her. "Here, take it. You look like you need it more than I do," he said.

She seemed confused about his generosity as if she had never experienced any. But she took the bread and began to eat it with relish.

"Thank you," she said.

"You're welcome," he replied, then entered the toilet room.

When Filip finally came out, Anna was gone. He looked around but couldn't find her in the crowd. He was surprised at how much he wanted to see her. He hoped to talk to her more. Instead, he went back to his seat.

"We're almost there," said Leszek.

The brakes engaged, and the train began to decelerate. The crowd hooted and hollered but quieted down when they saw German soldiers lined up all along the train station. Kassel was a bigger town than Fulda. Hundreds of people were waiting on the platforms, which were covered with a giant metal roof.

The train stopped, and the soldiers started to yell out orders. Filip and everyone else quickly evacuated their car. They were directed toward the back of the platform and lined up against a red brick building. A table was set up with a couple of clerks, who began to take down information to process all the Polish workers.

Filip scanned the crowd, looking for Anna, but he couldn't find her. It was as if she had never existed. *Was she a ghost?* he wondered. *Did I dream up meeting her?*

"Who are you looking for?" Leszek asked.

"Nobody," said Filip, not only because he wasn't sure if Anna existed but also because Leszek was famous in his village for stealing women from other men. Filip didn't want him to know anything about Anna.

Filip arrived at the clerk's desk and was asked his name. The clerk told him to write it down on a piece of paper, which Filip had learned to do in fourth grade—his last year of schooling. He also received his new identification documents and a badge with the letter *P*, which he was told to wear visibly at all times.

As soon as everyone was processed, the soldiers lined them up against the wall, and a group of about forty German civilians began to inspect them. The workers had to open their mouths and lift their arms and legs to show how healthy they were. Filip had done the same to horses and cows when his father took him shopping for farm animals at a market.

A well-built man wearing a green hat with a swastika pin pulled Filip out of the lineup, stood him next to a heavyset gal, and then disappeared into the crowd. In the meantime, Filip watched as Leszek was picked by another man, who pulled him away toward the other side of the crowd.

"I want to go with him," Leszek said to the man as he

pointed at Filip. But the man didn't listen and kept pulling him away. "I'll see you, Filip!" Leszek yelled, giving up.

Filip didn't know what to do. His instinct was to rush after Leszek to stay with someone he knew, but he also didn't want to upset his new boss if that was who the guy in the green fedora was. So he just waved at Leszek and remained standing where he was.

The green-fedora man emerged from the crowd again. He stood in front of Filip and the gal. "I am Herr Wolff. You belong to me now," he said in terribly broken Polish. Then he walked off toward a nearby horse carriage. He waved at them to follow.

Filip looked at the young woman. "What did he say?"

"I'm not sure," she replied. "Something about owning us. I'm Sabina, by the way."

"Filip," he said.

They followed Herr Wolff to his carriage. Filip wondered what awaited him.

5

MAY 1, 1941

Anna found three young women standing over her when she opened her eyes in the morning. She had slept deeply after arriving at the farmhouse in the middle of the night and now felt disoriented. She hardly remembered how she'd ended up in a bed.

The man who had brought her to the farmhouse didn't say anything and had just shown her to a room in the attic with several cots. She had lain down in one of them and fallen asleep immediately, forgetting about her unfamiliar surroundings. She was exhausted from the travel, and the bread the young man on the train had given her calmed her nerves. She had tried to remember his name. *Was it Filip?* she wondered. She hoped to see him again. He was the only one who showed her kindness during the trip to Germany. The rest of it was a blur of violence and brutality that made her numb. If her stomach hadn't constantly reminded her that she was alive, she would have thought it was a nightmare.

"You don't look like a farm girl," one of the women said in

Polish with an Eastern, Russian-like accent. She was sturdily built with a large, round face, and she held her hands on her hips like she owned the place.

"I'm not," said Anna, sitting up.

"Hmm. You're proud," said the woman, surprising Anna at how quickly she figured her out. "Is that how you ended up here?"

"What do you mean?"

"You know what I mean. You did something bad because you're proud, and now you're here working for Hitler. Am I lying?"

"Sorry, who are you?" Anna asked.

"I'm Dasha," said the woman. She nodded toward the other two women. "These are Misha and Slava. We're all Ukrainians from villages around Lwow. Who are *you*?"

Anna stared at the women, not sure if she was ready to share her name with them. They wore traditional peasant skirts and shirts over their strong, healthy bodies. One of them was pregnant, maybe seven months along.

"I'm Anna," she said finally. "Why am I here?"

"That's a good question," said Dasha. "You look weak. Not good for work."

"What are *you* doing here then?"

"We have strong farmer arms for work and wide hips to make strong babies," Dasha answered. "That's why Germans brought us here."

Anna understood the first part about the strong arms. Dasha could throw her over the house. But she didn't quite get the second part. Who was Dasha going to make babies with?

"You don't understand, do you?" said Dasha, immediately sensing Anna's confusion. "In my village, life is simple. You work in the fields, and then you make children, so there are more people to work in the fields. That's it. There's nothing else. I think life in a German village is the same."

"There are no Ukrainian men here," Anna remarked, unable to comprehend.

"You'll figure it out soon. The old man has not introduced himself to you yet. If I were you, I would not fight. A weak girl like you might get hurt."

Anna finally understood. She wished she didn't, but Dasha made it all too clear.

"Come on," said Dasha. "Let's get you ready for work." She pulled Anna out of her cot and stood her up. "You look like shit. Take it all off. Misha, get some water."

The pregnant woman ran off.

"I'm not taking my clothes off," Anna protested.

"You can't wear torn-up city clothes for farmwork," Dasha said, pulling Anna's jacket off her. "And you stink."

Anna tried to hold onto her clothes, the last reminder of her home, but Dasha and Slava made quick work of her. She was naked in seconds. She held her arms over her breasts while they examined her.

"Skin and bones," Dasha announced, shaking her head in disgust. "What am I supposed to do with this? Herr Uding must be running out of money."

"I'm sorry," said Anna. "I haven't eaten much in the last few days."

"What is that around your neck?" asked Dasha.

"It's the Black Madonna. From my hometown."

"Ah, good. At least you're not a pagan."

Misha returned with a bar of soap and a metal bowl filled with water. Dasha pulled a small towel out of her skirt's pocket, dipped it in the water, and then began scrubbing Anna from head to toe.

When they finally toweled her off and dressed her in farm clothes—the same type of skirt and shirt they wore—Anna saw a different person when she looked in the mirror. She was a Ukrainian farm woman. That didn't match what she was on the inside—a Polish city girl who once had ambitions to be a doctor.

"You look good enough," said Dasha. "Time to go downstairs."

Anna followed Dasha and the women downstairs and into the kitchen, where two men and a woman sat at a large wooden table, eating breakfast. The younger man, who was maybe in his forties and was the one who brought her there the night before, stood up and approached them. He was ugly, with eyes too close together and a big nose pointed up like a pig's. He seemed nervous when he spoke.

"Good morning," he said slowly in German, which Anna understood perfectly. "You look good. Better than yesterday, I mean."

"Thank you," Anna said, not wanting to be rude, even though she didn't trust him.

"Sorry. I wasn't sure if you spoke German. I'm Klaus Uding, and this is my wife Helma and my father Gustaf," he said, pointing back at his family members.

The father looked just like Klaus, with the same beady eyes and upturned large nose. But his hair was gray and deeply receding. He didn't acknowledge Anna. He only grinned creepily to himself as he continued to eat.

The wife also looked a bit like a pig. She was fat, with a large, round face and three chins. She glanced at Anna but quickly retreated to her plate of food as if afraid to say anything.

"I'll show her the farm and teach her what she needs to do," said Dasha. "You don't worry about a thing, Herr Uding."

"Thank you, Dasha," Klaus said.

Dasha pulled Anna out of the kitchen and closed the door behind them. "That wasn't too bad," she said. "I think he likes you." Misha and Slava snickered. "What are you still doing here!" Dasha yelled at them. "Get to work!"

They ran off quickly.

"It seems like you're in charge here," Anna pointed out.

"You can say that," Dasha admitted. "Helma doesn't do much. Just likes to sit around and eat. Klaus and Gustaf mostly do the heavy work, then go drinking at the tavern every evening. So we take care of everything else. Milk the cows. Feed the chickens. Collect the eggs. And, of course, we take care of the pigs. That's going to be your job. Come on, I'll show you."

Anna followed Dasha outside. It was daytime now, and she could finally see the farm. It consisted of the two-story farmhouse, where they slept, but there was also a large barn and two other buildings—one small and the other long and narrow.

"That's where we keep the cows," Dasha said, pointing at the small building. "And that's where you'll be working," she said, walking toward the long, narrow building.

Anna was following closely behind when an unbearable stench assaulted her nostrils. She gagged, coughing against the overwhelming putridity. It was as if she had thrust her head into the depths of a city sewer.

"What is that?" she asked.

Dasha laughed. "That's sixty pigs eating and shitting all day, every day. Don't worry. It's worse inside, but you'll get used to it over time."

It was much, much worse inside the building. Anna felt

vomit crawl up her esophagus, and she pinched her nose to stop herself from throwing up the little food she had eaten in the last few days.

"Don't be a baby, city girl," Dasha said, grabbing a shovel. "We need to feed them first, and then we shovel shit. We do this while they eat so they don't knock us down. You have to be careful. Pigs are assholes."

A wheelbarrow full of mashed-up vegetables and grain stood next to one of the many pens, each containing about five or six pigs. Dasha began to shovel the food into a trough inside one of the pens.

"You grab a pitchfork and start shoveling the shit out through that little opening in the wall," she said. "We use the shit later to fertilize the fields."

Anna let go of her nose and grabbed the pitchfork. Her eyes were watering from the smell—or maybe she was crying—but she managed to wiggle her way behind the pigs and began shoveling the shit out through the small waist-high opening. The pigs violently shoved each other to get to the food while grunting and squealing in excitement. They didn't seem to care that Anna was behind them. Otherwise, they would easily knock her down into the nasty excrement.

She was exhausted when they finally finished with all twelve pig pens. Anna got used to the smell, or at least it didn't make her want to hurl. But her muscles were on fire from fatigue, and huge blisters formed on both her hands. She sat down on the ground outside the pigsty and cried. She didn't want to cry; she wanted to be strong, but the emotions took over, and she had to release them.

Dasha sat next to her. "It's fine," she said, pulling pieces of cloth from her skirt pocket and wrapping them around Anna's hands. "They don't give us gloves because they are too expensive. But after a while, you will build calluses on your hands and won't form blisters anymore. See?" She showed Anna her hands, which looked like men's hands, with a big yellow callus below each finger. "You'll be fine," she said.

Anna nodded in agreement, but she now began to sob, her body heaving violently. She couldn't control herself. It was just too much to handle.

Dasha put an arm around her and pulled her in for a hug. "Don't you worry about a thing," she said. "I'll take care of you."

"I want to go home," said Anna.

"Oh, you poor thing. You can never go back."

Anna pulled away from Dasha and wiped her tears. "What do you mean?"

"Don't you know anything? Didn't Herr Uding tell you? You're one of those troublemakers. Your papers say that you're to be permanently incorporated into the Reich. You can never go back to Poland."

Anna's sadness now turned to anger. "I don't care what *they* say. I'm going back to Poland to my family."

Dasha stood up and shook the dirt off her skirt. "Sure, honey. You do that. But how about we eat some breakfast first?"

Anna knew Dasha was mocking her, but in her heart, she believed what she said was true. She decided right there and then that she was not going to shovel shit for the Germans.

6

MAY 2, 1941

Filip woke up when he heard footsteps outside his bedroom. The room was still dark, and he saw only a glimmer of light through the curtains. He got up and opened the window. It smelled like five o'clock—a curious mix of grass, pine trees, and cow dung. Looking out the window was his only pleasure since Herr Wolff had locked him up in this room two days before upon his arrival from Poland. He didn't have much of a view—just the farm itself, which consisted of the farmhouse and a huge barn—but it was better than being locked up in the cattle car.

The lock turned, and the door opened. Usually, Herr Wolff slid food into the room twice daily, but a female face appeared this time. Filip assumed this was his wife, Frau Wolff. She had a grin on her face, but not one of kindness. It was more like she was permanently pleased with herself about something. Otherwise, she was a handsome woman: older than Filip by about ten years, with sharp blue eyes, a hooked nose, and straight, thin lips. She could have passed for a man if it hadn't been for her braided blond hair and generous breasts and hips.

"Schnell! Let's go, you lazy Pole!" she shouted at him in broken Polish.

Filip didn't understand why she was so mad, but he quickly rushed out of the room. Sabina, the heavyset woman who'd arrived with him, also came out of her room. She looked just as confused as he felt. She seemed scared as well. Her small brown eyes bobbed nervously, her lips quivered, and her large frame backed against the wall as if she were trying to blend in with the whitewash. She and Filip had spoken to one another through their windows over the last two days, and neither could figure out why they were being kept in their rooms for so long. Sabina's theory was that the Wolffs were going to fatten them up and eat them. She told Filip about some ridiculous fairy tale about a witch wanting to eat a boy and a girl after luring them into a house made from gingerbread cookies.

Frau Wolff shoved Filip and Sabina down the stairs and out to the barn, where four cows were lined up against the wall. She yelled, waving her arms as if to tell them to milk the cows. Filip's father had owned three cows, and he knew his way around them. So he sat on a wooden stool next to one of the cows, put a metal bucket under her, and got straight to work. Sabina apparently also knew what to do because she did the same with another cow.

Frau Wolff left the barn, still yelling at them.

"What the hell was that about?" Filip said to Sabina.

"I have no idea."

"Well, I'm starving," he said, lifting the bucket to his lips and drinking the milk.

"Stop it, Filip. You're going to get us in trouble," Sabina said, horrified.

"The witch didn't feed us this morning, and I haven't had milk since I left my village."

Sabina didn't reply and continued milking the cow. She must have been hungry too, but she wouldn't help herself to the milk.

"You still think they're going to eat us?" said Filip.

"Don't make fun of me. There are pictures in my church of the devil eating people, and isn't Hitler the devil himself?"

"True," Filip conceded. "We had the same pictures in my church. But there were no pictures of the devil making people milk his cows."

"You're stupid," she said, giving up on the conversation. "Just do your job."

They finished milking all four cows and carried their full buckets inside the farmhouse. As soon as they entered the hallway, Frau Wolff rushed out of the kitchen, already yelling at them. She made them set the buckets on the ground and shuffled them from one chore to another around the farm the rest of the morning.

They finally ate breakfast around nine o'clock, after four hours of work. Frau Wolff gave them some bread with butter and one boiled egg each. Filip inhaled the food like it was the first time he'd ever eaten. They ate out of sight of Frau Wolff at a small table in the hallway, so he hurriedly licked the plate.

"Stop licking the plate, Filip," said Sabina. Before he could protest, she put a finger to her lips. "Listen."

Filip heard the faint sounds of heavy grunts coming from inside the house. He could recognize these from a kilometer away because he'd often heard them in his father's house.

"I hope he got better food for that," he said.

A few minutes later, Herr Wolff walked out into the hallway. Filip didn't recognize him at first because he wore a full military uniform. Frau Wolff followed behind, hiking up her dress while yelling at Herr Wolff in German. He must not have been amused by whatever she said because he turned away, grabbed a backpack propped against the wall, and stormed out of the house.

That upset Frau Wolff even more. She pulled out a whip tucked behind her belt and began to hit Filip and Sabina with it. Each blow felt like a knife slicing through Filip's skin. He pulled Sabina out of the building and into the garden. Otherwise, he thought Frau Wolff might kill them both. Instead of chasing them, she slammed the doors behind her and locked herself in the house.

That was the last time they saw Herr Wolff.

Frau Katherine Wolff sat at the kitchen table, her body shaking uncontrollably. Her husband had abandoned her, leaving her alone with two devils from Poland. She understood it was his duty to fight for Germany and secure the land the German people needed, but why now? Why leave her by herself on this damn farm with nobody to protect her? All alone with the slaves. She was scared to death of them. She heard stories of slaves stealing, raping, and murdering their owners. She couldn't believe her husband had brought them here without her approval, and she refused to let them out of their rooms until Herr Wolff left for the Eastern Front. She had no choice. She couldn't run the farm by herself.

Frau Wolff got up and walked to the cabinet where she displayed her mother's china. She opened one of the bottom drawers and pulled out a pistol. It was a Mauser Model 1914 that she'd inherited from her father, an officer during the Great War. It wasn't made for a lady, but her father had made her practice shooting with it, so she was not afraid to use it. She was going to show the devils not to mess with her.

She rushed out of the kitchen and into the hallway that led to the entrance. She turned the key and opened the front door. Both slaves were sitting on the stone stairs leading up to the house, but they sprung up as soon as the door opened. They backed away when they noticed the gun in her hand.

"Upstairs!" she shouted, waving the gun and motioning for them to get inside. "Let's go, you dirty pigs!"

They hesitated for a moment but followed her order. Frau Wolff chased them upstairs to their rooms and locked the doors. Relieved to be safe again, she hid the pistol inside her skirt and went downstairs. She then went outside, got on her bicycle, and rode as fast as possible. There was no time to waste. She couldn't live like this for even one more day.

The Bürgermeister's house was located near the main road running through the village. There were only eighty-seven houses in Rotenburg an der Fulda, but nothing was permitted to happen without Otto Koch's approval. He was a small man already in his fifties but more of a disciplinarian than the Führer himself. He made sure the village was in impeccable shape. Every roof tile had to be of the same shade of orange. All the houses had to be painted the same white. The streets had to be swept daily. Even the church bells had to be precisely on time per his watch.

Frau Wolff was nervous about talking to him when she got off her bicycle and knocked on his front door.

"What's the matter, Frau Wolff?" he said when he opened the door. Koch wore a white cloth napkin over his chest, and his long mustache bobbed up and down like a scared mouse as he chewed food.

Frau Wolff only now realized it was lunchtime and that she'd caused a great disturbance to his daily routine.

"Mahlzeit!" she said, wishing him a good meal.

"Mahlzeit!" he replied, as was customary.

"I'm sorry to disturb you, Bürgermeister Koch, but I have something very important I need to discuss with you."

"Well, what is it, woman? What's more important than a peaceful lunch?"

"My husband made a mistake," she said. "He went off to war this morning and left me all alone with two Polish slaves. They smell like pigs and look like they want to rob me and kill me. I'm a weak woman by myself and scared for my life. I'm afraid to be in the house with them."

Koch frowned in confusion. "Your husband did the right thing, Frau Wolff. How else will you harvest your crops and care for the farm?"

"Please, I beg you," she said, putting her hands together as if in a prayer. "Exchange them for a German helper. I'll give you both of them to do as you wish for just one German. He'll do more work than ten lazy Polish swine—"

"Frau Wolff," he said. "I don't know if you're aware, but we're about to go to war with Russia. Every able man in this country, including your husband and my own son, has been mobilized. There's no one I could give you even if I wanted to. I suggest you return to your farm and do the best you can with what you have to collect the grain our people and our soldiers will need this coming winter."

"But, Herr Koch," she pleaded. "I might not survive the night."

"I'm sorry," he said, closing the door in her face.

Defeated, Frau Wolff sat on the stairs leading up to the front door. If Koch didn't help her, then nobody else could either. She was left to deal with it alone and would do it the only way she knew how: fighting fear with fear.

7
JUNE 23, 1941

Anna tended to the pigs, just like she had every morning. She was alone this time because Dasha needed to help with the cows since Misha had just delivered her baby and Frau Helma was sick with a fever. She took turns shoveling food into the trough and manure out of the building while the pigs ate.

She was on her fourth pen when Gustaf showed up. He smirked at her, took a pitchfork, and got behind the pigs to shovel shit in the next pen. Anna wasn't sure what to do. He'd never helped in the pigsty before.

"What are you standing around for?" he said. "Get to work."

She obeyed his order and shoveled food into the trough in the next pen. Gustaf laughed, apparently pleased with himself for scaring Anna. He then got behind one of the pigs and thrust his hips back and forth at the pig's rear end. His laugh was loud and sinister, like that of the devil himself.

"You like it?" he said, grabbing his crotch.

Anna dropped her shovel and ran out, not stopping until she was inside the farmhouse. Her heart was racing. She pressed her back against the stone wall in the hallway and tried to take deep breaths. Her hands were shaking, and her legs felt weak.

"Pull yourself together," she said to herself.

After a few moments, she was able to calm down. She didn't know what to do next, except that she wasn't going back to the pigsty. Yet she couldn't just take the day off and hide somewhere. She had to keep busy or she would get in trouble.

She entered the kitchen. With two women out of commission, no one made breakfast. So she rolled up her sleeves and began preparing a meal. She'd learned how to cook from her mother, spending countless hours as a child watching her cook and helping her prep as a teenager. Many people complimented her mother's cooking, but Anna never looked for praise. She found cooking to be more like a form of meditation. Back in Poland, it had been her stress reliever from studying. She had memorized all the recipes and decided to try them on the Germans.

Anna had a feast ready when everyone gathered for lunch two hours later.

"What is this?" asked Klaus Uding.

"I prepared lunch," Anna replied, setting forks and spoons on their table as if it were her usual routine.

They sat down and began to eat. They seemed skeptical at first, perhaps worried about being poisoned, Anna thought. But their pace quickly accelerated, and they were shoving food into their mouths as if they hadn't eaten in days.

"It's good," Klaus said, smiling at Anna.

Anna was surprised at how much everyone loved the food. The men couldn't stop smiling as they devoured her meat pierogis covered with fried bacon bits and sweet plum knedle with sour cream and sugar for dessert. The only person not smiling was Helma, who quietly disappeared into her bedroom after finishing her meal. Anna knew she was jealous, but she was probably also happy to give up her work. Anna hadn't seen her do much since she arrived on the farm. Helma seemed content with just sitting around and staring out the window the whole day.

While Klaus sat on a small couch and drank his beer, Gustaf came up behind Anna with that same creepy smirk on his face. Anna tried to ignore him, but he just stood behind her, watching as she washed the plates. He then slapped her hard on the buttocks. She jumped forward in shock, slamming into the countertop with her stomach, which made him laugh.

Klaus didn't share the laugh but didn't protest either. "Come drink with me, Father," he said instead, pouring beer into an empty glass from a small barrel.

Anna collected herself and went back to cleaning. The act was so shocking that she almost didn't believe it had happened. But it did happen. She still felt the sting of Gustaf's hand on her buttocks. She was humiliated and couldn't do anything about it. Protesting would only make it worse. She decided that maybe it was better to ignore it. She waited for a good opportunity to leave unnoticed, and when both Klaus and Gustaf started to laugh about something, half drunk and half comatose from the food, she quickly ran out of the kitchen.

She lay in her cot that night, reminiscing about her home and family while trying to keep warm under a thin wool blanket. She was always so cold at night. Back in Poland, at her parents' house, she would cuddle up with her father in front of the fireplace every night to read books together. Then she would snuggle with her older sister under a thick comforter made from duck feathers that kept them cozy all night. She wondered where her sisters might be at that moment. Were they in Poland, released back to their parents? Were they in Germany somewhere, working as slaves just like Anna? Or were they dead in a mass grave somewhere?

Anna wanted to cry and feel sorry for herself, but she was not one to surrender easily. If she had one thing going for her, it was her pride. She had to prove to these Germans that a Polish woman was stronger than all of them put together. Her body might be failing her now, and her mind was vulnerable, but she would condition them both until they were stronger than a rock.

In the meantime, she hoped today's success in the kitchen might give her some relief from the hard labor in the pigsty. This would give her enough time to plan something else and avoid Dasha's prophecy about the old man Gustaf. Perhaps she could run away. After all, the Germans could always find a replacement for her. She heard slave workers were arriving from all over Europe every day. If she disappeared, another strong Ukrainian woman would be picked up at the train station.

On the other hand, the more she thought about it, the more she convinced herself the whole thing with Gustaf was nothing to worry about. It had been a couple of months already since her arrival in Germany. So, surely, Gustaf would have shown his bad intentions a long time ago if he had any. Even her roommates never really talked about it. Misha, now with her baby in a crib, never said much. Anna tried to ask her some questions about the baby once, but Misha just turned her back and didn't respond. However, Dasha, who always had something to say, also kept quiet. Whenever Anna met her eyes, Dasha would avert her gaze by staring at the wall. Maybe they were just trying to scare her, and there was nothing to worry about.

That was when she fell asleep. She dreamed about Poland and her family.

It happened in the middle of the night. The first thing Anna felt was a hard object on her backside. She initially thought it was a dream. But then, as she awakened, she figured it was just Dasha sneaking into her bed to cuddle for warmth, as she did on many occasions. It was only when Anna recognized Gustaf's smell and groaning voice that she realized what was happening.

She screamed in terror, jerking herself away and pressing against the wall. Gustaf's hand quickly cupped her mouth, and his right leg clamped her body down to the bed. Anna thrashed around, trying to find a way out in the darkness, but Gustaf was strong for an old man. She bit his hand, but he slapped her hard across the face, and the room spun around like she was on a carousel back in her neighborhood playground. Gustaf then pushed her down on her stomach, pulled her hair back, hiked up her nightgown, and spread her legs with his knees. She wanted to fight back, but her body didn't have enough strength to respond. Anna heard him snicker and lick his finger, then . . .

CRACK!

It sounded like a forest tree breaking in half. Gustaf went limp on top of her. Then a dim candlelight broke the darkness, and she saw Misha standing over her with a broken chair in her trembling hands. Anna now fully understood where Misha's child came from. Perhaps she'd known all along but didn't want to believe it.

She also knew she didn't have as much time as she thought.

8

JULY 4, 1941

It happened the night before the first harvest. After Frau Wolff locked Filip and Sabina in their attic rooms, Filip lay down on his straw mattress and began to doze off. That was when he heard the lock turn and the door squeak open. He looked up and saw Frau Wolff standing there. She stepped in and closed the door behind her.

"What do you want?" he asked, confused.

She hesitated, then said, "Just wanted to tell you that you did a good job with the horses today."

"I need to get some sleep," he said, flipping his body away from her.

"Good . . . Sleep well, Filip," she said. Then she left, closing the door behind her. This was the first time she'd called him by his name. Usually, she just called him a pig or a dog.

Filip heard the lock turn again and her footsteps pacing back and forth outside his room. Then she walked down the stairs.

He got up and, just in case, jammed a screwdriver from his

tool belt into the lock so Frau Wolff would not be able to unlock it. He stayed by the door, listening for a while to her footsteps downstairs. She then came up the stairs again and paced outside his door. Finally, she stopped and tried to unlock the door. She worked the keyhole, then swore loudly when she couldn't turn the lock. She kicked the door and walked back downstairs. Filip smiled to himself and went back to bed.

"What was that all about last night?" Sabina asked the next morning when they were eating breakfast in the hallway.

Filip shrugged as if he didn't know what she was talking about.

"Don't play stupid with me, Filip."

Filip had grown to love Sabina like a big sister, and he wanted to explain but was embarrassed to talk about it. Just then, Frau Wolff walked in from the kitchen.

"I have a surprise for you, stupid donkeys," she announced.

They paused and looked up at her, fearing the worst.

"Don't look like you just pissed your pants, Filip. I'm taking you both to see a show today."

Filip and Sabina looked at each other, surprised. This was definitely not good news.

"By the way, you're not allowed to return to Poland," Frau Wolff said as if it was of no consequence.

Filip's understanding of German had improved, but he looked at Sabina to verify. She just lowered her head, looking like she was about to cry.

Frau Wolff pulled out a newspaper and laid it on the table. She read it to them. "Due to an increase in war efforts, all foreign laborers are to stay in Germany indefinitely. Some foreign laborers working on the farms will be transferred to factory labor. Those who do not transfer will be given additional farms to care for until further notice."

Filip's head dropped. This sounded like a prison sentence, and he was not ready to give up his freedom or the dream of building a house back in his village. He wanted to run and get away from this place, but he was stuck. Even though there were no fences around the fields, there might as well have been. He was also in the middle of Germany. It had taken him and Sabina some time, but they'd finally figured out that their village of Rotenburg an der Fulda was about halfway between Fulda and a town to the north called Kassel. That put him about eight hundred kilometers from his home village—an impossible distance to travel without money. The train ride back would be expensive, and he probably would be arrested the minute he entered the train. Walking home was also out of the question. It would take him a month to walk back, and he would have to sneak around every town and village to avoid getting arrested.

Even worse, his hope for the return of Herr Wolff, who seemed more sensible, was diminishing. Sabina had learned he was fighting in Russia, near Stalingrad. She said Frau Wolff didn't get many letters and mostly kept them to herself. Then, a letter came one day, and she didn't mention him again. She wouldn't even bring the topic up to her sister, who visited occasionally.

Filip assumed Herr Wolff was dead or had just decided never to return. Either way, he figured Herr Wolff was better off without this witch—and a witch she was! She got worse as time passed, bothering Filip with constant complaints about the work and hitting him with the whip. Even worse, she began to look at him differently. There were long stares and inappropriate touches. And, of course, there was last night. It made the hair on his neck stand up.

"I paid the official so that both of you would stay here. But

Filip will also work on my sister's farm," Frau Wolff said. "Oh, one more thing. I can't pay you until you are released from your job here. That's what the paper says."

Filip thought that perhaps this German farm was destined to be his home for the rest of his life. According to Sabina, who was always tuned in to the local gossip, the Germans seemed to have taken over the whole world, so there was probably no hope of him being a free man again. Sabina said slave workers were arriving from France, Ukraine, Belgium, Greece, and other places he'd only heard of in schoolbooks. But most were from Russia, where Germany was having a lot of military success.

His father had told him that slaving for other countries was the luck of the Polish nation and that fighting was only going to get you killed. Filip hadn't wanted to believe it growing up, and he'd always hoped for something better. But it was starting to look like his father had been right all along.

On the other hand, it wasn't like his life in Poland was much better. He'd had the same routine: Wake up at five o'clock, work for four hours, eat, work for four hours, eat, work for five or six hours, eat, and then sleep. The only difference was that in Germany, he had limited contact with outsiders other than the neighbors and occasional visitors. Frau Wolff did not allow him and Sabina to wander around the village. The only real freedom Filip felt was when he was out in the fields by himself. That was rare, though, as Frau Wolff usually accompanied him.

The farm was large—about a hundred hectares—with fields and animals to care for. So Filip never had much time to think about his imprisonment anyway. Whenever he found himself alone, he would lie in the grass and look at the sky. The clouds moving past him toward the east made him wonder if his mother would see the same clouds in Poland. Frau Wolff did not allow them to send letters; she wouldn't even let them have a piece of paper to write on, so he wished he could write messages on the clouds. *What would I write anyway?* he wondered. He would probably write some nice things to make his mother happy, but he wanted to tell her how bad he felt about slowly forgetting her with each passing day. As days turned into months, the memories of his life in Poland became more and more distant, almost as if it were a dream. His mother's face started to blur in his mind. It looked like a cloud—just a white puff of vapor for her face and a black one for her hair.

"Come on, why are you just staring into space?" said Frau Wolff. "Let's go see the show, you lazy pigs."

Filip didn't know what she was talking about. He'd never been to any show except when a man came to his village and played a silent movie for the villagers inside their mayor's barn.

Frau Wolff shooed them out of the house and locked the door behind her. They walked through the village together, Filip and Sabina behind Frau Wolff. Filip had rarely walked through it before. He noticed a newsletter posted on a fence next to the road. They didn't stop to read it, but the fact that it was in both German and Polish made him nervous. Whatever it said, it couldn't be good news for Polish workers.

When they arrived at the village square, it was already packed with people, both Germans and foreign laborers. About two hundred people stood around talking passionately, yet quietly, about something happening at the front, where they were all staring.

Filip looked around, trying to figure out what was happening, and that was when he saw her. The gal from the train—Anna—sat next to several other women on a horse wagon at the back of the crowd. She was almost unrecognizable in the farmer clothes she was wearing. The last time he'd seen her, she'd been wearing a fancy city dress and jacket. But her porcelain-white face and long blond hair, which seemed like something from a painting, were unmistakable. He had cast her beauty in his memory and could never forget her. Filip wanted to go over and talk to her, but Frau Wolff pushed him and Sabina through the crowd to the front, where a horrific scene was unfolding.

"Enjoy the show," said Frau Wolff, smirking with satisfaction.

Four SS soldiers and three policemen surrounded the makeshift gallows. There were also two civilians with *P* badges —fellow slave laborers—standing on top of the gallows right next to a hanging noose. They held a young man, maybe nineteen or twenty, preventing him from falling to the ground. He was beaten and bruised, his body barely able to stand, his head hunched down. Filip didn't recognize him at first because the man's face was swollen. But it soon became clear that it was Leszek. Filip felt nauseated, and beads of cold sweat formed around his neck.

"I know him," he whispered to Sabina.

"Who is he?"

"His name is Leszek. He's from my village."

The SS officer stepped forward, and the crowd went silent.

"Heil Hitler!" the officer shouted.

"Heil Hitler!" the Germans in the crowd shouted back.

"I'm SS Sergeant Fritz Hinkelmann from the Buchenwald prison camp. That's where the Great German Reich gives lesser men the opportunity to contribute to our greatness, regardless of their digressions or where they came from. This man was also given an opportunity," he said, pointing at Leszek. "He came here to make an honest living and do his duty as a laborer for our great country. Instead, he chose to spend his time raping our glorious German women!"

The Germans screamed with hatred. The slaves hung their heads low.

"That's impossible," Filip whispered to Sabina. "Leszek didn't need to rape anyone. Women are attracted to him like bees to honey."

"Are you sure?" she said. "He looks guilty."

"They beat him like a dog. He can barely stand."

"The punishment is clear," continued Hinkelmann. "All those who choose to attack or weaken our superior German race will be punished by death!"

The Germans cheered. The foreigners clenched their teeth and cried.

"These Polish laborers volunteered to execute this man themselves." He pointed to the two civilians with *P* badges. "They understand that dogs don't bite the hand that feeds them."

The two men stood still, eyes pointing at the ground and unable to make eye contact with their comrades. It wasn't exactly a sign of enthusiasm for the cause.

"Let's get on with it!" shouted Hinkelmann.

The SS soldiers shoved Leszek and the two volunteers with *P* badges toward the noose.

"Don't look away!" ordered Frau Wolff.

Filip and Sabina didn't want to watch, but they stared ahead hopelessly. They stood frozen and unable to do anything. Although there were more slaves than Germans gathered in the main square, Filip still felt small and powerless, like a bug looking up at an elephant.

One of the volunteers stood Leszek up on a stool while the other tightened the noose around his neck. They stepped back and lowered their heads again as soon as they were done. Filip figured they must have done this before because they knew their jobs well.

The crowd was silent, not sure what to expect next. Filip had not seen anything like this before. He hoped it would end without Leszek getting hurt. Perhaps the Germans would only give a warning.

Then Hinkelmann walked over to Leszek and unceremoniously kicked the stool from under him. The whole crowd jerked back as Leszek's body dropped, and the noose snapped tight around his neck. His body twitched for a few seconds, his toes dangling just above the floor, then he became limp.

Sabina folded into Filip's arms and sobbed uncontrollably. Filip looked away, retching at the sight, while Frau Wolff grinned, watching Leszek swing back and forth for a while longer. Her eyes shone brightly with excitement as if she'd just received her Christmas present.

"Let's go, swine," she finally ordered.

Sabina and Filip shuffled after her as the crowd quietly dispersed. However, instead of leaving, Frau Wolff approached SS Sergeant Hinkelmann.

"Thank you for your service to the Reich," she said, smiling at him like a teenage girl at a dance party.

"The pleasure is all mine," Hinkelmann replied, smiling back.

"I wish we had strong men like you around more often. These foreign slaves are hard to control. They're like vermin," she said, pointing at Filip.

Filip looked up at the man and saw his brows furrow in anger, so he turned his gaze away, his eyes landing back on Leszek, whose feet still swung back and forth as if pushed by some invisible wind. He stared at the feet, now unable to look away, while listening to the bizarrely casual conversation between the two Germans.

"I wish I could be here for you, dear Frau," said Hinkelmann.

"You can call me Katherine," she said. "I'm widowed. My husband died in Russia."

"Pleasure to meet you, Katherine. You can contact me anytime you like if you ever need help."

"Thank you. I certainly will."

Frau Wolff bowed to Hinkelmann and pushed Filip and Sabina back toward the road.

Filip was glad to get away from Hinkelmann. It was like standing next to the Grim Reaper. He also wanted to see Anna. He scanned the crowd, looking for her, but the wagon was gone, and she was gone with it. This added to the despair created by the day's events, yet hope also entered his heart.

Anna was alive and lived somewhere nearby. Maybe he would see her again.

As Anna rested with the other women in their room, she pondered why Gustaf had driven them to another village to see the hanging. If it was to scare them, it worked. Despite living through the German invasion of Poland, Anna had never seen anybody murdered before. The sight of the poor Polish man hanging from the gallows made her throw up. She couldn't stop shaking for hours afterward. Were her hopes of escape from earlier just a naïve girl's silly dream? Was her fate simply to spend the rest of her life as a slave? Was she destined for rape and murder? It had never really occurred to her that she might just be an object in someone else's path—an object to be used and thrown away. What power did she really have? Her German masters controlled her life, and the smirk on Herr Gustaf's face after the hanging confirmed that.

She took the medallion off her neck and stared at the Black Madonna. Then she put it inside her pocket.

"What are you doing?" asked Dasha, sitting in a cot beside her. "You have to always keep it on your neck."

"What for?" said Anna. "It's just a made-up story about a virgin who got pregnant without a man."

"Oh my God!" Dasha yelled, crossing herself several times. "Spit that out of your mouth, girl. That's blasphemy."

"Then why did the young man die? If God exists, why did he let that happen? How about all the other people who have been tortured and killed?"

"My son will avenge us all one day," Misha proclaimed while rocking her baby boy in the crib.

"You first make sure he lives," said Dasha, who protected Misha's son like her own. "You keep him safe. I heard rumors that Germans take slave babies and put them in orphanages, where they turn them into Nazis. And you know Herr Uding doesn't like that he has another mouth to feed."

This was another reason they now moved a dresser every night to block the door to their room. This upset old Gustaf, but he dared not try to fight his way in. He was already embarrassed over the last time he'd tried something with Anna, and his son, Klaus, made it clear he didn't appreciate being woken up in the middle of the night. It didn't seem to bother Klaus that his father was raping his slave laborers. But at least Gustaf seemed to respect his son's sleep, which helped the women just the same. They still had to worry about Gustaf during daylight hours. He told Anna that he would get her one day. That was why she tried never to find herself alone with him. But at least she could get some sleep at night.

"He was there," said Anna.

"Who?" Dasha asked.

"Filip. The boy from the train. The one who gave me bread."

All three Ukrainian women sat up in their cots. Even Slava, who never spoke and whom Anna suspected of being mute, whimpered in excitement.

"What did he look like?" said Dasha, even though Anna had told her about the young man and what had happened on the train many times already. "Was he handsome?"

Anna smiled and stared at the ceiling, trying to reconstruct his figure in the darkness. She felt a weird, tingling sensation in her stomach whenever she thought of him. "He's tall and has bushy black hair," she whispered as if he were standing before her. "He looks strong, with big hands, like he could throw a horse over a building."

The women giggled.

"I bet you wouldn't kick *him* out of your cot," said Dasha.

"Stop it," said Anna, even though Dasha was right. She imagined herself engulfed in his arms, protected from the world like a small bird nestling under its mother's wings.

"Did he say anything to you?" asked Misha.

"No. He was far away," Anna said. "But I saw him looking at me. I think he wanted to come talk to me. Then this German woman pushed him in front of the crowd, and I didn't see him afterward."

"You love him!" Slava shouted.

Anna and the other two women were startled, mostly because Slava had spoken for the first time but also because *love* was a heavy word. Anna had never been in love with a man. Sure, she'd had crushes on boys when she was a little girl, but nothing that felt like this. Was she really in love? Just from a short encounter on the train? She didn't know anything about him. How could she love a complete stranger?

"Yes," said Dasha, standing over Anna and looking into her eyes as if trying to find the truth. "I see it now. You *are* in love, aren't you?"

"No, I'm not," Anna scoffed, turning away from them in her cot.

"Oh, yes," Dasha continued. "And it's serious too. He has a zaklynanya over you."

"What's that?" Anna turned back to Dasha, afraid of what disease Dasha might be talking about.

"It's a magic spell," said Dasha, twisting her face and body to impersonate a terrifying witch. "It's the worst thing you could ever imagine. It's very painful, and it will make you scream."

"What is it?" Anna shrieked.

"It causes a man's cock to enter your pee hole," Dasha announced, then laughed.

The other two women roared with laughter. Misha fell to the floor, holding her stomach. Slava accidentally farted. The baby started crying.

"You guys are stupid!" Anna shouted and hid herself under a blanket. She hoped Klaus would beat them in the morning for waking him.

9
JULY 5, 1941

Frau Wolff walked next to the wagon while Filip drove. It was the first day of the harvest, and the wagon was full of wheat bushels. She was exhausted from working in the field all day, but Filip wouldn't let her sit beside him. He said he needed to concentrate on leading the horses through the uneven fields. She didn't believe him, because driving the wagon wasn't that difficult. He was just upset that she ordered him around all day.

She watched his bulging arm muscles flex while he manipulated the reins, wondering if she repulsed him. She was about ten years older than him, after all. Yet she knew she was a handsome woman; that was what her husband used to say. He was gone now, of course—killed by the very same Slavic slaves who worked the German fields. Not that she'd liked her husband much anyway. But he did have sex with her, so she couldn't be too unattractive. Why didn't Filip want to sleep with her? It drove her mad that he kept locking himself up in his room at night. Any other young man would take an opportunity to have his way with her in an instant. He had his needs just like she did. Was he screwing Sabina or some other woman?

"That's the house," she said, pointing at a nearby farmhouse. "That's where my sister lives."

She didn't like coming here. Her sister, Helma, was fat and useless, and her husband, Klaus, spent most of his day drinking beer with his father, Gustaf. Their village of Braach was two kilometers away, making it inconvenient. But Frau Wolff had to at least try to help with their farm, as she had agreed with the authorities. Otherwise, she risked losing Filip altogether.

"Why don't you open the gate?" Filip said in his broken but rapidly improving German.

She hated him ordering her around, but it aroused her at the same time. So she did as he said while pretending to curse under her breath.

Filip seemed pleased with himself as the gate swung open. He drove the wagon inside the courtyard, which was filled with scampering chickens. She hoped that following his orders would make him more amiable toward her.

"Park it in front of the barn," she said. "I'll help you unload."

Klaus came out of the farmhouse, flipping suspenders over his shoulders. His face was red like a rooster's wattle, and his hair was disheveled, as if he'd been sleeping off a hangover.

Frau Wolff thought he should be ashamed of his drinking. The harvest was not a time to be lazy. "I did your work for you, Klaus," she announced.

"I didn't ask you to do anything," Klaus replied, his face turning even redder, if that was possible.

"I know. You never do. It's always my sister who has to

ask." She turned to Filip and said, "Come on. Let's get these bushels inside the barn."

Klaus swore, then stormed inside the house, screaming Helma's name. Frau Wolff was pleased with herself for rousing the big loaf into a rage. She hoped he would have a heart attack and drop dead so she wouldn't have to ever talk to him again. Of course, his death would also mean the farm's ownership would pass to her—a nice bonus. Klaus and her sister had no children, which meant the farm her father had let Helma manage when she married Klaus would automatically pass to Frau Wolff as the oldest sister. All she had to do was marry again and have a child to secure it as hers forever. Maybe she just needed a child. The marriage would be so people wouldn't talk. She would do whatever was necessary, marriage or no marriage.

Anna watched from the kitchen window as Filip stood on top of the wagon, throwing bushels of wheat at the same woman she'd seen him with at the hanging. He was very strong, and the woman was almost knocked down to the ground with every bushel he threw. It was as if he was doing it deliberately, grinning with every blow. The woman cursed at him angrily for trying to knock her down. Anna was surprised he could get away with it because the woman was obviously German.

Anna decided to leave her cooking and go outside to investigate. She took off her apron and fixed her appearance in the hallway mirror. By now, she looked like an ordinary farm girl. All the semblance of the city girl was gone. She wished she had her clothes from Poland—maybe the nice blue dress with white dots her father loved so much.

Filip froze atop the wagon when he spotted Anna leaning against the farmhouse's front door. He stared at her as if hypnotized. She wanted to laugh at him for being so easily enchanted with her, but she stared back at him instead. Their eyes were locked together for what seemed like minutes before the woman came around the wagon and spotted them.

"Who the hell are you?" the woman yelled.

Anna woke up from her trance and stared at the woman without answering. Something about her scared Anna. Her body language said she didn't mind hurting people. She maybe even enjoyed it.

"Are you mute?" the woman insisted. "Speak up!"

Helma appeared beside Anna. "This is Anna. She's our cook," she said.

"Is she one of Gustaf's new whores from Ukraine?" Frau Wolff asked and then laughed with exaggeration, trying to make it a funny joke.

"You've upset Klaus," said Helma. "Why didn't you tell me you were coming?"

"Am I supposed to announce it to him every time I do his work for him?"

The two women continued to argue, but Anna noticed that Filip never took his gaze off her. She smiled at him, feeling her cheeks swell with the warmth of a blush. He smiled back. She decided she wanted to talk to him and snuck around Helma toward the wagon. He was already on the ground when she circled the horse and got out of sight of the two women.

They stood there for a moment, staring at each other, unable to speak. Just like on that train, when they first met, words seemed unnecessary between them. It was as if they had known each other their whole lives.

"Do you remember me?" she said finally. "I'm Anna. From the train."

"Filip," he said. "My name is Filip."

"Nice to see you again, Filip. And thank you for the bread you gave me."

"You're welcome."

They stared at each other again for a moment.

"It's funny that we ended up with the sisters," he said.

She chuckled. "Yes, that's a nice coincidence."

"I hoped to see you again," he said. "You disappeared from the train, and I couldn't find you."

"Sorry," she said. "It was a long trip from Poland."

He nodded.

"Will you visit here again?" she asked.

"Yes, I will try to come every day," he said.

"You promise?"

Frau Wolff appeared from around the wagon. "What the hell are the two of you doing? Get back to work, you Polish dogs!"

Anna ran in the opposite direction without saying goodbye. She was deathly afraid of Frau Wolff, but she still smiled, knowing she would see Filip every day.

Filip couldn't stop thinking about Anna that evening. He sat at the hallway table across from Sabina and chewed his food, but, in his head, he wasn't even there. Instead, his mind kept replaying the earlier meeting with Anna. He analyzed every moment: Anna looking at him from the doorway, walking toward him, standing so close to him, and then rushing off like a frightened pigeon.

In his mind, her blond hair seemingly blew in the wind, even though it was a calm, hot day. Her light-blue eyes glistened like a stream of cold mountain water on a sunny day. Her voice was like a whisper of weeping willows, gently massaging his ears. Did she really speak to him? The moment seemed so brief that Filip wasn't sure it had happened. She had said she wanted to see him again. If she only knew about his desire to see her. He was willing to sleep on the floor beside her bed like a dog. He had never felt like this before.

"What's wrong with you?" Sabina said, interrupting his thoughts.

"What?" he asked, unsure if she was talking to him.

"You're acting weird today."

"No, I'm not."

She stared at him, then said, "Are you in love?"

"What? No!"

"Oh my God. You are! Tell me who it is."

He pulled his hair in frustration and averted her gaze. He could never get anything past Sabina. Like a big sister, she read him like a book. "It's the girl from the train," he said finally. "I saw her today."

Sabina let out an involuntary yelp, then put her hands over her mouth to stop it. "Oh my God," she whispered. "The girl you gave bread to? Did you talk to her?"

Filip nodded.

"What did she say?"

"She wants to see me again," he said, grinning uncontrollably.

That was when Frau Wolff burst in from the kitchen, waving her pistol. "What the hell is all the barking about, you dogs?"

Filip and Sabina hung their heads and chewed their food as

if nothing had been said. There was no sense in arguing with Frau Wolff when she had a pistol in her hand. She stood next to Filip, her hand on her hip as if she had something to say.

"You need to stop chatting up women all day and do some work around here," she said. "There are rules. You are here to do as I say. You understand me?"

Sabina nodded vigorously, but Filip didn't move. He'd never hit a woman before, but he now had a sudden urge to get up and punch Frau Wolff in the face. He had hoped she would leave him alone, seeing his hard work around the farm, but she kept getting worse. Her constant ordering around and sexual advances chafed on his nerves.

"Speaking of rules," she said, pulling a piece of paper from her shirt pocket and setting it down on the table. It was one of the leaflets Filip had seen hanging all over the village fences a few days earlier. She read it out loud, slowly pronouncing each word. "These are the new directives from our Great German Reich government. Number one, Poles are not allowed to leave their cities of residence. Number two, they are not allowed to leave the houses where they're staying without permission. Number three, they are not allowed to use public transportation without a permit from the authorities. Number four, all foreign laborers must always visibly wear the *P* insignia on their clothing. Number five, anyone who doesn't follow those rules or rouses others not to follow them will be sent to a labor camp for up to several years. Number six, Poles are not allowed to mix with Germans in public places. Number seven, Poles who have relationships with Germans will be punished by death." She stopped there and waited a moment for emphasis. "And finally, number eight, Poles are not allowed to talk or write about the rules."

Filip watched as she put the leaflet back in her pocket. He

couldn't believe what he had heard. Just a few minutes earlier, he was hoping things were getting better. Instead, things had gotten worse. Not only could he not go back to Poland, but they'd also now put him under house arrest.

"Go upstairs, Sabina," said Frau Wolff. "Filip, I want you in the kitchen."

Sabina quickly got up and ran upstairs. Filip looked up at Frau Wolff, who had a triumphant smirk on her face, and then stood up. He wanted to tell her to fuck off, but he walked to the kitchen instead. There was nothing he could say to make this all go away.

Frau Wolff closed the door behind them and turned the key in the lock. She took the key out, put it inside her bra, and smiled at Filip. He ignored her and sat at the kitchen table, casting his eyes down.

"I need you to start doing more things around the house, Filip," she said. "Things that I need."

She walked over to him and put her hand on his shoulder. He felt a shiver of disgust come over him. He wanted to punch her in the face and run to see Anna.

"Don't be a fool, Filip. Don't be like your Polish friend who was hanged. You know that all I have to do is tell the police that you tried to rape me, and you're a dead man."

He didn't move, paralyzed by Frau Wolff and her power over him. She confidently put another hand on his other shoulder and gently massaged it.

"Do we have an understanding?" she said seductively. "Will you do as I please?"

Filip swallowed hard, desperately searching for a way out of this. None came to mind.

10
DECEMBER 24, 1941

Anna couldn't believe six months had passed since she'd last seen Filip when he'd visited Helma's farm with her nasty sister, Katherine. He disappeared after that. Nothing. Not even a letter. Dasha thought she saw him once working the fields, but that was months ago already. Then, last week, Helma announced that her sister and her two laborers, Filip and Sabina, would join them for Christmas Eve dinner. Anna's heart hadn't stopped racing since then.

Today was the day, and the preparations were frantically coming to completion only minutes before their arrival time, which was six o'clock in the evening. The winter was harsh outside, with deep snow and very low temperatures, but Anna was sweating inside the kitchen. She spent all day cooking many different dishes—all the ones that Germans required and those that were traditional in Poland and Ukraine. There were twenty dishes altogether, including carp, potato salad, herring salad, borsch, pierogis, kutya, and many more. Enough to feed nine adults and a toddler. Plus, Slava was now pregnant and ate for two.

Anna squealed with joy when she heard the gate to their farm swing open. All three Ukrainian women who were helping her in the kitchen laughed at the same time.

"Calm down, girl," said Dasha. "Don't tear your panties."

Anna ran to the window. "He's here!" she announced. "What do I do?"

"You take your apron off and look pretty," said Dasha. "We'll serve the food."

Anna took her apron off and threw it into a corner. She nervously adjusted her clothes and hair, wanting to look her best for Filip.

Helma appeared in the doorway. "Is everything ready? We are ready to be seated at the dining room table."

"We're ready," said Misha.

Helma left, and a woman appeared in her place. She was larger in stature but had a friendly, round face and brown eyes.

"Hello!" she said, smiling at them. "My name is Sabina. And this is Filip."

Filip emerged behind her. His eyes immediately locked with Anna's. She smiled at him involuntarily. He looked handsome in a wool suit.

"Welcome," said Dasha. "Have a seat. We have to serve the Germans first, but they are allowing us to eat our dinner in the kitchen."

Filip and Sabina sat at the kitchen table and waited as the Ukrainian women hustled the food out of the kitchen for the Germans. Anna sat across from Filip. He twisted his neck, pulling at the collar of his white button-up shirt like he was nervous or embarrassed.

"I'm glad you came," she said to him.

"I wanted to earlier but couldn't," he said.

She nodded. "You're here now."

He smiled.

She liked talking to him. She could tell he respected her.

"Where are you from?" she said.

"Junno," he said. "It's a small village near Konin."

"I'm from Czestochowa."

"I'm from Junno," he said as if trying to confirm.

"Yes, Junno. You mentioned that," she said and laughed.

Sabina rolled her eyes. "Don't mind him. He's not as dumb as he looks."

All three of them laughed.

After months of darkness, Filip finally had a sliver of hope. He was sitting across from Anna at the kitchen table, feeling like he was meant to do this for the rest of his life. She was beautiful —delicate and thoughtful, yet so full of passion, like a painting of an angel Filip once saw in church. He was grateful to Frau Wolff for letting him come to the Christmas party, even though he wasn't sure why she did. She never took him or Sabina anywhere or gave them any breaks from work. He suspected she was worried about them escaping or stealing her things. Or maybe this was his reward for all his . . . work. The thought of it made him sick to his stomach. He preferred to pretend she simply found some goodness in her heart on Christmas. Whatever the reason, he was glad to be out of his prison and with Anna.

Filip shoved the food into his mouth like it was his last meal on Earth. It was as delicious as his mother's cooking and the best meal he'd had in a long time.

"She cooked it all," said Dasha, who sat across from Sabina at the kitchen table. "Anna's a genius in the kitchen. Whoever marries this girl will be a very lucky man."

"Stop it, Dasha," said Anna. "You're embarrassing me."

All the women laughed, including Misha and Slava, who sat at the end of the table.

"I wouldn't mind you cooking for me for the rest of my life," Filip said. He immediately realized his words carried more meaning than intended, as everyone at the table fell silent and stared at him. "I mean, who wouldn't? It's very good."

"I want to show you something," Anna said, getting up from the table. "Come with me."

He got up and followed her out of the kitchen. She handed him his fur coat, compliments of the deceased Herr Wolff, and put on her worn wool coat. Then they snuck out of the house into the still winter night.

The snow crunched under their feet as they ran toward the barn. She swung the door open, and they went inside. He remembered the barn from when he had visited in July. It was large and stacked with hay, including on the second floor above them.

"Turn around and wait for me to call you," she said.

He turned away and listened as she climbed the ladder.

"I'm ready!" she shouted after a moment.

When he made it up there, she was already lying on a bed of hay, covered with a thick wool blanket. She'd obviously had this all planned in preparation for his visit. He lay beside her, and she wrapped the blanket around them, snuggling up to his left arm. He couldn't believe this was happening. All he had dreamed about the last few months was to be close to her, and here she was, her warmth radiating through his body like the sun. He was paralyzed with shock.

"We are free up here," she said. "No one will find us."

"It's nice," was all he could muster.

"Tell me about yourself. I barely know you."

"Not much to tell. I grew up in a small village. I have a big family with ten siblings. That's all, really. How about you?"

"I'm a city girl," she said. "Parents were teachers. Three sisters. I'll probably never see any of them again."

"How did you end up here?" he asked. "I saw that the clothes you wore on the train were torn and bloody."

"I did something stupid, something illegal," she said. "They threw me in jail and beat me. Then they put me on a train and sent me here."

"Just like that?"

"Yes. I thought they were going to kill me."

"At least you're alive then," he said. "I'm glad for it."

She smiled at him and kissed his cheek. His heart stopped beating, and he forgot to breathe. All he could do was smile back.

"Have you heard from your family?" she asked.

He shook his head.

"My parents don't know where I am, and I'm not allowed to write," she said. "My three sisters were rounded up together with me, but I haven't seen or heard from them since."

"You are very beautiful," Filip said, swallowing hard as his heart, lungs, and brain restarted. His words embarrassed him, but he didn't know how to tell her he liked her.

Anna pushed away and said, "I'm telling you now about my sisters."

"I know. I just wanted to let you know . . ." he mumbled.

"What, that you don't care about my sisters and just want to roll around in the hay with me?"

Filip swallowed hard again. This was not going as well as he had hoped.

She laughed. "You're cute. I'm just joking with you."

He forced a smile, not sure if she was really joking.

Anna sat up. "Promise you'll take me back to my family," she demanded.

She said it with such conviction that it made Filip think it was somehow possible. He barely knew her, but he nodded in agreement for some reason. He didn't know what it was about her. Something strange had overtaken his mind. He'd heard of true love, but he'd come from a place where that kind of thing was more fairy tale than real life. Or maybe that's what this was, except he was lonely and wanted to escape Frau Wolff's strangle on his mind. Either way, he knew he must take Anna back to her family in Poland regardless of what happened.

"I promise," he said.

"Good. It's settled then," she announced, snuggling his arm again.

They lay beside each other, looking up at the stars through a tiny window. Filip felt like he was floating among them. This was freedom, and he didn't want the feeling to end. They fell asleep, embracing each other like an old married couple.

Frau Wolff woke up furious on Christmas Day. Filip had disappeared the night before, making her feel foolish for not having anyone to share her bed with—on Christmas Eve, no less. This was when she'd expected him to make her feel the most special. Instead, she'd cried half the night.

She got dressed, then stormed out of her room and into the

kitchen. Everyone was already gathered there. The Germans sat at the table, eating breakfast, while all the slave women were cleaning dishes from dinner. Filip sat on a chair near the stove, watching the women.

Frau Wolff wanted to yell at him for abandoning her but decided not to make a scene in front of everyone. Instead, she said, "Good morning," and joined the Germans at the table. They replied with the customary "Merry Christmas." Helma handed her a plate with bread, cheese, and ham. She took it and started eating, but her focus was exclusively on Filip. He didn't acknowledge her at all or even look in her direction. His eyes kept following one of the women around the kitchen—the same woman who had approached him when they delivered bushels during the harvest. Wherever she moved, his eyes went with her. It was as if his eyes were attached to her by a string.

"Filip! Come here!" Frau Wolff barked at him.

He looked at her as if realizing for the first time she was there. Then, reluctantly, he got up and walked over to the table. He stood beside her without saying a word.

"Get the horse ready," she said. "We're leaving."

The Germans looked at her with surprise.

"You're not staying?" asked Helma. "It's Christmas Day."

"Can't we stay for the Christmas Day meal?" Filip threw in.

"No!" she interrupted curtly, then calmed herself. "I'm not feeling well. I want to go home and get some rest."

Filip's face twisted in anger, but he didn't say anything. He simply left the kitchen. The slave woman stopped what she was doing and watched him leave the room. Frau Wolff sensed sadness and longing on the woman's face, and she didn't like it.

"What's her name?" she asked Helma, pointing at the woman.

"Anna," Helma answered. "She's from Poland."

"Anna from Poland," Frau Wolff murmured. "I'll have to keep my eye on her."

Then she got up and left the kitchen.

11

APRIL 5, 1942

Filip had nearly gone mad during the winter, but this morning brought a ray of hope.

Three months of harsh weather had anchored him at the farmhouse, where there was nothing to do except perform daily chores and hide from constant abuse by Frau Wolff. Worse, he hadn't seen Anna even once. She disappeared from his life just as quickly as she appeared. Filip suspected Frau Wolff had discovered his infatuation with Anna. He often offered to help at her sister's farm, but Frau Wolff refused each time. She said they didn't need any help during the winter months, but he knew she was lying. Pigs required constant attention, and Helma's farm had many of them.

Then a Ukrainian man collecting milk had handed him a letter that morning and told him it was from Anna. His heart almost jumped out of his chest. He'd hidden it in his jacket and run back to the farmhouse. Sabina was shocked when he grabbed her arm and dragged her from the kitchen to his bedroom.

"What is it?" she said when he closed the door behind them. Her face was pale like a ghost. "Did someone die?"

"Read it!" he ordered, shoving the letter into her hands. He could read in Polish, but he wasn't good at it. Sabina was much better, and he wanted to make sure he understood everything Anna wrote.

"Who is it from?"

"Anna," he said, smiling.

"You're a fool," she said. "You scared me to death."

"Please read."

She took the letter and began to read.

Dear Filip,

Many days have passed, but there hasn't been a single day when I didn't think of you. You are always on my mind, and I'll never forget our night together on Christmas Eve. I'm sorry it took so long for me to write to you, but we're not allowed to send letters. We're not even allowed to have paper or pencil. I had to give Vitko a whole ham, but he assured me that he'd deliver this letter to you, so I'm hopeful it will find you in good health. I pray to see you again soon.

Yours,
Anna

Sabina looked at him and said, "I think she loves you, Filip."

"She didn't say so," he argued, even though his body seemed to levitate from joy. He could hardly contain himself.

"No girl gives a boy letters if she doesn't love him."

Filip smiled with satisfaction. "You really think so?"

Sabina sighed and said, "I wish I had a boy to write letters to."

"Thank you, Sabina."

Filip put the letter back inside his jacket and went outside. He spent the morning doing his chores, mostly cleaning dung in the building where they kept the cows, horses, and a few pigs, but he wasn't even aware of doing them. It was as if his mind left his body to do the chores and floated in the air like a balloon, filled with the thoughts of Anna and memories of the night they spent together on Christmas Eve. He wanted to see her so badly. He needed to see her. He would see her, he promised himself.

When he finally returned to the farmhouse for breakfast two hours later, he found Sabina crying in the corner of the kitchen and Frau Wolff sitting at the table, staring at him. The skin on her face was tight, and her eyelids were narrow with anger. She was in one of her moods again.

"What is it?" he asked.

"No breakfast today," she said. "I'm going with you to deliver the eggs."

"Why is Sabina crying?" he demanded.

"That's none of your concern. Get the horse ready."

This annoyed Filip. Frau Wolff never accompanied him to deliver eggs and knew nothing about negotiating pricing. She would just slow him down, and he didn't want to be alone with her.

"I'm going by myself," he announced and rushed out of the kitchen.

He opened the gate, got on the wagon, and was about to

order the horse to pull the wagon out of the courtyard when Frau Wolff came running out of the house.

"Halt!" she yelled, trying to get on the wagon.

He ignored her, pulled a whip out of its stand, and smacked the horse to make it go faster. The wagon jerked forward, bumping her off to the side.

"You Polish swine! How dare you disobey me!" she screamed, her face beet red from anger.

"Leave me alone!" he replied and whipped the horse again.

"It's that whore, Anna, isn't it? She got into your head."

"You leave her out of this," he demanded.

"We won't have to worry about that," she said.

His heart dropped. He immediately knew something was wrong. He stopped the horse.

"What did you do?"

Frau Wolff laughed. "Your Anna is being sent near Nordhausen to work for my brother. No more letters, you foolish man."

"Letters?"

"You don't think I know about the letter she sent you? The one this morning was the first and the last. I promise you that."

There was no time to waste. Filip whipped the horse hard. It jolted forward, this time knocking Frau Wolff to the ground. She cried in anger but sprung back up and grabbed after the horse's stirrup. Filip had enough. He swung his whip around and smacked Frau Wolff in the back. He hit her harder than he meant to, but a year full of frustrations had finally boiled over, and his muscles exploded in violence.

She whirled in pain, falling face-first into the mud. "I will kill you!" she screamed, trying to stand up.

Filip drove the wagon from the farm onto the road without looking back. He tried to stay calm, but inside, he was shocked at what had happened. He feared what might happen to him and Sabina as a result of this disobedience. Would he hang for this? Would they hang Sabina as well? Yet he was desperate to find Anna. He couldn't let her go. He was sure he'd never see her again if he didn't go after her now. He was also sure he had reached a point of no return.

When Filip arrived at Frau Wolff's sister's farm, he found nobody inside except for one of the female laborers, Slava. She looked at him through the gate like he was a crazy person and wouldn't open it.

"Where is Anna?" he demanded.

"They took her this morning," she said.

"Took her where?"

"The train station. Where else? Don't you know she's leaving?"

Filip punched the gate and winced in pain. Then he unharnessed the horse from the wagon, jumped on it, and took off. He had to hurry, and riding the horse without the wagon would be faster. There was still a chance he could catch the train. There were usually only a couple of trains per day going through the station in Rotenburg, and there was a chance they'd left early with Anna just to be safe.

People paused to look at him as he galloped through the village, but nobody stopped him. When he arrived at the station about twenty minutes later, he hid the horse in nearby woods. He ripped his *P* badge off his jacket and walked toward the train station. Instead of going inside, he hurried directly to the platform, where a small crowd gathered. Only one policeman watched over the passengers and their belongings.

That was when he spotted Anna. She stood right next to the policeman, surrounded by the Germans from her farm—Helma, Klaus, and Gustaf—plus the two Ukrainian women—

Dasha and Misha—who were both crying. Anna stared at the ground aimlessly, seemingly numb to everything around her.

The locomotive's whistle sounded off in the distance, and the crowd moved to attention. A few minutes later, the locomotive slowly pulled into the station. Several people came off the train when it stopped, and then the crowd began to file on. Anna was one of the last ones to get on. She stood there for a while, looking around, until Gustaf pushed her. Filip didn't have a lot of time. He had to find a way to get on that train without a ticket.

When the locomotive started to roll again, loudly huffing and puffing while sending out billowing white smoke, Filip ran across the tracks and jumped onto the back of the train, which was an empty cattle car. But there was no way in, as the door on the side of the car was locked. He needed to find a hiding place to avoid being spotted at the upcoming stations.

Filip climbed on top of the car and walked on its roof to get to the other side. The next car was a regular passenger car, and its door was unlocked. He opened it and snuck inside. It was lined with individual cabins on its right side, each with its entry door, and a hallway on the left, which was empty. He didn't want to walk through the hallway, afraid someone might see him through their cabin door window. Filip looked around and saw a door close to him. He opened it to reveal a tiny closet with a broom and some towels. He got in and closed the door behind him.

He spent the next few hours thinking about what had happened earlier. He assumed Frau Wolff would surely inform the police and have him punished. It would not take them long to realize where he was going. She knew he would go after Anna. Nevertheless, it was too late; there was no turning back now. He had to figure out how to save both of them.

When the train stopped, he heard a big commotion outside and snuck out of his closet. Everyone was getting off. The sign outside said they were in Kassel, which was probably a big city because the train station was huge. He saw Anna walking toward another train platform with her German owners and the Ukrainian women. He guessed this was where they would have to change trains for their final destination.

Filip got off the train and tried to blend in with the crowd. The station was swarming with police and soldiers. He felt like a fox during a hunt, hidden yet fully exposed. It was unusual for a single man without any luggage to roam around. They might think he was a pickpocket or some other troublemaker, even if they didn't suspect him of being a foreign laborer.

He followed Anna and her group, keeping his distance. They went to another platform and waited for their train to arrive. He saw a broom leaning against a lamppost, picked it up, and began sweeping. That seemed to make him invisible to others. Nobody cared about the cleaner.

When the train arrived about twenty minutes later and everybody got on board, Filip got on the back of the train and found another closet to hide in. He thought himself clever for finding a way to travel undetected through Germany until his luck ran out an hour later. That was when a conductor opened his closet door and almost fell backward, shocked to find Filip inside.

"Scheisse! What are you doing here, kid?" the man yelled. He was an older man with gray hair under his conductor's hat. He seemed more startled than upset.

"Sorry, sir. I got lost." Filip tried to come up with an excuse.

"You're lost inside a cleaning closet?"

Filip couldn't think of anything to say, so he just shrugged.

"Where's your ticket?" the conductor demanded.

Filip searched his pockets as if a ticket was going to miraculously appear.

The conductor saw right through it. "Get up! You're out at the next station. I'm not even going to ask you for your papers. The police can deal with that."

"Wait," said Filip. He reached deep inside his jacket pocket and pulled out a handkerchief full of the coins his mother had given him when he departed Poland. He had never taken them out of his jacket, afraid Frau Wolff might steal the money if he left it in his room. "Will this be enough to pay for the ticket?"

The conductor looked at him suspiciously but grabbed the money from Filip. "I better not find you in another part of the train. You can only stay here," he said, shutting the closet door and leaving with what was left of Filip's past.

He felt guilty for betraying his mother. He was only supposed to use the money to return to her in Poland. But that seemed like so long ago. It had been almost one year since he left Poland, but it might as well have been forty because he could barely remember her. It was as if she was just a distant memory of a dream. He hoped she didn't think about him much.

Filip slept curled up on the floor until the train stopped a few hours later. He awoke disoriented, forgetting how he'd gotten there. For a moment, he thought maybe he had dreamed everything that had happened.

He stepped out of the closet and looked around. The sign on the station wall said NORDHAUSEN. This was where Frau Wolff said they were taking Anna to work on her brother's farm. He scanned the crowd and found Anna leaving the train station with her travel companions. Filip jumped off the train and ran across the tracks toward the side of the building, where he wouldn't have to go through any policemen.

Anna and her masters got on a horse wagon driven by another man. Filip followed them on foot. Fortunately, the horse was old and slow, so Filip could keep up easily. He avoided other travelers by hiding in bushes or switching sides of the road.

The sky was darkening when the horse wagon finally stopped at a farm in the village of Immenrode. Filip was glad because he hoped to find some food at the farm. He had left Frau Wolff's farm with nothing but the clothes on his back and hadn't eaten all day. His stomach grumbled angrily, trying to eat itself.

He watched everyone except Anna leave the wagon and enter the farm. She was alone, her head down as if resigned to her fate. Filip could no longer wait to be close to her again and ran toward the wagon. It was probably a mistake, but he was still acting impulsively. He needed confirmation that the Christmas night they'd spent together was just as special to her as it was to him.

He approached her quietly and said, "I'll be watching over you."

She jumped, startled, not realizing someone was near. Filip took his cap off in case she didn't recognize him.

"You forgot me already?" he asked.

"What are you doing here?" she whispered, jumping off the wagon.

"There's no time to explain. I just wanted to tell you that I intend to keep my promise. I will bring you back to Poland. Maybe not right now, but I will do it."

"Filip! They will kill you."

"Only if they find me. That's why I can't stay here. But I will be around. Everything will be all right. Just not a word to anyone," he said, pulling away to leave.

Anna clasped his arm and put something in his hand. He looked down and saw a golden medallion with the Black Madonna.

"It's for good luck," she said, kissing him on the cheek.

His heart swelled with joy. He had a reason to live again.

"I will see you soon," he said, then rushed off.

12

APRIL 6, 1942

Anna didn't sleep a wink the first night at her new farm. It wasn't just that she and the women had to sleep in the barn full of rats; Misha would scream every time she heard a noise, and Dasha would yell at her to shut up. It was more that she couldn't stop thinking about Filip.

He'd been foolish to chase after her. Ever since Helma told her two days before that she'd be taking Anna to her brother's farm, Anna had hoped he would, but she knew it would be foolish. Then, when Filip showed up at the new farm, her heart swelled with joy and fell into despair simultaneously because she knew he would hang for this. She couldn't see a way for him to escape without getting caught.

She also couldn't see a way forward for them. What would they do? Escape back to Poland? How? Yes, there was a glimmer of hope in her heart. Filip did escape and somehow managed to follow her on the train. Maybe there was a way.

Her thoughts were interrupted when a rooster sounded his morning wake-up call. Dasha and Misha stirred awake.

"I have to tell you something," Anna said.

"I'm tired," Misha answered.

"What is it?" asked Dasha, who was always interested in gossip.

"He's here," she said and smiled. The thought of it made her happy despite the danger.

"Who is here?" said Dasha.

"Filip. He's here."

"How do you know he's here?" asked Misha.

"I saw him yesterday evening when we arrived," she said. "He followed me here all the way from our village."

"That's impossible," Dasha announced. "Are you telling the truth?"

"I swear on the Black Madonna," she said, grabbing for her medallion. Then she remembered she had given it to Filip. It was the only thing she owned that reminded her of home, but she wanted Filip to know how much he meant to her. "He said he would take me back to Poland."

"How?" asked Misha.

"He didn't say."

"He's a fool if he thinks he can escape Germany," Dasha said. "They will catch him and hang him for sure."

"Dasha!" Misha protested, seeing Anna hang her head. "I'm sure Filip will find a way."

"Sorry," said Dasha. "I didn't mean it like that."

Anna knew Dasha was just being honest and saying only what Anna was feeling. "It's all right," she said.

Dasha got up and shook the straw out of her dress. "C'mon! Let's meet this brother and find out why we're here."

"They want us to work," Misha suggested. "What else?"

Helma never explained why she was taking them to her brother's farm. Anna suspected that it had something to do with Helma's sister, Katherine, who seemed to hate Anna and wouldn't let Filip out of her sight. Helma also didn't tell them anything about her brother and didn't let them meet him when they arrived.

Anna followed Dasha out of the barn, with Misha reluctantly trailing behind her. The daylight was breaking, and they could now see the farm. It was very small, with the barn and the single-level farmhouse the only buildings. There weren't any animals on the farm except a few chickens scattered around the courtyard.

"Her brother must be lazy," said Dasha. "There's nothing here."

It all became clear when they entered the house. The Germans were already gathered for breakfast in a hallway that seemed to serve as a kitchen. Helma, Klaus, and Gustaf sat at a table while another man, very skinny and with mangled legs, sat next to them in a wheelchair. He was younger than his sisters, maybe in his early thirties, and had a gentle, calm face covered in a thick blond beard.

Helma got up and stood next to the man. "Gunther, I would like you to meet my girls."

She introduced them to her brother, who smiled meekly, seemingly uncomfortable meeting so many women at the same time.

"It's very nice to meet you," Gunther said, his voice soft and steady.

"My brother has polio," Helma explained. "He doesn't have a wife, so he'll need some help around the farm this season. That's why you're here."

"I don't need much," he said.

"Yes, you do," Helma said, interrupting him. "This place is a mess."

"All of us will be staying here?" asked Dasha.

"Only for a couple of days. After we clean this place up, we'll be going home. Except for Anna. She'll be staying here permanently."

A knot tightened in Anna's chest. Gunther seemed like a nice man, but she wasn't ready to part with the girls.

"Don't just stand there," said Helma. "Grab some brooms and start cleaning the barn."

They filed out of the house and closed the door behind them.

"At least you don't have to worry about him raping you," Dasha said to Anna.

That was one way of looking at it. Another was that Anna would be alone on this farm with an uncertain future while the love of her life was somewhere out there, trying to survive.

Filip woke up wet from a morning dew that covered the underbrush of the small woods. He'd found the area just outside Immenrode the night before. He'd slept deeply, exhausted from the day's travel, but he was freezing and hungry as soon as he opened his eyes. He hadn't eaten in nearly two days and needed to find some food if he was going to survive. The excitement of seeing Anna seemed to have worn off already, and the hopelessness of his situation was now at the forefront of his thoughts. He had no food and nowhere to go. He was in an unfamiliar place and surrounded by Germans. Police were probably out looking for him.

There was only one thing for him to do. He got up and started walking. He didn't know where he was going; he just knew he had to move forward. He walked in the opposite direction of Immenrode because he knew he couldn't stay in that village. It was too small, and they would discover him quickly. So he walked through the woods, hoping to find another village that was far enough away that people wouldn't connect him to Anna in any way yet close enough that he could visit her on foot.

Filip stopped at a stream at the end of the woods and drank as much water as he could carry in his stomach—enough to last him all day. He then walked over a hill covered with several empty fields that, only months from now, would be overgrown with wheat. He was fully exposed with nowhere to hide, but nobody was around.

When he reached the other side of the hill, he saw a small town in the valley below. Beyond the town was another hill. A large chunk of it was missing, exposing white rock like a half-eaten birthdate cake. Filip thought this must be a mine chiseled out by human hands, and he suspected the rock was gypsum because it looked like the powder farmers spread on the fields here in Germany to better retain water. Hundreds of people moved about the mine like ants, amplified by its whiteness. Filip had never seen anything like that before. The operation looked busy. This gave him hope that he could hide among the crowd somewhere and maybe even get a job in the mine so he could buy food.

The name of the mining town was Niedersachswerfen, one of those long German words that Filip still had a hard time pronouncing. He traversed the main asphalt road among horse wagons full of gypsum and many workers walking in each direction. It was a busy town, and nobody paid attention to him. He followed the wagons, hoping to find work wherever they were going.

He eventually found a huge fenced-in yard filled with

mountains of gypsum and hundreds of barrels bearing German words he didn't recognize. Several horse wagons were lined up outside a small brick building, and a few men were standing beside it, smoking cigarettes.

Filip hesitated, scanning the area for policemen, but after seeing none, he walked inside the yard and into the brick building. Inside was just one large room, with several people standing in a line ahead of a single table, where a man sat giving out papers. The man started yelling and told everyone to wait quietly in line. Everyone quieted down, seemingly afraid of this man. This scared Filip, and he stepped back outside.

"Looking for work?" a man's voice sounded behind him.

Filip turned and saw a short, stocky man, maybe in his forties, with a big belly and a long mustache. The man smiled at him like he knew everything about Filip and why he was there. He had kind eyes, and Filip wanted to trust him but wasn't sure if he could. Maybe he had no choice.

"Yes, sir," Filip replied with caution.

"Do you know how to take care of horses?"

"Yes."

"Can you start right now?"

Filip nodded but was surprised to find work so quickly. He hoped this wasn't some swindle.

"Perfect!" the man continued. "My name is Peter Strauss. You can call me Peter. Come with me." The man walked toward two horse wagons standing off to the side. Each was stacked with many large barrels. "I need you to drive one of them," Peter said, mounting one of the wagons. "My assistant got drafted into the army yesterday, and I need help."

Filip stopped, realizing this might be a good time to push his advantage. "What about payment, sir?"

"I'll pay you one mark per day. You won't find anything better."

"And when will you pay me?"

"I'll pay you daily," Peter said, pulling a coin from his jacket. "I'll even pay you today before you do your work."

He flipped the coin in the air. Filip caught it and stared at it like it was a miracle. He'd been in Germany for a year and hadn't seen a single mark of wages.

"Can we go now?" Peter asked. "I need to get these barrels over to the mine."

Filip thought about it for a moment. "Can I have something to eat first?"

Peter sighed. "You're something else, kid," he said, pulling a thick sandwich out of a bag. "You're lucky I'm desperate for help. Now, get on that wagon."

Filip grabbed the sandwich and ran to the other wagon. He couldn't believe his luck. Not only did he miraculously escape from Frau Wolff without getting caught, but one day later, he also had a new job, money, and food. He was excited to discover what else was possible for him and Anna.

They led the two wagons back through the town and up the white gypsum hill. Filip ate his sandwich—two slices of fresh bread with melted bacon fat in the middle—while slowly snaking up the road. He was in heaven, dreaming of Anna. Then he saw the workers, and his mood quickly worsened.

There were hundreds of them, all wearing the same gypsum-smeared, gray-and-blue-striped uniforms, round caps in the same colors, and wooden clogs. The uniforms hung on them like potato bags because the workers were just skin loosely wrapped around some bones; there was no meat on their bodies. Filip had never seen humans that thin before. What shook him the most, though, were their eyes. They all had the same look of emptiness, as if there was nobody inside —no soul. He couldn't look back at them, feeling guilty for being happy and eating his sandwich.

As they came upon the gate, chills shot down his spine. The place looked more like a prison than a mine. It was surrounded by a tall barbwire fence, with sentries every hundred meters or so and SS guards with dogs at the gate. They all watched Filip's every movement.

Peter handed them a document, and the guards opened the gate. He then led the horses through the gate. Filip followed in his wagon, knowing he could be arrested on the spot if they asked him for his papers. They drove toward a large tunnel as tall as a house carved into the gypsum rock. As soon as they stopped, about two dozen workers started unloading the barrels.

Filip jumped off the wagon and approached Peter. "Who are these people?" he whispered.

"Prisoners from the Mittelbau-Dora camp, about a kilometer from here," Peter answered, also in a whisper.

"What are they doing here?"

"Storing this fuel in a safe place so the British can't bomb it. I think our fearless Führer is worried now that America has entered the war. But that's between you and me, kid. They'll shoot you dead if you ever talk about it to anyone."

Filip was both frightened and excited. On the one hand, he hoped not to experience planes dropping bombs on him again as the Germans did during the invasion of Poland a couple of years before. On the other hand, it was great news to hear that America had entered the war against Germany. His father once told him the Americans were the ones who beat Germany during the Great War, so Filip now had renewed hope of freedom.

The prisoners unloaded the wagons, and Peter and Filip left the mine. Filip was glad to leave.

"You have anywhere to stay, kid?" Peter shouted from his wagon once they were out of earshot of the prisoners and SS guards.

"No, sir," Filip replied, realizing he had forgotten about needing shelter. He had to find somewhere safe to stay close to Anna.

"You did a good job today," said Peter. "You can stay at my house in Kleinfurra. It's only a few kilometers from here."

Filip nodded in agreement, hardly believing his luck. This man was an angel sent by God. He had given him a paying job, food, and now shelter. It almost seemed too good to be true.

13
APRIL 12, 1942

As soon as the church bells rang on Sunday morning, Filip rushed down the stairs and into the kitchen, startling Peter, who was enjoying his breakfast. Filip stood before him, nervously twisting his cap, but the words didn't come out as planned.

"What's the matter?" Peter asked.

"May I have a day off today?" Filip blurted out. "Today is Sunday."

Filip had worked hard all week, helping Peter with deliveries and caring for his four horses. Peter had been good to him too. He gave him some of his clothes and a room in the attic, fed him three meals a day, and left him alone to do as he pleased after work. Peter didn't have a family and had only a small farmhouse with a barn outside the village of Kleinfurra, so Filip had nobody to worry about but himself.

"Are you going somewhere?" Peter asked.

Filip wasn't ready to tell him the truth, so he said, "I just want to take a stroll to see the area. It's a nice day, sir."

Peter stared at him for a moment. "I never asked you because I don't care, but are you sure you're safe walking around? Judging by your accent, I'm guessing you're not allowed to go wherever you please."

Filip knew Peter was right; he was putting himself in danger by going out there, but he couldn't wait any longer. He had to see Anna.

"I appreciate everything you've done for me, sir," Filip said, "but I need to do something."

"Fine," Peter said and went back to eating breakfast. "And please call me Peter, for God's sake."

"Thank you, sir," Filip said with a smile and rushed off.

He ran through the fields without stopping until he saw Anna's village of Immenrode. He approached cautiously, hiding behind whatever freshly blooming foliage he could find until arriving at the farmhouse where he'd last seen Anna. He peeked over the wooden fence, expecting to see her feeding the chickens or sweeping the yard, but he was disappointed to find the farm empty. There were no people or animals outside. It looked almost abandoned. He wouldn't dare go inside or approach the house, so he decided to lie under a wild gooseberry bush and wait.

About an hour later, Filip's patience was rewarded when he saw Anna pushing a man in a wheelchair down the road. The man's legs were deformed, and his body looked whittled down. He hid his face in his hand as if embarrassed by it all. Anna, however, was cheerful and as beautiful as ever. She was singing a love song in Polish that Filip didn't recognize.

He watched Anna pull the wheelchair up three steps and disappear inside the house. She returned seconds later to pick up a bag she had left at the bottom of the stairs.

Filip climbed halfway up the fence. "Anna!" he yelled in a

hushed voice, waving his arm so she would notice him. "Come here!"

She smiled brightly when she saw him and ran up to the fence. "Filip! It's too dangerous—"

"Meet me at the creek in the woods," he said. "I'll wait for you there."

"I missed you," she said, then ran back inside the house.

Filip's heart almost exploded with joy. He wanted to tell her he loved her and ask her to run away with him, but he needed to be patient.

Anna fed Gunther and then laid him in bed for his daily nap. She wanted to rush, but caring for him was a long process. He had been kind to her, and she didn't want to disrespect him, so she took the necessary time. Yet she yearned so badly to be with Filip. She watched the clock above the fireplace, minutes ticking by slower than expected.

"What is it, Anna?" Gunther asked, apparently noticing her nervousness.

"I'm sorry, sir," she replied, trying to calm herself. "I just have a lot of errands around the house and need to get them done before dinner."

He smiled. "Why don't you take the rest of the day off? You've been very good to me, Anna. You deserve some rest."

"Thank you, Herr Gottschalk," she said, tucking him in. "You just take your nap and don't worry about anything."

She ran faster to the stream than she had run from the police in her hometown of Czestochowa. When she arrived, Filip didn't waste time talking. He opened his arms and embraced her so warmly that it made her cry. Then he kissed her on the lips. Anna didn't resist. She closed her eyes and enjoyed the moment.

"What took you so long?" she said when he finally released her.

Filip smiled and pulled her down to the ground. "You wouldn't believe my luck. I found a job and a place to stay."

"Where?"

"In a village only a few kilometers away. A nice man helped me."

"A German?"

"I guess they're not all bad," he said. "What about your German?"

"I don't know. He seems good too."

"See, things seem to be getting better for us."

"Be careful, Filip. Maybe he's deceiving you."

"Don't worry, I'll be fine. Can you please sing me the song you were singing to that man in a wheelchair?" he said.

Anna smiled back and started singing, watching Filip close his eyes and relax on the grass beside her.

> Everyone is allowed to love,
> that's love's simple law.
> Because you love with your heart,
> and everybody has one.
> Everyone is allowed to love,
> that's love's simple law.
> Let the worries melt away,
> and let happiness last . . .

Anna sang for a few minutes, repeating all the lyrics she could remember. When she was done, Filip opened his eyes and gently patted her hair. She leaned over and kissed him on his lips.

"What is this song?" he asked.

"You've never heard it?"

He shook his head.

"It's called 'Everyone Is Allowed to Love' by Mieczyslaw Fogg," she said. "It was very popular in the city before the war. They played it on the radio all the time."

"You had a radio?" he asked.

She nodded. "My father even took me to Fogg's concert once."

Filip whistled in admiration. "We only had a guy with a fiddle in my village. Nobody could afford a radio."

Anna laughed. "I hope your fiddler was good."

Filip sat up, crossing his arms defensively. "Are you making fun of our fiddler? He was the best."

"How do you know? Have you seen other fiddlers?"

He stood up and walked over to the stream. "You're making fun of me."

"Yes," Anna admitted. Although she didn't like arguing with people, she enjoyed doing so with him for some reason. She was curious about how he would respond.

"You're probably right," he said. "Come to think of it, you're a much better singer than he was a fiddler."

They both laughed.

"Good answer," she said.

He sat next to her and kissed her. "I wish I could kiss you all day."

Anna wished for that too, but her mind darkened. She remembered they couldn't do this all day or every day. They were fortunate to have even this single moment. Unless they safely returned to Poland, they might not have many moments like these left.

"They're probably looking for you," she said.

"They'll never find me," he said. "I found a man who gave me a place to stay and is paying me to work for him."

"How long do you think that will last? He can give you or sell you to somebody else tomorrow."

Filip nodded in agreement. "I'll save the money and take us back to Poland. I think I found a way we can take the train."

"How long before we can do that?" she asked.

"I don't know. I get one mark per day, and it will probably cost a hundred marks for the train, plus another hundred for the bribes and food."

"That will take half a year to collect," she said, disappointed. "There has to be a faster way."

Filip shrugged, out of ideas.

"I have to go back," she said. "Gunther will be waking soon."

"When can I meet you again?"

"Tomorrow," she suggested. "At the same time."

Anna kissed him and stood up. Filip sprung up and kissed her, holding her close to him. She felt herself melting into his arms. It made her want to stay with him there forever.

"I love you," he whispered into her ear.

She froze. She had never heard those words come out of a man's mouth, and their effect on her was greater than she'd anticipated. Her knees wanted to buckle, her mouth dried up, and cold sweat dripped down her back. She was losing control of her body and needed to escape.

"I'll see you tomorrow," she choked out while pushing away from him.

She ran half-dazed and disoriented through the woods. She knew now with certainty she loved him.

Frau Wolff was sitting at the kitchen table with two policemen across from her when Filip burst through the door. Peter Strauss, the dumb guy who'd helped him, stood up as if trying to warn Filip. But it was too late, if that was what he was trying to do.

Strauss had admitted that Filip was staying with him, but only after the policemen told him about the witnesses who saw Filip at the gypsum yard and the mine. He wouldn't tell them where Filip went; he pretended he didn't like him and that he probably ran away. He probably hoped Filip would spot the police from outside.

Frau Wolff watched Filip just stand there, petrified. She could tell that his mind was telling him to run but that his body couldn't execute the order. Her heart ran fast with joy. Frau Wolff had spent a week working with the police to find Filip, and the dumb look on his face was her reward. As the two policemen put out their cigarettes and stood up, Filip collapsed to his knees.

"Filip Wolny?" asked one of the policemen, reading from a document he pulled from his pocket.

Filip nodded, his face pale. The other policeman went around Filip to block the exit.

"You're under arrest," said the first policeman.

"Peter, please save me!" Filip begged.

Peter hung his head and stared at the floor. His face seemed to say, "I'm sorry," but he, too, seemed paralyzed.

Frau Wolff stood up and approached Filip. "Nobody can

save you now," she said. She'd hoped to see him again, but only while hanging from the gallows. She wanted to see his feet twitch as he was hanged. "You will pay for what you've done to me."

"What is it that he's done exactly?" asked Peter. "You never explained."

"It doesn't matter," said one of the policemen. "He's a runaway. He's going to jail."

"I could really use him," argued Peter. "We're short of people, and they have orders from the highest SS officials to hide fuel inside the mines."

"I'm good with horses," Filip pleaded. "I can make ten trips per day with the wagon."

"Stay out of my business," Frau Wolff hissed at Peter. "You're lucky nobody is arresting you for harboring a criminal."

That shut Peter up, and he backed away. The policemen dragged Filip outside. He didn't protest as they threw him into a car.

14
APRIL 13, 1942

Fourteen of them packed a prison cell meant for two. Filip had passed out when they brought him to the prison in Weimar the night before, and he woke up only when a foul smell hit his nose in the morning.

He grunted, sore from sleeping on the concrete floor among the bodies of the other prisoners. He untangled his legs from someone else's and sat up, finding himself faced with another prisoner, who was sitting, naked from the waist down, on a metal bucket in the corner of the cell. The skinny man, who was probably in his late twenties and had a long, bony face and large, sad eyes, strained with effort while staring at Filip. That explained the putrid smell of feces engulfing the cell. Filip stared back, unsure what else to do.

"Good morning," said the prisoner when he finally finished.

"Good morning," Filip replied, still confused by the situation.

"My name is Sig Blau."

"Filip."

"Excuse me, please," said Sig. "I apologize for my disposi-tion. Unfortunately, I didn't have other options."

"Don't worry about it."

"You wouldn't happen to have some toilet paper or a piece of newspaper, would you?"

"No. Sorry," Filip said.

"Ah," Sig said as he stood and pulled his pants up. "I guess I'll just have to walk around with my asshole chafed."

Filip laughed.

"Ah, perfect," said Sig, sitting next to Filip. "It's always good to find a receptive audience for my jokes. Where are you from?"

"Junno," Filip replied.

"Ah, yes. The metropolis of Junno. Very impressive city. Remind me, how many theatres do they have there?"

"It's a small village in Poland," Filip replied, confused that there might be another Junno out there. "We don't have any theatres."

"Ah, pardon," said Sig. "I apologize for the confusion. I'm sure it's a lovely place. I'm from Berlin. Very nice to meet you, Filip."

Sig extended his hand, and Filip shook it with some hesita-tion, considering where Sig had been just a minute ago.

"Don't worry. I usually wipe with my other hand," Sig assured him.

Filip laughed again. It was nice to find some humor in his desperate situation.

"What do you do for a living, Filip?"

"I'm just a farmer. How about you, Sig?"

"Ah, I thought you'd never ask. I'm a famous comedian— well, at least in Berlin. I'm still working on expanding my popularity nationwide."

"What's a comedian?" Filip asked, embarrassed not to know this profession.

"Ah, right. Maybe this is not a well-known profession where you're from. What I do is entertain. I go up on a stage and tell jokes for money."

Filip's mouth dropped in astonishment. "People pay you money to hear jokes?"

"Yes, that's correct."

"I wish I had some money to hear your jokes," Filip said.

"Ah, well. I usually require a larger audience anyway. Maybe one day."

"We had a comedian in our village," Filip said. "Jasiu. But he didn't get paid. He was hilarious. Do you want to hear one of his jokes?"

"No, that's all right—"

"So, listen to this," Filip said. "Hitler, Stalin, and Churchill are flying on a plane. They see the devil on one of the wings, cutting the wing with a saw. Churchill says, 'Don't worry, I'll talk to him.' He opens the door and screams something at him, but the devil keeps cutting. Churchill comes back. They ask him, 'What did you tell him?' Churchill says, 'I offered him Africa, but he refused.' Hitler says, 'Don't worry, I'll go out there and talk to him.' He opens the door and screams something at the devil, but the devil keeps cutting. Hitler comes back and says, 'I offered him Poland and France, but he didn't care.' Stalin says, 'Don't worry, I'll talk to him.' He goes out there and talks to the devil, who suddenly stops cutting and flies away. Stalin comes back, pleased with himself. Hitler and Churchill, astonished, ask him, 'What in the world did you tell him?' 'Oh, nothing,' says Stalin. 'Only that if he keeps working so hard, I'll sign him up for the communist party.'"

Sig and several prisoners, who were now awake, laughed.

"That's not bad," said Sig. "My comedy is slightly more sophisticated, but I admit that was pretty good. I might have some competition in Junno from your friend Jasiu."

That was when the locks slammed and the door to their cell swung open. A large, burly man stood at the entrance. He was about a head taller than everyone else and had a chest twice as broad as Filip's. He wore the pants of a police officer but only a white shirt on top, with sleeves rolled up. There were small splatters of blood on his shirt.

"Shit! That's Detective Inspector Hubert Leclaire," whispered Sig.

"What are you cunts laughing about?" the man shouted, his voice booming.

The room quieted immediately. Everyone held their breath.

"Filip Wolny!" Leclaire yelled out.

"Try to breathe," said Sig, sliding away from Filip.

Filip didn't know what that meant and had no choice but to identify himself. "It's me," he replied while standing up.

"Let's go!" said Leclaire, leaving the cell.

Filip followed him through a path that other prisoners cleared for him. They looked at him gloomily as if they were seeing him for the last time.

A guard locked the door behind Filip and pushed him to catch up with Leclaire, who entered another room. Filip walked in.

"Close the door," Leclaire ordered.

Filip closed the door behind him.

"Sit down," Leclaire said.

Filip sat on a wooden chair at a small table, the only two objects in the room. Leclaire stood over him while reading some documents in a folder. Filip noticed the man's knuckles were red with blood.

"I'll be damned," Leclaire said finally. "You almost got away with it."

"Sorry, sir?" Filip choked out, his throat dry.

"You thought you could run away from your owner and pick another job?"

"I didn't run away . . ." Filip said. He wanted to make up a story, but just then, a fist smashed into his right cheek. He flew back, taking the chair with him, and landed hard, smacking his head against the floor. He became disoriented and dizzy. Black dots floated in space before his eyes. Then a hand grabbed him by the shirt and lifted him and the chair back up.

"Sit down!" Leclaire yelled.

Filip wanted to say something, but he wasn't exactly sure what. His face was numb, and nothing but an incoherent babble came out of his mouth.

"That's what happens when you lie to me," Leclaire said, rounding the table to get on the other side of Filip. "Now, it says here that you beat up Frau Wolff. Is this true?"

Filip shook his head. Immediately, a fist landed on his left cheek. This time, Filip flew off the chair and landed on the floor on his hands and knees. The room was spinning, and all he could do was watch as a trickle of blood dripped from his mouth to the gray floor.

A hand grabbed his shirt collar and pulled him back into the chair. Filip closed his eyes to collect himself.

"Did you beat her up?" Leclaire asked.

Filip was ready to admit it, but his body gave up. He couldn't speak or move. It was as if he wasn't inside his body anymore. His soul was just circling above him, ready to disembark at any moment.

"You can't talk?" Leclaire said, standing above Filip. "Don't worry. You'll talk."

Anna waited at the stream, just like they'd agreed, but an hour passed, and Filip was still not there. She wanted to stay longer and wait, but she had to return to care for Gunther, who would soon wake from his nap.

She marched slowly through the woods, hoping to see Filip run to her at any moment. Anna was planning to tell him that she loved him. She was no longer afraid to express her feelings. She was ready for it, but now she had doubts. Did something happen to him, or did he betray her? Her mother had always warned her about boys and their games. Filip wasn't like that, though. He'd chased after her across Germany and told her he loved her. She knew something terrible must have happened to him to prevent him from seeing her.

Gunther was already sitting up in bed when she returned to his farm. He looked at her sleepily and smiled. She smiled back and began preparing his dinner of boiled potatoes and breaded veal steak. She was thankful to be working for such a kind master. He never complained and was always happy to see her. He didn't like talking to other people—probably scarred by them looking down on him because of his polio disability—but he always wanted to talk to her.

"I'm glad to have you here, Anna," he said.

"Thank you. I like it here," she said.

"It feels like I have a wife."

Anna froze over the pot of potatoes in her hands. She dared not look at him, so she stared into the pot. This was unexpected, and she was caught entirely off guard. Why was Gunther saying this to her? He'd only known her for a week. Was he lonely?

"We might as well get married," he continued, trying to be

nonchalant. "I'm not much of a man, but you won't have to worry about anything. Your life in Germany would be safe. My father left me some land that I'm leasing to other farmers, so we'll always have money. It would make me happy."

Anna put the pot down and faced him. "I'm sorry, Herr Gottschalk, but I don't understand. I'm just a Polish slave girl."

"So what?" he pushed. "I can marry whoever I want. Who's going to stop me?"

"It's not possible," she insisted.

"Why? Why is it not possible?"

She had to stop this now. She knew he was serious and would not relent. If she let it continue, it would be Gustaf all over again. "I love someone else," she blurted out.

Gunther clenched his teeth and sat motionless on his bed. "Who is it?" he asked.

A horn sounded outside. Anna hurried to the window facing the road in front of the house. She was happy their conversation had been interrupted, but the urgency of the horn worried her. She pushed the curtains to the side and looked out the window. A woman exited a black car marked "Polizei" on its side, confirming her fears.

"Who is it?" Gunther asked.

"It's your sister," she said.

"What is Helma doing here?"

"Not Helma. It's Frau Wolff."

"What the hell is Katherine doing here?"

They heard a knock at the front door, but Frau Wolff was inside before Anna could run over to let her in. She entered the kitchen and stared at them triumphantly.

"What is it?" Gunther demanded.

Frau Wolff paused momentarily, as if reconsidering what she would say. Then she said, "Hello, brother!"

"Good day to you, sister. Now, may you tell me why you're here?"

"Oh my goodness," she said, pretending to be offended. "Is that how you welcome your own sister?"

"You haven't visited in five years," he rebutted. "If I recall correctly, which I do, you told me to go to hell after you found out how much land our father left me. That's the last time I saw you. At his funeral."

Frau Wolff sat down at the kitchen table. "Well, I'm afraid I'm coming with more bad news. In fact, it concerns both you and your little Polish whore."

"Don't call her that—" he demanded.

"I'm taking her with me."

Anna gasped. This news was much worse than she expected. A bead of cold sweat trickled down her back.

"You can't take her," Gunther protested. "Helma gave her to me."

Frau Wolff pulled a piece of paper from her purse and smacked it on the table with a loud thud. "Because of your whore, I lost my laborer, Filip. He chased her across Germany to this village. It took the police and me a few days to find him. Unfortunately, the police cannot release him back to me, so they granted her to me as his replacement."

"Where is Filip?" Anna finally spoke up despite being horrified by the thought of what she might hear back.

Frau Wolff gasped, faking an insult. "How dare you speak to me, bitch!"

"Don't speak to her like that!" Gunther screamed. He wriggled out of his bed and tried to get into his wheelchair, but it slipped from under him, and he fell to the floor.

Frau Wolff laughed. "My poor, crippled brother is in love,

isn't he? Our Führer thinks the likes of you make our Aryan race weak, and I must agree. You're a waste of a human being."

Anna couldn't take it anymore. "WHERE'S FILIP!" she screamed.

Frau Wolff's hand came across Anna's face like lightning. Anna stumbled back, shocked by the pain.

"Your Filip will be doing hard labor at the Buchenwald concentration camp for the rest of his short, miserable life!" Frau Wolff shouted while standing over Anna. "Now, go pack your shit before I have you thrown in there with him."

"You will pay for this!" Gunther screamed, knocking over a chair in frustration. He then started crying. "You can't do this to me."

"I can do as I please, little brother. And you will fall in line like a good German. Remember, this Polish swine is subhuman. Don't make me tell your neighbors about your pathetic little love for her. You've disgraced our family enough, don't you think?"

Anna ran off, crying. She feared this was the end of her love story and that she would never see Filip again.

15
APRIL 29, 1942

Filip held a metal spoon to his forehead to reduce the swelling. Two weeks of beatings had taken a toll on his body. Leclaire kept beating him almost daily, even after he admitted to his crimes. He was covered in cuts and bruises from the man's knuckles, which somehow refused to break.

And Filip wasn't the only one getting pummeled; Leclaire beat up half of the now twenty prisoners squeezed into this cell and probably countless others from other cells. The man had the strength of a bear, and his beatings never weakened. He was like a heavyweight boxing champion using the prisoners as punching bags to train for his next fight.

"How come you don't get any beatings from Leclaire?" Filip asked Sig, who was sitting next to him, whistling a happy tune. Sig would occasionally be pulled out of the cell, but he always returned unscathed. Other prisoners murmured that he might be a spy, reporting to Leclaire about what they were talking about. Filip didn't want to believe it, but his animosity toward Sig grew with each beating.

"I told you, I'm famous," said Sig. "People would be upset if they found out I was beaten in prison."

"But they're not upset you're in prison?"

"Ah, of course they are. I'm sure they miss my performances."

"Do they know why you're in prison?" Filip asked. "Because you never told me."

Sig scratched his head as if contemplating whether he should tell Filip. "Well, it's not that complicated. I'm a Jew."

"So what?" Filip asked, unsure why being a Jew would put Sig in prison. He'd heard in his village that the Nazis didn't like Jews, but he'd never heard of them being imprisoned.

"Haven't you heard?" said Sig. "Nazis put all the Jews in ghettos and prison camps and confiscated all their property."

"Why?"

"Good question. They seem to blame us for everything, but I'm guessing they mostly like to take our money."

"Are German Jews rich?" Filip asked because he knew only of the Jews who lived in a village close to Junno, and they were poor farmers just like everyone else.

"Some of them," Sig said. "Not me, that's for sure."

"I thought you were famous."

"Yes, famous. But not rich," Sig said, sighing. "That's the curse of a comedian."

That was when the lock slammed and the door swung open. Two policemen entered the cell and started pulling people off the ground, yelling at them to get up.

"Let's go! Get your asses up!" Leclaire shouted from the hallway.

Filip and Sig sprung up to their feet.

"What's going on?" Filip shouted at the policemen.

"Shut your mouth and get out!" yelled one of the policemen, pushing Filip with a baton.

"Where are you taking us?" Filip insisted.

Instead of answering, the policeman whacked him across the back. Filip hissed from the intense pain, which felt like a thousand beestings.

"Shut your mouth, Filip," Sig said. "You're going to get us killed."

"You're dead already," said the policeman. "You're not coming out alive from where you're going."

"Where's that?" Filip asked. He had to know in case there was a chance to let Anna know where he was going.

"Buchenwald," the policeman said quietly, as if he feared the word.

The other prisoners quieted down when they heard the name.

"What?" Filip asked, looking around for an explanation. "What's Buchenwald?"

"It's a labor camp," said Sig. "That's where they send you to die."

Armed soldiers marched Filip and Sig, along with two hundred other prisoners, through the town of Weimar and then the surrounding countryside in a driving, cold rain. Their group had many nationalities: Polish, Ukrainian, and Gypsy, but mostly German. They all marched quickly, covering themselves with whatever clothing they had to protect against the rain. The soldiers rode bicycles in front, behind, and beside their column, so there was no way to escape.

"Hey, you want to hear a good joke?" said Filip.

"Try to keep your mouth shut," Sig suggested.

"We have to find a way to survive this."

"I'm a Jew in Germany who's still alive. Stick with me, and you'll be all right."

Filip thought the opposite was true. He'd had nothing but bad luck since he met Sig. His fears were confirmed when the Buchenwald camp appeared to them an hour later on a hill through a forest clearing.

It was a formidable prison camp, even more tightly guarded than the gypsum mine camp Filip had delivered to just a couple of weeks ago at Mittlebau-Dora near Niedersachswerfen. It had electrified barbwire fences and watchtowers around the camp, along with sentries and dogs. Dozens of grim barracks—long structures built out of wood painted the color of red brick—stood behind the fence. There were only a few windows in each, and all were barred with metal rods. The buildings looked more like factories, but prisoners were moving about them, so Filip figured these had to be their living quarters. On the opposite side, he could see the chimneys of what appeared to be a factory.

As they approached the gate, he noticed a sign above it inscribed in stucco. "What does that say?" Filip asked, not able to read German very well yet.

"'My country, right or wrong,'" Sig read to Filip. "I would say wrong."

There was another sign in iron letters across the bars of the gate.

"'To each his due,'" Sig read again.

"What does that mean?" Filip asked.

"I think it means that death is meant for us."

The SS guards welcomed them through the gates by beating them with their guns and whips. Filip hid behind another prisoner, and Sig hid behind him, but they got their share of blows anyway. One of them hit Filip on the ear, and he thought he'd gone deaf until he heard Sig cry in terror. He turned to see Sig bleeding from a cut on his forehead.

The SS then made them run for about a half kilometer until they reached a fenced-in area. There, they were ordered to take all their clothes off. Filip hid the medallion he got from Anna in his mouth. It was the only thing to remember her by. He undressed as slowly as he could, hoping to keep something on, but the SS beat those who hesitated. Eventually, everyone ended up naked, hiding their private parts by holding a pile of wet clothes in front of them.

They stood like this for an hour, shivering in the cold spring rain, before the SS rushed them through the camp and into another open area where about twenty chairs were lined up. Behind each chair stood a prisoner holding what looked like shears. The guards created a line of prisoners behind each chair, and the shearing began. One by one, all the prisoners sat naked in the chairs while their heads were shaved bald.

Filip barely recognized Sig when they were done.

"You look like a prisoner," said Sig, apparently feeling the same about Filip.

"I don't think we're ever getting out of here," said Filip.

After everyone was shaved, the guards rushed them into a large, empty barracks. Inside were piles of camp uniforms, grayish white with blue vertical stripes, just like the ones Filip had seen prisoners wearing at the gypsum mine. Recalling their skinny bodies and blank faces, he realized he was one of them now. He feared the same destiny awaited him.

"Welcome to the meat grinder," said one of the prisoners, who was helping them sort through the clothing. He smiled, showing off a mouth full of black teeth.

It took another hour for everyone to dress. The uniform sizes were all messed up, and it took them a while to exchange with others for the correct size. Finally, the prisoner who seemed to be in charge and whom everyone called the kapo rushed everyone out to a large, muddy plaza, where they lined up in columns.

Hundreds of prisoners were gathered in the plaza, along with the ones Filip had arrived with, perhaps a thousand men in total. An SS officer climbed the gallows that stood at the edge of the plaza and started reading names. Each time he read one, a prisoner would respond with "Present." Those who stepped out of line or fell from exhaustion were beaten mercilessly by the SS guards. Thus, they stood in the rain for another two hours, waiting for everyone's name to be called. Filip's legs were still sore from the day's trip and the beatings of the last two weeks, so standing still for two hours in the cold was torture.

Finally, just as the rain stopped and the sun peeked from behind the clouds, the SS rushed all the newcomers across the camp to another plaza. Several tables were set up there, each with a different letter representing the beginning of a surname. An SS guard sat behind each table. The prisoners formed lines in front of the respective tables. Filip was the first one in line at the *W* table.

"Your name?" demanded the guard, who looked younger than Filip. He had blond fuzz barely showing on his face.

"Filip Wolny."

The guard flipped through some papers, then said, "Are you a Jew?"

Filip shook his head. "No, sir."

"You're a political prisoner," said the guard matter-of-factly.

"No, I'm not," Filip said. "I'm just a farmer."

"It says here that you are, so you are," the guard insisted, handing him two badges: a red triangle and a white rectangle with the number 131124. "Stitch them to your jacket and keep them there at all times."

Filip wanted to explain himself further but saw that it was pointless, so he took the badges.

"I'm assigning you to the quarry," said the guard, handing him a brown band. "Stitch this to your sleeve. Go to Block 4. The kapo there will tell you what to do."

Filip was about to ask a question but was quickly pushed out of the way by the prisoner behind him. He stood there for a moment, unsure what to do. If the quarry work was anything like what he saw at the gypsum mine, he would be dead within weeks. He listened to what professions men claimed at the other tables and noticed they were getting easier jobs.

Filip forced his way inside the line again. He hid his brown band in his pants, and after a while, he stood in front of the table again.

"What are you doing here again?" the same young SS guard asked.

"I forgot to mention that I'm also a barber," Filip replied, trying to sound confident about his fake profession, which he had just overheard someone else claim.

The guard stared at him for a moment, then handed him a green band and said, "Fine. We need barbers. Report to Block 7."

Filip thanked the guard and marched off to Block 7 with satisfaction. He didn't know how to cut hair but figured it couldn't be too difficult. His mother had cut his hair back home. He thanked his luck for being able to change jobs.

When he arrived at Block 7, he found a group of about twenty chairs standing outside. Almost all the chairs were occupied by naked prisoners who were squirming uncomfortably while being shaved and washed. The barber kapo put him to work right away. "Get behind one of the chairs and get to work," the kapo said, handing him the shears.

Filip had never used shears before but did as ordered and found an empty chair. He observed what other barbers were doing. It seemed easy, but there was a technique to it. It reminded him of when he saw his uncle shearing the sheep—smooth, quick actions across the head while constantly snapping the shears closed.

His first client had thick black hair down to his shoulders, and he didn't speak Polish or German. Filip sat him down and immediately started cutting, trying to simulate the other barbers. It was a lot harder than it looked, and he accidentally cut the man twice. The man started yelling as blood poured down his scalp.

An SS officer standing nearby quickly stepped in and slapped both Filip and the man across the face. He took his pistol out and pointed it at Filip's head. He looked familiar, but Filip couldn't remember if he had seen him before. His face was handsome, with high cheekbones, but his thick lips and large blue eyes tightened with apparent anger.

"Are you a fucking barber?" the SS officer screamed.

Filip froze in panic but managed to nod.

"Fuck you are! Get the hell out of here!" He pulled a brown band from his pocket and threw it at Filip. "Put that on, swine. Maybe some stonework will teach you a lesson. I'll see to it personally."

He kicked Filip, causing him to fall into the mud. Filip quickly crawled away and didn't look back until he was out of the SS officer's sight. When he finally stopped to catch a breather, he heard a voice above him.

"I told you to stick with me."

Filip looked up and saw Sig standing over him.

"Your band is brown too," Filip pointed out. "And whatever the yellow star means that's sewn on your jacket."

"That represents a Jew, which is never good. But at least I didn't piss off Sergeant Hinkelmann, who, from what I hear, is the worst piece-of-shit human being ever to exist," replied Sig.

Filip now remembered why Hinkelmann looked familiar. He was the same SS officer who hanged Leszek. "I don't know why he's so upset. I didn't do anything," Filip said.

"Really? Is that also how you got here? By not doing anything? I saw you go back in line. Which reminds me, do you know that joke about a Jew and a German going to the barbershop?"

Filip got up and walked away.

"That's fine. I'll save it for later," said Sig, following Filip. "You don't deserve my jokes anyway. And believe me, they're much better than your stupid joke about the devil on a plane."

"Stop following me," said Filip.

"I'm not following you," insisted Sig. "I'm going to Block 4. Where are you going?"

Filip threw up his arms. "Great! We're in the same building."

The barracks of Block 4 were lined with rows of bunks, four high and full of prisoners squeezed together like on a transport train. Filip and Sig walked along the bunks, trying to find an open spot, but other prisoners pushed them away. Filip was exhausted from the day and finally forced his way into one of the bunks. He was punched and kicked by four other prisoners as he did so, but he was able to fight his way in.

Sig tried to follow Filip but wasn't so lucky. He was kicked out and landed on the floor. Filip heard him sobbing like a child and thought about leaving him there. Sig had been nothing but bad luck. But Filip couldn't just let him sleep on the floor. He punched a couple of prisoners, grabbed Sig by the shirt, and pulled him into the bunk.

"Thank you," Sig whimpered.

"There's nothing to thank me for," said Filip. "We're both dead men anyway."

16

AUGUST 5, 1942

S weat poured from Anna and Sabina as they walked through the village of Rotenburg behind the horse wagon Frau Wolff was driving. It was a hot summer day, and they had just finished ten hours of wheat harvesting. Not used to heavy labor, Anna's hands burned with blisters from the scythe. She was no longer just a cook and had to do everything around the Wolff farm. This had been very difficult for her, but it had one significant advantage: She could leave the farmhouse. That was exactly what she needed to accomplish the day's mission.

"Where did you hide it?" Anna whispered to Sabina, who had been a great friend since Anna arrived. Sabina had welcomed her like a sister and kept her spirits up after the news about Filip. She was the only reason Anna had emerged from depression in the last few months.

"It's underneath the bushels on the right side of the wagon," Sabina replied. "The post office is also on the right side."

"And the distraction?"

"Should be there," said Sabina with a hint of uncertainty.

That was what Sabina had said the last three times, and each time, the diversion didn't work. However, they had no choice. The plan relied on Sabina's ability to create chaos through her gossip, which was significant but unreliable at best. Fortunately, Anna's fears were quickly erased when a heavyset woman ran out of the house that was on their left and across from the post office. She was heading straight for Frau Wolff's wagon and began screaming as soon as she was within their earshot, waving her fist threateningly above her head.

"You fucking whore!" the woman shouted at Frau Wolff, who stopped the wagon and stared at the woman in shock.

"Do it now," said Sabina.

Anna followed the order immediately and ran to the right side of the wagon.

"What the hell is wrong with you, Frau Spiegel?" Frau Wolff yelled back at the woman.

"Your husband is dead, so now you think you can fuck our husbands?" accused Frau Spiegel.

Frau Wolff turned toward the woman and paid no attention to what was happening behind her, giving Anna the time to search the wagon without getting in. She looked under one pile of bushels, then another, but found nothing. She glanced back at Sabina to ask for help, but Sabina didn't move from her spot. They'd agreed beforehand that she would stand in place no matter what to make sure Frau Wolff didn't get suspicious, and Sabina was now sticking to that plan.

"I wouldn't fuck your ugly husband if he were the last man in the Reich, you stupid bitch!" screamed Frau Wolff, not paying the slightest attention to Anna.

Anna searched frantically under each bushel, of which

there were at least forty just on the right side of the wagon. She only had a few minutes, or the plan would be ruined. She wiped the sweat from her eyes, her face now completely drenched. Finally, she found it at the very back of the wagon. Anna cursed herself for not starting at the back, then pulled out a small package wrapped in brown paper and tied with twine.

"From what I hear, you'd fuck anything that walks, you cunt!" screamed Frau Spiegel.

"How dare you! Your ugly husband has been looking at my ass for years because he's sick of fucking your fat behind. He probably can't even find your hole."

Anna decided this was the right moment and sprinted toward the post office with the package secured under her arm. She didn't look back until she reached the door. When she did, Frau Wolff stood on the wagon with the horse whip in her hand, ready to strike at Frau Spiegel on the ground below. Without hesitation, Anna entered the post office.

She was relieved to find only the clerk inside the one-room office. She stepped up to the counter and set the package on it. The clerk, an old lady with thick glasses, glanced at Anna's *P* badge but said nothing.

"I would like to send a package to Buchenwald prison camp," said Anna.

The clerk stared at her for a moment, then said, "You know that foreign laborers are not allowed to send mail, right?"

Anna had counted on the clerk's sympathy, but now she realized she'd been naïve to assume. She had to improvise.

"It's actually not from me," she said, setting a one-mark coin on the counter. "Frau Wolff sent me because she didn't want people to talk. It's a sensitive issue, and she would like to keep it a secret."

The clerk stared at the coin and then slid it into her pocket.

"It's two marks and twenty pfennigs to send the package," she said.

Anna counted the money and set it on the counter. She thanked God for Sabina, who somehow managed to collect enough money. Since Frau Wolff never paid them, Anna could only imagine the lengths Sabina went to.

"Thank you," said Anna.

"What's all the screaming out there?" the clerk asked, taking the money and the package behind the counter.

"One of the town gossipers is accusing Frau Wolff of something she didn't do," said Anna. "I don't know what kind of monster starts such rumors."

With that, she said goodbye and rushed out of the post office. Frau Wolff was still arguing with Frau Spiegel, but it looked like the argument was petering out because Frau Spiegel was walking back to her house. Anna quickly ran back behind the wagon and stood next to Sabina. They smiled at each other, both happy their mission was accomplished.

"What are you two pigs smiling about?" Frau Wolff yelled from the wagon. "You think this is funny?"

They lowered their heads, staring at the ground and trying not to burst out laughing. This was a good day, and they had hope again.

Filip cursed God under his breath and heaved a large stone onto his right shoulder. Judging by how much it compressed his bones, he guessed it was at least fifty kilograms, the weight of an average-size woman. He waited a moment to make sure the stone was well-balanced and wouldn't fall, and then he began his trek up the quarry hill again, joining hundreds of other prisoners.

It was his eleventh trip up the hill today and what seemed like the one-thousandth time since he began his work assignment in the stone quarry. It was brutal work, especially during these hot summer days, and Filip could feel strength seep out of his body. There were no mirrors in the Buchenwald concentration camp, but he imagined he looked as broken down as those poor prisoners he saw months earlier at the Dora gypsum mine. Heavy labor, combined with a lack of food—only a quarter loaf of bread and a bowl of leek soup per day—had reduced his body to a skeleton.

Worse, after several months of hard labor, he'd lost hope of seeing Anna again. There didn't seem to be a way out of this place other than as burned ash through the camp's crematorium chimney. That was where they burned the bodies of those who died of exhaustion, sickness, or a bullet. Smoke billowed daily from the chimney because hundreds died each day.

That was no respite for the other thirty thousand prisoners because new arrivals quickly replaced the dead. The beds remained full, and the food remained in short supply. Then another day would arrive, and hundreds more would die while Filip somehow stayed alive.

What is the point of this labor other than to kill people? Filip wondered. The Germans didn't do anything with the stones once the prisoners carried them to the top of the hill. They just lay unused in a huge pile, quietly mocking the prisoners below.

"Pick up the pace, you pigs!" yelled Sergeant Hinkelmann, standing at the top of the hill as prisoners marched past him. His black SS uniform reminded Filip of the Grim Reaper the priest at his village was always talking about.

Hinkelmann was the same SS officer who threatened to

shoot Filip for faking to be a barber. Filip wondered why he hadn't killed him then. He's seen him shoot dozens of prisoners since for no apparent reason and without any emotion. Perhaps Hinkelmann knew this work was worse than death and preferred that Filip experience its hell. Maybe he only killed those who had nothing more to give and stopped their suffering.

No, Filip realized. *The killings are not for mercy.* Hinkelmann just found those he killed to be no longer useful to him and his game of torture. They were already dead and couldn't see or feel anything around them. They were ghosts.

"Here comes the barber of Seville," said Hinkelmann, laughing as Filip marched before him.

Filip didn't know what Seville was, but the two guards standing beside Hinkelmann apparently did because they also started laughing.

"Keep your back straight," Hinkelmann ordered, smacking Filip with a short whip.

Filip winced in pain, his body wanting to jerk in response, but he stayed steady and straightened instead. The stone on his shoulder wobbled a bit but remained in place. Hinkelmann did this to Filip almost daily, so he'd learned to stay steady on his path and avoid another beating.

"Good boy," said Hinkelmann, walking beside Filip while stroking the whip against his gloved hand. "I thought you'd be dead by now, barber. What's keeping you alive, huh?"

Filip didn't say anything because prisoners were not allowed to talk to the SS officers. Even if he could, he wouldn't dirty Anna's name by mentioning it to this monster. She was the only reason he was still alive.

"Oh, I know," said Hinkelmann. "It's a woman, isn't it?"

Filip again said nothing. Then he felt a kick to his legs. He tripped and fell, his face hitting the dirt while he tried to hold onto the stone, which smashed down dangerously close to his head.

"Are you listening to me, you Polish dog?" screamed Hinkelmann, standing above him. "You Polish fucks murdered my father in 1921, and my family had to escape Silesia with nothing but the clothes on our backs. You're going to pay for that now, you piece of shit. Do you hear me?"

Filip didn't know what Hinkelmann was talking about. His father once told him about a Polish rebellion in Silesia against the Germans, but he didn't know anything else about it.

"Get up!" Hinkelmann screamed.

Filip scrambled to his feet and stood to attention like prisoners were ordered to do when near an SS officer.

"What the hell are you waiting for, you stupid pig?" Hinkelmann said, his angry face only centimeters in front of Filip's. "Pick up that fucking stone and get back to work."

Filip could smell onions and pork on Hinkelmann's breath and wanted to indulge in it for a bit longer, having not tasted such delicacies in months. However, he bent down instead and heaved the stone back onto his shoulder. A thought to smash Hinkelmann's head with the stone entered his mind for a split second but evaporated just as quickly.

Filip rushed off and stepped back in line with the other prisoners, who'd never stopped their journey up the hill to even look at what Hinkelmann was doing to Filip, much less do anything about it. Just like Filip, they were not ready to die yet. They had a reason to survive.

∽

Sig was moving packages from one stack to another when SS Technical Sergeant Hans Schmidt walked into the camp's post office. He wore his black SS uniform, just like all the other officers, but his kind face and dainty spectacles were more like those of an elementary school teacher, which Sig knew more closely represented the real man.

Schmidt glanced at the other three prisoners digging through packages on a table at the back of the room, then said, "I need canned ham. Do you have any?"

"Yes, we found three this week—two from Denmark and one from Poland," said Sig. He had the inventory memorized at all times because Schmidt made surprise visits, randomly requesting specific items. Sig had been running Schmidt's racketeering operation for seven years, first in Berlin and now, for the last several months, in Buchenwald. Schmidt was good at transactions but terrible at securing products, so he'd had himself and his family transferred to Buchenwald after Sig's arrest just to maintain his side income and the high-end lifestyle that came with it. Of course, this was not the only reason he'd transferred to Buchenwald.

"Good," said Schmidt. "My wife and daughter left for the day and won't be back until this evening. I would like you to bring those hams to my villa."

Sig and Schmidt were not only racketeering partners. They had also been lovers for the last ten years.

Schmidt was just an accountant when Sig first met him at the Eldorado—the best homosexual club in Berlin, where Sig performed. He was charming, in a gentlemanly kind of way, and made Sig feel special. They fell in love shortly after that and saw each other weekly even though Schmidt was married and had a child. Nothing would stop them from being together, not even when the Nazis came to power, closed all the homosexual clubs, and started arresting homosexuals and Jews. Sig lost his job at the club, and Schmidt lost his job at a Jewish bank that had to close down. That was when they decided to get into racketeering together. It was the only option for them to survive.

Schmidt even joined the SS to get connected to the movers and shakers of the new regime. It was also a way for him to save Sig—both gay and Jewish—from the Nazis. Sig and his contacts were also essential to securing goods from sellers and finding buyers. Meanwhile, Schmidt cleared the paperwork from the Nazi bureaucracy to move products across Germany.

"I will be there," said Sig.

"And we need to discuss the inventory," said Schmidt. "There's a huge demand for socks, meat, sugar, and coffee. Ever since Hitler decided to ration these, demand and prices have surged. I have a lot of customers waiting for delivery."

Sig loved the way Schmidt talked about business. It was their love language. His tone was so calm and calculating that it turned Sig on. They were stealing from people, which was illegal and wrong, but Schmidt somehow made it sound sexy.

"Don't worry," Sig assured him. "People keep sending packages. We have plenty of supply. But I need you to do me a favor first."

"What is it?"

"I have a friend in the quarry work unit—"

"What kind of friend?" Schmidt asked. He was a very jealous lover. It was his dark side, which seemed to emerge more often after he joined the SS. He'd acquired a taste for complete impunity for his actions.

"Nobody you have to worry about," Sig said. "He's just a nice kid from Poland. Helped me get through the Weimar jail. He's in love with this slave farm girl and wants to see her again.

I would like to help him any way I can, so I was hoping you could get him out of the quarry."

"The quarry?" Schmidt hissed, indicating he didn't like the idea. "You know Hinkelmann doesn't like to let anyone go unless they're leaving on a gurney."

"I know it won't be free, and you can't make Hinkelmann suspicious. But I'm counting on you, Hans."

Sig called him by his first name to make sure Schmidt knew how important this was to him. He employed this trick whenever he wanted something from Schmidt, and it worked every time.

"I'll see what I can do," Schmidt said, walking away. "But you bring those hams tonight."

Sig knew he would pay for it like he always did, but it was the kind of payment he enjoyed giving.

17
SEPTEMBER 23, 1942

Filip climbed the two scaffolding levels inside the trench and lay on a patch of grass below a small beech tree. No SS guards were around, so he took a breather from digging.

The work wasn't as exhausting as carrying stones in the quarry, but digging ditches all day was still backbreaking. The trench was deep—the height of two grown men. The man at the bottom of the trench would throw dirt up to the first scaffold, the man on the first scaffold would then throw it up to the second scaffold, and finally, the man on the second scaffold would throw it up to the ground level, where another man would put it in a wheelbarrow and dump it onto a pile. There were rumors that this was a military installation, but it seemed more like pointless work to kill more prisoners than anything for practical use.

One of the few advantages of this work was that Filip and about two hundred other prisoners got to work in a forest outside the camp without the constant watchful eyes of the SS.

Of course, the biggest advantage was that Sergeant Hinkel-mann was not in charge of this work unit. Filip didn't know how he got so lucky to get out of the quarry. Everything seemed so random in Buchenwald, like a roll of the dice, but he knew he probably would have been dead already if he had stayed there.

Filip watched the clouds lazily pass above him and wondered what Anna was doing at that moment. Judging by the sun's position, it was probably two in the afternoon, so Gunther was taking his nap, and Anna was free to do whatever she pleased. Maybe she was watching the same clouds as Filip. Was she wondering, like him, whether they'd ever see each other again? What if she had already decided she never would and had moved on with her life? Filip couldn't blame her if she did. After all, it was common knowledge that labor camps were a death sentence. Even if he somehow miraculously survived, it might be years before he got out. He would not be the same man either. He would be broken physically and mentally. Anna was a beautiful woman, and there would be many suitors tempting her to marry. Maybe it would be Gunther himself. He was crippled but still young, and he had a house and probably money. Why would Anna wait for a dead man?

"Get up!" a man shouted.

Filip sprung to his feet and saw an SS guard before him. The guard carried a rifle, which he pointed at Filip.

"Schnell!" the guard yelled.

Before Filip could respond, the guard's leg lashed out at his stomach. The blow landed with power, and Filip stumbled backward, teetered on the edge of the trench, and fell into it. He crashed through the top scaffold, hit another prisoner on the second, and landed feetfirst on the bottom. His knees buckled, and he collapsed into the mud that filled the bottom of the trench like a small swamp.

He tried to get up and quickly go back to work, not giving the SS guard a reason to shoot him. But his right ankle gave in, and he fell back into the mud again. He screamed, excruciating pain surging through him. He glanced at his ankle and saw that something wasn't right. His foot was pointing sideways instead of straight. He screamed again, and then there were prisoners above him, lifting him.

"What's wrong with my ankle?" Filip yelled at them.

"Shut up!" screamed one of the prisoners. He was about the same age as Filip but broader and more muscular. He lifted Filip up with ease and stood him up against the dirt wall of the trench. "They'll kill you if they think you can't work. Pretend you're digging for now. We'll look at your ankle back in camp."

Someone handed Filip a shovel. He looked up and saw the SS guard standing at the top of the trench with his rifle pointed down, so Filip took the shovel and began digging. The pain surged through him with each stroke. It was as if someone was hammering nails through his ankle. Yet he bit his tongue and didn't scream. He just kept shoveling until the guard above him disappeared.

"What's your name?" asked the young man who'd helped him earlier.

"Filip Wolny. From Junno."

"I'm Beniek Helonski. From Lodz."

Filip sat down on a plank of wood. "Thank you," he said. "You saved my life."

"I think your ankle is broken," said Beniek. "I saw a guy from Britain break his ankle like that when I was at the 1936 Olympics. He was high-jumping and landed weirdly, like you."

Filip didn't know what the Olympics were, but it confirmed

what he already knew: His condition was desperate. His chances of surviving Buchenwald had just decreased dramatically. Perhaps he wouldn't even survive this day.

"What happened to that guy?" asked Filip.

"I don't know. He never competed again. But don't worry. We'll get you fixed up. It's not like you have to be an Olympian."

"I'm a dead man," Filip said. "They'll shoot me dead if they see me like this. I need to go to the infirmary."

"I wouldn't do that if I were you," said Beniek. "Several comrades from our barracks went to the infirmary and never came back. There are rumors the Nazis experiment on people and then give them a shot at the end that kills them to erase evidence."

"How do you know this?"

"You can ask the doctor. He works there."

"What doctor?"

"Dr. Ciepielowski," said Beniek. "You'll meet him later."

Whistles blew above them, a sign the work was ending. It was time to march back to the camp—except Filip could barely stand, as his right foot was utterly lame.

"Let's go," said Beniek, rushing to Filip's side with two other prisoners.

"What's going on?" Filip protested.

"Don't talk," Beniek ordered.

They lifted Filip above their shoulders, and two other prisoners on the scaffold above pulled him up. They, in turn, lifted him to the top scaffold, where two other prisoners pulled him up. The same thing happened at ground level. The whole thing was like a synchronized circus act Filip had once seen in his village.

"Are you all right?" asked Beniek, standing beside him.

"How did you do that?"

"Teamwork. Something you learn in the Olympics."

Beniek and another prisoner lifted Filip off the ground, stood him up between them, and trotted to the column of prisoners already forming on the path back to camp. Filip promised himself he would find out more about the Olympics. *It must be something amazing*, he thought.

Another whistle blew, and the column marched off in the standard rows of five. Filip was in the middle of the row, carried by Beniek and other prisoners, who switched at intervals to refresh while maintaining the brisk pace of the march.

It seemed like a miracle when they finally reached the Buchenwald camp about thirty minutes later. Filip was relieved to be still alive.

"Thank you, Beniek," he said when they laid him down in his cot. "I owe you my life."

"Don't worry about it," said Beniek. "I'll check up on you later."

Beniek was true to his word. When Filip stirred awake sometime in the middle of the night, Beniek was above him with two other men.

"What's happening?" Filip asked, half asleep and confused by this sudden visit.

"I brought the doctor with me," said Beniek. "He'll fix you up."

"Hello, comrade. I'm Dr. Marian Ciepielowski," said one of the men, smiling at him as if nothing was wrong. He had a large head with a receding hairline, a prominent nose, and thin lips that, in their sum, somehow seemed reassuring. "You can call me Marian."

"What's going on?" asked Sig, who had just stirred from his sleep beside Filip. Filip figured that Sig must have gotten back to the barracks after he'd passed out from the pain in his ankle. Sig was always coming back late from his work unit at the post office.

"Keep it down," Beniek ordered. "Are you ready, Filip?"

"For what?"

Beniek nodded to the other two men, and they sprung to action. Ciepielowski positioned himself at Filip's feet while the other man placed a twig inside Filip's mouth.

"Bite on that," said Beniek. "And try not to scream."

Before Filip could respond, he heard a loud crack and a bolt of excruciating pain rushed through him like a thunderbolt. He couldn't stop himself from screaming, but a blanket was already over his head, muting the savagery that came out of his mouth. He then felt a sudden weakness, like his soul leaving his body, and he passed out.

Frau Wolff found the package under the floorboards in Anna's room. She ripped it open to make sure, but the Buchenwald address and its contents made it clear: socks, gloves, underpants, salami, sugar cubes, jam, and dried bread. Anna wasn't just sending packages to Filip; she was also stealing from Frau Wolff. Anna wasn't paid and couldn't leave the house, so the items could only have come from the house. Sabina had to have helped her too. It would be difficult for just one person to scrounge all this stuff undetected.

She grabbed the package and rushed downstairs to the kitchen. She sat at the table with it before her and waited for the two women to return from milking the cows. This was unacceptable. How dare they scheme against her like this in her own house? This was after all she had done for them—

feeding them and clothing them—even though they were just slaves, easily replaceable with new arrivals from Russia. For what? For that worthless piece of shit, Filip?

How was he still alive anyway? Sergeant Hinkelmann promised her he would suffer and die within two months. It had been five months already. His official sentence would expire in another three months, and he was apparently still not dead, surviving on food sent from her own house, no less. This was outrageous, and she would make Anna pay.

Anna and Sabina walked into the kitchen just as Frau Wolff was about to angrily slam her hand on the table. Instead, she placed her hand on the package and watched them step back, spilling some milk out of their buckets as they did so.

"Stop!" yelled Frau Wolff.

They froze, and she could see their fear. She was going to enjoy this moment.

"What is this?" she said, pushing the package forward.

Neither one of them spoke, so she stood up, lifting the package off the table.

"I'll tell you what it is," she said, dropping it on the floor before them. "My clothes. My food. For that criminal, Filip. You stole from me to give to that scum!"

Anna spoke up. "The money was from Gunther—"

Frau Wolff slapped her across the face before she could finish. "My brother's money is my money. Everything that's yours is mine. You own nothing. You are nothing. Do you understand me?"

"You can't treat us like this," Anna said. "We're still human."

Frau Wolff stared at her for a moment, then burst out laughing. "Who the hell do you think you are? Are you not my property? I can do whatever I please with you," she said, grabbing her by the hair and pulling her to the floor. "I can mop the floor with you if I want."

"Please, Frau Wolff—" Sabina said, trying to stop her.

"You keep your mouth shut," Frau Wolff said. "I'll deal with you later."

Anna screamed in pain while Frau Wolff dragged her by the hair across the kitchen floor and then up the stairs to her room. She fought her all the way, but she was small and weak compared to Frau Wolff.

"You're going to learn your lesson today," said Frau Wolff. "And I'm going to make sure that piece of shit, Filip, dies in Buchenwald like he was supposed to."

She slammed the door behind her and locked the room. This was the same room Filip had stayed in when he was at the farm. He used to block her from entering at night—the fool that he was—and Anna would now pay for both of their sins. She would learn her place. She would learn how to be a property of the great German nation.

18

JANUARY 23, 1943

The winter was taking a toll on Sig and everyone else at Buchenwald. Twelve-hour workdays six days a week were hard enough without the bone-chilling cold seeping through the uninsulated doors and windows of every building.

At least Sig was inside, unlike some poor bastards working in the quarry or other external units. On some days, the ground was littered with bodies of those who didn't make it back. For days, they lay frozen on the snow-covered ground in their blue-striped uniforms that resembled pajamas. It was as if they had left their houses in the morning to get a newspaper from their front porch and just dropped dead on the way there. Every day, the SS would announce on the loudspeaker, "Corpse carriers report immediately to the gate!" and a prisoner work unit would go out to clean up the bodies.

Hanukkah, Christmas, and New Year's Day were no different. Prisoners tried to celebrate the best they could, but there was no extra food and nothing to cheer about. They mostly just listened to the SS singing and drinking in their houses outside the camp. At least the business was good and kept Sig busy. Families still sent packages to the prisoners for the holidays, even though Germany was living in austerity due to the war. The post office had a large pile that grew daily because the mail was always delayed by a few weeks. The four prisoners assigned to the work couldn't keep up.

Sig had ripped another package open that morning when he noticed a letter lying on the floor. It was in a brown envelope with a drawing depicting a green meadow with a meandering blue stream. That was not unique. Many people drew pictures on their letters to draw attention or express their love. What was different about this one was the addressee's name in large letters: "Filip Wolny"—Sig's Filip and his best friend since Weimar prison.

Sig picked it up and checked who sent it. It said "Anna Kogut, Rotenburg an der Fulda."

"Oh my God!" he cried out.

The other three prisoners stopped their work and looked at him like he was crazy.

Sig regained his composure and said, "Where is the package for this letter?"

They shrugged in unison. Sig sighed in frustration, knowing he had asked a pointless question. Hundreds of letters were strewn on the floor from the thousands of packages they'd opened in the last month. There was only one chance to find out what Anna had sent to Filip. Sig opened the letter and asked one of the Polish workers to come over.

"Can you please translate this into German for me?" he asked.

The man read it slowly, translating each word carefully. Sig cried as it was read.

He rushed out of the post office as soon as his shift was over. With a package under his arm, he ran down Caracho (meaning "with gusto") Path, the street leading to the camp entrance. He entered through the main gate, where the SS guards waved him in. They knew he was under Sergeant Schmidt's protection and didn't bother checking what he was carrying. He then sprinted across the roll call square to Block 4.

Filip was already back from work and passed out in his cot next to two other prisoners. Sig shook him violently to wake him up. Filip was always exhausted after working in the forest work unit, where he chopped trees all day, so waking him up required some effort.

"What?" Filip finally mumbled.

"It's from her!" Sig shouted, waving the package excitedly. "Your Anna!"

Filip sat up, now wide awake. "Don't tease me!" he warned.

"I'm dead serious, Filip," said Sig, setting the package in front of him. "Open it up!"

"But it's been nine months," Filip said, staring at the package as if unable to comprehend it. "Are you sure it's her?"

"It's her name and address, isn't it?"

Filip pulled the letter off the package Sig had delicately glued together just an hour earlier and stared at the picture of the meadow. "This is where we met last time," he said. "We lay down and kissed right by the stream."

"What does it say?" said one of the prisoners next to them.

Filip opened it. "I can't read Polish that well anymore," he said.

"Let me see it," said the prisoner, grabbing the letter. "How can you not read Polish? It's your native language. Maybe she should be my girlfriend."

"Shut up, you fool," said Sig. "Just read it."

"Here we go," the prisoner said and began to read.

Dear Filip,

Not a minute goes by when I don't think about you. It's like you're captured inside my heart. Or maybe I'm captured inside yours. Either way, your spirit hovers next to me all day and all night. It seems I couldn't live without it. It's part of me the same way my own arms and legs are. Except it's not enough. It makes me long for you with such power that sometimes I feel like fainting. Maybe it's like an arm that's been cut off, and my brain thinks it's still there, trying to move its fingers and touch my face. But the arm is not there. It's just a ghost.

I don't know how much longer I can live without you. How much can a person suffer in the prison that Frau Wolff created for me? She brought me to her farm and tortures me relentlessly. She hates our love and means to destroy us at all costs, but slowly and painfully. Sometimes, I wonder whether death would be easier than this. The only thing that keeps me going is the hope of seeing you again one day. I have no word of whether you're dead or alive, but if this package finds you, I hope the undergarments, socks, and gloves keep you warm in the cold autumn and winter months while *the meat, sugar, and toast sustain you in life until your release from Buchenwald.*

With love,

Anna

Sig, Filip, and all the other prisoners around them had tears coming down their faces. They were the solemn tears squeezed out of a man's body by the weight of a burden heavier than any stone they could find in the Buchenwald quarry. It was the weight of despair, a feeling each of them suppressed through their daily survival routine but which they now remembered.

Filip slowly unwrapped the package. Inside were the items Anna mentioned in her letter, which Sig had spent an hour collecting from piles of items that the post office had confiscated under the order of the SS. Filip would never know the difference. He held onto the letter, staring at it as if he could understand the words, while the other prisoners gaped hungrily at the loot from the package.

"Don't you even think about it," Sig barked at them.

"He doesn't need it," said one of the prisoners. "He's filled with love."

Sig put everything back in the package and placed it in Filip's lap. "I have to work for Schmidt tonight," Sig said. "They're having a party, and he wants me to work as a server. You hang onto that package and try not to get killed by these barbarians."

Sig wasn't telling the whole truth. There were other reasons why Schmidt wanted to see him. But they didn't need to know that.

∽

Sergeant Hinkelmann sat in an oversized leather chair, sipping champagne, and smiled politely at Schmidt's story about another one of his rampages through the brothels of Berlin. It was full of vulgar jokes about his conquests in the company of the top Nazi party functionaries. Hinkelmann didn't believe any of it. It was all so outrageous. He just couldn't imagine the meek-looking Schmidt doing any of it. However, Camp Commandant Pister, a short, stocky man with a boxer's face, and his crew of drunk officers ate it up, rolling around on the villa's posh living room furniture like a band of baboons. Hinkelmann refused to indulge in the stupidity. He preferred to keep his mind sharp and his eyes open.

"Can I get you more champagne, sir?" said a server who appeared next to his chair with a tray of glasses.

"No," said Hinkelmann.

"C'mon, Hinkelmann," Schmidt said, laughing. "You're so uptight. Have some fun, for God's sake. Take another glass from Sig."

Hinkelmann reluctantly replaced his half-full glass with a full one. "It's excellent champagne," he said, watching the skinny, long-faced server walk off. "Where did you get it, Schmidt?"

"Where did I get it? How did I get it? How much did I pay? Why do you always want to know?" asked Schmidt.

Hinkelmann realized he needed to be careful. Over a year before, the previous camp commandant, Colonel Karl-Otto Koch, and some of his officers were indicted on corruption and embezzlement charges for stealing 200,000 deutsche marks from the Reich. Hinkelmann believed the stealing was continuing under Pister, led by Schmidt and others, but he didn't want them to think he was a snitch. He needed to pretend to be one of the boys, or he'd be shunned, and his career would be in jeopardy.

"I apologize," he said. "I didn't mean to offend. I'm just amazed you can still find champagne of this quality. I'm grateful for that. Thank you for sharing it with us."

"Don't mention it," said Schmidt.

"Curious-looking fellow," Hinkelmann said, pointing at Sig, who was now standing by the door.

"Sig?" asked Schmidt. "Yes, but more importantly, he's a great server. I believe he worked in one of those fancy restaurants in Berlin. And before you ask, no, you can't have him."

The other officers laughed.

"Schmidt wouldn't let him go even if I paid him," said Commander Pister.

"Speaking of moving prisoners," said Hinkelmann. "I've had several of them from Block 4 moved out of my quarry in the last few months. Any idea why that is?"

They all looked at each other as if confused. Pister shrugged.

"Could we please not talk about work, Hinkelmann," said Schmidt. "Try to have a good time."

"What barracks is your Sig from?" asked Hinkelmann.

"What are you implying?" said Schmidt, his tone serious.

"Now, now, gentlemen," Pister interrupted. "Let's not ruin this evening. You have plenty of workers in your quarry, Hinkelmann. The same goes for Schmidt at the post office and the cantina. There are hundreds more coming from the Eastern Front every day."

"Not for very long if we lose Stalingrad," said Hinkelmann.

"The Führer will never let that happen," said Schmidt. "We will be marching into Moscow by springtime."

Silence fell upon the room. *It's just another wild boast by*

Schmidt, Hinkelmann thought. They all knew the situation in Stalingrad was desperate and expected General Paulus's Sixth Army to surrender at any moment.

"Well, you did it again, Hinkelmann. You ruined the party," said Pister.

They all laughed uncomfortably.

"I'll leave you on that note, gentlemen," said Schmidt, springing from his chair. "I apologize, but I have some paperwork to finish tonight. Please feel free to stay as long as you'd like." Then he turned to the server. "Sig, come with me."

Schmidt left the room with his server following. Hinkelmann was happy to see them go. The opulence of Schmidt's villa, with its modern alpine design and two-car garage, as well as the way he behaved like some kind of nobility, offended him greatly. Hinkelmann shared his villa with two other officers, and their accommodations were much more spartan.

Hinkelmann listened to Pister and his officers brag about their accomplishments for another hour before he decided to leave.

"Excuse me, gentlemen," he announced, standing up. "It's time for me to turn in."

"It's only ten o'clock," one of the officers pointed out.

"I apologize," he said. "It was a long day today."

"I expect nothing else from you, Hinkelmann," said Pister. "I'll send you more prisoners tomorrow."

"Thank you, sir," he replied, then left the room.

Hinkelmann entered the foyer and put on his wool winter coat. He was about to leave when he heard a strange noise upstairs. He paused to listen. It was very faint and almost sounded like a mouse squealing. Perhaps it was nothing, but he was curious. He had seen some crazy stuff in Buchenwald and remained on guard for prisoner mischief.

He climbed the intricately carved spiral staircase to the second floor and followed the sound to the first door in the hallway. He paused momentarily, trying to determine what the sound might be, but it wasn't any clearer from this distance. He pressed the handle and slowly opened the door.

What he saw shocked him.

Schmidt lay sprawled half-naked with his pants down on a lounge chair while his servant, Sig, was on his knees pleasuring him. They didn't notice him, so he stepped inside and closed the door behind him with a loud bang.

"What the hell. . . " Schmidt growled as he scrambled to cover himself.

"So, this is what you do with your prisoners?" asked Hinkelmann.

While Sig hid behind him, Schmidt stood up, zipped, and said, "How dare you—"

"Shut up, Schmidt!" Hinkelmann barked. "You'll do as I say from now on."

"This is none of your business, Hinkelmann," Schmidt said. "Please leave."

"Oh, this is very much my business. I'm in charge of imprisoning Hitler's rejects, including homos like you. You belong to me now."

"I'm an officer of the SS," Schmidt protested.

"Fine. I'll just go downstairs and tell Pister what I saw here," said Hinkelmann, spinning back toward the door.

"No! Wait!"

Hinkelmann turned back. "Yes?" he said.

"What do you want?"

"Now you're understanding me," said Hinkelmann. "I want 50 percent of everything you make."

"That's outrageous. My salary is barely enough to sustain my family," said Schmidt.

"Don't play stupid with me, Schmidt. I'm not talking about your salary. I'm talking about the money you make selling what you steal from the prisoners and the cantina. You don't think I know how you pay for all your luxuries?"

Schmidt hesitated, then said, "Twenty-five percent. That's my final offer."

"Fifty percent, Schmidt. And your boyfriend, Sig, is now part of my quarry work unit."

"No—"

"Yes!" Hinkelmann said. "Trust me. It's better for you that way."

With that, Hinkelmann opened the door and left. His fortunes had just taken a turn for the better. No more spartan living. He was finally going to have a taste of the good life.

19
MARCH 31, 1943

Filip couldn't take it any longer. Each day was the same as the one before, as was the day after. The only difference was that he grew weaker each day. Instead of getting used to the hard work, he was finding it more and more difficult. His energy sagged, and he felt like he was moving against the current of a river. The double speed the SS tried to force upon them seemed humanly impossible, especially with his ankle still healing. Prisoners would often fall to the ground from exhaustion. Some of them never got up.

They had Sundays off, like today, and this was their only time to recover. Except that was when the barracks were at their fullest and became more crowded as new prisoners arrived from Russia. The kapo told Filip there were about fifty thousand prisoners in Buchenwald, more than double what it was supposed to hold. They worked in two twelve-hour shifts, most in the munitions factory next to the camp.

As soon as Filip's barracks were emptied in the morning, the night shift would fill it back up. On Sundays, both shifts were in the barracks, and there was barely any air to breathe. On top of that, the latrines were always clogged, and the smell of feces constantly violated their nostrils. The food was worse than what he'd fed the pigs back at the farm. The warm soup or potatoes they received from time to time were the best meals. Otherwise, it was just stale bread or boiled old rutabagas. Half of the prisoners suffered from various stomach problems, which made the latrines smell even worse. Then there were lice and typhus. Constant itching and fevers drove everyone insane or dead. Some even ran into electrified fences to end it.

Filip began to eat whatever edible plants or creatures he could find. The camp was utterly void of life forms, but he sometimes encountered a mouse or a bug while working in the quarry. He shared whatever he could with Sig, who seemed to be dying before his eyes. They had both somehow ended up back in the quarry work unit, and Sig wasn't made for hard labor. His body was just bones. There didn't seem to be any meat on him. He could barely make it back to the barracks after work. His spirit was broken too. He would just lie in their bunk and not talk to anyone. Filip had to do something, or they would both be dead within a month—and he would never see Anna again.

Filip swung out of his bunk and walked to a wood stove in the center of the barracks, where some prisoners were gathered. These were primarily political prisoners, what the SS called communists, and they were the leaders in these barracks. He sat next to Beniek and Ciepielowski, who had their hands over a meager fire fueled by whatever twigs prisoners could find.

"We have to find a way out of here," Filip whispered.

They looked at each other suspiciously.

"What are you talking about?" asked Beniek.

"I'm talking about an escape," said Filip. "Sig might not make it another week, and I'm not sure how much longer I can keep up in the quarry with my bum ankle. We must do something."

"You have the red triangle of a political prisoner. Are you a communist, Filip?" Ciepielowski asked.

"Sorry, I don't even know what that is," said Filip.

"Do you believe that all humans are equal and that we all deserve the same treatment as everyone else?"

Filip didn't see the world working like that, even though he was a Christian. There were always those in charge and those who worked for them. That was how it was in his village, and it sure worked like that in Germany. Nevertheless, he needed help escaping, and these men were his only hope.

"That would be nice," said Filip.

"Well, then you're a communist," said Ciepielowski.

"Am I?"

"You sure are," said Beniek. "Nazis make us out to be the devil, but that's only because they want to rule the world. They think they are the chosen ones and everyone else is their slave. Just like us in this camp and millions working in their factories and farms."

"So, will you help us escape?"

"Yes, we can help you," said Ciepielowski. "But first, you have to prove yourself as a communist."

"Tell me. I'll do anything," said Filip.

"Are you sure? This could mean death."

"I'm dead already."

"In that case, I'll have you and Sig moved to the infirmary, where you'll work as my test patients on the typhus vaccine. You'll find out the rest later."

"I heard they kill people in the infirmary," said Filip.

"Exactly," said Ciepielowski. "Death will set you free."

Anna opened the window in her room and squeezed through it onto a steep roof. She stood at the ledge, looking at the ground two stories below, and her head started spinning. She didn't think she was scared of heights, but for some reason, she imagined herself crashing to the ground and snapping her neck like a dry twig. Thankfully, the rope Sabina was supposed to throw up to the roof was there. She crawled over to grab it and held onto it for dear life.

"C'mon, Anna!" yelled Sabina from below.

Anna took a deep breath and slid down the rope. Her long skirt snagged on the orange roof tiles, but she freed herself and eventually landed on the ground.

"What took you so long?" Sabina asked, looking around in a panic. "Frau Wolff will be back any minute."

"Sorry. I'm not a monkey," said Anna, remembering the swiftness of the monkeys at a small zoo in her hometown. "I'm not good at climbing."

"I've never seen a monkey, but forget it," said Sabina, handing her a small bundle. "Here's your stuff for the road. Enough food to last you two weeks."

"Hopefully, I'll find him sooner," said Anna.

She wasn't so sure she could. It had seemed like a good idea after months of being locked up in her room by Frau Wolff, but now that she was on the ground, it occurred to her that their plan was fraught with holes. For one, she didn't know how she would find Buchenwald. Neither Sabina nor anyone else in Rotenburg knew the way there. Two, she wasn't sure if taking a train to wherever it was would work. It worked for Filip once.

He took trains to follow Anna before. Nevertheless, he could have easily gotten caught. And finally, she had no idea how she would get him out of Buchenwald. She had a plan, but the chances of it working were slim.

"C'mon, let's go!" Sabina pleaded as she collected the rope and hid it inside the barn. "I'll take you to the river."

"Did you send the letter?" asked Anna, referring to her only hope of getting Filip out of Buchenwald.

"Yes, of course."

"Thank you, Sabina. I couldn't do this without you."

They slid through the wooden fence's back door and ran toward the Fulda River, which snaked through Rotenburg. She hoped to follow the river to a larger town like Erfurt, where she could learn about Buchenwald's location.

They were already at the river when Anna noticed the horse wagon charging toward them across a field. Frau Wolff stood on top of it, wailing like a madwoman and whipping the horse to go faster. There was nowhere to hide. They were stuck between the river and Frau Wolff.

"Let me talk to her," said Anna, stepping before Sabina. "This is my problem, not yours."

The horse wagon came to an abrupt halt in front of them, and Frau Wolff jumped to the ground with such ease that it seemed inhuman. Her face was red, and her muscular body was tense with adrenaline.

"I can explain everything," said Anna.

Instead of pausing to listen, Frau Wolff punched her in the eye and ran toward Sabina. Anna fell to the ground, disoriented, and watched through a fog in her eyes as Frau Wolff tackled Sabina into the riverbank.

"You fucking traitor," she screamed at Sabina, wildly

throwing punches at her. "I knew I shouldn't trust you, you slave pig."

"Frau Wolff, please! What did I do?" pleaded Sabina, thrashing in the water as she tried to keep her head above the surface.

"Don't play dumb!"

"We were just going for a walk—"

This enraged Frau Wolff even more. She kneeled on Sabina's chest and held her head underwater. She was bigger and stronger than Sabina, who struggled to get leverage.

"Frau Wolff, please!" Anna screamed, trying to get up from the ground.

"I don't know what you thought you were doing, but you will never see Filip again," said Frau Wolff. "That is my promise to you. I swear it on my grave."

Sabina stopped moving, and Frau Wolff let her go. "That should teach you a lesson," she said, standing over her motionless body.

Frau Wolff and Anna waited for Sabina to get up, but she never did. Frau Wolff breathed heavily, trying to calm herself from the rage. She looked around to see if anybody was nearby. "You see what you've done?" she said finally.

"You killed her!" screamed Anna.

"It's all your fault! *You* killed her!" screamed Frau Wolff. "None of this would've happened if you didn't try to escape."

Anna stood up and stumbled over to Sabina's body. She pulled her onto the shore, but Sabina remained motionless. "Oh my God! She's dead! She's really dead."

"Put her on the wagon," ordered Frau Wolff.

"No, I'm not," said Anna, tears pouring down her face.

"Fine! I'll do it myself, you useless swine."

Frau Wolff grabbed Sabina under her arms and pulled her

to the wagon. She then heaved the wet body onto it as if it were a bag of potatoes. "Let's go!" she ordered Anna as she got up on the wagon and pulled the reins.

Anna followed the wagon to the village, staring at Sabina's body as it shook with each pothole. She had never seen a dead person before and somehow hoped Sabina would wake up.

As they made their way up the main road, people stopped what they were doing and stared at them. Anna realized they must've looked distraught—she herself with a bruised face and Frau Wolff still wet from the river. Two farmers approached them and looked inside the wagon.

"She's dead," said Frau Wolff. "She drowned in the river."

"How?" asked one of the farmers.

"I have no idea. Just an idiot slave. I can't seem to get any good ones."

The two men scratched their heads but didn't say anything.

Anna knew it wouldn't make a difference if she told them the truth. Nobody would believe her anyway. She followed the wagon to the constable's house and watched numbly as they unloaded Sabina's body. She didn't say anything to him either. He would probably arrest her instead. There was no point.

It was just her and Frau Wolff now.

20

JULY 7, 1943

I t was darker than the devil's asshole when Filip snuck out of his bed, but it was finally time for his first assignment from Ciepielowski.

It had been three months since the doctor had promised to help him and Sig escape, but they were still at Buchenwald. At least they were now in the infirmary's Block 46 and not in the quarry. They had their own warm beds and better food: bread twice daily, morning rye coffee, and daily warm soup with potatoes. Ciepielowski injected them with some medicine a few times, but he said it was fake; he called it a placebo and said it was harmless. Filip had no choice but to trust him. They would have been long dead if they'd stayed at the quarry.

Filip woke Sig and Beniek up. They stirred lazily but didn't complain. They'd been planning this night for days and were quickly out of bed, following Filip to the door. Filip pulled the door handle and swung it open. The door creaked, but none of the other nine patients in their room woke up.

"Now it's your turn, Beniek," said Filip, closing the door behind them.

Beniek nodded and led them down a long hallway lined with rooms on each side. When they were close to the main lobby, Beniek motioned for them to hide inside one of the rooms. This was the part of the plan where Beniek was supposed to fake illness to pull the SS guard from the lobby.

Filip opened the door and snuck in with Sig. Soon, they heard Beniek wailing in pretend pain and an SS guard yelling at him to get back to his room. Beniek would not succumb so easily, so the boots of the SS guard quickly followed. As soon as the guard passed them, Filip and Sig rushed out of the room and up the lobby stairs.

They ran into the laboratory where the vaccines were stored. Nobody was up there, but the SS guard made his rounds through Block 46 every half hour, so they only had about twenty minutes to complete their task.

"Get the empty containers," Filip said when they entered the lab. "I'll get the vaccines for the army."

Sig did as ordered and rolled a large metal can, the same as the one farmers used for milk storage, from under a table. Filip did the same with two cans full of liquid, each with a sticker with writing explaining the contents. One said, "Typhus vaccine," and the other, "Placebo."

"Now we pour the vaccines for the soldiers into the empty can, then refill it with placebo and fill the placebo can with the real vaccine," said Filip, more to remember what he was supposed to do than to explain it to Sig.

This was a simple but daring plan. They were switching vaccines, which were for the German soldiers fighting the Russians on the Eastern Front, with the placebo, which was usually given to the sick Buchenwald prisoners only as part of medical experiments. This meant soldiers would not get the actual typhus vaccine and would keep dying by the thousands while many prisoners' lives would be saved from typhus. Filip, Sig, Beniek, Ciepielowski, and every other prisoner working in the lab, guilty or not, would be shot dead if the SS found out.

"I know this already," said Sig. "Just open the container."

Filip grabbed the large cap on top of the can and tried to twist it off, but it wouldn't budge. He pulled his shirt off and put it over the cap to get a better grip, but that didn't work either. The cap was stuck.

"It's sealed," said Filip.

"What do we do?" asked Sig.

"We need a hammer."

"Hammer? You can't make a noise. The guard will hear you."

"Just find a hammer or something heavy I can hit the cap with," said Filip, looking around the room. There was nothing but glass test tubes on the table. "Check the drawers. I'll check the cabinet."

"We only have about ten minutes left," Sig protested. "Why don't we try again tomorrow?"

"There is no tomorrow. The vaccines will be shipped tomorrow. Just check the drawers."

Filip rushed to the cabinet. Seeing he would not change his mind, Sig started going through the drawers. It was difficult to search in the darkness; Filip had to feel for it rather than see it, but he finally found something heavy. It seemed to be a metal base with an attached rod, perhaps part of some medical test apparatus. He rushed back to the can.

"Hold the can," he ordered. "And hold my shirt over the cap."

Sig sat on the floor and grabbed the can's base with one

hand and the shirt over the cap with the other. "You're going to get us killed, Filip," he said.

"Ready?" asked Filip.

Sig nodded, and Filip swung the base against the cap with all the strength he could muster. He hoped to dislodge it with a single stroke to minimize the noise, but the vibration was louder than expected. Even through the cloth of his shirt, it sounded like a church bell ringing on a quiet Sunday morning. Filip jumped on top of the can, absorbing the noise, but the initial strike was already enough for the whole building to hear.

"We're in trouble!" said Sig.

"Shut up and hold the can," said Filip, twisting the cap. He used all his strength, and it finally released. "Hurry up. Get the empty one."

Sig held the empty can as Filip filled it with the vaccine.

Then a door slammed closed somewhere.

"Where was that?" asked Sig.

"I have no idea," Filip answered because it was impossible to tell if the noise came from the first or the second floor. When empty, the building echoed like a cave. "Get the placebo can!"

"Someone is coming, Filip. Let's get out of here," Sig pleaded.

Filip grabbed the can himself and pulled at the cap, but it was also sealed. "Fuck!" he hissed.

"Filip, we're going to die—"

"Hold the can."

Sig did so again, holding the shirt over the cap. Filip swung the base at the cap, and again, the can rang like a bell. Filip jumped on it a bit quicker this time, but the noise rang audibly for everyone to hear anyway. Filip twisted the cap off and poured the placebo into the vaccine can. Sig drifted toward the door to listen for any noises.

"Someone's coming," he whispered.

Filip didn't stop. He put the cap back on the can with the vaccine sticker, then poured the vaccine liquid into the placebo can, twisting the cap back on that one when he was done. "Put the empty can back," he ordered while dragging the full cans back to their place.

They heard boots approaching, but Filip grabbed his shirt and quickly wiped up the liquid he had spilled on the floor earlier. "Cabinet," he said and pulled Sig inside it, closing the squeaking door behind them.

Hidden among the lab coats, they heard the door open and the guard's boots walk around the room. The boots squealed as if slipping on water. The guard stopped. Filip felt the cold sweat dripping down his back and sensed Sig shaking next to him. He grabbed Sig's hand to calm him down. But the guard walked again, the door closed, and the boots stomped down the hallway. Filip opened the cabinet, and they quietly slid out.

"How do we get back to our room?" Sig asked.

"Just like we planned," said Filip. "When he's at the back of the building, we go back down the stairs to the first floor and back to our room."

"Right, but he's now really paying attention. What if he sees us running down the hallway?

"Then we die," Filip said as he swung the door open and ran.

"Shit!" Sig uttered and took off after him.

Sergeant Hinkelmann stormed into the SS camp commandant's office, his blood still boiling, but he stopped when he saw Pister's adjutant officer, SS Lieutenant Wolff Simon. He paused to calm himself because he had to approach this properly, regardless of the severity of his complaint. Pister could block his career advancement if he perceived him to be difficult.

"Heil Hitler!" Hinkelmann said as he saluted.

"Heil Hitler!" Simon answered.

"I would like to meet with SS Oberführer Pister," Hinkelmann said. "Immediately. Please."

"Commandant Pister is busy at the moment. I can take a message."

Hinkelmann grunted but tried to control himself. "It's urgent," he said. "Is he by himself?"

"Yes, but—" said Simon.

Hinkelmann ignored him and knocked on Pister's door. He didn't wait for an answer and walked in instead.

"Sergeant Hinkelmann! This is an outrage!" yelled Simon.

Hinkelmann didn't hear anything after that because he shut the door behind him. He focused on Pister, who sat in a lounge chair by the window, observing the camp. He had his jacket off and only suspenders on over his white undershirt. His feet, boots off, were on a stool.

"Don't you think it's crazy that only a few hundred of us manage to control fifty thousand prisoners?" Pister asked. "I mean, they could overrun us if they wanted to."

"They're subhuman, Oberführer Pister," Hinkelmann answered. Pister was known to have fits of melancholy, and Hinkelmann didn't like it. He considered it a weakness that didn't have a place in prisoner camps. Nevertheless, he couldn't say that to Pister. "They're not able to organize themselves."

"Ah, subhuman." Pister sighed. "That's what the Romans

called Germans when they came to conquer us. They thought we were barbarians."

"We overran Rome, sir," said Hinkelmann.

"Exactly," said Pister.

"Sir, I have a complaint I would like to discuss with you."

"What complaint?"

"Sir, this morning, I received an order to release Prisoner 131124, a Polish laborer named Filip Wolny from East Prussia," said Hinkelmann. "Sir, I would like to understand why."

"It's very simple, Hinkelmann," said Pister. "I received a request for his release from his owner in the village of Rotenburg an der Fulda—some Frau Wolff. She says she needs him back on the farm for the harvest. His sentence was for six months, and he's been here for fifteen. I don't know why he's still here, in fact. Any idea, Hinkelmann?"

Hinkelmann grunted, trying to control himself. He couldn't believe 131124 was giving him this much trouble. The prisoner had first managed to get himself reassigned from the quarry to forest duty. Then he'd somehow managed to get reassigned again from the quarry to the vaccine-testing infirmary. "Sir, the prisoner didn't follow orders on several occasions. I had to extend his sentence."

"Does he know that?"

"Sir, I'm not in charge of distributing orders to the prisoners—"

"You just write them, right?" Pister said. "Look, Hinkelmann, why do you care so much about this prisoner?"

"Sir, I don't care about any prisoner. He means nothing to me. But rules are rules. The law must be followed."

"Perfect!" said Pister. "I am the law here, so the prisoner will be released. Send a telegram to Frau Wolff that he'll be back on her farm next week. Understood?"

"Yes, sir." Hinkelmann saluted despite the anger boiling his blood. "Heil Hitler!"

He spun around toward the door, hiding any anger that might show on his face. His mind was made up, though. Pister could say whatever he wanted, but Prisoner 131124 was his and was not leaving Buchenwald alive.

21

JULY 12, 1943

Frau Wolff arrived in Buchenwald on Monday in the late afternoon wearing her best dress—a floral design her deceased husband bought on their honeymoon trip to Frankfurt. She wanted to look her best and even arranged her hair in the latest fashion with a red bow.

After the taxicab dropped her off at the camp's administration building, she was told to wait for Sergeant Hinkelmann at his villa, which was a Bavarian-style two-level house with a two-car garage in the basement and a large terrace on each level overlooking the Thuringian countryside.

The butler, who had a French accent, let her in and left her in the living room. She waited on a plush couch, admiring the hardwood floors covered with colorful rugs, wallpaper with a floral pattern similar to her dress, carved cherry furniture, and chandeliers made from deer antlers. It was all quite elegant for an SS sergeant. She was impressed with Hinkelmann's ability to live in such luxury while the rest of Germany struggled to survive under ever harsher war rations.

"Welcome, Frau Wolff," said Hinkelmann when he finally entered the living room about an hour later.

She stood up, wanting to get straight to the point, but she now felt nervous. She was taken aback by how handsome he looked in the SS uniform. Or maybe she just had a thing for uniforms. "Thank you for having me, Sergeant Hinkelmann," she said.

He smiled. "I love your dress. Would you like to join me for supper?"

"Yes," she said, surprised by how much she wanted to spend time with him.

He put his arm out, she grabbed onto it, and he led her to the dining room. She was amazed to see the abundance of food on the table: beef roast, potatoes, salad, mushroom soup, fresh bread, wine, and cake. It was as if they were at some fancy restaurant.

The butler pulled the chair for her and then served them their portions. "Bon appétit, mademoiselle," he said, then left the room.

"Enjoy," said Hinkelmann.

"Thank you," she said.

The two of them ate quietly for a while until Hinkelmann finally spoke up. "Are you enjoying your meal?" he asked.

"Yes, of course," she said. "I have not been able to afford beef for a year now. I forgot what it tastes like. It's delicious."

"Excellent. I'm glad you like it."

"Thank you," she said with a satisfied smile. She sat in silence for a moment, then spoke again. "I'm really impressed with the camp. I saw it from a window inside your administration building. It's very well-organized. You've done a great job."

"Thank you. That's very nice of you to say. We do what we can to keep the filth occupied."

"Is your butler a prisoner?" she asked.

"Yes, he was one of the top chefs in Paris. I couldn't get into his restaurant when I visited Paris five years ago. Now he'll wipe my ass if I wanted him to."

She chuckled. They ate in silence again for a moment. "You're probably wondering why I'm here," she said.

"Yes, you can say that. I thought my telegram was clear about the prisoner's release this week. We can't release him any sooner. Bureaucracy . . . I'm sure you understand."

"I want you to keep him here," she said.

"Pardon?" he said, his brows furrowing in confusion.

"The letter you received wasn't from me. It was from Filip's Polish bitch back at home. She pretended to be me so you would release him."

Sergeant Hinkelmann stared at her for a moment. "I hope you had her arrested," he said finally.

"No. She's worse off with me."

He smiled devilishly. "What did he do to you?"

"He . . . didn't do his job," she said, not keen to get into all the details, parts of which Hinkelmann might think reflected poorly on her.

"Well, anything can be arranged . . . for a price," he said.

She smiled. "What did you have in mind?"

"Well, I'm not short of money, as you can see. But there are other forms of compensation. You see, I'm not married, and I work a lot, so . . ."

"Agreed!" she yelped. It slipped out a bit more enthusiastically than she wanted.

An hour later, Frau Wolff lay naked in bed and watched as Hinkelmann leaned over and grabbed a cigarette from a nightstand.

"You're a tough woman to please," he said, lighting the cigarette.

"Will you do it or not?" she replied coldly.

"I'm a gentleman. Of course I will do it. In fact, I can kill him for you if you wish."

"Not so easily!" she protested. "I want him to suffer while he's dying."

He smiled. "A woman after my own heart."

"But I want him to really suffer. Something special."

"Like I said, you're a tough woman to please."

Sig and Beniek stood and watched as Ciepielowski prepped the needle for Filip, who lay in a hospital bed. His face was paler than gypsum, and Beniek's was not much better. Sig imagined his face was the same. It was so quiet in the room that they could hear their hearts beating. Nobody dared to speak. None of them had been able to talk since that morning, when Ciepielowski laid out their escape plan. They'd hoped it would be something simple and less risky, but they immediately understood there was nothing simple about Buchenwald. Unfortunately, it was their only way out.

"What is that?" Sig asked.

"A mixture of nightshade and opium," said Ciepielowski. "I designed the concoction myself, but these have been used by doctors for anesthesia for centuries."

"Nightshade? Like the poisonous plant?" asked Filip. "My parents said that witches used it to kill people."

"Yes, we found it growing in the surrounding forest. It's deadly only in large quantities. In the right quantity, it puts you into a sleep that will only *look* like death."

"Are you sure this is going to work?" asked Beniek.

"No, I'm not sure," said Ciepielowski while pointing the needle at a vein in Filip's arm. "You're my first test subjects."

"I can't do this!" Sig cried, standing up as if to leave the room.

"Sig, this is our only chance," said Filip.

"What if we're poisoned to death? What if the guards send our bodies to the crematorium instead of the ditch in the forest? What if they bury us in the ditch before we wake up?"

"Crematorium ran out of coke fuel. They can't burn any bodies today," said Ciepielowski. "That's why we have to do this now."

"I'm sorry, but I'm out," said Sig. "I made up my mind."

"I need you, Sig," said Filip.

"I can be the body carrier, but I'm not taking the poison," Sig offered.

"We're dead if we stay here," said Beniek.

"I'll find a way to survive," said Sig.

"Suit yourself," said Ciepielowski, stabbing Filip's vein.

Filip winced in pain as Ciepielowski injected him with the substance. They watched him for a few moments to see if he'd die. Instead, his movements calmed, and he stared at them blankly with half-open eyes. It was almost as if he was going to sleep.

"I will see you after the war," Filip slurred, grabbing Sig's arm. "Please come see me in Junno."

"You have your medallion?"

"Yes."

"Where is it?"

"You don't want to know . . ." Filip said, then his face froze mid-sentence.

"Is he okay?" Sig asked Ciepielowski.

"Yes, the substance acts quickly. Beniek, you're next."

While Filip passed out, Beniek lay in another bed and pulled up his sleeve. Ciepielowski picked up another needle and injected him. He was out within seconds. Ciepielowski checked his pulse, then Filip's.

"Now it's up to you, Sig," said Ciepielowski while writing something in a patient chart. "I've marked their time of death. Now, get the corpse carriers and take them to the pile of bodies going out for burial in the forest ditch. Try to avoid anyone checking their pulse. It's much lower than normal, but you can still feel it if you take your time. We have about three hours."

It took Sig twenty minutes to round up the corpse carriers. The two prisoners didn't ask any questions as they loaded Filip's and Beniek's bodies onto a two-wheel cart with a flat top. They probably carried hundreds of bodies daily, including many from the infirmary, and couldn't care less about another two.

"Be gentle," said Sig, walking beside the cart as they rolled it through the camp and the bodies bounced around like rag dolls.

"Why?" asked one of the prisoners, a young Russian who barely spoke German—probably one of the recent arrivals from the Eastern Front.

"They were my friends," said Sig, but he quickly realized he was raising suspicion. "Never mind. They're dead now."

They approached two young SS guards, barely out of high school, who were standing at the pile of naked dead prisoners, arranged on top of each other like wood logs. Several prisoners were loading a truck with emaciated bodies.

"Who are they?" asked one of the SS guards.

"Died from experimental typhus vaccine," said Sig, handing over the papers that Ciepielowski gave him.

Apparently afraid of getting infected, the guard put on his gloves and took the papers. He read through them, then walked over to Filip's and Beniek's bodies. He circled the cart, inspecting them, but hesitated to touch them. "Why don't they have any signs of typhus?" he asked.

"You give the vaccine before they get typhus to see if it prevents it," said Sig. "They died before we could find out."

"Well, I guess the vaccine worked against typhus," said the guard, laughing. The other guard laughed as well. "Take their clothes off and take them to the crematorium."

"They're meant to be buried in the forest," Sig protested.

"The crematorium is finally operational, and we have no more room in the truck."

"But I have specific orders—"

"I don't give a shit about your orders!" yelled the guard.

"Dr. Ding-Schuler requires all the test subjects to be buried," Sig lied. Ding-Schuler, the SS doctor in charge of the vaccine development, was so clueless that he couldn't tell the difference between a vaccine and a placebo under a microscope. They'd put him in charge only because he was an SS officer.

"Move!" ordered the guard, pointing his rifle at Sig's stomach.

Sig felt his body heat up with anxiety. He only had a couple of seconds to figure out how to prevent Filip and Beniek from getting cremated. "Forgive me, sir," he said. "May I offer you something for your inconvenience? It would save us a lot of time by not having to drive this cart across the camp to the crematorium and would, at the same time, make Dr. Ding-Schuler very happy that I followed his orders."

"Shut up and move," the guard ordered.

"Hold on," said the other guard. "Let's see what the Jew has to offer."

"Why don't I just kill him and take what he has?" the first guard asked.

"That's bad business, my friend," said the other guard. "Why steal only what he has on him when he can bribe us many times in the future."

"That's very smart," said Sig, pulling a pack of cigarettes from his shirt pocket. "I'm sure this won't be our last delivery from the infirmary. And I always have something worth your time."

"Are those Neue Front?" said the guard, throwing his rifle back over the shoulder and grabbing the pack out of Sig's hand.

"Yes, sir," said Sig. "Five pfennig outside Buchenwald, but here it cost me my shoes. It's free to you, though."

The truth was Sig had gotten them for free as a makeup present from Schmidt, who still felt guilty for ruining their racketeering scheme at the post office. Things hadn't been the same since Hinkelmann caught them together. Sig didn't want to run Schmidt's business anymore and was happy to be reassigned to the vaccine-testing unit with Filip. He enjoyed knowing that Schmidt was struggling to manage his business with other prisoners, only to give most of his profits to Hinkelmann. Sig had been offended by the gift of cigarettes and was relieved to give them to the SS guards.

"Fine," said the guard. "You can fuck off."

Sig waved the corpse carriers to move. They unloaded Filip and Beniek onto the pile of naked bodies and marched back to the infirmary. It was now out of Sig's control whether Filip and Beniek would live. He hoped to see them again one day.

22

JULY 13, 1943

Anna awoke to the sound of chains being pulled from the door handles. She didn't know how long she'd been trapped inside the basement cellar because it was pitch black, regardless of the time of day. It seemed like days since Frau Wolff had thrown her in there with some food and water without telling her for what. The daylight blinded her when the door swung open.

"Good morning, sleeping beauty," said Frau Wolff, standing over the opening. "Time to get your ass back to work."

Anna climbed up a small ladder and crawled out to the ground. She sat for a moment, trying to get used to her surroundings. Her legs were weak from being unable to walk inside the cellar, which had a low ceiling.

"C'mon, the cows are not going to milk themselves," said Frau Wolff, kicking Anna in the ribs.

"I'm not doing anything unless you tell me what's going on," Anna insisted.

"What's going on? You're my slave, and you do whatever I tell you to do. It's very simple."

"Why did you lock me up?"

"If you must know, I had nowhere else to put you while I was on a little holiday," Frau Wolff said, then kicked her again. "Now, get up and get to work."

"No, I'm done with it!" Anna shouted. "I'm not doing any more work for you. Go ahead and kill me if you want."

"Are you refusing to follow my orders, you useless piece of shit?"

"Yes!"

"I can have you thrown into Buchenwald together with Filip for insubordination—"

"So, Filip is alive?"

Frau Wolff hesitated as if she'd revealed too much. Then she said, "He might as well be dead. Despite your efforts, you'll never see him again."

"What are you talking about? What efforts?" Anna pretended not to understand.

"You don't think I know about your letter to the camp commandant using my name and asking for his release? Did you think you could get away with it?"

Anna thought she had gotten away with it but didn't care about it anymore. She was just happy to hear Filip was alive. Throughout all those months, she'd never gotten a single word from him. She'd sent letters and packages but never heard a single word back. With Sabina dead, there was nobody to keep her spirits up, and she'd lost all hope that she'd ever see Filip again—until now.

"He's alive," she said and laughed. "He's alive!"

"Shut up, you stupid bitch!" Frau Wolff yelled and kicked her again. "I told you. He might as well be dead. I made sure he would suffer worse pain than in purgatory. He'll pay for what he did to me."

"What did he do to you that's so terrible?" Anna challenged. "What did I do to you? You've treated us like dirt from the beginning. You're the one who should be in purgatory."

Frau Wolff smiled as if a new torture had just occurred to her, then said, "He never told you, did he?"

"Told me what?"

"That we were lovers, that's what," Frau Wolff said triumphantly. "He didn't mention that he used to fuck me every day?"

Anna stared up at Frau Wolff, trying to comprehend what she was talking about. Was she lying? She had to be making things up to hurt her. Yet Anna sensed that it was true. Something inside her told her Frau Wolff was not lying this time.

"But he hated you," she said, trying to justify the feeling away.

"Yes, that's true. Except when he fucked me, I guess. And when he lay in my bed for hours afterward. He seemed to love me then."

The thought of it made Anna feel sick. The man she loved and thought was pure of faults was now the man who'd climbed willingly on top of this monster. He'd made love to her like she was an ordinary woman. What was worse, he'd lied to Anna about it. It didn't matter that he'd just avoided the truth. To her, it was the same as lying. Frau Wolff was right; Filip might as well be dead.

~

"He's dead," said the clerk.

Hinkelmann had spent all morning trying to get Filip reassigned back to the quarry, and now this. "What do you mean he's dead?"

"It says here that he was declared dead yesterday," said the clerk, pointing at his logbook. "We keep very good records at the infirmary."

How could Filip be dead one day after Hinkelmann promised Frau Wolff he would make his life a living hell? Something wasn't right.

"Where the hell did they take the body?"

"I don't know, sir. I'm sorry."

Then a familiar person appeared, walking down the hallway with a doctor behind him. It was the homosexual butler from Schmidt's party.

"You!"

Sig froze.

"What the hell are you doing here?"

"He's a test patient for the typhus vaccine," answered the doctor.

"And who the hell are you?" Hinkelmann asked.

"Dr. Ciepielowski. I run the experiments for Dr. Ding-Shuler."

"He looks healthier than when I last saw him at Schmidt's house," said Hinkelmann. "Granted, he was on his knees then."

"The vaccine must be working," said Ciepielowski.

"Great! I'll make sure he's transferred back to the quarry."

Sig looked at Ciepielowski as if begging him to do something.

"He's not allowed to leave the hospital," said Ciepielowski.

"Bullshit! I won't let him and his friend Filip get away from me this time. Now, where is his body?" Hinkelmann said to the clerk.

"Probably cremated already," said Ciepielowski.

"Actually, it says here that he was scheduled for burial in the forest," said the clerk.

"I better find him there, or heads will roll," Hinkelmann said, storming out of the infirmary.

He marched quickly through the camp toward the area where they collected bodies for disposal. Two young soldiers, barely out of their mothers' bosoms, sprung up to a salute when he arrived.

"Heil Hitler!" they shouted.

"At ease," Hinkelmann said. "I'm looking for someone and need your help."

"Yes, sir! How can we assist?" said one of the soldiers.

"Were you here on duty yesterday?"

"Yes, sir. All week."

"Did you process any bodies from the infirmary?"

The young soldier thought about it for a moment, then said, "Yes, sir. Two, I believe."

"What happened to them?" Hinkelmann asked.

"They were sent to the forest, sir."

"Why not the crematorium? I thought we had orders to dispose of all bodies at the crematorium."

The soldier looked back at his colleague as if searching for support.

"What is it?" Hinkelmann challenged.

"Sir, yes, sir, but . . . the corpse carriers had orders from the infirmary doctor to bury the bodies. Dr. Ding-Schuler is also an SS officer, and we followed his order."

"Is it normal for the infirmary to bury the bodies instead of cremating them?"

The soldier hesitated again, then said, "No, sir. They usually want to cremate so that the disease doesn't spread."

"And you ignored this?"

"Sorry, sir. We just followed the orders."

Hinkelmann sighed. "Scheisse!" he swore. "I need you to take me there immediately in your truck."

A truck was parked next to a pile of dead prisoners, and Hinkelmann marched off toward it before the soldiers could even answer.

"Sir," said the soldier as he ran after Hinkelmann. "There are dead prisoners inside the truck. They didn't take off their uniforms yet."

"Don't worry," said Hinkelmann. "We'll bring them right back."

"But, sir—"

"Get in the truck!" Hinkelmann ordered.

The soldiers looked at each other and followed him, scared of getting in trouble if they didn't.

Filip heard someone vomiting next to him and opened his eyes. Tree branches were swaying high above him but nothing else. He figured he must be outside, perhaps in a forest. He tried to remember where he was, but being in a forest didn't make sense. Maybe he was dreaming. Shouldn't he be at the infirmary? *And what are the muffled voices and scraping sounds I've been hearing?* he wondered. He tried to get up, but there was a weight on him he couldn't overcome.

"Filip! Get up!" Beniek said, appearing above him, completely naked.

"Where are we?" Filip asked.

"In the forest ditch. Don't you remember?"

Filip now remembered Ciepielowski's plan. "How long have we been out?"

"Longer than we were supposed to. I vomited all over myself. He must've given us more than we needed. It's already the next day. I hear the work unit approaching."

Filip now heard people talking and marching toward them. They couldn't be more than a hundred meters away. "I can't move," he said.

"C'mon! We have to go," Beniek insisted, pulling on Filip's arms.

As Beniek lifted him, Filip realized his naked body was covered by the bodies of other naked dead prisoners. There was a ditch full of them—the same ditch he'd dug months earlier. It wasn't a military installation after all—just a mass grave.

Filip's limbs began to climb clumsily toward the top of the ditch, but that was when the first prisoners appeared above them.

"They'll see us if we try to get out," Beniek said, pulling him against the dirt wall of the ditch.

Filip scanned the area. There was nowhere to hide. The forest was a few meters past the ditch, and they would easily be spotted if they tried to run toward it. The SS guards would shoot them dead. "We can blend in with the prisoners and then try to sneak out. They don't have us in their count," he suggested.

"Filip, we're naked," Beniek protested. "How can we blend in?"

"Is that you, Beniek?" somebody said from above them.

They looked up and saw one of the prisoners they knew from their barracks.

"Zbychu?" Beniek replied.

"Yes, it's me," Zbychu said. "What are you doing down there?"

"We're trying to escape. You must help us," Filip whispered.

They heard the rumble of a truck engine quickly approaching.

"Hold on," said Zbychu. "Somebody is coming."

The truck engine turned off, and then they heard Sergeant Hinkelmann's echoing voice somewhere above them. "Has anyone seen the body of Filip Wolny?"

"Shit!" Filip swore under his breath. "Zbychu, cover us with dirt!"

"I'm coming," said Zbychu, then he jumped into the ditch.

They hid under some bodies while Zbychu shoveled dirt on top of them. It was enough to hide them but leave some room to breathe. They remained motionless while listening to what was going on above them.

Moments passed, and then shouts erupted right next to them.

"Search the bodies," Hinkelmann ordered, seemingly standing right over them.

They heard people swearing in German—probably the SS guards. Then everything stopped, and people started talking nearby.

"They're not here, sir," someone said.

"Then they escaped," Hinkelmann announced. "I want every guard searching this forest. They can't be far."

"But, sir, what about the other prisoners?"

"I don't give a shit about the other prisoners! I want Filip Wolny! Get your men into the forest, now!" Hinkelmann ordered.

"Yes, sir!"

They heard more shouts and then nothing.

"Are you alive?" asked Zbychu, pulling dirt off them.

"Yes, we're fine," said Filip. "Where did Hinkelmann go?"

"He took all the guards into the forest to search for you."

"Why is he after you?" asked Beniek.

"I don't know," said Filip. Hinkelmann seemed to hate every prisoner equally, so it was unusual for him to seek out Filip specifically. Whatever his reason, it couldn't be good. "We need to get out of here."

"Wait! I have an idea," Zbychu said, then ran off.

Moments later, two bodies flew into the ditch next to them. They were fully clothed in their prison uniforms, and Filip thought at first they were alive, but he quickly realized they were dead. Filip and Beniek looked at each other, unsure what to think.

"Put on their uniforms and get on the truck," Zbychu ordered.

The two men quickly followed his direction, undressing the two dead prisoners and putting on their clothes. Zbychu then pulled them out of the ditch. They rushed into the back of the truck as the prisoners from the ditch-digging work unit watched them in awe and admiration. Not many dared try to escape Buchenwald.

"Why don't we hide somewhere in the forest?" Filip suggested as they hid themselves among the bodies in the truck. "This will just send us back to the camp."

"The forest is crawling with the SS," said Beniek. "There's nowhere to hide. At least this gives us a chance to stay alive."

"We can jump out when the truck drives back to Buchenwald," said Filip.

"It's the only way," said Beniek, nodding in agreement.

They lay there for a few minutes, trying to think of other ways to escape, until they heard the SS guards screaming orders on their way back.

"Keep looking! I want them found!" ordered Hinkelmann

from near the truck. "I will take the truck and scan the road back to Buchenwald."

"Yes, sir," a soldier answered.

"You two, on the back of the truck," Hinkelmann said. "I want you scanning the road behind us."

"Yes, sir," somebody else said.

Filip watched two soldiers climb on the back of the truck where they were hiding. With that, his plan of jumping out before reaching Buchenwald was ruined.

The truck engine turned over, and they were off. The ride through the forest trail was bumpy. Filip tried not to squeal every time they hit a pothole and the bodies on top of him crushed him with the force of all the knees and elbows. He was relieved when the truck stopped a few minutes later, even though it meant they were back inside the Buchenwald prison camp and the chances of their escape had dissipated.

"Come down!" Hinkelmann ordered, and the two soldiers at the back of the truck jumped down. "I need you to come with me to the crematorium. We need to search it in case he somehow found a way to escape through there."

"Yes, sir," the soldiers said.

Filip heard boots marching off. There were no noises after that.

"I'm going to look outside," Filip said.

"Be careful," Bieniek whispered. "The guards might be near."

Filip pushed the bodies off him and crawled toward the tailgate. He peeked outside and saw a group of corpse carriers moving dead prisoners from carts and throwing them on a large pile of bodies. There were no SS guards around.

"Come on!" Filip said, climbing out of the truck.

"Where are we going?" Beniek asked as they walked toward the corpse carriers.

"We have to get back to our barracks before they find us," said Filip.

"Let's just walk there," Beniek suggested. "We're already inside the camp."

"We're Jews now," Filip said, pointing at the Star of David badge on his newly acquired uniform, the same as the one Beniek had on his. "Jews can't just walk around the camp. I learned that from Sig. We need an excuse so no one will stop to question us. Shalom!" he said, greeting the corpse carriers, who all had Stars of David on their uniforms.

"Who are you?" asked one of the carriers, unamused by the greeting. He was a tall, handsome man with intense eyes who seemed in complete control of his surroundings.

"We're corpse carriers like you," said Filip. "The Nazis took our cart, so we need to take one of yours back to camp. There are more bodies we need to transport here."

"You're a fucking liar," said the carrier. "You're not even Jewish."

"What do you mean?" asked Filip.

"You have too much meat on your bones to be Jewish. You don't look half dead like we do."

Filip thought the carrier had a point. Staying at the infirmary the last few months had given them a chance to fatten up and their bodies an opportunity to recover from the grind of heavy labor. They were never going to convince anyone they were Jews, who received the smallest food portions and worked the worst jobs. This left Filip with the only way of reasoning that worked in Buchenwald: bargaining.

"I tell you what," he said, searching his pockets for anything he could offer. Unfortunately, the prisoners had been robbed immediately after dying, and the pockets were empty. "I will give you two potatoes per day for a week if you let us borrow one of your carts."

"Four!" the carrier demanded.

Filip looked at Beniek for help, but he just shrugged. They both knew they had no potatoes to offer.

"Fine," Filip said.

"Deal," said the carrier. "My name is Emil Carlebach, and I'm in Block 26. I want my potatoes starting tonight. You better bring them, or I'll be looking for you. And when I find you, you'll be going back with me on my cart."

"Deal," said Filip.

He and Beniek grabbed one of the carts and rolled it back toward the camp.

"Now what?" asked Beniek.

"Now we survive," said Filip. "Just like we did before."

23

DECEMBER 25, 1943

Anna trudged through the snow with the last bit of strength she had left. Her clothes were soaking wet after what seemed like hours in the storm, and each step was more difficult than the one before. She tried to protect herself from the howling wind, but it smacked her face with frozen snow like a thousand tiny knives. She pushed on, knowing that, as night turned into day, she might be discovered before reaching her destination.

She'd escaped while Frau Wolff and most Germans were sleeping off the Christmas Eve meal. After almost two years in Germany and nearly a year slaving away for Frau Wolff, she'd had enough. She couldn't be a caged animal anymore. She had to be free. Or dead. She accepted that possibility—especially since she was no longer waiting for Filip.

Who was he anyway? After learning he'd been Frau Wolff's lover, Anna couldn't help but wonder if she really knew Filip after all. They'd spent only a few precious moments together. She didn't know much about him. Maybe he wasn't at all what she imagined him to be. Maybe time had given her the proper perspective. She still harbored hope of seeing him again, but it was fading. After almost two years of suffering, she just wanted to be free.

The sun was peeking over the horizon when Anna finally reached the Uding farm. The Germans would still be asleep, but she slipped into the back building, knowing that at least one of the Ukrainian women would be milking the cows. She collapsed to the ground and cried when she spotted Dasha, her beloved friend.

"Praise the Lord!" Dasha yelled out and ran to Anna's side. "What in the world are you doing here, you poor girl?"

"I ran away," Anna said, her voice trembling. Tears would have poured down her face if her eyeballs weren't half frozen.

"I can see that, but why?"

"She beats me every day and tortures me. I can't do it anymore, Dasha. I'm no good at being a slave."

"Well, you can't stay here," said Dasha, looking around as if expecting someone to appear. "Frau Wolff's sister will call her if she finds you."

"I can hide in the barn," Anna offered. "They'll never find me. As long as you feed me, I'll never leave the barn. Even if I have to live there for the rest of my life, it would be better than living with that witch."

"Jesus Christ," Dasha said with a sigh. "Come on, I'll take you there."

"Thank you, Dasha. You're an angel."

"I'm definitely not an angel," said Dasha, lifting Anna off the ground. "You might regret living under my control."

They went outside and slipped across the yard into the barn. Anna's clothes were soaked, and her hands were shaking from the cold. But with Dasha pushing from below, she managed to climb the ladder to the loft. She then collapsed on the bales of straw stacked almost to the ceiling.

"I will bring you some warm clothes and food," said Dasha, covering her with the straw. "Don't go anywhere."

Anna closed her eyes and fell asleep immediately. When she woke up, Dasha was leaning over her as if trying to figure out if she was alive.

"What?" Anna said, startled.

"You're so pale, I thought you were dead," said Dasha. "C'mon, Misha. Help me get her clothes off."

Misha appeared from behind Dasha. "Thank God you're alive," she said.

"Misha! How is your son?" Anna asked, smiling at the thought of seeing Misha's son again.

"Yuri is fine," said Misha, lifting Anna from the straw. "He'll be happy to see you."

"If you live," said Dasha, pulling Anna's clothes off.

It took them a few minutes to take her soaked, half-frozen clothes off and dress her in new, dry ones. She felt as if a warm blanket was pulled over her. The comfort was so satisfying that she fell back onto the straw like a newborn calf.

"Thank you," she said. "I feel like I'm reborn."

"You have to eat," said Dasha, forcing a spoon of warm stew into Anna's mouth.

"And tell us about what happened to Filip," added Misha.

"I don't know," she said. "It's going to be two years in April since I last saw him, and I haven't heard from him since then. But I do know from his lover that he's probably still alive."

"His lover?" asked Dasha, puzzled.

"Frau Wolff."

Both women gasped at the name.

"No! That can't be," said Misha.

"Are you sure?" asked Dasha.

"That's what she told me," Anna confirmed.

"What if she's lying?" said Misha. "They're all liars. They'll lie to get whatever they want."

"Maybe she forced herself on him like Gustaf does on us," Dasha suggested.

Anna had considered this possibility, but over the last few months, she'd convinced herself Filip had slept with Frau Wolff willingly. He was strong and could fight back, not like some weak woman. "I don't know. It's been so long, I don't know what to think anymore. I just want to go home."

"Anna, don't be stupid," said Dasha. "Everyone who came to this god-forsaken country has done something they are not proud of. There's a lot of evil here. We do what we must to survive, and we hang onto whatever good we can find. Filip chased after you across Germany because he loves you. Don't give up on that."

Tears poured down Anna's cheeks. She knew deep down that Dasha was right. The suffering of not knowing made her want to forget, but the hope was always there, gnawing at her day and night like a mole digging holes in the underground darkness. After Sabina's murder, there'd been no one to remind her. Now Dasha rekindled her hope once again.

A door slammed somewhere. They jumped, startled.

"Misha! Where the hell are you?" screamed Gustaf from what sounded like the courtyard. "Your bastard is crying!"

"Shit!" Misha murmured.

"Stay here," said Dasha to Anna. "We'll come back with more food later. Whatever you do, do not leave this place."

Anna watched them scramble down the ladder.

"I'm right here," Misha yelled to Gustaf as she closed the

barn door behind them. "Dasha and I were cleaning up the barn."

"Where the fuck is my breakfast!" he screamed.

Anna hid deep inside the bushels of straw. She stared at the ceiling and wondered if Filip had the will to survive. Was he even alive?

Filip pushed the cart filled with naked, emaciated bodies, trying not to slip on the frozen dirt road leading to the crematorium. Beniek pushed next to him while Carlebach walked behind them as always. This was how they'd operated for over five months. Carlebach was the chief inmate of Block 26, which gave him special privileges—like not having to push the cart and being able to wear a long coat to protect him from the cold winter. He was their boss and acted like it.

"Pick them up," ordered Carlebach, pointing at two dead prisoners lying on the side of the road.

They stopped the cart and threw the bodies onto it. This was one of hundreds of pickups they'd made over the last few months, and it didn't faze them anymore. They'd seen too many prisoners run into the electric fence or past the borders of external work units so they could get shot by sentries simply because they couldn't take the suffering. Some days, the gunshots came every couple of hours. Then the SS would announce, "Corpse carriers to the gate!" over the loudspeakers. Very soon afterward, the chimneys would send out smoke that smelled like burned flesh, an unforgettable smell that made Filip want to vomit.

After a while, nobody even blinked an eye or thought about it. Each one of the prisoners was concentrating only on surviving the next few minutes. There was only a narrow tunnel of space and time in front of them. Nothing outside of that existed. Bodies of perished prisoners, sometimes piled four or five high, littered the camp. The surviving prisoners stopped seeing them, even as they stood by or ate near the fallen. It simply became part of the landscape.

"Search them," said Carlebach.

He didn't have to tell Filip and Beniek because they were already going through the sewn-in pockets inside the prisoners' uniforms. It was standard practice for prisoners to hide valuables that way. Filip had his own hidden pockets, where he kept extra food, Anna's medallion, and all kinds of other trinkets he had picked up the last few months in Buchenwald.

"They were already robbed," Filip announced, finding nothing.

"Goddamn it!" Carlebach fumed. "Fucking vultures!"

"We're no better," Filip pointed out.

"Are you complaining?"

"No, sir," said Filip. "I'm just pointing out that we steal just like everyone else."

"I've been hiding you in my block and feeding you all this time, and all I get is complaints," said Carlebach. "Would you prefer to be on top of this cart?"

"C'mon, Filip," said Beniek. "There's no point arguing. Let's just do our job and get back to the barracks before we freeze to death."

"At least one of you has a brain," said Carlebach.

Filip and Beniek got behind the cart and pushed ahead while Carlebach walked a short distance behind them.

"You should've never offered those potatoes to him," said Beniek. "I'm tired of trading everything I have for them."

"How was I supposed to know that Jews don't get potatoes?" said Filip.

"We need to get out of this work unit and find a job under a roof with some heat. Maybe the crematorium?"

They approached a large building with smoke billowing out of its tall, brick chimney like a locomotive.

"You know they kill anyone who works there after a month to erase all evidence, don't you?" said Carlebach, opening the door for them. "And I didn't put a gun to your head on the potato deal. There are consequences for not fulfilling your side of the bargain."

They pushed the cart inside the building and up a long corridor. Filip didn't like spending five months repaying the debt, but a deal was a deal, and twenty-eight potatoes proved to be a lot harder to come by for a Jew, even a pretend one. Nevertheless, Carlebach kept them alive, and that was all they could ask for in Buchenwald.

"Fucker hears and sees everything," Beniek whispered.

"Then shut up already," Filip suggested.

A wave of heat hit them as soon as they entered the furnace room. Several prisoners, with their jackets off, worked six large furnaces. Two of them staggered over and unloaded the bodies from their cart onto a metal shuttle that stood on rails leading into the furnace. They opened the furnace door and unceremoniously pushed the shuttle with the bodies inside the furnace. An SS officer and two guards stood in the corner, laughing at something. They seemed uninterested in the operation.

Carlebach approached one of the prisoners, who handed him something. He hid it inside his coat and walked back. "They need help with the ashes," he said to Filip and Beniek. "Let's go!"

They took the stairs to the level below.

"What did he give you?" asked Filip.

"Gold and silver teeth," said Carlebach. "He wants to buy food for his crew."

"Did you agree?"

"Of course. It's the least we can do for these bastards before they end up in the oven themselves."

Four other prisoners worked on the level below the furnaces. They collected the ashes and unburned bones and processed them through a grinder. The final powder was poured into urns.

"Grab the cart," said Carlebach, pointing at a cart stacked with urns.

They pushed the cart outside while he held the door for them.

"Where are we dumping them this time?" asked Beniek.

"Follow me," said Carlebach.

They pushed the cart through the camp until they arrived at an open field near two large barns where the Germans kept their farm animals.

"Dump it," Carlebach ordered.

"Here?" asked Filip.

"Yes, here."

"Isn't this the garden where they grow vegetables for our canteen?"

"The Germans think it's a good fertilizer," said Carlebach. "Now get on with it!"

Filip and Beniek looked at each other, shaking their heads.

"I'm not doing it," said Filip. "This is sacrilege."

"Me neither," said Beniek.

Carlebach laughed, and then his face tightened into a death stare. "What do you think this is? Some kind of holiday that you're on? This is a death camp. People are murdered. Their bodies are burned. Their ashes are made into fertilizer. We eat vegetables made out of their ashes. Then we die, and our ashes are turned into fertilizer. Then more people die. Until no one is left. All you can do is live as long as you can. But you will still die. You will still be ash. There's nothing you can do about that."

Filip lifted one of the urns and poured the ashes on the frozen ground. Beniek watched him and then did the same. It took them about an hour to spread the ashes all over the ground, trying not to step on them, which was futile. The wind blew the ashes everywhere, including all over their clothes and faces and inside their mouths and eyes. Filip tried not to think about it so he wouldn't go mad.

All he could do was try to survive as long as he could.

24
MARCH 21, 1944

Anna woke to the rumble of a car engine. After three months of hiding in the barn, all the sounds woke her because her ears were all she had been using. Her other senses had become muted without any interaction with the outside world, but her hearing had become sharp like a dog's. The car engine was also unusual for the village, where most farmers still drove around on their horse buggies. She became alarmed immediately and rushed to a tiny window near the ceiling overlooking the courtyard.

Down below stood a large black car. Its doors swung open, and four people emerged: three policemen and Frau Wolff. They were met by Helma, Klaus, and Gustaf Uding, all three standing on the stairs leading to their farmhouse. Anna knew why they were there but had nowhere else to hide, so she just stood there and listened.

"What brings you here, Frau Wolff?" asked Klaus.

"Don't play stupid with me, Klaus," said Frau Wolff. "You

know why we're here. Just tell us where she is before this gets worse for you."

"What are you talking about, sister?" Helma protested. "Have you lost your mind?"

"You stay quiet, Helma. Go back to your room and take a nap."

"Fuck you, bitch!" Helma screamed. "Get the hell off my farm."

One of the policemen stepped forward. "Excuse me, Frau Uding, but this is a police matter. We have a search warrant. We suspect you're harboring a fugitive foreign worker who has run away from Frau Wolff. Her name is Anna Kogut."

Anna felt nausea crawl up her throat. There was now no doubt about why they were there. They would surely find her if they searched the barn. Various options ran through her head, but none of them seemed feasible. Run? But where? She had nowhere to go. Hide somewhere else on the farm? Maybe the pigsty, inside a pile of shit, where they would not search? There was no time for that, and they might spot her. Come out and beg for mercy? She knew they had none.

"We're not stupid. Why would we hide a fugitive?" said Klaus.

"Maybe you're fucking her," Frau Wolff suggested.

"How dare you?" Helma screamed while climbing down the stairs toward her sister. "My husband loves me, unlike yours!"

"You're a fat cow! How can a man love that?"

The policeman got between the two sisters. "That's enough! We're coming in whether you like it or not. Let's go!" he yelled, waving at the other two policemen, who entered the farmhouse.

Anna scrambled around, trying to find a hiding place. That

was when she heard a noise downstairs, somewhere by the barn's back entrance.

"Anna! Come down here!" Dasha yelped from the ground level.

"I need to hide," she said, climbing down the ladder.

"No time for that. You need to run away to the forest."

"Forest! It's still March. I'll freeze to death."

"There's a group of runaways living deep in the woods. They're all Russian, but they might take you in. It's the only chance you have. You just have to be careful."

"What do you mean by that?" Anna asked, worried about how Dasha spoke.

"There's no time to explain," said Dasha, handing her a piece of paper. "Here's a map I got from someone a while ago. I was going to run away myself, but I was too scared."

"I'm scared too, Dasha," Anna said. "Maybe I should give up. What's the point of running?"

"Don't give up, Anna," Dasha pleaded. "Don't be like us. Give us all some hope. Do it for us, please."

Anna hugged her. Then she ran. She ran as fast as she could through the back door and straight to the forest behind it, trying to get as far away from the Uding farm as possible. She didn't stop until she collapsed with exhaustion in a meadow overgrown with spring grass.

She caught her breath and opened the map—a simple drawing with shapes outlining the forest and the villages, with an X in the middle. It also indicated where north, south, east, and west were located. She looked up to see where the sun was and decided to head toward it, or east, then follow the tree line south toward the highlands.

Three hours later, trekking up the hill through a thick pine forest, Anna arrived at the X spot, which appeared to be an old hut. She'd walked around the village of Eckardtshausen a few kilometers earlier, and there had been nothing but forest since then. It occurred to her that she had no one to save her. Whatever lay ahead, she would have to rely only on herself.

She approached the hut and swung the door open. It took her eyes a few seconds to adjust to the darkness, but when they finally did, she saw a single empty room. At first sight, it seemed abandoned, but looking closer, she noticed several cots with blankets, metal bowls with leftover food, and a fire in the hearth still smoldering. People lived there and had left not long before.

"Who the fuck are you?" said a man's voice from behind her. He spoke German.

Anna turned around and saw five men staring at her like hungry wolves, waiting for the signal from their alpha to attack. They all wore ragged clothes to keep them warm, and each held a wooden club made from tree branches.

"I'm Anna," she said. "Dasha sent me."

"Who the fuck is Dasha?"

"She's a Ukrainian woman from the farm in Braach," she said, raising her map. "She gave me this map and told me I can hide here."

"We hate Ukrainians. They fight alongside Hitler against Russia," the man said and stepped closer to her.

"I'm not Ukrainian," she said, understanding why Dasha didn't want to come here. "I'm from Poland."

"We hate Poles," he said, stepping even closer. "They killed my brother when we invaded Poland in '39."

Anna wanted to argue about why they invaded Poland in the first place, but this was probably not a good time to do that. "I'm not a soldier," she said. "I'm here only because I don't want to work for the Germans anymore, just like you."

"Kill her," said another man.

"Why kill her? Let's play with her a little," said a third man.

"Be quiet!" ordered the first man.

"I'm a great cook," said Anna, taking advantage of the sudden silence. "I can clean the place up too. You won't regret taking me in."

"We don't need another mouth to feed," said the man. "Tie her up and throw her in the hole."

"Wait—" she managed to say before the other four men pounced on her and stuffed her mouth with a gag. She wanted to fight, but they were strong men. They bound her with ropes in seconds, like a hopeless calf, and threw her into a shallow pit behind the hut. Before she could glimpse the sky for the last time, tree branches covered the opening, then something heavy was placed on top of them to prevent her from crawling out.

Anna wept because that was all she could do. No matter what she did, she couldn't escape her cage. Like a wild animal in the zoo, she seemed destined to die a captive. And no matter how hard she tried, she was no closer to seeing Filip.

Sig operated the lathe as carefully as he could, but he was no good at it, even after the last eight months of training from the German foreman. Schmidt would have laughed at him if he'd seen him pretending to be a machinist. At least he lived. Otherwise, it would be certain death at the hands of Hinkelmann after he discovered Sig at the infirmary.

Ciepielowski had managed to give him a different identity —one of a former Jewish machinist who'd worked at the Gustloff-Werke factory attached to the Buchenwald prison camp and died of typhus at the infirmary. Three thousand prisoners worked at the factory every day, and with their shaved heads and pajama-like uniforms, they all looked alike to the Germans, so switching identities wasn't that difficult. The Nazis were overwhelmed by an increasing number of prisoners arriving from the East and probably assumed all prisoners would die in the camp anyway.

Of course, nothing came free, as it always was with Ciepielowski and his underground resistance friends. Not only did Sig have to learn how to operate the lathe and machine precision metal parts, but his task was also to sabotage the production. The factory produced rifles, artillery components, and fine mechanics for rockets, and he did everything possible to slow down production and make the parts defective. That proved to be much more difficult under the watchful eyes of both the Nazi guards and the civilian workers obsessed with precision.

"Hey, Number 154799!" yelled a man over the noisy lathe.

Sig turned around and saw his foreman, Herr Meyer, a spectacled, bald man in his fifties, holding a clipboard. He seemed more pissed off than usual, his face tense in deadly seriousness.

"Yes, sir!" Sig yelled.

"Turn off the machine," said Meyer. "Someone is here to see you in Schaeffler's office."

Sig turned off the lathe and followed Meyer. This couldn't be good. Schaeffler was the factory manager, high above Sig in the organization's hierarchy. Was he found out? Did they figure out he was dumping the coolant into the drain and screwing up the machining tolerances on the rifle barrels?

Meyer opened the door to Schaeffler's office and nudged Sig inside before closing the door behind him. The room was more plainly furnished than he expected—just a simple metal desk and chair. The man sitting in it wasn't Schaeffler, however. It took Sig a moment to recognize him in his SS uniform, but Schmidt grinned, and Sig could never forget that smile.

"I finally found you," said Schmidt, standing up with controlled enthusiasm.

"What the hell are you doing here?" Sig asked, pretending to be mad at him for abandoning their relationship after Hinkelmann discovered them having sex at Schmidt's villa. The truth was, he could never be mad at him for too long, and he missed the one and only love of his life.

"I'm sorry, Sig. Hinkelmann threatened to report me. It would've destroyed my career and my family. I might've ended up here as one of the prisoners."

"At least we would've been together," Sig pointed out, even though being a prisoner in Buchenwald was the last thing he would have wished on anyone.

Schmidt approached Sig. "I'm very sorry, Siggy. I kept an eye on you at the infirmary but just couldn't get close. I was heartbroken when you disappeared. I thought you died. Then, when Hinkelmann came to me, demanding that I give you up, I knew you were alive. That was one of the happiest days of my life. And today is even better because I can see you and . . . touch you," he said, placing his soft hand on Sig's cheek.

Sig didn't resist. He wanted to feel his touch. "I missed you too," he said, tears trickling down his face.

Schmidt kissed him on the lips. "I love you so much."

"I love you too."

"And it's a good thing I found you now," said Schmidt. "You need to hide tonight."

"Why?"

"They are rounding up all the Jews and sending them to

Auschwitz-Birkenau for extermination. Two trains. Five thousand Jews. Anyone wearing the Star of David."

"Why are they doing this?"

"They don't tell me anything. I only run the canteen and the post office and keep my mouth shut. Only Hitler and Himmler know what's going on. The Allies invaded Italy, and the Soviets beat us in Stalingrad. So maybe they want to get rid of the Jews in case we lose the war."

"But where do I hide?" Sig asked. "They count everybody before we go back to the camp."

"I don't know, but you have to find a way," said Schmidt, pulling a wrapped bundle out of his pocket. "Use this to bribe your way out of it. Sergeant Zollner, Hinkelmann's friend, runs the factory work unit, so I can't do anything for you. You're on your own."

"Thank you," said Sig.

"I have to go, but I'll be back to check on you in a couple of days," said Schmidt. He kissed Sig on the cheek and walked toward the door.

"Wait! Have you seen or heard anything from my friend Filip?"

"All I know is Hinkelmann couldn't find him because he accused me of hiding him. But that was months ago. He's probably dead by now."

Sig thought the opposite. If Hinkelmann couldn't find Filip, then there was a chance he was still alive. After all, it had taken Schmidt months to find Sig among the tens of thousands of prisoners in Buchenwald. Thank goodness Filip wasn't Jewish and would be safe tonight.

∾

Filip was hovering over a hole, relieving himself in the latrine, when the sirens blasted and searchlights from the guard towers sliced through the evening darkness of his barracks. Then he heard shouts from the SS guards and a couple of gunshots. He stood and pulled his pants up, looking around for a way out, but he was trapped. The doors led back to where the shouts were coming from, and the windows were barred.

"They're everywhere!" Beniek screamed, appearing in the doorway. "It's a roundup!"

"There's nowhere to go," said Filip.

"Inside the latrines," Beniek offered.

They looked down into the hole filled with excrement. It was a foul swamp buzzing with flies that no sane man would want to enter.

"It's our only chance," said Beniek.

"Maybe they're just relocating us?"

"Nothing good has ever come out of a roundup. We're not going anywhere better."

Beniek had a good point. Buchenwald was hell, but at least he and Filip knew how to survive there. Whatever the SS was planning would probably make their situation worse, not better.

"You go in first," Filip offered.

Beniek didn't hesitate and jumped right in. Filip looked back at the door and the sounds of chaos beyond it, then jumped in. He had to survive.

They both gagged, standing chest-deep in shit. The smell was putrid. It was one thing to smell it from above and another to be immersed in it. They pinched their noses, but the intensity of the smell was so great that it seemed to seep in through their mouths and ears. Filip vomited, then leaned back against the wall, closing his eyes and taking only the smallest breaths through his mouth.

"There's a hatch at the end of this trench where they pump the shit out," Beniek murmured. "We have to try to get out through there, or we'll suffocate."

Filip nodded and followed Beniek while trying to keep his nose, mouth, and eyes closed. The excrement was thick, and it took them a few minutes to wade their way to the end.

"That's the hatch," said Beniek, pointing at a small metal door about a meter above them.

"How the hell do we climb up there?" asked Filip because there was no ladder.

"I'll climb on top of you and get it open."

"Why can't I climb on top of you?"

"I'm an Olympian and a lot more agile than you."

"Fine," Filip capitulated.

"Put your hands together," Beniek ordered. "I will then climb on your shoulders."

"But that means I'll have to unplug my nose."

"Just hold your breath until I'm up."

Filip took a deep breath and stuck his hands in front of him. Beniek didn't waste any time. He put his foot into Filip's hands like they were a stirrup and hefted himself up. Using Filip's head for balance, he placed his other foot on his shoulder and then grabbed the wall above him to lift his other foot onto Filip's other shoulder.

Filip, feeling Beniek's full weight, let the breath out of his mouth. Holding onto Beniek's feet, he had no choice but to inhale the smell through his nose. He gagged again, trying not to vomit.

"I got it," said Beniek.

Filip heard the heavy metal hatch scraping against

concrete, and a sliver of the black sky showed above them. With it came a rush of fresh outside air, and he gulped it down. Then the weight was off his shoulders, and Beniek climbed out.

"Grab on to this," Beniek said, dangling his jacket down.

Filip snatched the sleeves but couldn't lift himself out of the swamp.

"Use the walls to climb up with your feet," Beniek suggested.

Filip found a groove in the wall with his foot and lifted himself. He grabbed Beniek's arm, then climbed over his back and out of the hole. He collapsed against the back wall of the barracks, exhausted from the effort but hidden in the darkness from the commotion on the other side of the building. Beniek sat next to him, and they listened to the shouts of the SS guards, the barking of their dogs, and the screams of the panicked prisoners.

"I want everyone with the Star of David at the roll call plaza!" someone shouted, seemingly just around the corner from them. "I'll court-martial you if you miss even one Jew!"

"Now what?" Beniek whispered.

"We need to get out of these clothes," said Filip. "We smell like shit."

"And how do you suggest we do that? Nobody will take our Jewish uniforms."

"I don't know," said Filip, shrugging. "Maybe we need to find Ciepielowski. Maybe he can smuggle us out of the camp again."

"He nearly killed us last time," Beniek protested. "I'm not doing that again. Plus, how will we make it all the way to the infirmary with all the searchlights?"

"They're all pointing at this block right now. It's our only chance while they're distracted."

What other choice did they have? None. Ciepielowski was the only one who might be willing and able to help them. The kapos in the other barracks would quickly give them up to the SS since Filip and Beniek had nothing to bribe them with. There was nowhere else to hide, and they would quickly be captured and shot whenever they emerged.

"Fine," said Beniek, standing up. "We must hide in the dark and circle the camp until we reach the infirmary. Follow me."

He ran off toward the neighboring block behind theirs. Filip followed, dodging lights and prying eyes of the prisoners staring out of their windows to see the commotion. They finally reached the back of the camp—an empty, dark field that offered no protection.

"Which way?" Filip asked.

"We have to stay close to the barracks so we have somewhere to hide. They'll shoot us like pheasants in the open field."

"This way then," Filip offered, then took off to their right.

They snuck around the quiet portion of the camp and arrived at the infirmary a few minutes later.

"Now comes the hard part," said Filip. "The front door is locked, and there's a guard inside."

"Through the window, then?" Beniek suggested. "They're not barred."

"They're all locked from the inside, and if we break the window, they'll search the place as soon as they find it."

Shots rang out nearby—a salvo of them.

"What was that?" asked Beniek.

They scanned the area around them, unsure where the shots came from as the sounds bounced off buildings.

"There," said Filip, pointing at another barracks, where a group of SS guards stood with rifles pointed at two prisoners standing against the wall. Bodies of two dead prisoners lay at their feet, apparently shot by the previous salvo.

The guards fired again, and the two prisoners fell dead to the ground. An officer walked over and inspected the bodies.

"I think that's Hinkelmann," said Filip.

"Must be some kind of retribution," said Beniek. "Taking advantage of the chaos to settle some scores."

That might be, Filip thought. *Or just a random killing of innocent prisoners.* Who could know these things? It would remain one of the unsolved mysteries of Buchenwald.

The guards marched off, leaving the bodies on the ground.

"Let's go see," Filip said, running off toward the crime scene before Beniek could protest.

"What do you plan to do?" Beniek asked as they stood over the bodies.

"We take their uniforms. They're political prisoners, so better than being Jewish."

"But they got shot. What if the SS is after them? They'll kill us if they match their prisoner numbers."

"It's still better than having the Star of David on our uniforms. That's death on sight," said Filip, undressing one of the prisoners, who'd been shot in the head and had very little blood on his uniform.

"Are you sure about this?" asked Beniek, undressing another dead prisoner.

"No, not at all. It's just the only option."

Then a bloody hand rose from the pile of bodies. A meek voice screeched something.

Filip moved closer to the prisoner and leaned over, close to his mouth. "What is it?"

"Report . . . to Pister," the prisoner murmured. Then he went limp.

"What did he say?" asked Beniek.

"Something about Pister. Does he look familiar to you?"

"I don't know. They all look like assholes to me."

"Doesn't he look like one of the guards from the quarry work unit?"

"Forget it," said Beniek. "Let's get out of here."

They ran away, looking for a place to hide until the morning. Who knew what tomorrow would bring for their new identities. Filip wondered what the dying prisoner meant and if it would help him survive.

25
MARCH 22, 1944

L et me have her, Sergey," a man said in Russian.

"Stop acting so horny, Andrey," said another man. "We need to understand who drew that map for her. If she found us, then the Nazis will too."

Anna cracked her eyelids just a little so they wouldn't know she was awake or that she understood Russian, which she'd picked up from the Ukrainian women on the Uding farm. She saw two Russian men she met the day before staring at her like a piece of meat.

"She's awake," said the man who sounded like Andrey.

"What's your name?" said the other man in German, whom she recognized as the leader of their gang. She decided he must be named Sergey.

Anna opened her eyes wider. She wanted to kick and punch them but realized her hands and feet were still tied. She looked about her and saw they were inside the hut. A fire was burning in the hearth.

"Did you hear me? What is your name?" asked Sergey.

"I won't tell you anything unless you cut me loose," she said.

Andrey kicked her in the ribs. "Who the hell are you to make demands?"

"Don't hurt her!" Sergey ordered. Then he turned to Anna. "I promise he won't hurt you again if you tell me everything I need."

"I told you," she said. "I'm a runaway who needs shelter. My Ukrainian friend told me where to find you and that you could help."

"Why are you running away?" Sergey asked.

"My master is a witch, and I'm tired of living in a cage like a zoo animal."

The two men looked at each other, frowning like they were impressed.

"Please let me have her," said Andrey in Russian. "She'll be a lot of fun, this one."

"Shut up, Andrey. She's a prisoner, just like us," said Sergey, also in Russian. Then, in German, he said, "Who drew the map for you?"

"I don't know. I got it from my Ukrainian friend. I told you already. She didn't say who drew it."

"Is there a chance that others saw the map?"

"I have no idea. I had to run from the police after she gave me the map. I'm sorry."

Sergey scratched his head, then said, "I believe you. Untie her, Andrey."

"Are you serious?" said Andrey. "Are you going to let her go?"

"She's going to help us pack. We have to move to another location. It's not safe here anymore."

"Where are we going? Where will we find another hut like

this with a hearth?"

"I don't know. We'll live in the forest if we have to. It's better than dying. Now, get the others and start moving out."

Andrey grumbled but untied Anna. He shoved her toward the sleeping cots. "Roll the blankets and put the cooking pots inside them," he ordered.

Anna and the men spent the next hour packing everything up. They left the hut just as the sun reached its peak in the sky.

As the six of them trekked through the pine forest, staying off the beaten paths and away from any German tourists hiking in the mountains, Anna wondered if it would be better for her to escape or stay with the Russians. How would she survive on her own? Spring had not arrived yet, so there were no plants or fruits to eat, and she had no idea how to trap and kill wild animals. She would die of hunger within days. The only other option would be to turn herself in and hope for the best, which was probably prison or death.

She looked back at Sergey, who was walking about two meters behind her, to see if he was paying attention to her. He smiled at her like they were taking a stroll in a park. Andrey and the other three Russians were far ahead, but she could not get away from Sergey if he decided to chase her.

She sat on a large stone and said, "How did you end up here?"

"We need to keep walking," he said. "The guys will be upset if you slow them down."

"You're avoiding my question."

He sat down next to her. "We were captured at Leningrad. Then they sent us to the Buchenwald labor camp—"

"You were at Buchenwald?" Anna asked.

"Yes, but we escaped."

"It's possible to escape Buchenwald?"

"It's not easy, but possible," he said, standing up. "Keep walking."

Anna got up and pushed forward. "Did you meet any Polish guys there?"

"Why do you ask?"

Anna considered if it was safe to tell the Russians about Filip. What would they do if they found out she loved someone? "Someone I love is there," she said, deciding it might keep them at bay if she had a man. "His name is Filip Wolny. Do you know him?"

"No. Never heard of him," he said. "There are tens of thousands of prisoners there from all over Europe. Even some Americans."

"Tell me about the camp, please."

"I don't like talking about it. It's a horrible place."

"Please, I want to know what my Filip is going through."

"Fine. But I promise you won't feel better about it after I tell you," he said.

He then told her about the hunger, the hard labor, typhus, and people dropping dead every day, hundreds of them. He told her about the crematorium and trenches full of naked bodies, nothing but bones held together by skin. He told her about their escape from the truck on the way to another labor camp in Dora, where the Nazis were building rockets inside mountain caves. He told her about surviving the winter in the mountains and stealing food from the local farms.

"Why don't you hunt in the forest?" she asked.

"We're all just factory workers from Leningrad. We don't know how to hunt. And we don't have any weapons. We killed a boar once with spears, but that meat only lasted for about a month. That's why we have to steal food to survive."

They entered a forest clearing, and a village appeared below in the valley.

"And you're going to help us," he said.

Anna's stomach grumbled, reminding her she hadn't eaten in a few days. She had never stolen anything before; her parents had made sure she knew it was wrong, but it was either that or death. She decided to choose life.

"What do you want me to do?" she asked.

"You'll see," he said. "Let's hope you're quick."

Somebody nudged Filip awake. He opened his eyes and saw a prisoner standing over him. He was a short man with a round face that looked puzzled.

"Who are you?" asked the man.

"Where . . . are . . we?" Filip countered, his teeth chattering from the cold.

"Block 17. Why are you sleeping outside?"

Filip nudged Beniek, who lay on the ground next to him.

"What is it?" asked Beniek.

"It's the roll call," the man said. "They'll shoot you if you miss it."

Filip wondered if the person from whom he had stolen the uniform the night before was from this block, but he got up anyway and followed the man to the roll call plaza. They couldn't risk not going.

They stood in the roll call square for an hour, waiting for their numbers to be called, but they never were. While everyone else rushed off to their respective work units, Filip and Beniek stood without a purpose, looking dangerously idle and being easy prey for the SS snipers in the towers surrounding the camp.

"Why weren't our numbers called?" asked Beniek. "The SS usually don't erase the numbers from the roll call for a few days after the prisoner dies. This is all very suspicious."

"These guys must've been special," said Filip.

"So what do we do now?"

"We have to find out who they were and what work unit they were from."

"What if we show up to the work unit, and they check our numbers and realize that we're supposed to be shot to death? They'll just put us against the wall and shoot us."

"Good point," Filip agreed. "So that leaves us with only one option again."

"Ciepielowski?"

"Yes. We have to get his help to hide us somewhere. He's the only one with the connections to do it. Let's go."

They marched to the infirmary, where the SS guard met them.

"What do you want?" the guard asked.

"We were told to see Dr. Ciepielowski," Filip lied.

"What about?"

"He's looking for more patients for his studies," said Beniek.

"Fine," said the guard, waving them in. "He's in his lab on the second floor."

They climbed the stairs and found Ciepielowski alone in the same laboratory where Filip and Sig had swapped the real vaccines that were supposed to be given to the soldiers at the Eastern Front for the placebo.

"What are you two doing in the camp?" said Ciepielowski with astonishment upon seeing them.

"Your potion worked too well," said Filip. "It knocked us out for many hours, and Hinkelmann chased us back to the camp."

"Hmm, that's interesting," said Ciepielowski, writing something down in his notebook. "I'll have to adjust my formulation. Perhaps the strain of the nightshade plant in the local forest is more potent than the one I used in Poland."

"No offense, Doctor." said Beniek. "But we've been stuck for months working for the Jews as corpse carriers, and yesterday, we had to run away from the roundup when they took them all away. So we're more worried about staying alive than your formulation."

"Yes, that's a pity," said Ciepielowski. "We had some good comrades among the Jews."

"Do you know if Sig was taken?" asked Filip.

"Fortunately, he's safe at the factory, where I got him a job. But how did you escape the roundup?"

"We climbed out through the sewer in the latrines and stole uniforms from some prisoners that were shot," said Beniek.

"And stricken immediately from the roll call record," Filip added. "It was Hinkelmann who had them shot, and I suspect it had to do with his business. So, our stolen prisoner numbers might be blacklisted."

"Hmm, very interesting," said Ciepielowski, again writing something in his notebook as if another chemical compound had just come to his mind. "I'll have to investigate this. Perhaps this can somehow help us in our cause. Are the bodies still there?"

"They were still there by Block 17 when we left earlier," said Beniek. "They took all the Jewish corpse carriers away, so the bodies are probably still there."

"Can you help us?" Filip asked.

"Yes, of course. I can have your identities replaced with those of our dead typhus patients and find you a job on one of the work units."

"Can you put us together with Sig at the factory?" Filip suggested.

"I'm afraid not. I ran into some issues with the SS officer there. But I have a job at the dog kennel if you want it."

"That should be easy," said Beniek.

"Quite the opposite, I'm afraid," said Ciepielowski. "They shot four prisoners there yesterday because they stole food from the dogs. The beasts are better fed than the prisoners, so resisting the temptation is difficult. Not to mention the constant barking. They're trained to attack the prisoners, and they just want to tear you apart. It's quite maddening, in fact."

"We'll take it," said Filip. "It can't be worse than corpse carrying."

"Of course, you have to do something for me," said Ciepielowski.

"Sabotage again?" asked Beniek.

"Yes."

"What possible sabotage can we do in the kennel?" Filip asked.

"Actually, something very critical to the resistance," said Ciepielowski. "The Allies have invaded Italy, and there are rumors of them invading France. The Soviets are also pushing from the East. It's just a matter of time before Hitler and his armies are destroyed. We suspect that, in case of an eventual invasion of Germany, the SS will murder the remaining prisoners. We must start preparing for armed resistance here at the camp. Our objective will be to overwhelm the guards, take control of the armory, defend the camp against any German army units, and wait until the Allied forces arrive. So, your objective will be to smuggle poison into the kennel, hide it in a secure place, and then feed it to the dogs when the signal is given."

Filip looked at Beniek to see his reaction and whether he felt the same as Filip did about this task. They'd almost gotten caught sabotaging the vaccines. But switching containers was one thing. Killing SS dogs was another. The SS guards cherished their dogs more than anything in the world, and they would kill on sight anyone who tried to harm them. Beniek, however, didn't show any emotion.

"Did, by any chance, the four guys who got shot for stealing dog food also have this exact assignment?" Filip asked.

Ciepielowski cleared his throat and said, "Do you want this job or not?"

"Yes, we'll take it," said Filip. "But I also want you to find a way for us to escape. We'll kill the dogs if we're still here, but I'm not planning to stick around to see what the SS or the Allies will do. I have someone waiting for me on the outside."

"Don't we all," said Ciepielowski. "I can't promise you anything, but I'll try to find a way. Pister has clamped down on everyone, and there's currently no way I know of to escape. Perhaps we'll get some help from the Allies soon."

"I have faith in you, Doctor," said Filip. However, he wasn't so sure. Ciepielowski had almost gotten them killed last time and seemed more interested in the resistance than helping them escape. Filip would have to find his own way out of Buchenwald or die trying.

Hinkelmann sat next to Schmidt in one of the chairs in front of Pister's office, trying not to scream accusations at him in front of the camp commandant's staff. He knew there could be only one reason Pister asked to see them both: He'd found out about their racketeering operation. Schmidt was doing a terrible job of running the business, and Hinkelmann suspected him of trying to find a way out. Perhaps he was the one who'd told Pister about it to gain his favor. Schmidt simply wasn't trustworthy. That was precisely why Hinkelmann had already planned to eliminate him. He would have to be more creative about it now that Pister suspected something.

Then the phone rang on the desk of Pister's adjutant officer, SS Lieutenant Simon. He picked up the receiver, listened for a few seconds, then said, "Yes, sir," and put it back down. "He's ready to see you," Simon announced.

Hinkelmann sprung out of his chair first, wanting to show Schmidt his superiority, then entered Pister's office. "Herr Kommandant," he announced himself.

"Sit down," said Pister from behind his large oak desk.

Hinkelmann sat in one of the two chairs opposite the desk. Schmidt closed the door behind them and sat next to him.

Pister stared at them for a while and then said, "Hinkelmann, I got your report about four missing guards not showing up for duty this morning. Any idea what might have happened to them?"

"No, sir," he said. "I suspect desertion, sir. Kids worried about the Americans invading Germany."

"Four of them at the same time? All from your quarry work unit? What are the chances of that, Sergeant?"

"I don't know, sir. I'm terrible with math."

Pister slammed his fist on the desk. "Are you being a fucking smart-ass, Hinkelmann?"

"No, sir," he lied. "I didn't mean any disrespect."

"Do you think I'm stupid? You think I don't know what the two of you have been up to?"

"Sir?" Schmidt asked, pretending to be confused.

"Shut up, Schmidt," Pister snapped at him. "Do you forget that my predecessor, Koch, was prosecuted and sent to jail for corruption? Believe me, I'm sympathetic. Our salaries are shit. I don't mind my officers taking some money from the prisoners to supplement their income. But I'll be damned if I have to go to jail for your fuckups. I will bury both of you in the forest myself if I find out you had anything to do with those four men disappearing. Do you understand me?"

"Sir, what are you accusing us of?" said Hinkelmann, faking innocence. "You can't possibly be suggesting I had anything to do with their disappearance. I resent this attack on my integrity. My reputation is at stake, sir."

"You can kiss your reputation goodbye, Hinkelmann," said Pister. "You can be assured that I won't be recommending you for a promotion. Whether or not you had anything to do with it is beside the point. What's already unacceptable is that you lost four of your men. This is grounds for demotion. In fact, I'm reassigning you to the factory. We've had some complaints from the army about the quality of the munitions built there, and we suspect there was sabotage. If you prove yourself by fixing this problem for me, I'll consider keeping you on as a sergeant. Otherwise, you're off to the Eastern Front as a corporal. Is that clear?"

Hinkelmann boiled with anger and wanted to snap Pister's neck, but he knew that fighting this would be a mistake. So he collected himself and said, "Yes, sir."

"As for you, Schmidt," Pister continued. "I'm taking you off the canteen and post office duties. Your new assignment will be at the kennel. Good luck trying to make money there. And those dogs better be fed well. If I see ribs showing on even one of them, I'll send you to the Eastern Front together with Hinkelmann. Is *that* clear?"

"Yes, Herr Kommandant," Schmidt answered, sweat pouring down his pale face as if he were dying of some terrible disease.

Hinkelmann should also have been worried because his SS and racketeering careers were likely over, but he was weirdly excited. He was bored with the whole thing. He wanted to get his hands dirty again.

"You're dismissed," Pister ordered.

They exited his office and marched out of the headquarters building.

"What the hell did you do, Hinkelmann?" Schmidt asked through clenched teeth as soon as they were out of anyone's earshot.

"I'm running my business," he said. "And you stay out of it."

"You mean our business? Because I'm the one running it while you're taking half the money."

"Listen, ass-fucker! You're lucky I don't have you and your love toy shot."

"Is that what you did to those four SS guards?" Schmidt asked.

"They wanted part of the action and threatened to go to Pister if I didn't. I had to eliminate them."

"Well, that didn't work, did it? Our business is dead now. We could've just bribed them like I've done with half the SS in the camp already."

Hinkelmann had enough. "Fuck it! I don't give a shit. I'll do my thing at the factory, and you do your thing."

"Not if they find the bodies," said Schmidt. "You'll be court-martialed and hanged. And me with you."

"Don't worry, Schmidt. I had the bodies cremated this morning. They had prisoner clothing, so nobody will find anything. You can sleep well tonight with your fake wife."

"You will pay for this, Hinkelmann," Schmidt said, his face red with anger. "And you're not bringing me down with you."

"Fuck off! Just stay out of my way and keep your mouth shut," he said, walking off.

He'd lied, but he didn't want Schmidt to worry. He wanted him dumb and happy when his death came. He was too much of a liability to keep alive.

26

JULY 21, 1944

Anna crawled through the mud toward the chicken coop. The sun was just peeking from behind the mountains, and the rooster had crowed his wake-up call, which was the best time to steal the chickens. Everyone was still asleep, and farmers assumed chickens made noises because they were waking up. She'd learned this trick over the last few months from the foxes—her competition for food. She used a hole under the fence, probably dug by the fox, to get inside the fenced-in chicken run. She hoped the farmer's carelessness in not finding and repairing the hole also meant her work today would be easier.

She stood up when she reached the door to the chicken coop. There was no lock, but the chickens clucked loudly, sensing her presence. She would have to hurry to stop them from making too much of a commotion.

She opened the door and ran inside, arms over her head, expecting an aerial assault from the rooster. The attack came swiftly, as usual, but she swiped at the rooster, and he bounced off her into the door. She ran to the roosting bars, where the chickens were perching, and grabbed the fattest one by its neck. She stuffed it inside her jacket and turned back toward the door, where the rooster stood waiting, flopping his wings and puffing his orange feathers to intimidate her. The rooster was a large one and no easy opponent. One just like it almost cracked her skull open about a month earlier.

She put her arms over her head again and charged at the rooster and the door. The rooster flew at her head, clawing at her with his sharp talons. She closed her eyes and smashed through the door, hoping to dislodge him. She landed in the mud, and when she got up to run away, the rooster was gone. Instead, an older man was standing over her with a hunting rifle.

"Don't you fucking move, or I'll shoot, you vermin!" the man shouted.

"Please don't kill me," Anna pleaded, releasing the stolen chicken out of her jacket. "Take it back. I was just hungry."

"Who are you?" the man asked.

"I'm nobody. Just passing through. I'll be on my way and never come back. I promise."

"The hell you won't. You're one of those runaways, aren't you? The police warned us about you. Are you Russian?"

"No, sir," she said. "I'm from Poland. My master was cruel. She beat me every day, so I ran away. I don't want to go back there."

"Get up!" he ordered.

She stood up.

"I'm taking you to our constable," he said, poking her with his rifle to make her move. "He'll know what to do with you."

She walked through the gate, out of the chicken run, and down a dirt road leading to the center of the village. The man followed her, his rifle pointing at her at all times. He seemed ready to fire if she tried to escape.

"Please let me go, sir," she pleaded. "They'll hang me if you take me to the police."

"You should've thought about that before running away. It's a sin to disobey your master and steal. God willing, they will give you proper punishment."

Anna thought that Germans, not God, enslaved other people and made all the rules, but she didn't say anything. This old man obviously wasn't willing to listen to reason.

"The one on the left," the man said, indicating a large house.

She turned and entered through a gate. The man knocked on the front door and waited. After a few moments, a tall, thin man opened the door.

"What is it, Neumann?" he asked.

"Sorry, Herr Adler, but I caught this one stealing my chickens. I would be very appreciative if you could take her off my hands."

"Excellent! We finally caught one," Adler announced, grabbing Anna by the collar. "I'll take it from here. Thank you, Neumann."

Adler pulled Anna inside the house and closed the door in Neumann's face. He pushed her into a small room and sat her on a chair opposite his large wooden desk. He positioned himself on the other side of the desk in an oversized leather chair.

"Have you seen any Russians in the forest?" he asked.

She shook her head.

"Probably a good thing," he continued. "They would have ripped you apart, those heathens. What's your name?"

Anna hesitated, unsure whether she should tell him her

real name. "Anna Kogut. From Poland," she said, realizing it probably didn't matter.

He moved a large pistol from a pile of paper folders on his desk, shuffled through them, and pulled one out. He read the papers inside it, then said, "Yes, this is you, young lady. Wanted by the Weimar police for illegally leaving her place of employment."

"I had to leave. My master was abusive," she said.

"That's not how they feel. It says here that you've already been sentenced and that I must take you directly to Ravensbrück. Any expenses to be paid by the Weimar police."

"What's Ravensbrück?"

"I've never heard of it, but I guess it's a female prison near Berlin. It's a six-month sentence, so I guess you'll get to know it pretty well."

"Six months?" she yelled.

"Don't you raise your voice in my office!" he shouted. "Law is law, and we must obey it."

"But I didn't even have a trial or a lawyer," she argued.

Adler laughed, then said, "Who do you think you are? You're not a German citizen. You're just a slave. Plus, we don't have enough people to process all the infractions by all you foreigners. None of you know any discipline. You should thank God the Almighty that it's not a hanging."

Anna didn't want to cry and show weakness, but the tears came anyway. Her life had just gone from bad to worse, and her chances of ever seeing Filip had vanished into the thin mountain air.

"Crying is not going to help you, young lady," he said, getting up from his chair. "C'mon. I must lock you up in a cell until we leave tomorrow morning. Try to get some rest tonight. You'll need it."

He shoved her inside a small windowless room and locked the door behind her. She sat on a cot, the only piece of furniture, and stared at the darkness. There was nothing else she could do. She was now a prisoner.

Filip stood at the roll call square and watched as thousands of prisoners gathered, much more than usual. He noticed that prisoners from both day and night shifts, and from all barracks and work units, were there. The square usually held no more than a couple thousand at a time, but now there were probably more than fifty thousand prisoners and several hundred SS guards stuffed together shoulder to shoulder.

Something is wrong, he thought.

"They're gonna bomb us all to hell," said Beniek, who stood next to him.

Filip had the same thought exactly. All these men conveniently gathered in the same spot? If the Allies were getting near, dropping bombs on the prisoners would be the quickest way to kill them and destroy all evidence at the same time.

"The guards are still here," Filip pointed out, trying to convince himself not to panic.

"Hitler wouldn't think twice to sacrifice a few hundred Nazis to kill fifty thousand undesirables."

"I hope you're wrong."

Then Camp Commandant Pister walked up the stairs to the gallows at the front of the square and put a megaphone to his mouth.

"Prisoners of Buchenwald!" Pister shouted, his voice booming like that of a god. "Today is a sad day for Germany.

Yesterday, several traitors and terrorists attempted to murder our Führer, Adolf Hitler."

A collective groan rumbled through the crowd. Prisoners turned to each other with shocked faces, whispering their hopeful opinions.

"Hitler must be dead," said Beniek.

"Then the war must be over," said Filip. "Are they letting us go?"

"SHUT UP!" one of the SS officers shouted somewhere nearby.

"QUIET!" Pister bellowed, and complete silence fell upon the prisoners again. "Our Führer has dedicated his life to serving our Reich and us, its children. Germany would still be a slave to France and England for losing the Great War if not for him. Fortunately, he is blessed by God himself and was unharmed. He gave a radio proclamation earlier today and promised to continue his work for the German people."

Another groan came over the crowd, but a different one this time—more of disappointment. Whispers again broke out all over.

"Fuck!" Beniek swore under his breath. "That fucker is like a cockroach. You can't kill him."

"SHUT UP! SHUP UP!" screamed the SS guards.

"Now!" Pister shouted. "To celebrate our Führer's life, let's have a minute of silence. This, and our daily hard work, is how we pay respect to him and what he has done for our country."

Pister turned off his megaphone and lowered his head. A hush slowly came over the crowd as everyone reluctantly followed his direction. The prisoners and guards stood in silence, with only occasional barks from the dogs.

"Heil Adolf Hitler!" Pister said finally. "Go back and honor our great leader through your work!"

The crowd dispersed. Filip and Beniek marched toward the dog kennel.

"This is bullshit!" said Beniek. "We'll never get out of this damn place."

"At least we're not dead," said Filip.

"Is Buchenwald better than death?"

Filip wasn't sure anymore. Was living in purgatory better than being dead? Every day, more prisoners arrived, and every prisoner had less food to eat. He was so weak he could barely walk. Only skin hung from his bones. The crematorium couldn't keep up with all the bodies they had to burn each day. The SS were on edge and trigger-happy. What was the point? He started to regret hope because it was the only thing keeping him alive. The hope of seeing Anna again. The hope of going back to Poland. These were bitter, bitter hopes.

"They say the Allies landed in Normandy," he said, trying to convince himself to keep putting one foot in front of the other.

"Hitler will never let them enter Germany," said Beniek. "And he'll keep us slaving away until we die."

"That's why Ciepielowski is preparing a rebellion," said Filip, feeling the poison for the dogs hidden in his shoe.

They joined a group of prisoners and their commanding SS officer, Sergeant Schmidt, who walked them through the main gate. The SS guarding the entrance often searched random prisoners but never the kennel work unit. Filip knew of Schmidt through Sig and suspected the guards were afraid to bother him. He was very well-connected and ran a massive racketeering scheme. Filip also tried to avoid him since it was never a good idea to get yourself noticed by the SS.

Filip and Beniek passed the gate and walked toward the kennel, a one-story building just outside the camp's electrified fence. As soon as they entered the building, they rushed off to their task of feeding the animals, forty dogs in total, each in its separate stall. It was one of the worst jobs at the kennel because the dog food was better than what they served the prisoners—usually something meat-based—so it took a great effort not to eat it and to avoid the guards thinking they had. On top of it, the dogs barked at them ferociously from behind the bars, flashing their evil smiles of white fangs.

Other prisoners tended to different tasks, such as cleaning and upkeep, but none of those tasks were easy. Several SS guards watched like hawks, including Sergeant Schmidt, who made his rounds about every half hour. Even the most minor mistakes were punished with often deadly beatings.

"Tell me when you're ready to hide the poison," said Beniek when nobody was paying attention to them.

Their task was to stash the poison until later, when the dogs would have to be killed. They had already hidden several bags, but they had another batch today.

"I'm ready," said Filip.

They walked inside a large industrial kitchen, where all the food was prepared for the dogs. It was empty, so they rushed to their hiding spot on the floor. Beniek lifted a large ceramic tile while Filip took the bags of poison out of his shoes.

"You might want to hide it somewhere else," Schmidt said behind them.

Beniek nearly dropped the tile on Filip's hands as they swung around in a panic. Filip hid the bags of poison behind his back.

Schmidt stood calmly, hands crossed over his chest, staring at them through his professorial glasses. Filip wanted to explain himself, quickly making up lies about special nutrients for the dogs. But prisoners were not allowed to speak to SS officers, so he said nothing.

"It's all right," said Schmidt. "I know who you are, Filip. I don't know how you switched your prisoner number because I distinctly remember 131124 when I got you moved from the quarry to the forest trenches. Either way, you're safe with me. You can talk to me."

Filip shook his head in protest, but Schmidt seemed so sure of his identity that it seemed senseless to resist. Plus, how else would Schmidt know about the change in work units? Sig never told him, but it now made sense how Filip had been saved from the quarry and Hinkelmann.

"Yes, I'm Filip," he said.

"I don't care about what you're doing," said Schmidt. "But there will be an inspection of this facility tomorrow, and you will surely be discovered. They will shoot you and every other prisoner who works here from both shifts. I might get in trouble as well."

"I'm sorry, sir," said Filip. "We'll throw it in the drain."

"That won't be necessary. Just give it to me, and I'll hold onto it until you need it. Come on, give it to me."

His hands shaking, Filip handed his bag of poison to Schmidt. He still suspected a trap and that he would shoot them both, but Schmidt just put the bags inside his pocket and smiled.

"Remember this when the Allies take over the camp," said Schmidt. "Put in a good word for me. I'm tired of this war and of Buchenwald. I just want to go back to my old life of working in the bank and for Sig to go back to performing his terrible routine at the club. Those were the good days."

"Yes, sir," said Filip.

"Now, go back to your work and keep quiet about this," Schmidt said. Then he walked out of the kitchen.

Filip and Beniek looked at each other and hugged. They were still alive.

Hinkelmann stalked the Gustloff factory floor for months without finding any saboteurs. He shot several prisoner workers just as a warning, but there was no proof of any actual wrongdoing. He almost gave up hope until he ran into a familiar face, the butler named Sig, who'd sucked off Schmidt at his party.

Schmidt had hidden him at the infirmary, where Hinkelmann accidentally ran into him while he was looking for that Polish pig, Filip Wolny, whom he'd promised Frau Wolff to kill. Then Sig disappeared. Hinkelmann watched Schmidt for weeks, trying to get a lead, but found nothing. So, it wasn't Schmidt who'd moved Sig around the work units, Hinkelmann decided. But if it wasn't him, then who had? And why? How did a Jew manage to miss the transports to Auschwitz and stay alive in Buchenwald?

Hinkelmann suspected a grander scheme was in play and observed Sig for a few days before finally making his approach.

"Very clever," he said, sneaking up behind Sig without him noticing.

Sig jumped, startled. He took his cap off and lowered his eyes to the ground like all prisoners were supposed to around an SS officer.

"Number 154799, huh? What happened to your old number, Sig?" he asked, but he didn't get an answer. "Whoever is pulling your strings is very clever. But nothing is free in Buchenwald, so how did you pay for your new identity? Is Schmidt somehow involved? Is he paying for you? Or is there something else going on? Maybe both?" He waited a moment, but his patience ran out when Sig said nothing. "Answer me! It's an order!"

All the prisoners working nearby stopped what they were doing and ran off.

"I'm a simple machinist," Sig answered, keeping his eyes lowered to the ground but now fidgeting with his cap.

"You were also a butler from a famous French restaurant, according to Schmidt. Then, according to our records, Sig Blau is also a homosexual from that famous Berlin cabaret. So, who are you really?"

Sig didn't say anything.

"Do you know my theory on who you really are? I think you are a saboteur, perhaps a spy of some sort, sent to Buchenwald to disturb our efforts to get rid of the sorts of you."

"I'm just a simple Jew trying to survive," said Sig.

"Really? Then why are you dumping machine oil into the drain when nobody is looking? Why are you falsifying records of the tolerance measurements on the parts that you're machining? Why are you producing only five parts per day when you can make twenty?"

Sig turned pale, and tears welled up in his eyes.

Hinkelmann laughed, then said, "I've been watching you for many days, whoever you are. I can have you shot right now, and nobody would blink an eye. However, you can still save your life. Do you want to live?"

Sig nodded.

"Perfect! All you have to do is tell me who sent you here. I want the person in charge of the sabotage. Who is giving you orders?"

"There's nobody," Sig said. "It's just me."

Hinkelmann felt his blood pressure jump. He was sick and

tired of prisoners lying to him. He smacked Sig across the face. "You're a fucking liar! Tell me who's behind this!"

"I swear to God. I'm telling the truth."

Hinkelmann pulled his pistol out of the holster and pointed it at Sig's face. "I'm asking you for the last time. Who is giving you orders?"

Tears poured down Sig's face, and he began sobbing.

"TELL ME!" he screamed.

Yet Sig said nothing. He seemed resigned to dying.

Hinkelmann so badly wanted to pull the trigger and teach this Jew a lesson, but that would not get him back in good graces with Pister and the SS. He needed to destroy the whole underground organization, not just kill one useless Jew.

"Fine," he said, sliding the pistol back into the holster. "We can do this the hard way if that's what you prefer."

He grabbed Sig by the collar and dragged him outside into the parking lot, where two SS guards stood next to the goat—the infamous flogging device—which was his favorite form of torture. He appreciated its ingenious simplicity. It was just a low table with a box at its feet, but it was highly effective.

"Strap him in," Hinkelmann ordered.

The two goons grabbed Sig, who dug his feet in as soon as he saw the goat, and dragged him to it. Despite his screams of resistance, they locked his feet inside the box at the bottom and bent him over the table, holding down his arms and head.

Hinkelmann pulled Sig's pants and underwear down and stood behind him with a bullwhip. "Are you ready to tell me, or do you prefer that I first ruin for Schmidt your delicate white ass?" he asked.

"I don't know—" Sig pleaded.

SNAP! The whip cracked the air and sliced Sig's bottom

before he could finish his sentence. Hinkelmann smiled as Sig roared in pain like a wild animal.

"Don't fuck with me, Sig," he said. "I'll slice you up like butter if you keep lying."

Sig cried violently, like a child. This was the part Hinkelmann enjoyed the most—turning a grown man into a small child. They all eventually gave in to the whip, but he appreciated that Sig needed only one lash. It made him feel gleeful to possess such power over another man. He lifted the whip again and swung it in the air.

CRACK!

Sig howled in pain again, his voice breaking as if unable to find a pitch high enough to express the suffering.

CRACK!

CRACK!

CRACK!

Hinkelmann hit him again and again, over and over, sweating from the effort, until he realized Sig had stopped making any noises. He just lay motionless on the goat, his bowels emptied on his legs and pants. Hinkelmann lowered the bullwhip and tried to catch his breath. He noticed now the horror on the faces of the two SS guards. They were covered in blood and shit. He looked down and saw that so was he. How many times had he hit Sig? He'd lost count. Twenty could kill a man if the job was done right.

"Take him away," he said. "I never want to see this fucker again."

He didn't want to see Sig again because an overwhelming feeling of guilt had come over him. He hated it, but it happened every time he had an outburst of anger like this. He just wanted to forget it ever happened.

He needed a drink and a nap.

27

AUGUST 24, 1944

Filip and Beniek were shoveling dog feces onto a pile of manure outside the kennel when the sirens sounded. The SS had blasted these many times before, but nothing ever happened, so Filip just ignored it. It was a hot and humid day, the sun already at its peak, and his head pounded with a headache. The smell of the boiling dog shit made him dizzy and sluggish.

Then the roar of engines filled the sky. Dozens of dark planes moved slowly above, like little bugs crawling on the water's surface.

"Is that the Americans?" asked Beniek.

Filip had no way of telling from this distance. "Or the Germans flying to bomb the Americans," he speculated.

He was quickly proven wrong when the ground shook and giant explosions erupted near the SS barracks only a few hundred meters from them. Filip didn't know where to hide; a bomb could land anywhere, so he just dropped to the ground and covered his head. Beniek did the same next to him. They watched as tall plumes of smoke rose into the sky. Seconds later, the debris—wood, paper, bricks, and random other objects—fell all around them. A cloud of dust filled the air, blocking their view.

Moments passed, then more explosions—this time farther down, near the Gustloff factory. The ground shook with each explosion, dozens of them, one after another in quick succession.

Then silence. No noise at all. Not even the sound of birds. It was as if time and the Earth stood still.

Filip stood up. The dust cloud cleared, revealing a strange sight. To his left, beyond the electrified fence, the camp's prisoner barracks stood completely intact, unscathed by the bombing. But to his right, the world lay in ruins. Most of the buildings used by the SS, including the officers' villas and the factories, were destroyed. Some of them were burning.

Somehow, the Americans had managed to wipe out everything that mattered to the Nazis while keeping the prisoners unharmed. Of course, Filip knew many prisoners had probably died. Many of them worked at the factories and other SS facilities. He was lucky the kennel was so close to the prisoner barracks, or he might have been dead already.

Filip stepped forward, thinking the attack was over, but that was when another wave of bombs fell from the sky. These were different, however. Instead of piercing holes and collapsing buildings, the bombs exploded into an inferno of fire. He collapsed to his knees and watched in horror as all the areas that had been bombed before now turned into a sea of flames. He saw people, their clothes and hair on fire, run out of their hiding places, screaming madly and then collapsing to the ground like piles of burning coal.

Unlike the silence before, now the air was filled with

hissing noises and a strange smell, like that of a burning chemical compound Filip could not identify. It was as if a thousand red-hot irons had dropped into a thousand buckets filled with putrid water.

"Are we in hell?" asked Beniek, standing up.

Filip looked to his left and saw the prisoner barracks still standing intact, untouched by the bombardment.

"I think we're alive," he said.

The sirens sounded again. Then there was the shouting of the SS guards as they sprung to action. One appeared out of the kennel, pointing his rifle at them.

"Let's go!" he screamed. "To the fire brigade!"

Filip and Beniek looked at him, unsure if they still had to follow his orders now that his world was destroyed, but the rifle convinced them otherwise. They rushed toward the burning buildings, joining hundreds of other prisoners, all of them being pulled from their barracks. Someone handed them metal buckets, and the SS guards herded them toward what used to be the Gustloff factory.

They found only a burning skeleton of the building when they arrived. Hundreds of prisoners stood in lines, moving buckets filled with water from a nearby forest pond toward the fire. Prisoners dove to the ground from time to time as munitions exploded inside the factory. The SS guards, with their dogs, forced everybody back to work immediately, and the bucket chain continued.

"To the back," said Filip, pulling Beniek toward the pond.

They worked for many hours, until the night came, but the factory still burned. Exhausted, the prisoners began to slow their efforts. Even the guards lost their focus. They were mainly gathered near the factory, where they concentrated on rescuing their German comrades from the rubble.

"I'm leaving," said Beniek.

Filip looked around to make sure there were no guards. He didn't want another broken ankle. Then he stopped what he was doing and said, "What do you mean you're leaving?"

"Look around. There are no guards. All we have to do is sneak out into the forest and disappear. It'll be days before they realize we're gone. We'll be a hundred kilometers away by then."

Beniek was right. This was the opportunity they'd been waiting for—his chance to escape and see Anna again.

"C'mon, Filip. Come with me before it's too late," Beniek pleaded.

Filip dropped his bucket and said, "You're right. Let's go."

They crouched and ran alongside the pond's shore into the forest. Nobody seemed to be paying any attention to them. People were either too preoccupied with the fire or too tired to respond.

Filip was also tired, but the thought of freedom exhilarated him, and his legs somehow found the strength to churn forward. He followed Beniek through the thin brush for a few minutes, until they reached a dirt road.

"I think this leads to Ettersburg," said Beniek. "That's where they bring the building materials from. If we follow the road, we can find the town and then go on to Weimar, where we can catch a train back to Poland."

"I need to go back to Rotenburg to find Anna," said Filip.

"You do what you need to do, but you still have to find a train station. We can't stay around this area."

"Shouldn't we take the forest instead of the main roads?"

"It's too easy to get lost in the forest," said Beniek. "We'll walk all night and accidentally circle back to where we started.

The road is less safe but leads us to exactly where we need to go. We'll be fine traveling at night."

Filip knew Beniek was right, so he nodded in agreement, and they took off down the road, away from the glow of the burning Buchenwald.

They'd been running for only a few minutes when Filip noticed a strange object on the side of the road.

"Beniek, do you see that?" he said.

"Yes, I see it. Let's walk inside the forest, just in case," Beniek suggested.

They walked along the tree line until they got closer to the object. At first, Filip couldn't make out what it was, but then he gasped in horror when he realized what he was looking at.

Hanging on a cross, his body beaten and sliced to a pulp, was Sig.

"Oh, my dear Lord, have mercy on his soul," said Beniek, collapsing to his knees.

Filip's heart sank, but he moved closer and saw Sig's chest moving in shallow breathing.

"He's alive!" he said.

"Filip, look at his body," said Beniek. "He might as well be dead."

"He'll die for sure if we leave him here."

"What are you talking about? We can't take him with us."

Filip looked at Sig, his old friend, and made up his mind. "We need to take him to a doctor," he said. "I'm not letting him die out here. He pulled me from the quarry and saved my life."

"Are you mad? No German will help us. They'll arrest us immediately."

"Then I'll take him back to Ciepielowski. Whatever it takes."

"I'm not going back there for a dead man," said Beniek, walking away. "You're on your own."

"Beniek!" Filip yelled after him.

Beniek stopped and looked back.

Filip knew this might be the last time he'd ever see him. "Good luck, my friend," he said.

Beniek walked back and hugged Filip. Then he took off running.

Filip watched him for a moment, pondering whether he'd made the right decision. This might have been his last chance to escape Buchenwald and find Anna. Yet he couldn't imagine living his life in peace knowing he'd left Sig to die on this cross. He thought Anna probably wouldn't love a man like that and wouldn't want to live with a miserable one ridden with guilt.

He looked up at Sig and then went to work. The cross wasn't very tall—only the height of two men—and Sig was held up by rope around his ankles and wrists, so Filip first untied the rope around his ankles. He then climbed up and untied the rope at each wrist while holding Sig to make sure he didn't fall to the ground. When he was done, he lowered Sig gently to the ground.

"Sig, can you hear me?"

Sig mumbled something, but his voice was barely audible, as if he couldn't push air through his lungs. His eyes were closed, so it looked like he was talking in his sleep.

Filip lifted him onto his back, pulling Sig's arms over his shoulders to hold him in place. Sig's body was slack, and Filip had a hard time holding onto him, but he slowly walked back toward Buchenwald—back to the inferno.

~

Anna sat in her isolation cell, rocking her body wrapped in a straitjacket and trying to block the sounds of wailing women. She had already spent a month at Ravensbrück prison for women and one week in isolation for resisting the guards, but she still couldn't get used to the screams that went on all night. The woman in the neighboring cell had told her that most of the wailing was done by some famous opera singer who had gone mad, but she wasn't the only one. There was a chorus of them every night, like at some never-ending funeral. Anna had a hard time falling asleep; she would black out from exhaustion for a couple of hours, then wake again to the wailing. The same thing happened night after night, and she was now near her breaking point.

The lock slammed, and the door cracked open. Aunt Emma, the assistant to the head guard whose real name was Emma Zimmer, walked in. She was a short, older woman, maybe in her fifties, with wide, thin lips and intense blue eyes that seemed to shoot icicles whenever she looked at you.

"Wakey, wakey, princess," said Aunt Emma. "Time to see the boss."

Two other female guards walked in and untied Anna's straitjacket. They lifted her and dragged her out of the cell.

"Don't forget," said Aunt Emma, walking behind them. "One more infraction, and then you will go away. You know where. Just one way. Up the chimney."

Anna wasn't sure if it was true or just a rumor, but she'd heard from other prisoners that the SS burned people in the prison's crematorium, which seemed to billow smoke out of its large chimney on a daily basis. Perhaps they were just trying to scare her.

The guards threw her into a room where the head guard, Johanna Langefeld, sat behind a desk. She was a beautiful woman with long blond hair, full lips, and large blue eyes. However, just like the first time they'd met, chills ran down Anna's spine when Langefeld spoke in her cold, calculated style.

"Sit down, Miss Kogut," Langefeld ordered.

Anna sat on a metal chair across from the head guard. "What did I do?" she mumbled, unsure whether she was allowed to speak.

"Well, what haven't you done? That's a better question. I have a letter here from Frau Wolff accusing you of many things. She claims you stole from her and failed to perform your duties, for example. But that's nothing compared to you running away from her farm, which is illegal, and stealing from the farmers. All of that in itself is punishable by death."

"But I'm still alive," said Anna.

"Yes, indeed."

"Why?"

Langefeld smiled and said, "I like you. I don't think you've made too many good decisions, but you seem like a smart girl. So, I'll be honest with you if you promise to be honest with me. Deal?"

Anna didn't trust her but sensed a sincere ray of goodness in Langefeld. Plus, what did she have to lose? Things couldn't get worse for her, could they? So she nodded in agreement.

"Good," said Langefeld. "It's very simple, actually. The reason you're here is that they want us to find out about the Russians you cooperated with."

"I didn't cooperate with anybody," said Anna. "They tied me up."

"But you were with them for some days, correct?"

"Yes, but we were not friendly."

"Well, we need to know everything you learned from

them," said Langefeld. "The Soviets are at our borders, and we can't have them running around inside Germany, causing havoc for our troops building defenses. I expect that you Poles don't have much love for the Soviets, so I hope you can understand our concern. They're animals that have nothing but rape and stealing on their minds."

"They didn't seem different than the Germans," said Anna, immediately regretting it.

Langefeld's brows furrowed, and her facial muscles tightened. "I'm disappointed, Miss Kogut. God made our German nation great to be an angel of light among other nations. We gave you a job, fed you, and gave you purpose in life. Is this how you repay us?"

Anna needed to keep her mouth shut, but she was offended by the arrogance of yet another German woman. "Do you really think God exists?" she asked. "The same God that preaches equality, goodness, humbleness, and forgiveness? Do you think he would create so much hate, pain, suffering, and death? You're not an angel of light. You're an angel of death."

Langefeld stood up abruptly. "How dare you speak to me like that!"

"Have you read the Bible?"

"I read the Bible every day."

"Then tell me, where in the Bible does it say that it's acceptable to conquer, murder, and imprison fellow Christians? In fact, where does Jesus say it's all right to do that to any human being?"

Langefeld stared at her blankly, then said, "I don't have to prove anything to you. Guards!"

The door opened, and the two guards came back inside. They grabbed Anna by the arms and stood her up.

"Take her back to the bunker," said Langefeld. "Let's see if another week of isolation will refresh her memory."

As they dragged her away, Anna wondered how much longer she could resist the cage. How long before she just sat in the corner and stared lifelessly at the world around her? How much isolation and how many more beatings would it take for her to stop resisting? How much longer before she gave up on seeing Filip again?

28

AUGUST 25, 1944

Filip watched as Ciepielowski tended to Sig's battered body. With the benefit of daylight, he now saw the full extent of the injuries. Among dozens of open wounds from the bullwhip, there were also swollen bruises all over Sig's face and burns on his toes and fingers. Dried-up blood covered the rest. Filip could only imagine the damage inside Sig's body. Whoever did this to him had taken his time and enjoyed it.

"Will he live?" he asked.

Ciepielowski shook his head while stitching closed one of the wounds. "I don't think so. It will be a miracle if he does. That's if the SS don't find him here first."

"Can't you hide him?"

"I can only do so much. I'll have to switch his identity with another prisoner who died this morning, but the Nazis are not completely dumb. I might have only a couple of days to hide him. But if whoever put him on that cross finds him missing, the first thing he will do is come looking for him here. We're the only infirmary within a thirty-kilometer radius."

"Can't you hide him somewhere else?"

"Where? There's nowhere to hide in Buchenwald for someone in his condition. Plus, he will need constant care."

"So, what do we do?"

"Pray," said Ciepielowski. "That's all you can do."

"I'll stay here and take care of him then," Filip offered.

"No, I can't hide you both. You have to go to the roll call. They've been counting the survivors all morning. If they don't find you, they'll assume you tried to escape and will go after you until you're dead."

"I can't go back to the kennel. It's torture. Maybe I can escape again and try to catch up with Beniek. There's still chaos out there."

"Forget Beniek," Ciepielowski urged. "You'll get shot by the sentries in the daylight. It's a certain death. Go back to your barracks and try to survive. We just got word that the Americans liberated Paris, so it's a matter of time before they arrive here."

Filip wasn't so sure. It seemed impossible that Hitler's massive armies would let anyone on their soil. Nevertheless, Ciepielowski was probably right about the window being closed on the escape. The SS were quickly reorganizing, and he'd barely been able to sneak back into camp with Sig.

"Thank you, Doctor," he said. "I will be back to check on Sig."

Filip left the infirmary and snuck back to the roll call plaza, where all the camp's prisoners were gathered, standing shoulder to shoulder in their thousands. Just like him, many were straggling in, lots of them injured by the bombing or the fight to put out the fires. The SS guards and their dogs were in bad shape too, but their zeal for order prevailed, and they lashed out at the prisoners for the slightest violations.

The SS officer standing on top of the gallows yelled out each prisoner's number individually through the megaphone, and every time he didn't get a response, the SS guards and the kapo of each barrack scrambled to find the prisoner. There were many missing, so the process took forever. They stood in the plaza for many hours, some prisoners passing out from exhaustion. They would be beaten back into consciousness and stood back up. It took Filip a tremendous amount of effort to maintain an upright position. It was a hot summer day, and it felt as if his body was melting into the ground like an old candle.

Then, as the day turned to night, the SS made them sing the Buchenwald song over and over again while they shined the searchlights on them from their guard towers.

> When the day awakes, before the sun laughs,
> the forest is filled with a thousand joys.
> We inmates of Buchenwald
> know it will be better someday.
> O Buchenwald, I cannot forget you,
> because you are my fate.
> Who leaves you, only he can appreciate
> how the freedom breathes.
> The rain beats the barrack's roof.
> We laugh as it hits us.
> We do not whine, we have but one cry,
> We want to be free from misery!
> O Buchenwald, I cannot forget you,
> because you are my fate.
> Who leaves you, only he can appreciate
> how the freedom breathes.
> Even when we are treated badly,
> we have to look life in the eye.

Hell has many names,
but we will not despair.
O Buchenwald, I cannot forget you,
because you are my fate.
Who leaves you, only he can appreciate
how the freedom breathes.

SS Sergeant Hinkelmann walked among the prisoners with his pistol drawn, daring them to move. He shot those who moved too much or had no strength to stand up. Filip felt him standing next to him at one point, but he never raised his head to look at him.

"Back straight! Head up!" screamed Sergeant Hinkelmann as he smacked Filip's stomach with a bamboo stick.

Filip lifted his head, seemingly heavier than a boulder. He did not dare look at Sergeant Hinkelmann, so he closed his eyes. He was not sure when Hinkelmann walked away.

Finally, the SS officer announced that 388 prisoners were killed in the bombing. Then Hinkelmann got up on the stage and said that 23 prisoners were shot while attempting to escape, and anyone else who tried would be hunted down and killed like a dog.

The prisoners were released and allowed to go back to their barracks. There would be no work this day. Filip dragged himself back to his bunk, wondering if Beniek was one of those who were shot. It seemed like they would hang the escapees on the gallows to make an example instead of shooting them and not showing the bodies. Then he passed out and dreamed about eating meat stolen from the guard dogs while Beniek stood over him and laughed.

Hinkelmann stood at attention as Pister paced his office. The camp commandant had been on edge since the bombing, his hands trembling and his voice hoarse. It was as if the Americans were about to enter the camp and he was scrambling for excuses or a way out.

"This is a fucking disaster, Hinkelmann!" Pister shouted. "What are we supposed to do now? Without the factory, all we're left with is fifty thousand useless mouths to feed. Who's going to pay for that?"

"Sir, if you allow me to speak . . ." said Hinkelmann.

"Go ahead. What is it?"

"Well, sir. This might be a blessing in the sky. No pun intended."

"How do you mean?"

"As you well know, sir, we're already thirty thousand over our twenty thousand capacity. We could lose half the prisoners to starvation and still have plenty left to do whatever jobs we need."

"Are you mad, Hinkelmann? They would start a rebellion if we didn't feed them. We can't fight them all if they decide to storm our positions. We can barely hold them in the camp now. Twenty-three of them escaped without a trace just last night. I'm sure more are planning the same as we speak."

"They're still scared of us, sir," said Hinkelmann. "I have twenty of my best men waiting in a truck outside. Just give me the order, and we'll hunt them all down and kill them right in front of this mob. That will keep them quiet for a while."

"I don't know," said Pister. "I need all the men I can get to keep guard on the camp. We already lost eighty men in the bombing."

"Please, sir. The fear will do the job of a thousand guards. Without it, we'll never have enough men to hold them back."

Pister sighed while staring out his window overlooking the camp. "Fine. Take your men and find them. But you better find them, Hinkelmann. You never found the ringleaders of the factory sabotage, so this is your last chance to prove yourself."

"Yes, sir!" Hinkelmann shouted, snapping his officer's boots in salute.

He ran downstairs, where a truck full of SS men stood waiting. He got inside the cab on the passenger side and ordered the driver to take off.

"Where to, Sergeant Hinkelmann?" asked the driver.

"Ettersburg," he said. "It's the closest town."

29
SEPTEMBER 12, 1944

Filip took a hit of the cigarette, held it in his mouth for a few moments, savoring the taste, and then blew the smoke into Sig's mouth. Sig inhaled it, closed his mouth, then swallowed and coughed.

Filip laughed and said, "You smoke like a five-year-old boy."

Sig spat out some phlegm and cleared his throat. "I don't know why you think this is relaxing. It's like trying to eat smoke from a campfire."

There was nothing else to do. They had been sitting around for weeks, waiting for the Nazis to give the prisoners something to do. With the factories destroyed, there was no point in doing anything. Most of the work now centered around clearing the debris and burying bodies, but there just wasn't enough to go around for all fifty thousand prisoners. It wasn't like they had much energy to do work anyway. Their food portions were cut in half, down to a quarter loaf of bread and a bowl of watery soup per day. The prices of food on the black market also skyrocketed. The prices of everything else, like cigarettes, tumbled because the prisoners were only interested in food. Not able to afford food and with Sig finally somewhat recovered from his injuries, Filip decided to at least enjoy cigarettes.

"What else can we do?" said Filip. "At least we're eating burned tobacco. There's nothing else."

"You should sell Anna's medallion," Sig suggested. "You could probably buy a loaf of bread with it."

"Forget it," Filip snarled. "That's all I have to remember her by."

"Don't you think she'd prefer that you survive rather than find your dead body with the medallion around your neck?"

"I said forget it. What about your friend Schmidt? Can't you get him to give us some food?"

Sig cleared his throat again and shifted his body. "He's not my friend."

"You ran his business for him, didn't you? I thought you were on good terms."

"He doesn't want anything to do with me anymore," said Sig.

"What do you mean? What happened?"

Sig shifted his body again. "I should probably tell you the truth."

"What are you talking about?" asked Filip.

Sig cleared his throat again. "Schmidt was my lover."

Filip didn't know what to say. Homosexuality was rampant in the camp since there were no women, but he'd never heard of a prisoner doing it with their SS overlords. This was a bit of a shock, especially since Sig had never given him any indication. They'd been friends for two years, and he never mentioned anything about being a homosexual.

"Did he make you do it?" Filip asked.

"No," said Sig. "We've been together for many years, even before the war."

Filip's jaw dropped. He couldn't believe it. His best friend for two years was a completely different person.

"I met him at my club, and we hit it off right away," Sig continued. "He kept it secret from his wife and everyone else. Then the Nazis came and started rounding up Jews and homo-sexuals. We had to survive, so he joined the SS, and we started a business. It was illegal, and I had to hide. But we bribed every-one, so the business was good. Then I got caught outside one time, and they arrested me. It was stupid. This one local policeman recognized me, and I wasn't wearing my Star of David. So Schmidt decided to follow me. He pulled a lot of strings and paid many bribes to get himself transferred to Buchenwald. We continued the business here until Hinkel-mann stole it from us and tried to kill me. Now he doesn't want to have anything to do with me."

"Why?" Filip asked, mostly to give himself more time to process the information.

"Have you seen my body?" said Sig, pulling his shirt up to reveal several ugly red scars. "He's repulsed by me. Plus, he's more worried about his own skin. He's probably trying to find his way out of Buchenwald before the Americans come."

"How come you never told me any of this before?"

"Why do you think? Would you still be my friend if I told you?"

Probably not, Filip thought. Not if he was being honest with himself. He'd never heard of homosexuality before coming to Buchenwald and would have been repulsed by the thought of it. He also would not want anything to do with any risky busi-ness like what Sig and Schmidt were involved in. Now, two years later, while he still didn't approve of homosexuality, he at least understood and accepted it as something that was part of this world. That risky business also saved his life by taking him out of the quarry work unit and providing extra food Sig brought to the barracks.

Filip understood now why Sig didn't tell him. He was glad for it. Otherwise, he would have never had the chance to become friends with one of the most decent men he'd ever met.

Then the sirens wailed, and the speakers blasted an announcement ordering everyone to gather at the roll call plaza.

"Let's go, my friend," said Filip, standing up and extending his hand to Sig.

Sig winced in pain as he stood up. "Here we go. They're gonna let us go."

"Or bomb us all to hell."

They walked to the plaza, where thousands more were gathering. Many were talking and pointing at the gallows, on top of which stood several SS officers, including Pister and Hinkelmann. Between them stood four prisoners, half naked and severely beaten. Filip stared at them for a while until he finally recognized one of them as Beniek. His muscles tensed, feeling the sudden urge to run up the gallows and pull Beniek to safety, but he remained frozen in place, knowing any attempt to help him would mean certain death.

"Is that Beniek?" asked Sig, realizing the same.

"There's nothing we can do," said Filip.

Then Hinkelmann stepped forward and put a megaphone to his mouth. "Prisoners of Buchenwald!" he shouted. Silence came over the crowd. "The war is not over, and Germany will be victorious. The German army is strong and will not allow foreign invaders on our soil. Just days ago, we launched a new weapon at the enemy, the V-2 rocket. It's an indestructible bomb that can fly hundreds of kilometers on its own without being shot down. And it can kill thousands of enemy soldiers in one strike. We have thousands of these rockets. All made here in Buchenwald, Dora, Ravensbrück, and many other labor camps across Germany."

The crowd whispered in simultaneous awe and despair. They had assumed the war was nearly over and that it was just a matter of days before the Allied troops showed up at the camp. This new development changed everything.

"Did you know about these rockets being built at the factory?" Filip asked Sig.

"I had no idea. We were making parts for their weapons, but they never told us what weapons exactly."

"Do you believe them?"

"I don't know," said Sig. "Hitler might have another trick up his sleeve, but the factory is destroyed, isn't it? How will they make these rockets now?"

"Silence!" Hinkelmann screamed at the crowd from the gallows. "Our Führer demands that the production at Buchenwald resume. Starting today, you will begin the rebuilding process. We have one month to restart production at the factory. You will have to work harder than you've ever worked to make this happen. And for those who think they can cheat and hide, here's a lesson for you," he said, pulling Beniek to the front while taking out his pistol.

Beniek stood up straight, apparently sensing his opportunity. He scanned the crowd and shouted, "You may murder us by the millions, but we will win. It will be our turn yet!"

Then Hinkelmann shot him. A cloud of blood exploded out of his brain, and Beniek's body fell off the gallows like a limp mannequin.

"Anyone thinking of escaping or not following orders will be executed!" Hinkelmann shouted through the megaphone.

Tears streamed down Filip's face, and Sig whimpered as they watched Hinkelmann shoot the other three prisoners. Complete silence came over the crowd. Any hope the prisoners might have had of their Buchenwald nightmare ending fizzled like air out of a balloon.

Hinkelmann stood victoriously over the crowd and shouted, "Now, let's get back to work! Tables have been set up behind me to register you for new work units. We are looking for bricklayers, carpenters, and machinists. Line up now!"

The prisoners lined up behind twenty tables like sheep waiting to enter their pen. Filip stared at Sig's weakened body and wondered what else they would have to do to survive. With less food, more work, and the winter months ahead, they would need a miracle.

The guard pushed Anna inside the room and locked the door behind her. She stood there, scanning the room, which had a desk, two chairs, and a metal cabinet. There was no window, and a single light bulb on the ceiling gave very little light, making the room look sinister. It also smelled like cleaning chemicals combined with feces, perhaps one trying to camouflage the other. The stench seemed to come from a bucket of watery, reddish liquid standing next to the desk. Then she noticed red stains on one of the walls.

But before she could investigate, a man in a dark-green flannel suit walked in through a door on the other side of the room. He was a tall, handsome man despite his receding hairline and grimace of disdain, which seemed to foretell bad things to come. He closed the door behind him, placed a short leather whip on the desk, and sat in one of the chairs.

"Sit down, Miss Kogut," he said with the calm of a gentleman asking a woman to sit across from him at a coffee shop on their first date.

Anna sat in the chair on the other side of the desk and put her hands together on her lap to stop them from shaking. She had a bad feeling about this man, and her mind frantically searched for escape options.

"My name is Ludwig Ramdohr, and I'm the chief Gestapo inspector at Ravensbrück," he continued, opening a folder with several documents inside. "I understand that you unlawfully escaped from your assigned place of work and then spent many days with several Soviet POWs sabotaging our farms. Is that correct?"

"I don't know of any sabotage," she said as calmly as possible so she wouldn't upset him. "We were hungry, and I stole a couple of chickens. Nothing else."

"Those chickens were meant for hungry German soldiers," said Ramdohr. "Therefore, you sabotaged the efforts of our nation to defend us against the Bolsheviks—those blood-sucking communists. What else did you and the Soviets do?"

"Nothing else. I swear!" Anna implored. "We were just trying to survive."

"Did you see them making any maps? Did they have a radio?"

"No! I don't know. I didn't see anything."

"Miss Kogut," said Ramdohr, picking up the leather whip with his right hand. "You leave me no choice."

KNOCK! KNOCK! KNOCK!

The urgent sound came from the door Anna had entered through.

"Who is it?" asked Ramdohr, frowning with irritation.

"It's Langefeld," said the woman on the other side of the door.

"I'm not to be interrupted," he said.

"It's urgent. Open up, please!"

Ramdohr grunted but got up and walked over to the door. "This better be important," he said as he swung it open.

Langefeld didn't wait for the invite and barged right in. "You're violating the prison protocol, Lieutenant Ramdohr," she said.

"I'm in the middle of interrogation—"

"That's the problem, isn't it?" she said. "You pulled a prisoner from my isolation cell and are interrogating her without my approval."

"Frau Langefeld—"

"Head Guard Langefeld."

"Sorry, Head Guard Langefeld," he said, seemingly intimidated by her assertiveness, "but we don't have any more time. She's been here for weeks, and we still don't know anything about the Soviets roaming our mountains. The Soviet army is at the German borders, and we need to know if they're planning any sabotage actions. I am taking over this prisoner's interrogation, whether you like it or not. Gestapo has the overriding authority in this prison camp."

"Not without the proper paperwork it doesn't." Then Langefeld turned to Anna and said, "Get up!"

Anna stood up slowly, unsure if this would get her in trouble with Ramdohr.

"I will file a complaint," he threatened.

"C'mon, prisoner! Let's go! I don't have all day," the woman yelled at Anna, who staggered toward the door. Langefeld turned to Ramdohr and said, "I look forward to discussing your complaint with the camp commandant. I'm sure he'll be happy to hear about your complete lack of procedural professionalism in his camp."

Langefeld grabbed Anna's arm, and they walked out, leaving Ramdohr stunned into silence. They walked down a long corridor until they reached an open cell. Langefeld pushed her in.

"Thank you," said Anna.

"It's not about you. We must have order," Langefeld said and shut the door.

Anna didn't believe her. Something in Langefeld's eyes said something else. Or maybe Anna just wanted to believe there was some good in Langefeld's heart. Either way, she was safe from Ramdohr—at least for now.

30

JANUARY 5, 1945

Filip shook violently from the extreme cold despite being huddled with Sig and five other prisoners in a corner of an unfinished building. The chill permeated his prison uniform, then soaked into the emaciated flesh and into his bones. The Nazis had run out of building materials a few months earlier and out of coke and other heating materials about four weeks before, so there was nowhere to hide from the cold. Even their barracks were unheated, and Filip often awoke with frost in his hair.

The Germans were determined to rebuild the factory, but as the outside visits by Nazi officials subsided and the news of the approaching Allies increased, the SS guards lost their enthusiasm for pushing the prisoners. They still sent them to work on rebuilding what had been destroyed by the Allied bombing in August, but the prisoners had no materials to finish the job or to warm themselves, nor did they have any food to keep their spirits up. It was as if the Nazis were purposefully sending them out there to either starve or freeze—usually both.

"We're gonna die, Filip," said Sig, his voice trembling from the cold.

Filip couldn't deny the possibility and was too tired to find encouragement, so he said nothing.

"We need to sell that medallion," Sig suggested with irritation.

"No," Filip replied. He understood why Sig was upset and wasn't mad at him. Buchenwald's prisoners got easily irritated. "If I give up the medallion, there's no hope. I will have no more hope."

Sig looked at Filip but said nothing. They both knew having hope was more important than having food.

Then the bell rang to end their shift. It was time to return to the barracks and get their last meal of the day—probably some watery soup.

"I have an idea," said Filip.

"What is it?"

"C'mon, let's go!"

Together with thousands of other prisoners, they walked back to their barracks. Bodies lined the road, and many others dropped dead on the way. Stacks of bodies also lay in front of each barracks—those who had died in their sleep. Filip stopped in front of one of those stacks.

"What are we doing?" asked Sig.

Filip lifted one of the corpses that looked recently deceased. The man must have died less than an hour before because he'd barely turned pale. His eyes were still open, and he had a smile on his face. Perhaps one of his last thoughts was about his home or family.

"I'm not a corpse carrier, Filip!" Sig protested.

"Do you want to live or not? I'm doing this with or without you."

Sig grumbled but grabbed the dead man from the other side and swung one of the arms around his shoulders.

"Now what?" asked Sig.

"Let's get in line," said Filip.

Filip and Sig dragged the body to the food line, where Sig finally understood. He smirked at Filip.

"You're smarter than you look," said Sig.

When they reached the front of the line, the SS didn't even blink. Most of the prisoners in the camp looked half dead anyway, so they gave the dead man his portion of food. Overjoyed to score extra food, Filip and Sig had turned to go back to their barracks when a figure in a black SS uniform blocked them.

"There you are," said Hinkelmann.

Filip's heart stopped. Sig dropped his bowl of soup.

"Drop the dead guy and come with me," Hinkelmann ordered, marching off toward a nearby storehouse.

The sea of prisoners parted as Hinkelmann walked. Sig and Filip followed in his wake, leaving the dead guy lying on the ground among many other corpses scattered around the camp. Thinking this might be his last meal, Filip drank his soup, sharing half with Sig as they walked. Neither one dared to speak. Filip could only ponder the many different ways Hinkelmann could kill them. He hoped for a quick death.

They entered a storehouse and followed Hinkelmann into a small room, where he closed the door behind them.

"I'll get straight to the point," said Hinkelmann, slowly pulling off his black gloves as if preparing to bludgeon them to death with his bare hands. "I have a deal for you."

Filip and Sig looked at each other in utter confusion because those were the last words they expected to hear from him. Filip couldn't imagine what Hinkelmann planned to propose. Other than Anna's medallion, he possessed nothing to offer in exchange.

"I'm sure you're wondering why you're still not dead," Hinkelmann continued. "I'm surprised myself, to be honest. I've been hunting you two assholes for months and dreamed about shooting both of you in the head. However, when I stumbled upon you in the food line, I had an epiphany. Would you like to hear it?"

Filip and Sig nodded. Filip didn't want to speak for fear of a trap, and he saw in Sig's eyes that he felt the same way. Neither one of them seemed to comprehend what was happening.

"Perfect!" Hinkelmann proclaimed. "What occurred to me is that we just might be able to help each other. You see, it's just a matter of time before the Americans or the Soviets get here. Then I'll need some kind of an escape plan. Since you two somehow managed to survive inside this camp by changing your identities, I want you to do the same for me. I want to sneak out of here as one of the prisoners with a completely new identity and live the rest of my life in peace. What do you say?"

Filip now understood. Hinkelmann hadn't killed them only because it benefited him not to. All they had to do was find a way to let this monster live out the rest of his life without any consequences for what he had done at Buchenwald.

"And what do we get in return?" asked Sig.

Hinkelmann laughed, stepped closer to them threateningly, and said, "Suddenly, the Jewish swine speaks as soon as there's something in it for himself. Fair enough, I expected you to want something in return. It's simple: Your reward is that I won't kill or torture you. Just your lives in return, that's all. Which, by the way, I could take easily. I can shoot you right now, and nobody would even ask me why. I mean, I would be breaking promises to a certain lady, which would be a tremendous hit to my reputation. But I'm willing to live with that."

"What promises?" asked Filip.

Hinkelmann searched his breast pocket, fished out a pack of cigarettes, lit one up, and blew smoke into Filip's face. "First, I'll have to break a promise to Frau Wolff that I would torture you until eternity, Filip Wolny. I have no idea what she sees in you, honestly, but you must've had quite an impact for her to be so vicious. But, worst of all, Sig Blau, I'll have to break my promise to our Führer to kill every Jew in Germany. He is going to be very, very disappointed in me."

Filip was shocked by all of it, but most of all by Hinkelmann calling them by their names. The SS always called prisoners by their numbers, with no exceptions. The fact he used their real names made his offer feel real. He wasn't bluffing. He wasn't going to pull out his pistol and shoot them in cold blood. Filip believed Hinkelmann. The question was, could they help him? Ciepielowski was the one who'd helped them assume new identities. Would he agree if they asked him to help hide an SS monster like Hinkelmann?

"We'll do it," said Sig before Filip could decide what to do.

"Perfect!" Hinkelmann announced, extending his hand. "It's a deal!"

Filip watched Sig shake Hinkelmann's hand, then reluctantly did the same. He felt dirty, as if he had just signed a deal with the devil. But, at the same time, he would perhaps live another day.

Maybe he would get to see Anna after all.

Johanna Langefeld kneeled in front of the altar, made a sign of the cross, and began her prayer. She started with her standard Hail Mary but found herself just mouthing the words without emotion.

Instead of connecting to the higher power, like she always tried to do, she couldn't stop thinking about the young woman from Poland—Anna Kogut—and what she'd said to Langefeld about God. Her words stung more than she had expected. They confirmed what she'd felt for a long time: that she wasn't helping people as a head guard.

When she first joined the German prison system, she felt it was her calling to help women get on the right path. But now, all she was doing was helping the Nazis murder innocent people. Most of the female prisoners at Ravensbrück were not criminals. They were just innocent foreigners brought to Germany to slave in the factories feeding the Nazi war machine, which was built to kill more people. This went against everything she believed in as a Christian, and she had to do something about it. She could not go on like this anymore.

Langefeld crossed her heart and stood up. She stared for a moment at the statue of the compassionate Virgin Mary, then walked over to the front pew, where her seventeen-year-old son, Herbert, sat yawning. She would normally scold him, but it was seven a.m., and the church was empty, so she decided to forgive him this time. Some people said she spoiled him, her only child, but she just couldn't resist his tousled blond hair and brown puppy-dog eyes. She thought he was a good boy who followed her orders without complaining, even if it meant stopping at the church every morning before going to school.

"Are you ready?" she asked.

"Yes, Mother," he complied.

They got up and left the church. It was a cold winter day, and the snow crunched under their boots. Fortunately, with her salary as the head guard at Ravensbrück, she could afford warm wool coats and hats for both of them. Things had not been easy since her husband, Wilhelm, passed away ten years earlier, and she appreciated her new job and its financial benefits, including free housing and schooling for her son. She prayed for things to stay the same in the future, even with the Allied forces pushing against the western border of Germany.

"Mother?" asked Herbert.

"Yes, son?"

"I was wondering. Some boys were talking . . ." He stopped, twitching nervously.

"What is it, Herbert?"

He cleared his throat and said, "I'm thinking about joining the army."

Langefeld stopped and turned to her son. "Don't you even think about it!" she yelled. "I didn't sacrifice my life to raise you just to have you killed in the war."

"But, Mother, our country is under attack," he said. "Our Führer needs us."

"I don't want to hear it. You're still only seventeen and in high school. You don't even qualify to join the army."

"I can join the national militia," Herbert pleaded. "You can join at sixteen."

"Forget it!" she yelled, walking away from him.

They walked in silence until they reached the school.

"Have a blessed day, son," said Langefeld, kissing Herbert on the cheek. "We'll talk more at home."

"Yes, Mother," he said, then walked inside the school.

She trudged through the snow toward the concentration camp, disappointed with herself for getting angry at Herbert.

As a head guard at Ravensbrück, she was known for always staying calm and collected, but it was different with her son. He was all she had in her life. He *was* her life. She used to believe in the Führer and wanted to help make Germany great again, but losing her son was a price she was never willing to pay.

When she finally arrived in the office and took off her winter coat, it was already eight a.m., and a stack of papers sat on her desk, waiting to be addressed. She grabbed the first one from the top and marched toward the office of the camp commandant, SS Major Fritz Suhren. She already knew the outcome of this meeting but knocked on his door and walked in before hearing an invite anyway.

"Ah, Frau Langefeld," said Suhren from behind his desk, even though she had asked him many times to address her by her official title of Oberaufseherin. He was a tall, slim man with a mop of blond hair. He was only in his late thirties and had the disposition of a bartender, but he'd proven many times over that he was not to be trusted. "You're punctual as always. Please have a seat. I'm just finishing up with Edmund."

By the window stood SS Lieutenant Bräuning, the adjutant to Suhren. He was an older man, probably in his late fifties or maybe even early sixties, but he was dating Dorothea Binz, one of the younger female guards under her command, and flirted with all the other guards like a dirty old man. He'd even taken several passes at Langefeld.

"Are you sure?" asked Bräuning.

"Yes, of course," said Suhren. "Frau Langefeld should know about this."

"Know about what?" she asked.

"Well," said Suhren. "We have an order from Reichsführer-SS Himmler to build a gas chamber here at Ravensbrück. I'm told he believes the prisoner population has grown too large, and we need to find faster ways to liquidate. You worked as a head guard at Auschwitz, Frau Langefeld, so perhaps you can advise us on implementing such a process."

Langefeld shuddered at the memory of Auschwitz. She'd been sent there to run the female part of the camp but had asked to be reassigned back to Ravensbrück as soon as she realized that Auschwitz's commandant, SS Lieutenant Colonel Rudolf Höss, didn't want to listen to any of her advice on how to run a proper prison for women and simply wanted to turn the camp into a murder factory.

"I'm afraid that's beyond my level of expertise," she said, trying to avoid appearing uncooperative.

"That's what I'm trying to tell you, Fritz," said Bräuning. "We don't have anyone who knows how to build and run a gas chamber."

"So, you want me to defy Himmler's direct order?" asked Suhren.

Bräuning cleared his throat and said, "Of course not."

"Then what do you suggest?"

"I suggest you get somebody else for the job."

"Fine," said Suhren. "Then I want your letter of resignation and you out of here within an hour. I don't want to see your face ever again. Understood?"

"Fritz—"

"SS Major Suhren to you. And if I were you, I would catch the earliest train out of town before I write a letter to Himmler about how you refused his direct order. You're dismissed."

Bräuning glanced at Langefeld, looking for help, but she turned away and said nothing.

"Heil Hitler!" Bräuning said, saluting, then left the room.

"What can I do for you, Frau Langefeld?" asked Suhren.

"I actually have a solution to your population problem, Major Suhren," she said. "I have a list of prisoners here whose sentences have expired and who are due for release. The first one is Anna Kogut—"

"Stop with the nonsense," Suhren said. "You've been asking me for releases every day for months now, stubbornly following the procedure, but you already know your request is denied. These prisoners are here to work in the local factories, and none are to be released."

"But, sir, we have plenty of workers. The rest are dying of freezing cold and hunger, and now you're talking about spending money to simply kill them in a gas chamber. I just don't understand the logic."

"You're not here to think, Frau Langefeld. Neither am I, for that matter. We're here to follow orders. And that's exactly what I intend to do."

"Sir, I have not seen any official orders to keep prisoners here past the expiration of their sentence," she pushed.

"The orders don't have to be written," he said. "I'm interpreting verbal directions from the SS command in Berlin. Don't you think they would order me to release prisoners if that's what they wanted instead of ordering me to build a gas chamber?"

Langefeld realized it was pointless trying to convince Suhren to do the logical and humane thing. He was an SS officer through and through, and he would do whatever possible to please Himmler and advance his career.

"Understood, sir," she lied. "I'm sorry for bothering you again about this."

"You're dismissed, Langefeld," he said, looking through his desk's documents.

"Heil Hitler!" She saluted and left his office.

She closed the door behind her and stared at the empty desk of Suhren's secretary, Aunt Emma, who was always sleeping on the job and whom Langefeld purposefully assigned to this position just to annoy Suhren. Langefeld remembered Anna Kogut, the young woman who'd lost her religion after years as a slave laborer in Germany, and felt an impulse to help her. Maybe it was God speaking to her, or maybe she just wanted to spite Suhren. But she decided to do it.

Langefeld walked behind the secretary's desk, took Suhren's official stamp, and imprinted it on Anna's release order. She then faked Suhren's signature, which she'd seen a thousand times, and ran down the hallway.

Bräuning was packing in his office when she found him.

"What else does he want?" he asked, frightened to attention.

"I'm not here for him," she said. "I need a favor."

"Why should I help you? You didn't help me in there with his ridiculous gas chamber idea."

"What did you expect me to say, Edmund? I can't afford to lose my job."

He waved his hand dismissively and said, "What do you want, Langefeld?"

"I need you to take a prisoner back to her farm," she said, handing the release document to him. "It's signed by Suhren."

"I don't work for him anymore. Why would I do this?"

"You're not doing it for him. You're doing it for me. Also, remember that your girlfriend, Dorothea, works for me. I can be extra nice to her."

He took the document reluctantly and looked it over. "Fine, I'll do it. Rotenburg is on my way home to Frankfurt anyway."

"Thank you, Edmund. I'll meet you at the gate," she said and walked off.

"You better do something for Dorothea!" he yelled after her.

She ran back to her office, put on her boots and jacket, and went outside. Freezing wind smacked her face as she exited the camp through the main gate. She then went out on the frozen lake next to the camp, where about twenty women worked, chipping the ice and collecting it for use in the prison morgue. A wooden shed stood nearby, where the guards hid from the cold with a campfire.

Langefeld entered without knocking. To her surprise, she found two male SS guards with their pants down and Dorothea Binz half-naked between the two.

"What the hell is going on here?" Langefeld screamed, turning away from the scene, appalled at its vulgarity.

"I apologize, Head Guard Langefeld!" yelled out Binz. "Just trying to keep warm."

Langefeld turned back when the clasping of belt buckles subsided. "You might want to make the fire bigger instead of whoring with every man in town, Binz."

Binz was a tall blond woman in her twenties with voluptuous breasts and buttocks that seemed to attract men like flies, and she made sure to treat every one of them with honey. She was already sleeping with old Bräuning and probably four other officers, but she apparently wasn't above doing it with regular soldiers too.

"Yes, ma'am," said Binz.

"I'm reassigning you to be Suhren's secretary. Aunt Emma will take your place."

"Ma'am, isn't that a promotion?"

"It's a favor I'm doing for Bräuning," she said. "He was let go by Suhren and was asked to leave the camp within an hour."

"Thank you, ma'am," said Binz. "Why is Bräuning being let go, ma'am?"

"You can talk to him about that yourself. Right now, I need you to bring me Number 125312. Her name is Anna Kogut, and she's being released today."

Binz seemed confused and wanted to ask a question but decided not to push her luck. "Yes, ma'am! Right away, ma'am!" she yelled and rushed out of the shed.

Langefeld glanced at the two guards with disgust and followed Binz out. As she got closer to the group of prisoners, she noticed that one of them wasn't working. Instead, the woman lay on the ice and was engulfed by it like an ice sculpture. She stared at the unfortunate creature, transfixed by the innocence on her face under such brutal circumstances, until two figures appeared before her.

"Reporting with Number 125312, ma'am!" Binz shouted.

"Why is she like this?" Langefeld asked, pointing at the frozen woman.

"Sorry, ma'am. She fell in a few days ago and froze in the lake before we could take her away. It's too difficult to pry her out, so I decided to wait until the lake thaws. It's a good reminder for the prisoners to work hard."

Langefeld looked at Anna Kogut's petite figure next to Binz, trying to read what Anna thought about this situation, but the prisoner's eyes pointed down, as was expected in the guards' presence.

"Binz, you order the prisoners to chip that poor woman out of the lake and burn her body in the crematorium. You're coming with me, 125312," she said, turning back toward the camp.

"Yes, ma'am! Heil Hitler!" said Binz. Then she ran off, shouting at the prisoners.

Langefeld, with Anna trailing behind, walked back to the

camp in silence until they reached the gate where Bräuning was already waiting.

"Here are her papers," she told one of the guards, showing him Anna's release document with the faked Suhren signature. "She's being released."

The guard nodded and went back to marching.

"Take this with you," she said, handing the document to Anna. "If anyone tries to arrest you, just show them the paper."

Anna lifted her eyes to Langefeld's, a look of puzzlement on her face. "You're letting me go?" she asked. "I don't know anyone else who was released."

"Yes. Your sentence has expired," said Langefeld, pointing at Bräuning. "That man will take you back to your farm. You stay there until the war is over. Then you go back home and find your God again."

Tears came down Anna's face. "Thank you," she said. "I will repay you for this one day."

"If you're lucky, you'll never see me again," said Langefeld.

"Let's go," said Bräuning. "The train leaves in forty minutes."

Langefeld pulled money out of her pocket and handed it to Bräuning. "Here's twenty marks for the fare and some food for her. I better not hear she never made it back, or you'll have to deal with me, Edmund."

Bräuning grabbed the money and pulled Anna away. Langefeld watched them for a while, trudging through the snow, Bräuning in his fur coat and elegant hat and Anna in her blue-and-white striped prison uniform.

She hoped God would fix this world soon so she would never have to see such things for the rest of her life.

31
APRIL 1, 1945

Filip lay on a straw mattress inside his bunk with Sig, Ciepielowski, and Hinkelmann. Work stopped in the camp with the sounds of American artillery only a few kilometers away, so both day and night shifts had to stay in the barracks at all times. All four levels of the bunks were stuffed with prisoners—about five hundred instead of the maximum two hundred and fifty the barracks were designed to hold.

"Pister will kill us all if we don't attack now," said Ciepielowski. "There's no way he's going to let us be taken by the Americans."

Ciepielowski told them prison camp leaders were somehow able to receive radio signals and were beginning preparations for an uprising. There were thousands of former Polish and Soviet soldiers imprisoned in Buchenwald, and they were itching for revenge. Filip was ready to join them if asked, even though he had no military training.

At the same time, the SS had begun to act differently, spending less time monitoring the camp and torturing its prisoners. They were all opportunists and, thus, experts at surviving and thriving in any situation. Most of them had gotten rich by ripping off prisoners and their own country, and now they were preparing for life without Hitler, trying to find ways to save their skins. The SS didn't change their attitudes toward prisoners; they were simply more disengaged. In fact, this made the prisoners worry because they feared the camp was inconvenient evidence of Nazi atrocities, and they might want to wipe it off Earth's surface.

"I don't believe that," Hinkelmann whispered, trying not to bring attention to himself and his new identity. He had grown a beard, had smeared his face with dirt, and wore the filthy uniform of a prisoner who died in the infirmary. "Pister doesn't have the balls. He'll maneuver his way around both Hitler and the Americans to make sure he doesn't get in trouble with either one."

"And what if you're wrong?" Ciepielowski pushed.

"I'm not wrong. But I have my trusty friend just in case," said Hinkelmann, patting his chest, where he carried a Luger pistol.

"Easy for you to say," said Ciepielowski. "What about the other prisoners who might be slaughtered? Maybe you're telling us lies on purpose so our resistance doesn't kill your SS buddies."

"Are you calling me a liar?" said Hinkelmann, his face red with anger. "If I wanted the SS feeling safe, I would have shot you already, Ciepielowski."

"Stop it, you two. Let's just see what happens," said Filip, trying to diffuse the situation. He'd wanted to expose Hinkelmann as soon as they hid him in the barracks two days earlier, but he followed them around with that Luger wherever they went. Filip had no doubt Hinkelmann would shoot them all for even the slightest hint of betrayal. But he also wanted to keep him around in case they needed his help to escape. Hinkelmann knew the SS security better than anyone, as well as all the roads and towns around Buchenwald. "It can't be too much longer before the Americans arrive."

"We'll starve before they come," said Ciepielowski. "They haven't fed us in two days and blew up the water pumps yesterday. People are starting to get desperate. They're running out of whatever they had stashed in their mattresses and uniforms."

The sirens went off. Everyone froze, looking up at the ceiling and listening. Then a deep rumble of plane engines filled the sky. Panic broke out among the prisoners because they all had terrible memories of the last bombing but also because there were rumors of the German air force bombing the barracks to kill all the prisoners and wipe out all evidence of the camp's existence.

Filip and everyone else streamed out of the barracks and into the wide-open roll call plaza, running away from the buildings, which were easy targets. However, instead of bombs, about twenty parachutes appeared from the sky, each carrying a tubular white container. The prisoners watched in awe until the containers hit the ground and the contents spilled all over the plaza. That was when the madness broke out.

Bread! The ground exploded with loaves of it, and thousands of prisoners madly dove after it.

Filip dove into the melee of prisoners, tearing at each other like animals. He was right in the middle of it when he saw Sig get kneed in the face and knocked out cold. Filip tried to get to him, but he was now under the pile, and he could only watch as others went through Sig's pockets and robbed him of every pathetic belonging he had.

Then thousands of leaflets fell on them like snow, and the SS started shooting. The prisoners ran back into the barracks while the guard dogs brutally tore at them. Filip finally got out from under the pile, stuffed a leaflet into his pocket, then grabbed Sig and dragged him back to the barracks.

Ciepielowski helped revive Sig and tended to Filip's multiple bruises from kicks and punches, but others weren't so lucky. Hundreds of prisoners lost their lives, scattering the roll call plaza with their bodies like seeds during planting. Only Hinkelmann and a few others in their barracks came out of it with some bread, which they had to share for fear of losing their lives. Filip only got a tiny morsel but saved it for Sig. He wondered how many more days it would have to last them.

"What does it say?" asked Hinkelmann, grabbing the leaflet from Filip's hand.

"I don't know for sure," said Filip. "It's from some kind of general."

"Paulus," said Hinkelmann, reading the leaflet. "The traitor that surrendered Stalingrad."

"What does he say?" asked Ciepielowski.

"It doesn't matter," said Hinkelmann.

"I think it says that Hitler is kaput and for the German soldiers to give up," said Filip.

"It's all lies. The Führer will never surrender," said Hinkelmann.

Filip hoped he was wrong.

Anna pulled the heavy metal ball attached to her right ankle with a chain and carried a bucket full of milk back to the house. After three months, her leg had grown stronger, and the ball didn't feel as heavy. But it still made escaping from Frau Wolff's farm impossible. The farthest she could travel without fatigue overtaking her was only a kilometer. She had a better chance at freedom by biding her time and waiting for the Americans to liberate her. Their guns were pounding the Germans night and day, so it had to be just a matter of time before they showed up in Rotenburg.

"Move it, you donkey!" yelled Frau Wolff, stepping out of the farmhouse. She waved around her late father's pistol, which she always carried in her hand as if it would make Anna drag the ball and chain any faster.

"I'm hungry," said Anna, setting the bucket of milk at the doorstep.

"What do you want *me* to do about it? We're down to one cow and two chickens, so you can drink a cup of milk. I have to collect the rest of it for the soldiers. The eggs are mine. The grain was all taken by the army, and the bakery shut down, so there's no bread. So, what would my Polish princess like me to serve her for breakfast?"

Anna expected this reply because she had received a similar answer the last few days, but it didn't make her feel less hungry. She was already stealing a cup of milk every day in addition to the one Frau Wolff allowed her to drink, but it wasn't enough to fill her stomach. The cellar was emptied of all the potatoes, carrots, and jarred preserves, and the spring hadn't yet produced any fruits or vegetables. Anna would have been dead already if it hadn't been for some dandelions and birch tree sap.

"I'm too weak," said Anna. "I can't work without food."

"You'll do what I tell you," said Frau Wolff, pointing the pistol at Anna's head.

Anna was about to shuffle off to the barn when a bicycle

rang its bell and a policeman appeared at the gate. His name was Zimmermann, and he was an older, large-bellied man responsible for their village.

"Good morning, Frau Wolff," said Zimmermann.

"Heil Hitler!" Frau Wolff said as she saluted.

He raised his hand in a salute but skipped the words. "Have you seen any foreign laborers passing by your farm?" he said instead. "We had a couple of them escape from the village yesterday."

"That's outrageous," said Frau Wolff. "Those damn pigs should be shot. That's why I keep mine on a chain."

"So, have you seen anyone?" he repeated, seemingly uninterested in the outrage.

"No, I have not. But I will shoot them myself with my father's pistol if I find any."

"Right. How about her? May I ask her?" he said, pointing at Anna.

"She's dumber than a tree. It's not worth talking to her."

Anna wasn't allowed to talk to anyone without Frau Wolff's permission, but she shook her head to let him know she hadn't seen anyone. That wasn't true; she'd seen people sneaking across the fields and into the forest from her window, but she wouldn't tell him that even if she was allowed to speak.

"Fine," he said, turning to leave. Then, he stopped and turned back. "By the way, I wouldn't be doing my duty if I didn't tell you that the Americans are probably going to come through here soon. I've been informed that the army was not able to hold them back and to prepare for citizen defense. However, we have limited resources, and most able-bodied men were already drafted, so most people are leaving the village and heading toward Berlin."

"Why Berlin?" asked Frau Wolff.

"The Führer is building up defenses there, and rumor is that he's planning a counteroffensive to push the invaders out of Germany. I don't know if that's true, but either way, you don't want to be here when they come through. The paper said that they're raping all the women."

Anna's heart dropped. This never occurred to her before, but what if the Americans, whom she hoped would liberate her, were killing and raping everyone they came across inside Germany, regardless of whether they were German or not? She glanced at Frau Wolff and saw fear on her face.

"Thank you, Herr Zimmermann," said Frau Wolff.

He tipped his cap and rode off on his bicycle.

"Maybe we should go to your brother's village," said Anna. She asked not because of just the fear of rape but more because Frau Wolff's brother, Gunther, was friendly and might even have some food. More importantly, his farm was closer to Buchenwald. "I'm sure the German army won't let Americans that far north."

"Do you think I'm stupid? You don't think I know you're already planning your escape?"

"You can keep me chained. I won't escape, I promise," said Anna.

"Don't play dumb with me," said Frau Wolff.

"I swear it. I'm not planning to escape. I just don't want to be raped by the Americans. They might do worse things to a German."

Frau Wolff scratched her head, then said, "Fine, get the horse wagon ready. But if I even think for a second that you're running away, I will shoot you with this pistol and send you to hell to join your Filip."

32
APRIL 9, 1945

Filip had been hiding inside a small, dark hole in the ground under the barracks, together with Sig, Ciepielowski, and Hinkelmann, ever since the SS had announced Ciepielowski's name with forty-five others as ringleaders of the resistance and began massive camp evacuations.

They listened for three days as the SS and their dogs rounded up thousands of prisoners and walked them out of the camp under heavy guard. Their hopes of uprising were quickly fading with the guards' increasing brutality. Those who didn't follow orders were shot or beaten to death. Filip, Sig, Ciepielowski, and Hinkelmann were happy to escape this fate—except they'd run out of food and water two days before.

"I can't do this anymore," Hinkelmann announced.

"What are you talking about?" asked Filip.

"I need to get out of this goddamn hellhole," said Hinkelmann. "I'll just tell them I was kidnapped and held prisoner. It'll blow my cover, but at least I won't starve to death."

"So you can tell them about us?" asked Ciepielowski. "You're not going anywhere, Hinkelmann."

"Who's going to stop me?" said Hinkelmann, pulling a pistol out of his jacket.

"You can't kill all three of us," said Ciepielowski. "By the time you fire the first bullet, the other two will be on top of you. Not to mention the SS guards who will hear the gunshot and kill you before they recognize who you are."

Then the cover above them lifted and a head appeared. Hinkelmann pointed the gun at the man, but it was just another prisoner.

"They have orders to transport us to Berlin," said the prisoner. "Nine thousand people. Everyone from this barracks and seventeen others."

They all looked at each other with anxiety.

"Why Berlin?" Filip asked.

"Who knows, but I bet it's not for Hitler's birthday celebration on April 20," said the prisoner. "They probably need slaves to dig trenches to defend the city."

"We should start the rebellion," said Ciepielowski. "It's now or never."

"It's too late. They have already evacuated half the guys from the attack troop. We don't have enough trained people to overwhelm the guards."

"We should hide out and wait for the Americans," said Sig.

The sirens blasted, and the sounds of dogs barking and people yelling quickly followed.

"I have to go," the prisoner said, then he disappeared, closing the cover above them.

"We'll die here before the Americans show up," said Hinkelmann.

"We'll die if we go," said Ciepielowski.

"Maybe we can escape from the transport," said Filip. "It's probably chaos out there. They may not have enough guards to watch over so many people."

"I'm leaving," said Hinkelmann, pushing the cover open.

Ciepielowski dove at his legs, but Hinkelmann kicked him and lifted himself out of the hole. Filip rushed to help Ciepielowski.

"Go after him!" Ciepielowski screamed. "Make sure he doesn't talk to the SS."

"C'mon, Sig!" Filip shouted.

"I'm not going," said Sig, leaning back against the dirt wall.

Ciepielowski grabbed his arm and pulled. "You're coming with us. You have a better chance of surviving if we stick together."

Filip pushed Sig up, then climbed out with Ciepielowski behind them. Hundreds of prisoners ran in a panic all around them. The SS guards surrounded the area and used their vicious dogs to force the mob toward the camp's exit.

"Where is Hinkelmann?" asked Ciepielowski.

Filip saw a dirty, bearded man pushing through the crowd toward the SS guards and ran after him. Unlike Hinkelmann, he was used to fighting other prisoners for space and caught up with him quickly after shoving several people to the side.

"Don't even think about it," he said, pulling Hinkelmann back into the crowd.

Hinkelmann tried to break free, but Ciepielowski was already there and grabbed his other arm. Sig pushed him from behind.

"You assholes are going to pay for this," Hinkelmann hissed.

"Better keep moving," said Ciepielowski. "The prisoners would tear you apart if we told them who you are."

Hinkelmann stopped resisting, and they slowly moved out of the camp with the crowd. They marched together with thousands of prisoners, looking back at Buchenwald with shock, realizing it might be the last time they saw it. Some people refused to follow the column, either too disturbed to leave a place they had lived in for many years or too exhausted to walk. They were met with kicks, punches, and whips from the SS and bites from the dogs. Those who still refused were shot in cold blood.

The prisoners quickly reached the local road leading to the nearest big town of Weimar. The guards were all around them, marching or biking alongside the column. There were also horse-drawn wagons with machine guns in the front and back.

"Where is our train?" asked Filip. "I hope they're not planning on marching us all the way to Berlin."

"We should have hidden in the camp," said Sig.

"The Allies have full control of the sky," said Ciepielowski. "They probably bomb any trains going anywhere near a factory."

"He's right," said Hinkelmann. "There's probably a train waiting for us in Weimar."

When they arrived in Weimar an hour later, they were shocked to find the town in ruins. They'd heard the sounds of explosions over the last few months, and rumors had run rampant about Allied bombings across Germany. But nothing prepared them for the level of destruction in the city. Only skeletons of buildings remained. All the windows were shattered. Graves were scattered all around. The city was reduced to rubble.

The SS guards stopped the column near the train station and made the prisoners sit on the cobblestone streets. Filip was the closest prisoner to a half-broken wooden fence with a garden behind it. He looked around and saw that the guards were preoccupied with taking a smoke break and talking to some civilians.

"We should try to escape," he whispered to Sig, who sat beside him.

"Are you crazy? They'll shoot us like dogs," said Sig.

"C'mon, Sig. We can sneak off through the fence. Nobody's paying attention right now."

"It's certain death if they see us. I'd rather wait for the Americans to save us. The Germans won't kill us if they haven't done it already."

Then whistles blew, and the SS made everyone stand up again. The column of prisoners moved forward, and they were pushed into the half-bombed-out train station, where they were loaded into the same type of cattle cars that had brought Filip to Germany. The four of them were squeezed in like sardines with about a hundred other prisoners, standing shoulder to shoulder with no room to sit down.

"We can't escape now," Filip told Sig.

"We can't be going far," said Sig.

"It will take us all day to get to Berlin," Ciepielowski said.

"How the hell are we supposed to survive in here?" asked Hinkelmann.

"Some won't," said Filip.

The train lurched and rolled forward. Within minutes, they could no longer see buildings through two small barred windows near the ceiling. They could only see a blue sky and some white clouds from time to time.

"Lift me up," said Filip.

"Why?" asked Sig.

"So I can see where we're going."

Sig put his hands together, offering a stirrup. Filip put his foot into it and lifted himself to the window.

"What do you see?" asked Ciepielowski, helping Filip stay up.

The train was traveling through open fields with nowhere to hide if they jumped out. Filip also noticed that the SS guards were all in the last train car with machine guns on top of the roof, ready to fire at anyone who dared to attempt escape.

"If we kick this window out, we have a chance to squeeze out," said Filip.

"They'll shoot you dead if you try," said Hinkelmann. "The machine gun in the back will also shred this car into pieces and kill everyone inside."

Then plane engines roared above them. Filip couldn't see much, but all hell broke loose. Bombs exploded all around them, violently shaking the ground and shattering their eardrums. Machine gun fire rattled off in spurts, tearing through the air like hammers. Filip jumped down, tipping Sig and several men next to them into a pile of bodies. He heard men scream in agony and saw that there were now large bullet holes in the walls. He couldn't tell if they were from the Allied planes or the SS machine guns. He crouched down, closed his eyes, and prayed to God to save him one last time.

The train stopped, and the planes roared away just as quickly as they'd appeared. A momentary silence was replaced by screaming from the SS guards.

Filip opened his eyes and saw that everyone around him was still alive. "Are you all right?" he asked Sig, just to make sure.

Sig nodded.

Then there was another explosion somewhere outside, sounding closer to the front of the train.

"They must've blown up the locomotive," said Ciepielowski.

Some prisoners started banging on the door and yelling for somebody to let them out.

The only response was more shouts from the SS guards.

"What are they saying?" Filip asked Hinkelmann.

"I can't make it out, but it sounds like they're leaving."

"Are they going to let us out of this trap first?" asked Sig.

"Lift me up," Filip ordered.

Ciepielowski lifted him, and he looked out the window again to see one of the kapos standing below.

"Open the door!" Filip shouted.

"I can't do that," said the kapo, a large man in his fifties with a Polish accent. "Only the first eight cars are being let out."

"What about us?"

"I don't know."

"Please open the door. The SS won't even notice in all this smoke."

"I can't. They'll shoot me."

"Where you from?" Filip asked.

"Czestochowa," said the kapo.

"The girl I'm trying to get back to is from Czestochowa," said Filip. "I need to get out of here and find her. I need to make sure she's alive."

The kapo looked up at Filip's face, hesitated, then disappeared.

"Is he going to open the door?" asked Sig.

Filip shook his head. Then the lock slammed, and the door slid open.

"Get out!" shouted an SS officer outside.

The prisoners jumped out, and Filip kissed the ground.

"What now?" asked Ciepielowski.

They got the answer immediately as the SS guards organized the survivors into a column and marched them down a dirt road alongside the train tracks, leaving the burning locomotive and the cries of hundreds of wounded behind.

"What now?" asked Sig.

"I guess we're walking to Berlin," said Hinkelmann.

Anna pushed a two-wheeled cart while Frau Wolff walked beside it with her pistol in one hand to make sure they wouldn't get robbed again by any of the thousands of refugees traveling on the same road toward Berlin.

In her other hand, Frau Wolff held a leash that was tied around Anna's neck with a lock to ensure she wouldn't run away. Anna was happy not to have to drag a ball and chain around anymore. They'd abandoned both when the German army confiscated their horse. She had to push the cart instead, but the leash felt like the last step in her domestication as a wild animal. She felt humiliated by her lack of mental strength to fight it.

At least the refugees around her were too downtrodden to notice. Coming from towns all over southeastern Germany, they seemed like ghosts of their former selves. In their dirty clothing and with suitcases full of scraps of their past lives, they were nothing like Europe's master race. They looked more like the many slaves they'd brought in cattle cars than their masters.

"Stop," ordered Frau Wolff, pointing at a house on the side of the road. "This is it."

Anna realized they were standing before Gunther's farmhouse. Even though she had spent a few months there before, her mind was so numb from the grueling travel that she hadn't recognized it.

Frau Wolff opened the gate, and Anna pushed the cart into the courtyard, where Gunther sat in his wheelchair next to a water pump.

"I don't have any food, but I can offer you some water," he said, which sounded like a prepared speech he had spoken many times before.

"Gunther, it's me—your sister," said Frau Wolff.

He paused and stared at their dirt-covered bodies. Then, his face brightened in recognition. "Oh my God," he said. "Katherine, what are you doing here? And is that Anna?"

"Yes," Frau Wolff acknowledged.

"Why is she on a leash?" he asked, horrified.

"What do you care about Anna? Welcome your older sister properly."

Gunther stared at Frau Wolff, his face tightening in anger, then said, "Let her off the leash so she can help me welcome you. She knows her way around the house."

"Fine," said Frau Wolff, unlocking the leash from Anna's neck. "I keep forgetting that you're a cripple."

"That's funny because I feel like you never let me forget it," he said. "Anna, please help me up the stairs."

Anna was relieved to be free of the leash and smiled for what felt like the first time in years. "Yes, Gunther," she said, pulling his wheelchair up the stairs into the farmhouse.

"There's a bowl of water in the hallway," he said. "Why don't you wash yourself and change into some of my clothes? Then you can help me cook some eggs. I also have a loaf of bread hidden under my bed."

"Thank you, Gunther," said Anna. "Has anyone been helping you?"

"My neighbor, but she left with her family yesterday. I was actually wondering how I would survive until you showed up. I'm very happy to see you. It's a miracle."

"I hate to break up this love affair," said Frau Wolff, following them inside the farmhouse, "but Anna is not here to work for you. I'll be taking over the farm to get us ready for the defense against the Americans."

"What are you talking about? What defense? We can't stop the Americans."

"I expected you to say that since you were never a real patriot. Our Führer needs us more than ever. The German army is building defenses from Hanover to Leipzig and preparing for a counteroffensive. That's what the soldiers who took our horse told us. I plan to help them."

"Have you gone mad just like Hitler? The war is lost, sister. The bombings have crippled the production of military equipment. They're also running out of oil and gasoline for their tanks since they've been cut off from the Middle East. There's no food supply. Half the soldiers have been captured. They're drafting boys and old men to fight well-supplied and much larger armies on three fronts. We only have a month at best before they take over the country. Hitler should have capitulated months ago."

Frau Wolff pointed her pistol at Gunther and shot him three times. He slumped over and fell out of his wheelchair. "That's what you get for betraying our Führer, you piece of shit!" she shouted.

"NO!" Anna screamed in horror, dropping to her knees next to Gunther's body. "What have you done?"

"He would only slow us down," said Frau Wolff. "Plus, it's one less mouth to feed."

Anna sobbed as tears poured down her face. "He was your brother . . ."

"It's people like him who held us back from winning the war. And you're not going to hold me back either. Get down to the cellar," Frau Wolff ordered.

"Why don't you kill me already!" Anna screamed.

Frau Wolff pointed the pistol at her and said, "You might get your wish. For now, I still need you to help me run Gunter's farm. So get in the cellar."

Anna got up and walked over to a rug on the floor. She lifted it, revealing a wooden hatch. "You're an evil person," she said. "God will punish you for this."

"Shut up and open it!"

Anna opened the hatch.

"Get in!" ordered Frau Wolff.

Anna stepped down a short ladder into a dark, cold, and empty cellar that was not much higher than she was tall.

"I'll let you come out when our Führer liberates Germany from the Americans," said Frau Wolff from above. Then she dropped the hatch.

Anna was engulfed by complete darkness, and a lock snapped shut above her. She wondered if this would be her grave.

33

APRIL 10, 1945

The sun peeked over the horizon, blinding Hinkelmann. He stumbled and fell into a puddle. His muscles burned from twenty straight hours of marching, but he got up quickly to avoid getting shot by the SS guards traveling alongside the prisoners on confiscated bicycles and horses. They killed, without mercy, anyone who fell behind the column.

He hoped to finish his one remaining task and slip off during the night into one of the forests they passed by, but the guards, perhaps spooked by the sounds of approaching artillery, didn't let them stop—not even to drink some water from the streams or relieve themselves. Those who had to defecate did it in their pants, chafing their legs and buttocks raw. Those who passed out from exhaustion had to be carried by others; otherwise, they were shot.

Hinkelmann got his opportunity after they crossed a bridge across the Saale River and the SS stopped the column in the large town of Halle. Thousands of prisoners collapsed to the ground in exhaustion on the bank of the river while about two dozen SS guards began to install mines on the bridge, apparently deciding to destroy it and block the Allied advance.

With the guards distracted, Hinkelmann quickly formulated a plan: Kill Filip, Sig, and Ciepielowski—the only people who knew of his new identity—and then slip into the river and float away. The only question was how to kill them without raising an alarm. The easiest way would be just to shoot them with his pistol, but that would be loud and make him an immediate target for the guards. He was thinking about how to find a quiet place away from the guards to give himself time and cover for the escape when a couple of guards approached the area where he was sitting.

"We need a hundred volunteers to carry sandbags!" shouted one of the guards.

Hinkelmann raised his hand immediately. He was the only one.

"What are you doing?" asked Ciepielowski. "We don't have the strength to carry sandbags."

"This might be our chance to escape," he whispered.

"We should wait," said Sig.

"What's your plan?" asked Filip.

"You'll see," Hinkelmann said, standing up. "C'mon, let's go."

The four of them stood, and a few other prisoners did as well. The guards rounded up the rest and marched them to a nearby factory, which was empty except for hundreds of sandbags stacked on top of each other in its warehouse.

"You need to carry the sandbags to the bridge entrance," said the guard. "We'll have to build a defensive fortification for our troops, which will be withdrawing this way sometime today." He hefted a sandbag and threw it over his shoulder. Others followed suit, and they marched toward the bridge.

"What is your plan?" Filip asked again, walking behind Hinkelmann.

"The river," he said.

"How?"

"There are only two guards. That's not enough to watch a hundred prisoners walking single file. One of them will have to stay at the factory. The other one will be somewhere on the bridge. There are a few hundred meters in between. We find the right time to jump into the river, and they'll never find us. Nor will they want to bother with it."

"They have guards on the bridge," said Filip. "They can shoot at us like ducks with their rifles."

"The river bends about three hundred meters past the bridge," Hinkelmann said. "We'll have to run through the city first, then jump into the river." He thought the guards would be too preoccupied with mining the bridge to notice them, but running through the city would give him a chance to shoot the three prisoners in the back.

"That's a good plan," said Filip, then he repeated the plan to Ciepielowski and Sig behind him.

They carried the bags up a slope and dumped them near the bridge. The only guard watching over them was the one who had followed them from the factory. He was now sitting on the bags to rest. They walked down the slope back toward the factory.

This is our chance, Hinkelmann thought. Then the earth exploded all around them. He dropped to the ground as chunks of dirt flew above him and massive blasts pierced his ears. He looked around but couldn't find the source of the bombs.

"It's the American artillery!" shouted Filip. "They must be on the other side of the river."

"Schnell!" screamed an SS guard appearing above them. "Back to the road!"

Dozens of guards rushed down the slope from the bridge, collecting prisoners along the way. Some prisoners were dead, and they left them behind. The column was already on the march when Hinkelmann and the others caught up with them.

Hinkelmann cursed the panicked guards who forced them to run in fear of the approaching enemy. His plan was ruined, and he now had to wait for another chance to escape before getting killed by either Americans or the SS.

Filip fixed his eyes on the ground beneath his feet and tried not to think about the numbing fatigue crippling his body.

They had walked for many hours since the morning's bridge disaster, but the frightened SS guards would not allow them to rest. Filip decided it wasn't a matter of escaping just to get back to Anna. He had to escape to survive the march. Otherwise, he would simply collapse and get shot in the head. Except there was nowhere to hide—other than maybe one of the drain ditches running alongside the road. But he would be easily spotted if a guard decided to gaze into it. Fewer guards were watching over them, some probably drifting off during the chaos, but a couple were still walking beside Filip's group of about a hundred prisoners. Many more were watching thousands of prisoners in the column behind them.

Then, as if by a miracle, a truck arrived, and the two SS guards jumped on the back and rode off. Filip looked around to see if other guards would step in for the two who left, but nobody seemed to care. Their group simply continued to walk without any guards watching over them.

"Did you see that?" Filip asked Sig, who was walking beside him.

"What?" said Sig, startled out of his marching trance.

"The guards left. Nobody's guarding our group."

"Oh," Sig said, but he continued marching.

"Where is Ciepielowski? Have you seen him?"

"No, not since the bridge."

"How about Hinkelmann?"

"I'm pretty sure he's in front of our column," Sig said. "I saw him trying to wait for us, but one of the guards kicked him forward."

"We have to escape," said Filip.

"What? Are you crazy?" said Sig, looking around. "There are still guards back there. They'll shoot if they see us. Why not just wait for all the guards to leave?"

Sig was probably right. There were still many guards left, and they were in the middle of Germany—seven hundred kilometers from his home in Poland—with soldiers and police swarming all around. But what if the Americans were unsuccessful and never arrived to liberate them? What if that was just wishful thinking?

"We're walking farther and farther north," said Filip. "The longer we walk, the farther we'll be from Anna. Escape with me, Sig. I'm begging you, please."

"I didn't survive three years of Buchenwald only to get shot now," said Sig.

Filip wouldn't have survived Buchenwald without Sig, but while his brain was telling him to listen to his friend, his heart was telling him to follow his instinct and escape. Perhaps it was just the thought of seeing Anna again and the promise he'd made to take her back to Poland. For the first time in three years, she seemed within his reach. The open landscape, without barbwire or watchtowers, made him feel like he might see her alongside the road, working in one of the fields.

"I'm leaving," said Filip. "Please come with me."

"I can't," said Sig.

Filip looked back. The closest SS guard was about forty meters behind him, staring at the ground below him, like everyone else.

It was now or never.

"Wait," said Sig. "I need to tell you something."

"What?" asked Filip. "I don't mind that you're a homosexual if that's what you want to tell me."

"No, it's worse than that."

"What is it?"

"I'm not a famous comedian," said Sig. "I was just a second-rate backup at my club, and nobody knows who I am. I'm much better off running accounts for criminals than I ever was as a comedian. I'm sorry I lied to you."

Filip smiled and said, "I already knew you're not a good comedian. I haven't heard you tell a good joke in three years. But I still love you."

Sig laughed. "Thank you, Filip," he said.

"Goodbye, Sig." Then Filip dove face-first into a drain ditch running alongside the road, quickly covering himself with grass, weeds, and dead leaves. He went completely still, trying not to breathe, and prayed as he listened to the footsteps marching by. Every second seemed to be an hour long, and the longer he lay there, the more he realized how stupid it was for him to risk an escape. It made no sense to escape this way; it was far too obvious. They would surely discover him. He closed his eyes like a little kid who thinks nobody could see him back.

Yet time passed, and finally, the footsteps faded away. Was it possible nobody saw him dive into the ditch? Was it so obvious that nobody expected it? Or perhaps nobody cared anymore?

Filip wanted to get up and run as far away as possible, but he was paralyzed with fear and exhaustion, so he stayed in the ditch. The muddy soil was cold, and he thought it might have frozen him. He thought about Sig. Was that the last time he would see his friend? He was already missing his companionship. It hadn't occurred to him until that moment, but as horrendous as the suffering had been back in the camp, at least they'd had each other.

Now he was all alone and more scared than ever.

34

APRIL 11, 1945

Filip opened his eyes to the dark night sky sprinkled with bright stars. He had fallen asleep and lain in the drain ditch for many hours.

He sat up and slowly crawled onto the empty road. There was nothing but flat, barren fields all around him. He stuck out like a sore thumb. If anyone was out there, they would easily see him—except that he could also see there was nobody out there. The column of prisoners and their SS guards must have passed a long time ago. He was all alone with the ever-present sounds of far-off artillery.

He looked both ways at the road, then decided to walk back to where he'd come from. He had to find a way back to Anna's village and formulated a plan in his mind. He would first find a way to cross the Saale River, probably not using the same bridge the prisoners had crossed earlier. He would then find his way to Kleinfurra, where he hoped to get a horse and some new clothes from Peter Strauss, his former employer, for whom he'd transported barrels of fuel to the Mittelbau-Dora gypsum mines. Finally, he would trek back to Rotenburg an der Fulda, to the address on the package Anna had sent him at Buchenwald—which was where he hoped to find her. All he had to do was travel what he guessed was about a hundred fifty kilometers while slipping around German and American soldiers without getting shot. *Piece of cake compared to surviving three years at Buchenwald,* he thought.

Filip walked along the road for a while until he came upon another road leading to a village a distance away. His stomach growled, reminding him he hadn't eaten anything in many days. He had to find some food if he hoped to survive his journey.

He'd followed the road for about twenty minutes when he finally reached the village. The lights were out in every house, probably because they didn't want to give Americans bombing targets. He expected some people to still be awake and possibly see him approaching, so he crouched down and crept behind bushes growing along the road.

Filip didn't waste any time sneaking inside the first barn he spotted. He climbed up the ladder to the loft and covered himself with hay, burrowing deep inside the pile, with only a small opening for air. He finally felt safe and quickly fell asleep despite his hunger.

After what felt like only seconds later, the sound of a woman shouting woke him up. He sprung to his feet, ready to run away, believing she was yelling at him. But the voice came from outside the barn. He crawled out of his hideout and looked out a small round window. It was still dark, but an older woman was in the middle of the courtyard, screaming at a couple of cows as they streamed through the main gate. He thought it must be early morning already and that she was probably sending them out to the pasture.

The woman went back inside the farmhouse. Filip scanned the courtyard, but he saw only some chickens scurrying around. He waited before climbing down the ladder. Once on the ground, he immediately spotted a door to the chicken coop attached to the barn. He rushed inside, saw it was empty of hens, and quickly grabbed three eggs, leaving a few others in their nests so the woman wouldn't get suspicious. He then quickly climbed back to his hideout, where he ate the eggs raw, clumsily spilling the contents all over his face and hands, which shook from excitement and fatigue. He relished the taste of the eggs, which had been forbidden and almost forgotten at Buchenwald. When he was done eating, he covered himself with hay and waited. He then fell asleep again.

Filip woke up to some noises outside the barn. He looked out the window and saw it was still nighttime, but the same woman from before stood at her front door, locking up the house. She then picked up a large suitcase and left through the front gate.

He went back into his hideout and waited for a while. But finally, his curiosity prevailed, and he climbed down the ladder. He peeked through the barn doors, looked around to make sure nobody was there, and then ran to the farmhouse's front door. He wiggled the door handle and pushed against it, but it didn't budge. Spotting an old knife lying on the ground, he tried to jimmy the lock, but it still didn't move.

Filip was afraid to break the window, not wanting to wake up the neighbors. Seeing no other door, so he gave up. He would have to find food somewhere else. The cows were gone, and the eggs had already been collected from the chicken coop, so he chased the hens. Unfortunately, they were very quick, and he was very weak. He kept falling into the mud, so he gave up on that. He had no choice but to leave the village before the sun came out and try to find food elsewhere.

He opened the gate and peeked out. The road was empty, and the village dark and quiet, seemingly still asleep. He stepped outside, closed the gate behind him, and ran as fast as he could. With the sky clouded, he couldn't tell which way he was going, but he guessed he was moving west, which was where he wanted to go. He had a limited understanding of German geography, but he was pretty sure he was northeast of Buchenwald. He also knew Kleinfurra was north of Buchenwald. So, he guessed he was about forty to fifty kilometers east of his destination.

The village was small, with only a few houses along the road, and he quickly found himself in some woods. He stopped running and walked for a few minutes, hoping to stumble upon a road sign to tell him which way to go, but the woods ended, revealing nothing but empty fields beyond. Instead of continuing on the road and risking exposure in the open, he trekked along the tree line, hoping to find another road.

Then he heard the sound of approaching planes, which quickly turned into a roar. He couldn't tell if they were small planes flying low or large planes flying high. He looked up at the dark sky, the noise getting louder with each second. The memories of the Buchenwald bombing flooded his mind. He ran again but tripped and fell on his face.

"Goddamn trees," he said, wincing and looking back at the culprit. But it wasn't a tree branch like he'd suspected. Leaning against each other were four rifles.

Filip sprung to his feet and pumped his legs, wanting to get away as fast as possible. Then a thunderous noise erupted inside the woods, and he fell again. Salvo of antiaircraft fire flared into the sky, turning night into day. He now saw the planes high up, gliding toward their destination.

He got up and ran again. He didn't know how long he ran; it seemed like only seconds passed, but he was suddenly on the road. The thunder of plane engines and artillery fire finally subsided, and the night went dark again. Maybe he'd run for an hour? How did he find the strength to do that? He lay down for a minute, trying to catch his breath. Finally, he got up and followed the road.

The sun was finally peeking over the horizon when Filip stumbled upon a village. As he made his way through it, he quickly realized it was the same village he'd left hours earlier. In fact, the barn he'd hidden in before was standing in front of him again. He'd spent all that time going around in a circle, almost getting killed in the process.

He snuck inside the barn, still in the same condition as when he left it, and climbed back into his hideout.

He passed out from exhaustion.

Sig and the column of prisoners marched all day and night until the SS guards finally decided to rest at a small village. He collapsed to the ground and lay on a patch of grass. He couldn't feel his body. He was numb.

"They're planning to split up the column," said Hinkel- mann, appearing above him. "They think this will give them better chances of avoiding the American planes and getting to Berlin."

"How do you know this?" asked Sig.

"I overheard the guards talking. Where are Ciepielowski and Filip?"

"I don't know," Sig said, unsure if he could trust him. But what could he do? Filip was already gone, and Hinkelmann was just looking after his own skin. "I haven't seen Ciepielowski since the bridge, and I think Filip escaped."

Hinkelmann's face furrowed in shock. "How?" he asked.

"I don't know. I think he just dove into a drain ditch."

"When?"

"I don't know. Why?"

"Never mind," said Hinkelmann. "We should escape too. It will be easier if they split us up. Fewer guards to watch over us."

The SS guards started shouting for the prisoners to get up. Then they split them into groups of about one hundred each and marched them out at different time intervals in all directions. Each group had only one or two guards, except Sig's group, which marched off into a forest trail with eight guards—four on two sidecar motorcycles with attached machine guns.

"Why do we have so many guards?" asked Sig.

"I don't know," said Hinkelmann.

They marched until they reached a small farmhouse in the forest.

"Inside the barn!" ordered one of the SS guards.

"What's going on?" Hinkelmann asked him.

Sig stepped away from him, expecting the guard to shoot the man.

"We'll rest here for a few hours," the guard said, then walked away.

The prisoners shuffled inside the barn and lay down on the hay. With so many people, it was tight quarters but comfortable. The guards left the barn door open, which gave them enough air to breathe. It was much better than what they'd had at Buchenwald.

Sig closed his eyes, ready to go to sleep.

"Stay awake," said Hinkelmann, nudging him in the ribs. "This might be our chance to escape."

"Why do you want me to escape with you?" asked Sig, confused. "Why don't you escape by yourself? I'm too tired to run."

"We need to find Filip and Ciepielowski."

"Why? What for?"

"They might be in danger. They don't know Germany like I do. They need my help."

That didn't make sense to Sig. Why would Hinkelmann try to save their lives after spending three years in Buchenwald trying to kill them? Why would he do that? *Maybe I need to escape from him,* Sig thought. He got up and said, "I need to take a shit."

"I'll go with you," said Hinkelmann.

"No, I'll be back. I don't need company taking a shit," he said.

Sig walked out of the barn and into the woods unnoticed. Most of the guards were inside the farmhouse, and the two guarding the barn were sleeping under a tree. He took his pants down and crouched under a bush. He had to think fast. Hinkelmann would come looking for him if he stayed away for too long. Did the German want to kill him, or was he really trying to help them? Sig had to make a decision quickly, or his life could be in danger. *Stay with Hinkelmann or run away?* he wondered. That was when he heard shouts of the SS guards and the barn door slamming shut.

He wiped with some leaves, pulled his pants up, and crawled close to the barn. All eight guards were now outside the barn. Four of them sat on their motorcycles, the machine guns pointed at the barn, while the other four threw torches inside it through openings in the walls. Prisoners inside screamed in terror as the hay quickly caught on fire. They banged on the door, but it was locked with chains and wouldn't open. Within seconds, the barn was engulfed in flames and smoke. The screams slowly subsided. The guards smoked cigarettes and chatted, waiting for the barn to burn down.

Sig crawled back and ran away through the woods. The fear gave him strength he didn't know he had. He felt sickened to see so many people die. Why did the SS kill them? What was the purpose? It seemed so senseless. At least Hinkelmann was dead. He was the only one who deserved it.

Filip woke around noon to the sound of car engines. He got up and looked out his window. He didn't see anything at first, but then a small vehicle appeared, driving down the village road. He had never seen one like it. It was dark green and had no roof. A white star inside a circle was painted on top of the hood. Two soldiers were inside it. They were wearing green uniforms, not the gray ones the SS guards wore.

He climbed down the ladder and ran for the gate, but when he finally reached it, the road was empty. He hesitated, unsure whether leaving his hideout in the daylight was safe, but he was desperate to continue his search for Anna and decided to leave.

He stayed close to the fence along the road, following the strange vehicle's direction. As he made his way through the village, he spotted two women talking next to one of the houses. He wanted to back away, but they saw him and stared for a while.

"Don't call the police!" he finally yelled out.

Immediately, one of the women sprinted inside the house. Filip ran, hoping to pass them quickly, but he was still weak, and he tripped over his own feet right in front of the second woman. As he tried to get up, the first woman appeared above him, extending her hand. She held a slice of buttered bread.

"Eat," she said with a smile.

Filip was dumbfounded, and he sensed his jaw drop open. He couldn't recall the last time anyone was kind to him in this godforsaken country. He stared at the bread suspiciously. What if she was trying to trick him into eating some poison? But the aroma of fresh bread was just too much to resist. He took it from the woman and ripped into it with his mouth as he'd never ripped into anything in his life. The crust was crunchy and the inside still warm, and butter oozed all over his face and hands. He could only imagine how pathetic he looked at that moment, with his prison uniform torn up, his body covered in dirt and hay, and his face smeared with egg and butter.

The women watched him with amusement. He wasn't sure if that amusement was sympathy or the same look the Nazi guards in Buchenwald had given him—the look of a bully tormenting a child. Either way, he was starting to understand why the SS called the prisoners swine. They looked and behaved like pigs, reduced to basic animal instincts while trying to survive.

Filip thanked the women and walked until he reached a paved road and spotted a vehicle that looked like the one he had seen earlier. It was parked under a tree, and two soldiers sat on the grass next to it. They stood up and stared at him as he approached. He stared back at them. Both had dark-brown skin and curly black hair, which was something he'd never seen before—not even in pictures. He'd heard about Black people from his elementary school teacher but never imagined they existed. He might have as well been looking at Martians.

The soldiers were looking at him in much the same way. He might have been an alien from another planet as well—a skeleton of a man covered in dirt, hay, egg, and butter.

One of them said something in a strange language that had to be American.

Filip didn't understand him, but he saw the concern on the soldier's face and realized he might be offering help. "Can I please have some water?" he asked in German.

"Water?" the soldier repeated in German.

"Yes. Please."

The soldier handed him a canteen, and Filip gulped down every drop. As soon as he was done, the other soldier extended his hand with what looked like chocolate cookies. Filip quickly ate one but stopped when he became nauseated. It was too much food too fast after not having any for a very long time.

The American soldiers sat him in the back of their little green car, and they drove away. They gave him a pack of cigarettes called Camel, a strange name—and he smoked one as they drove through the countryside. He stuffed the rest of the cigarettes inside his uniform, saving them for potential future bargaining. A pack of cigarettes would buy a week's worth of food back at Buchenwald.

They arrived in a town called Nordhausen about two hours later. The Americans dropped him off at an old school, where they gave him soup, a blanket, and a comfortable sweatsuit to wear. They also made him take a bath and burn his prison clothes.

There were only three other refugees at the school, all former prisoners, but none spoke Polish or German. Nevertheless, he was able to figure out from one of them that the Americans were gathering all the camp prisoners in that building. There were twelve of them by that afternoon.

With the bath, new clothes, blanket, and food, Filip fell asleep on a nice bed with a mattress. He slept like a baby until he felt something tickle his ear. He swiped at it a few times, but it kept tickling him. He finally got mad, and that was when he heard a familiar laugh.

"Wake up, sleeping prince," said Sig.

Filip sprung up in shock. He grabbed Sig and gave him a big hug. "I thought . . ." He choked up.

"What, that I was dead? Come on, Filip. I'm the invincible Jew."

They both laughed.

"How did you escape?" Filip wanted to know.

"Just barely. You were right. I should have escaped with you. The SS walked with us for another twenty kilometers, but then they threw all of us into a barn and set it on fire. The only reason I got away was that I had to take a shit in the woods and they forgot about me. When I came out of the woods, the barn was on fire and the Germans were laughing. I ran for I don't know how long until the Americans found me and brought me here."

Filip's face turned pale. "Nobody survived?"

"Hinkelmann was inside too," said Sig. "I don't think any of them lived."

"We're blessed, Sig," said Filip.

There were about fifty other refugees now at the school. *Were these the only survivors out of the thousands that initially marched out of Buchenwald?* Filip wondered. What about the thousands of others who'd marched out before them?

From the other refugees, they learned of horrific acts by the SS. One prisoner told a story of a few hundred who were cut down by SS machine guns in an open field. Another said that some were left locked up inside a train for days, dying of dehydration and hunger.

"We should go see the town," Filip said finally, unable to listen to the stories anymore. "Maybe we can find a way to Rotenburg so I can find Anna."

Sig agreed, and they ventured out into the town. Nordhausen was swarming with Americans, so they felt safe strolling the streets. They figured that the Germans had all evacuated because garbage was strewn all over.

Filip picked up an abandoned bicycle. "You have to come with me," he proclaimed, getting on it. He pointed to the crossbar. "Get on, Sig."

"I don't know . . ." Sig took a step back.

"I must do this," Filip insisted.

Sig shook his head and said, "Sorry, it's too dangerous. There are still Germans everywhere. We'll get shot for sure."

"I can't sit here waiting while the Germans kill her or drag her to Berlin."

Sig sighed in disgust. "What's the point? You never listen to me anyway."

"You finally said something smart," said Filip, grinning.

Sig went silent, then tears rolled down his face. "Did you hear that joke about a Jew and a Pole riding a bicycle together?" he muttered.

Filip shook his head and said, "I didn't say goodbye properly last time."

They embraced for the last time.

"Thank you," said Filip.

Sig nodded. And with that, Filip got on the bicycle and rode away. Sig ran behind him for a while, then stopped and waved.

That was the last time Filip saw Sig.

35
APRIL 12, 1945

Anna lost track of time in the dark cellar, but it had to be at least two or three days since Frau Wolff locked her up. She couldn't tell whether it was day or night. The only light she saw was when Frau Wolff occasionally cracked open the hatch door and threw down food, usually stale bread and a water canteen. She spent most of her time cuddled on the cold floor with some old rags she found in the corner, thinking about the person she used to be—that brave girl who was too stubborn to give up, the one who spread anti-German flyers in Poland. What happened to that girl? Was she still inside her?

There was only one way to find out. She had to do something. Anything.

She got up and felt her way around the walls. She stumbled upon some shelves, blindly knocking over what she assumed were tools and farming supplies. Then something metallic fell to the floor. She crawled on her hands and knees until she found it.

It was a screwdriver.

She stumbled to the hatch door and poked at it with the screwdriver. She listened for noises on the other side but heard nothing. She thrusted repeatedly, chipping at the wood, until her hands and arms hurt. She was weak, but the effort made her feel better. She continued for a few minutes, dislodging chunks of wood around the door hinges, until she heard footsteps above her. Then the lock turned. She hid the screwdriver in her pocket and dropped to the floor, covering herself with rags. The hatch swung open.

"Get up!" shouted Frau Wolff, climbing down the steps, which were illuminated by the flickering oil lamp she carried. She also clutched a large suitcase under her arm, which she dropped with a thud across from Anna.

"What do you want from me?" Anna asked, covering her eyes from the blinding light.

"Just shut your mouth and keep quiet," said Frau Wolff, pointing a pistol at Anna while closing the hatch.

"It's the Americans, isn't it?" declared Anna. "They're going to kill you and all the Germans for what you have done."

"I told you to be quiet," warned Frau Wolff. "If I'm going to die, then you will too."

"So what if you kill me? Why should I care?"

"Don't you want to see your precious Filip again?"

"You evil—"

"Evil?" Frau Wolff asked. "You're my goddamned property. I do what I please with you and your life. Remember that."

Anna wanted to tear Frau Wolff's throat out. She would have stabbed her in the eyes with the screwdriver if it hadn't been for the pistol.

"You will pay for everything," said Anna.

"You keep quiet," said Frau Wolff, sitting against the wall

opposite Anna. "I will shoot you before I let any Americans get in here."

They stayed silent for the next two hours while Frau Wolff stared at Anna, her gun squarely pointed at her head. Anna tried to think about how she could kill her. There were not many options. Other than rushing right at her and getting shot in the process, there was nothing in the cellar to help her.

Then Frau Wolff's eyelids flickered, and her head slumped forward. The pistol drooped down to the floor as she fell asleep.

Anna waited a few minutes, then quietly walked over to Frau Wolff and gently pulled the pistol out of her hand. Frau Wolff startled awake, but the gun was already pointed at her chest.

"Your life ends here, you witch," said Anna, pulling the trigger.

But nothing happened. The gun didn't fire.

"The gun isn't loaded," said Frau Wolff with a smirk, pulling bullets out of her pocket.

Anna threw the gun at her and then punched her in the face. She had never punched anyone before, but the hatred guided her fist so accurately and forcefully that it knocked Frau Wolff out. Anna wondered if it had killed her, but her chest rose up and down with each breath.

She didn't know how to load a gun, so she pulled the screwdriver out of her pocket and stood over Frau Wolff. She wanted to stab her and finish the job, but stabbing someone wasn't as easy as pulling a trigger. The thought of forcing the screwdriver through the skin made her feel sick.

She put the screwdriver back in her pocket, opened the hatch door, and climbed out of the cellar. She rushed out of the farmhouse and onto the empty road, trying to get as far away from Frau Wolff as possible.

She was free at last. Except she had no idea where to go.

Anna ran through the curiously deserted village. All the refugees were gone, and no villagers were in sight. It seemed to be completely abandoned. Was everyone dead? Was she the only one left alive in this damned world?

She sat on the ground and sobbed.

Filip arrived in Kleinfurra midafternoon and found Peter Strauss washing a horse outside his farmhouse. Peter's jaw dropped when he saw him.

"You're alive!" Peter cried.

"Yes, sir," said Filip. "I'm surprised myself."

"I wrote letters to the SS, asking them to release you, but they never replied."

"Don't worry. Very few ever got out."

Peter pulled up a stool and said, "Sit down, Filip. You are so thin."

"Thank you," said Filip, sitting down. "I'm glad to see you still have your horses."

"Only one. The SS killed the other three for food. They left me this one so I could continue delivering to Dora. I stopped for a few days, but now the Americans are here, and they asked me to deliver food to the prisoners. They are taking care of all the foreign workers there now."

"They're doing the same in Nordhausen. That's where I came from."

Peter scratched his head and said, "If you don't mind me asking, why did you come here?"

"Well," said Filip, uncomfortable with asking for a favor, "I need your help, Peter."

"Anything for you, Filip. What is it?"

"I need to get down to Rotenburg an der Fulda to get my girlfriend, Anna, and I wanted to borrow one of your horses. But since you only have one and are helping feed the prisoners, I must find another way."

"Wait," said Peter. "You mean that young lady you told me about who used to live at Gottschalk's house? The guy in a wheelchair?"

"Yes, that's the one. Why?"

"I think she's there now. A friend of mine who sells me milk for the prisoners lives in Immenrode, and she told me that Gottschalk's sister came to his house a few days ago, pulling a young Polish woman on a leash. She thought it was the same one who used to care for Gottschalk months ago."

Filip leaped from his stool. "I have to go," he said, getting on his bike.

"Wait!" Peter shouted. "Take my horse. It will be much faster and less tiring. It's only twenty minutes from here if you ride through the fields."

"Thank you, Peter. I won't forget this."

"Hold on," said Peter, rushing off into his house. He returned only a minute later, holding a small suitcase. "Inside are your old clothes and the money I owe you for the work you've done here. I also threw in a loaf of bread and some cookies I got from the Americans."

"Those are delicious," said Filip, getting on the horse. "Thank you for everything. You've been a good friend."

"Just return the horse to the Dora camp. I'll pick it up later."

Filip waved and kicked the horse forward, holding onto its mane. His heart pounded in anticipation as he rode through the empty fields. He was afraid of what he might or might not find in Immenrode. The whole world was upside down, and a lot could have changed in a few days. Plus, it had been over two years since he and Anna had last seen each other. What if she forgot about him or fell in love with someone else?

Immersed in his thoughts, he reached Immenrode. His heart dropped as he rode through the deserted village and pulled up to Frau Wolff's brother's house. The place seemed abandoned. The gate and door were wide open, as if everyone had left in a hurry.

Filip walked into the kitchen and immediately stumbled backward because Frau Wolff sat at the table, staring at him as if he were a ghost. She looked terrible. Her hair was disheveled, and a streak of dried-up blood covered half her left cheek. She held a pistol that pointed straight at Filip.

"Welcome home, Filip!"

"Where is Anna?" he asked, struggling to remain calm.

"What? No 'Hello' or 'Nice to see you'?"

"Where is Anna!" he screamed.

Frau Wolff laughed. "Your floozy ran away like the weakling she is. Who knows? She's probably shacked up with some Americans by now."

"When did she leave?"

"Do I look like your goddamned secretary? I don't work for you. You work for me, remember?"

Filip hesitated, trying to decide what to do, then turned to leave. That was when the pistol fired, and a bullet hit the wall about a foot above his head. The sound of the shot itself made Filip duck to the floor.

"Where the hell do you think you're going, slave!" yelled Frau Wolff, standing up. "You belong to me!"

∾

Anna heard the gunshot as she searched the village near Gunther's house. She froze, unsure whether she should continue or run away. Her curiosity won, and she ran until she reached the house. She then peeked through the gate. A horse stood in the courtyard, but there were no people around. The German army had confiscated all the horses, so she wondered if this horse belonged to a soldier. *What if it's a Russian or American soldier?* she thought. *Did he kill Frau Wolff, or did she kill him?*

There was only one way to find out.

She snuck inside the courtyard, creeping alongside the house. She heard yelling and peeked around the corner. That was when she saw Frau Wolff pushing Filip out of the house with her pistol.

Filip was not afraid of dying. That fear was gone long ago. What he was afraid of was dying without ever finding Anna. That was why he let Frau Wolff push him out to the yard without fighting back. He needed to find out if Anna was still alive and where he could find her.

"You will get the horse wagon ready, and we will both drive it all the way to Berlin if we have to. You understand me?" screamed Frau Wolff, poking Filip with the pistol.

"I'm not going anywhere until you tell me where Anna is," he declared.

"I don't give a shit about your dumb Anna. You need to forget about her. She's been nothing but trouble for you, has she not? She's the reason you went to prison and almost died. I'm the one who took care of you and gave you shelter. I even let you fuck me. What do I get in return? A whipping and a bunch of insults?"

"You deserve every piece of misery that ever came your way," said Filip. "Go ahead and kill me. Then you can live the rest of your miserable life alone."

Frau Wolff pointed the pistol at Filip's head. "Fine, you stupid man. You leave me no choice."

Anna stood frozen, pressed against the wall. Tears streamed down her tortured face. She had been so hopeless for so long that it was difficult for her to find courage. Was she going to let Frau Wolff destroy her life again? Or would she dig deep inside and take control of her life? To find strength, she thought about all those terrible moments of the last few years: the hanging of the innocent Polish man, Sabina's death, and Filip's imprisonment.

She pulled the screwdriver out of her dress pocket and gripped it hard with both hands in front of her chest.

Filip was staring down the barrel of Frau Wolff's pistol when he saw Anna run out from behind the corner of the house. She screamed the most horrific scream he'd ever heard, freezing both him and Frau Wolff. They watched in shock as Anna raised what looked like a screwdriver over her head and charged at Frau Wolff.

Unfortunately, Anna was about twenty meters away, and Filip watched in horror as Frau Wolff swung the pistol away from Filip and straight at Anna.

Filip didn't hesitate. Anna was alive, and he intended to keep it that way. He leaped at Frau Wolff, knocking her violently to the ground. The pistol flew out of her hand and into a large puddle.

Anna closed her eyes as she ran toward Frau Wolff. She could not bear to watch Filip's or her own death. She hoped the screwdriver would somehow miraculously find its destination.

Then she felt strong arms grabbing and holding her in place. Her feet went up in the air, and she shrieked in anger. That was when she opened her eyes and saw Frau Wolff lying face-first in the mud.

"It's over. You can let go now," said Filip, pulling the screwdriver out of her hands.

Anna fell into his arms, tears pouring down her face. "Did I kill her?" she asked.

Filip smiled. "No, she's fine. You didn't kill her."

"What happened?"

"I found you. That's what happened," he said, beaming with happiness.

Anna kissed him, then said, "What took you so long?"

They stared into each other's eyes as if looking for what they had missed during all those years. Maybe it didn't matter. What mattered was they were together again. Forget the past. The future was what mattered.

Filip pulled the medallion from his sweatshirt and hung it around Anna's neck.

"I don't need it anymore," he said.

Anna smiled and kissed him again. "God brought you back to me," she said.

Frau Wolff moved her legs and arms, then flipped onto her back. She lifted her head, watching Filip and Anna embrace.

"I order you to stop," she whimpered. "You belong to me . . ."

Filip felt sorry for Frau Wolff. "Let's go home," he said to Anna, pulling the horse toward the gate.

"Stop!" screamed Frau Wolff, crying as they left the farm. "I will send you back to Buchenwald, I swear it!"

Anna sat behind Filip as they rode the horse. It was a nice spring day, and the tree blossoms flew gently across the empty road just outside the village. This peaceful moment was not lost on them. It was a gentle reminder that despite the chaos around them, nature was going about its annual life cycle, undisturbed. Perhaps this was a sign that their lives would also return to normal.

Then a gunshot rang out in the distance. It wasn't very loud, but Filip and Anna had heard enough gunshots to know what it was. They looked at each other in acknowledgment because they both knew where it came from. Without saying a word, they simply rode away.

36

MAY 22, 1945

Two weeks after Nazi Germany capitulated, Filip and Anna were still stuck at the Mittelbau-Dora concentration camp, where the Americans were providing housing to several thousand foreign laborers. The conditions at the camp were dire. Hundreds of former prisoners were still dying daily from malnutrition and various diseases. Filip and Anna both volunteered at the infirmary, trying to help anyone they could, but stopping the flood of dead bodies seemed like an impossible task. The Nazis would have been pleased to know that their killing machine continued to work even after their defeat.

"I'm going to see if I can find better food for these guys," Filip said to Anna, who was bandaging a leg wound on one of the prisoners. "I'll meet you back in the barracks if I don't return."

Anna kissed him on the lips and said, "I love you. Don't get into any trouble."

He loved how things were between them. They could kiss

and make love whenever they wanted. There was no one they had to hide from. No one to threaten them. It was a feeling he had never had before, and he hoped it would stay like this forever.

He moved past hundreds of beds filled with suffering patients and exited the infirmary. It was a warm spring day, and he hungrily inhaled the fresh air to replace the stench of the interior. He walked through the camp, past many barracks filled with still skinny but cheerful former prisoners, now all dressed in civilian clothes, and past the now wide-open main gate. American soldiers sat nearby in their green vehicle, which Filip learned was called a Jeep, but they had little to do besides play cards. People were free to come and go as they pleased.

Any food arriving at the camp was quickly accounted for, so he strode toward the rail station, where food could be acquired. He approached a train, where several men were unloading bags of flour from one of the cars. Filip approached the large, burly one—Bogdan Romanowski—who was in charge. Filip had befriended and bribed him with medical alcohol from the infirmary, which was the only plentiful source they possessed. Romanowski sold it to the Russians, who used it to make moonshine.

"Good morning, Bogdan," said Filip. "Do you have any meat for the patients?"

"You know how hard it is to find meat these days?" asked Romanowski.

That meant he had some but didn't want to share for free.

"C'mon, I know you have some. The poor bastards can't eat bread all day. They need meat to give them strength."

"Talk to my new guy at the warehouse," said Romanowski. "But I warn you, he's a tough negotiator."

Filip laughed and said, "Don't worry. I negotiated my way through Buchenwald. I can deal with your new guy."

He walked past the train and into a long warehouse building near the tunnels inside the gypsum mountain where he used to deliver fuel with Peter Strauss and where the Nazis later built the V-2 rockets. The warehouse was full of people moving various materials from place to place, but he entered a small office where all the orders were processed.

The office was small, with a desk and some chairs. Only one man sat behind the desk. The man, who had a long black beard, lifted his head from hundreds of papers on the desk and stared at him. Filip stared back in shock for what seemed like minutes, unable to move or speak because the bearded man he was looking at was Hinkelmann.

"Ah, there you are," said Hinkelmann. "I was looking for you."

Filip stepped back, wanting to run away and call the Americans.

"I wouldn't do that if I were you," Hinkelmann said, pulling a pistol from his jacket.

"What do you want from me? The war is over."

"I can't have any witnesses who know about my new identity. I'm the camp's new chief procurement officer, and I'd like to keep it that way. I think I can use my experience from Buchenwald to make a career out of it. I'm sure you understand, Filip. Don't you?"

"Any witnesses? Only three people know about your real name. Ciepielowski and Sig are still out there even if you kill me."

"I wouldn't worry about them, my friend," said Hinkelmann, rising from his chair. "I'm watching them just like I've been watching you. Now, I want you to walk with me somewhere."

"I'm not going anywhere!" Filip shouted.

Hinkelmann walked over to Filip and poked him in the chest with the pistol. "I'm afraid I must insist," he said. "That's if you want your girl Anna to live."

Anna kneeled before the altar at the camp chapel and said her prayers. She prayed for Filip to be alive and safe. She had searched the barracks and the camp kitchen but could not find him. Nobody had seen him since the morning—or about eight hours since she'd kissed him and watched him leave the infirmary. It was unusual for him to disappear like this. He had helped Peter Strauss with the horses before and gone on a few delivery runs with him, but he always told her about those beforehand. After a three-year separation, neither of them liked to leave the other's side for long or without telling each other about it.

She stood up and left the chapel, heading for the warehouse near the railway station, where Filip sometimes acquired food and other goods for the infirmary. The warehouse was busy as always, but there was no sign of him. So she walked into the small office, where she found a man with a long black beard sitting behind a desk. She had never seen him before, but that was normal at the camp. People constantly left for their home countries, and new ones took over their jobs.

"Hello," she said. "I'm Anna Kogut from the infirmary. Who are you?"

"Good afternoon," he said, smiling. "I'm Johann Weber, the

new chief procurement officer for the camp. What can I do for you, young lady?"

"I'm looking for Filip Wolny, who was supposed to bring some food back for the patients. Have you seen him?"

"Ah, yes, Filip. He was here earlier today, but I haven't seen him since."

"Do you know where he might have gone?" she asked.

"Well, he was looking for meat, so I told him to go into the tunnel, which we use as a meat locker. Maybe he's still over there."

Anna couldn't imagine what Filip could possibly be doing in the tunnel for eight hours, but he did help around the camp whenever he could and maybe got stuck working on some project.

"Thank you," said Anna, turning to leave. "I'll try there next."

"Wait," said Weber, pulling a lantern up on his desk. "The lights in the tunnel don't always work very well. It's better if I take you there."

"That's kind of you, but I can just take the lantern with me. I'll return it as soon as I'm back."

Weber scratched his head nervously, then said, "I'm sorry, Fräulein Kogut, but I just met you, and I don't want to get fired if this lantern disappears or some meat gets stolen. I hope you understand."

She did. The Americans liked order and punished all those involved in any thievery. She also didn't mind someone escorting her through the dark tunnels. They were spooky and reminded her of crypts she and her friends explored in a cemetery near her house in Poland when she was a little girl.

"Yes, I understand," she said. "Thank you for taking the time to help me."

"Don't mention it," he said, leaving the office. "We have to help each other after this horrible war."

She followed him into the tunnel, the lantern lighting the way. The place was deserted, and she became increasingly frightened the deeper they went.

"Don't be afraid," Weber assured her, apparently sensing her uneasiness. "There are people working inside."

"How much farther?" she asked.

"Not far. Just around the corner."

They turned right and walked for a few more minutes until they reached a metal door.

"This is it," said Weber, opening the door for her. "This is our meat locker."

"You said there would be people here," she said, hesitating to go in.

"Yes, they're inside in the butcher shop."

It made sense. The meat and all its processing had to be kept in the cold so it wouldn't spoil. She stepped inside, and horror gripped her immediately.

There was only one person in the room—Filip—but he lay on the floor with his hands and feet tied together with a rope. When he saw her, he screamed through a rag stuffed inside his mouth.

"What is this?" she screamed, rushing to Filip's side.

"Your final reunion," said Weber, smiling. He pointed a pistol at her. "This one is for eternity, I'm afraid."

"Who are you?"

"Technical Sergeant Hinkelmann, at your service," he said, bowing like an aristocrat.

Fear gripped her heart. It couldn't be. Not Filip's torturer from Buchenwald. Filip had told her all about him and his cruelty, but he'd also said that the man had died in a barn fire.

How could he be alive? She couldn't let him kill them. Not now. Not after everything they'd been through. She pulled the rag out of Filip's mouth.

"What are you doing? Put that back!" Hinkelmann ordered.

"He can't fire the gun!" Filip yelled, gasping for air. "The gunshot would alert the Americans."

"I will shoot if I have to," Hinkelmann warned, waving the pistol at them.

Hinkelmann didn't fire, so Anna untied Filip's hands. "No, you won't," she said. We know your kind. You're too worried about your own skin."

Filip untied his feet and stood up. "We're not afraid of you anymore," he said.

Hinkelmann hesitated, then simply ran away, slamming the door behind him. The room turned pitch black with the lantern gone. Anna couldn't even see her own hands. She could only hear the distant sound of running feet and Filip's shallow breathing.

"Now what?" asked Filip.

She clasped his hand and said, "I was worried sick about you. Why did you let him tie you up like that?"

"I didn't realize he couldn't fire until he tied me up and left me here to die."

"Don't you ever leave me like that again."

"Trust me. I won't," he said. "Nobody's going to tell me what to do ever again. I'll do what I want to do, and that's be with you."

She smiled. "And I with you. But what about Hinkelmann? He might come back."

"Don't worry. I won't let him hurt us or my friends."

"C'mon, then," she said. "Let's go get him."

37
JULY 15, 2005

Filip moved back and forth in his rocking chair and stared through the open balcony door. His fifty-square-meter government-allocated apartment was on the fourth floor, which made it difficult on his old legs, but it gave him an excellent view of the surrounding Owl Mountains, one of the most picturesque places in Poland.

The morning breeze blew the window sheers like a lady's dress and brought the smell of the morning dew with it. It made his nostrils flare and reminded him of the summer of 1945—sixty years earlier—when he was young and energized by new opportunities as he traveled back to Poland from Germany. Looking down at his body, weakened by prostate cancer, he couldn't help but wonder how time could have possibly flown by so quickly.

He got up from his chair, not able to tolerate the pain any longer. He needed to lie down, but he was never one to stay still. The events of sixty years ago had taught him that every minute of life must be lived like it's the last. This day was not an exception, even though he knew his end was near.

He pulled down a small metal box from the top of his closet cabinet and opened it. There it was, after all those years—the gold medallion that was the only reminder of his life's love. Every time he touched it, Anna appeared in his mind, standing before him in her young glory, golden locks flowing in the wind and those light-blue eyes smiling at him like they did the first time they met on a train to Germany.

He missed her so much.

He sat down and stared at the wall filled with family pictures. His grandchildren from America—Marek and Marysia —were visiting him today. He wished he could always be with them, taking them on trips around Poland like he used to when they were small kids. Instead, he was stuck in his apartment, held prisoner by his disease. He wouldn't tell them for fear they would feel sorry for him, but today was a bad day. The cancer was making itself known.

The doorbell rang, and a smile came over Filip's face. He'd been waiting for their visit all day. He rose gingerly, his ankle springing to action despite the pain, and rushed toward the front door.

"Come in, come in," Filip said, opening the door.

Marek and Marysia entered and gave him big hugs. Both were in their early twenties, and after ten years of living in America, they looked like real Americans: Levi's jeans, Nike shoes, and brand-name shirts. They were in Poland on vacation.

"How is your ankle today, Grandpa?" asked Marysia.

"What ankle?" Filip responded, smiling.

"Ah, you're always pretending like everything is fine."

"We brought the video camera," said Marek. "Are you finally going to tell us about the concentration camp?"

Filip had been avoiding this for years. What was the point of talking about such unpleasant things? But he understood that his grandson's curiosity came from love. Marek wanted to know more about his life so he could have more memories of him. The young man sensed Filip didn't have much time left.

"Well, that depends," said Filip. "Will you have a shot of cognac with me?"

The boy smiled. Filip had known the kid couldn't hold his liquor ever since he'd had him take a sip of vodka when he was five years old. He'd had a disgust for it ever since.

"You're on," said Marek. "I'll drink with you today."

They drank and talked for hours. Filip told them everything he could remember, which was not too much anymore. Anna had forbidden him from talking about her time in Germany, and he'd kept his promise. When he finished speaking, he felt like a stone from Buchenwald's quarry had been lifted off his shoulders.

"I'm tired," he said finally.

"But how did you get back to Poland?" asked Marek.

"It was a twelve-day train ride, and the Soviets stopped us every few hours, asking for bribes. We almost got killed, but somehow, we survived. Together with your grandma, we could survive anything. But that's a story for another day."

"Oh, that's so romantic," said Marysia.

Filip never thought of it that way. It was just pure love—not romantic. Like two magnets, they couldn't resist each other. It just was. They just were.

"How come you didn't go to America?" asked Marek.

"Your grandma wanted to go back to Poland to find her

family. I wish we did go to America instead of living here in poverty. I could have met you there," he joked.

They laughed.

"If you went to America, we would've never been born, silly," said Marysia.

Filip thought about the stress of the last twenty years, with Poland mired in economic depression following the breakup of the communist bloc. He and Anna had struggled to put food on the table. Still, none of those things seemed very difficult compared to what he went through in Germany. He recalled those days each time he was in a bad situation. People asked him why he was always so happy. He didn't know how to explain it, but how could he not be happy compared to the alternative?

"So, you never looked for Sig after the war?" asked Marysia.

Filip shook his head. "I didn't know how to find him. I doubt he stayed in Germany. Now I can't even remember his last name."

"And what happened to Hinkelmann?" asked Marek.

"All I had to do was shout his name and say that he was wearing a black beard. Everyone knew and hated him. They found him hiding in a lavatory a few hours later."

Marek prepared his grandfather's favorite drink—warm tea with cognac. Filip drank and stared through the window at the surrounding hills. He tried to forget it all again, but now everything was refreshed. He could see the events of those days as if they'd occurred the day before. They were etched in his brain, whether he liked it or not.

He would not sleep well tonight.

"I have something for you," he said to Marysia, pulling the medallion out of his pocket.

"What is it?" she asked.

"Grandma would want you to have it. It's a good luck charm," he said, handing the medallion to her.

She took the medallion and cried. "Thank you, Grandpa," she said, placing it around her neck. "I'll wear it every day."

"Just don't give it to a boy. He'll follow you around until you die," he said.

They laughed.

"Now I can rest," he said, lying on his couch.

AFTERWORD

I loved my grandparents very much and always wanted to write a story about how they fell in love while working as slave laborers in Nazi Germany based on the bits and pieces I heard growing up from my grandfather. The story intrigued me because I read very little about slave labor in the volumes of information about World War II I inhaled over the years, and I thought people should know more about the enormity of the suffering and death it caused.

However, my grandparents (names changed to Anna Kogut and Filip Wolny to protect the family) never wanted to speak about what happened to them. My grandmother refused completely; she didn't even discuss it with her children. Then, only a few years before his passing, my grandfather finally agreed to talk about what happened to him and allowed me to record it. The few hours of video recordings I acquired convinced me this story had to be told to the world. Then, the more I researched slavery and concentration camps in Nazi Germany, the more I realized this book needed to pay respect to and acknowledge not just my grandparents' story but also the stories of other, mostly ordinary, people who went through it on both sides of the conflict. Therefore, I expanded the story to include real events and people of the Buchenwald and Ravensbrück concentration camps that my grandparents probably were never part of or met but could have.

One such person was Dr. Marian Ciepielowski, who indeed helped develop the vaccine for typhus and also later sabotaged the vaccines going to German soldiers on the Eastern Front by replacing them with placebos. Ciepielowski spent the final days before the liberation of Buchenwald in hiding, with the SS hunting the camp for him. He was liberated by American soldiers and spent several years working as a medical inspector for the Red Cross and the Exhumation and Identification Department of the International Tracing Service of the Allied High Commission for Germany. Ciepielowski married a fellow Polish survivor in West Germany and, in 1951, emigrated to the United States. He worked at Roosevelt Hospital in New York and became deputy director. He died in 1973 and was buried in Metuchen, New Jersey.

Another such figure was Emil Carlebach, a tough leader of the Jewish barracks in Buchenwald. He was known to be a great leader who managed to save some people from the Nazis. He was active in the illegal resistance organization inside the concentration camp. Following his designed plans, he launched the call to mutiny on April 4, 1945. He was going to be shot by the SS on April 6, 1945, for his efforts in the camp revolt, but he was hidden by other prisoners and survived until liberation. A change of identity (a common technique in Buchenwald to evade death) saved him from being murdered. He survived the war and published extensively on history and politics afterward. He was a Communist

Party Member of Parliament in the Hessian state parliament in 1946. In 1948, in the city council meeting of Frankfurt am Main, Carlebach helped draft the first Hessian state constitution after the end of National Socialism. He co-founded the Union of Victims of Persecution of the Nazi Regime. He also acted as editor of the weekly paper, delegate for the printing and paper union, chair of the Former Buchenwald Inmates' Advisory Board at the Buchenwald Memorial, and vice president of the International Committee of Buchenwald-Dora and Subcamps. Carlebach died in Frankfurt am Main on April 9, 2001.

Beniek Helonski is not a real person but was inspired by a Polish-born Jewish Olympian and champion weightlifter, Ben Helfgott. He was only a teenager when he was sent to Buchenwald and didn't achieve his Olympic accomplishments until later in life, after he moved to Great Britain and represented that country.

The character of Sig Blau was mostly fictional, but my grandfather's best friend in Buchenwald was indeed a Jewish man named Abram. I have not been able to find him, but I found inspiration in the famous German stage comedian and film actor Sig Arno. He escaped Hitler's persecution in 1933 and later moved to the United States, where he had a long film career. However, he was not a homosexual.

On the other side of the conflict, many of the Nazis from Buchenwald and Ravensbrück mentioned in this novel were real people. These included:

- Technical Sergeant Fritz Hinkelmann (tried at Buchenwald Trial, sentenced to death, commuted to life imprisonment)
- Technical Sergeant Hans Schmidt (tried at the

American military tribunal at Dachau and executed by hanging)
- Senior Colonel Hermann Pister (tried at Buchenwald Trial, sentenced to death but died of a heart attack prior to execution)
- SS Detective Hubert Leclaire (found guilty in three cases by First Grand Criminal Chamber in Düsseldorf but later acquitted)
- Dr. Erwin Oskar Ding-Schuler (arrested by US troops but committed suicide)
- Major Fritz Suhren (tried by the French military court and executed)
- Gestapo Inspector Ludwig Ramdohr (tried at Hamburg Ravensbrück Trial and executed)
- SS Lieutenant Edmund Bräuning (missing since the end of the war)
- Head Guard Johanna Langefeld (imprisoned in Cracow, Poland, where she awaited trial and likely execution but escaped)
- Guard Emma "Aunt Emma" Zimmer (tried at Ravensbrück Trials and executed by hanging)
- Guard Dorothea Binz (tried at Ravensbrück Trial and executed by hanging)

Although they were all notorious for their brutality, little is known about their true personalities and actions. However, what struck me while doing my research was how ordinary they were. Mostly brought up in middle-class Germany, they seemed to show no propensity for violence before their indoctrination by the Nazi party. I'm not able to explain why ordinary people became so brutal in their treatment of other human beings, but I recommend watching the Netflix documentary *Ordinary Men: The "Forgotten Holocaust,"* which tried to do just that.

It is worth mentioning that Ravensbrück Head Guard Johanna Langefeld was indeed recognized by some of her Polish prisoners as more humane than most. In fact, some of her former prisoners helped her escape from a prison in Poland, hid her in a monastery for ten years, and then smuggled her back to Germany, where she lived out her remaining years in relative obscurity until she died in 1974.

What I know of my grandparents' activities in Germany is limited. Regarding my grandmother, very little is known except that, together with her three sisters, she was sent by force to Germany to work as a slave laborer. Also, per the International Tracing Service (ITS), it was confirmed she was registered on February 12, 1941, in the village of Immenrode in the rural district of Nordhausen. She also appears on a list of persons wanted by the Weimar police on December 3, 1941, with the remark: "arrest." Whether she was, in fact, arrested and where she was incarcerated remains a mystery, but she didn't arrive back in Poland until 1945, so she somehow remained in Germany for another three and a half years. She met my grandfather in her village sometime during her five years in Germany, but when, precisely, is unclear. I used Ravensbrück as her place of incarceration because it was the largest prison for women, and the Nazis destroyed all documentation before abandoning it, which could explain why the ITS had no further information about my grandmother's stay in Germany.

Regarding my grandfather, almost all the events described in the novel really happened. He traveled to Germany in a cattle car for work, which was supposed to be for three paid months but ended up being five unpaid years. He was indeed sexually abused by the woman, name unknown, who owned the farm where he worked in Rotenburg an der Fulda near Kassel. He was arrested in June 1942 for insubordination and breach of contract and held at Weimar prison for two weeks, then transferred to Buchenwald concentration camp. He was arrested because he hit that woman with a horse whip as retribution for her abuse and then left her farm without permission.

While in Buchenwald, my grandfather encountered most of the predicaments described in the book, such as breaking his ankle, which nearly cost him his life, and constantly searching for food and jobs that wouldn't kill him. He also escaped from the death march (probably toward Berlin) and was saved by American soldiers after hiding for a few days in a chicken coop. He then trekked across Germany and found my grandmother. Like many prisoners, they spent some time housed in the nearby Mittelbau-Dora concentration camp until the Americans figured out how to send all these people back to their countries.

My grandparents were offered the opportunity to emigrate to the United States but traveled back to Poland instead. They settled in Silesia in southern Poland, where the Polish government provided jobs and free housing. My grandmother's three sisters, who all survived the war, settled in the same town. My grandparents performed various jobs until they became live-in custodians of an elementary school, where they worked until retirement and where I created many wonderful memories. My grandfather didn't go back to his hometown in the north of Poland until years later, but he learned through letters that all his family members survived the war as well, including his mother. He took me there when I was a child, and I got to meet his extensive family.

As I mentioned, my grandparents never talked about what happened to them in Germany. They were very fun and easy-going people who were focused primarily on their family. It wasn't until after my grandmother passed away in her sixties that Germany announced reparations for all former concentration camp prisoners. My grandfather decided to apply, and that is when we all learned about everything in more detail. He eventually received reparation of few thousand dollars from the German government, only about forty-five years after his forced labor and imprisonment at Buchenwald concentration camp. He gave most of the money to his children and grandchildren, but it gave him some moments of bliss toward the end of his life, in his seventies and eighties, after living most of his life on a meager income in an extremely poor and oppressed communist Poland.

I must admit that writing this novel was an agonizing process that took several years. While the desire to tell my grandparents' story drove me to complete it, I had to pause several times because it physically hurt me to go through the grim research and the process of imagining what they went through in Nazi Germany. As I tried to put myself in their shoes, the thought of them being humiliated, beaten, and starved by their masters was excruciating. However, I am glad I persevered. At least now, my children will know an important part of their family's history. I hope you, the reader, also found this story interesting and learned from it about the horrors of fascism and dictatorship. Tell others about this story, and let's work together to prevent it from happening again.

For more information about slavery and concentration camps in Nazi Germany, I found the following books instrumental in my research:

- *The Buchenwald Report* by Albert G. Rosenberg, translated by David A. Hackett

- *Survivor of Buchenwald: My Personal Odyssey Through Hell* by Louis Gros
- *Buchenwald: Hell on a Hilltop* by Flint Whitlock
- *Ravensbrück: Life and Death in Hitler's Concentration Camp for Women* by Sarah Helm
- *Wearing the Letter P: Polish Women as Forced Laborers in Nazi Germany, 1939–1945* by Sophie Hodorowicz Knab
- *The Tattooist of Auschwitz* by Heather Morris
- *The Apprentice of Buchenwald: The True Story of the Teenage Boy Who Sabotaged Hitler's War Machine* by Oren Schneider
- *Night* by Elie Wiesel

Also, the Buchenwald Memorial website was a great resource.

ACKNOWLEDGMENTS

First and foremost, thank you to my wife for giving me the freedom to pursue my passion of writing and to my children for their support.

I would also like to thank my fellow writers and beta readers for their feedback and constructive criticism: Brenda Hasse, Donald Levin, Rob Mackenzie, Tom Leins, Maryann, Nell Dickerson, Dan Zetterlund, Gwen, Nazire, Eva, Agnes, and all the guys at the Creative Writers' Workshop (led by the amazing Terry Hojnacki).

Finally, many thanks to my wonderful editor, Kristy Phillips, and the cover designer, Konah Buckman. You made my work look good.

www.ingramcontent.com/pod-product-compliance
Lightning Source LLC
Chambersburg PA
CBHW061925170626
46813CB00006B/2301